THE RISE OF HUANG ZHOU

Book 1 of the FORBIDDEN CHRONICLES

By Perry Lake

OTHERMIND BOOKS

ISBN-13: 978-1-7375041-3-9

Cover design by: Hephaestus Entertainment

Printed in the United States of America

Dedicated to
Seph Caseni, Ian Farly, Jackie Powers,
T.J. Guccione, Wyntur Henderson,
and all members, past and present,
of the bi-weekly Write Club,
who have provided so much help,
ideas, and inspiration to this series.
Thanks, from your elder statesman.

CONTENTS

A CENTURY OF HUMILIATION

1. The Mandarin

In the Celestial Empire, the mountains of Hunan Province rise like pinnacles of stone, vertical and daunting to all who might look up at them in awe. The early morning mists waft lazily between these imposing towers and the verdant forests that surround them. Here, a week's winding walk from the great provincial capital of Changsha, a scholar made such a walk, carrying a sack containing his brushes, rolls of paper, and bottles of ink of various hues. In the style imposed by their foreign overlords, his hair had been shaved in front and in back unshorn and plaited in a single long braid. Behind him obediently followed a small, silent child, wearing pajamas of a nondescript color and a fur-lined cap with ear flaps.

Their destination at last came into view, the ancient castle of Sang-Wah, home of the Order to which the scholar had dedicated his life. This was the palace of the mandarin of Hunan Province.

The boy followed his father up the steps and into the palace. After speaking to fellow dignitaries, his father turned and walked down a hallway. Keeping his head down, the boy observed a floor decorated with scaly dragons, fiery phoenixes, serene turtles, and rampaging tigers.

At the end of the hall stood guards in gilded armor, with heavy swords hanging from their green sashes and long muskets in their hands. These men bowed and opened the great double doors.

The boy followed his father inside an elaborate chamber, filled with the echo of their footfalls and the scent of pungent incense. At the far end sat a large dais carved with great skill from alabaster, on which sat a gilded throne. Upon the massive back of this throne had been engraved and painted a peacock in full display. On either side stood beautiful women with elaborate gowns and gems in their tall coifs.

His father faced the throne and bowed deeply. The boy followed suit, as he had been instructed.

Rising, the boy saw that a man in green robes, emblazoned in white with another peacock, sat on the throne. Upon his head rested a cap covered with red tassels, trimmed in black fur, on which was surmounted a small pink ball. The older man wore a long, gray beard, forked in two strands, each terminated with tiny jade beads. The boy had been told that this was the Mandarin Shu.

"Your Excellency," said his father, "I have brought my son to you that you might examine him and determine his worthiness. He has obtained his cycle of years and thus it is appropriate that his destiny be decided, as is the custom of the Children of Liu Lei. His horoscope is most auspicious. His given name is Fang."

The mandarin gave a slight nod. "A good name, at least, Master Lieu."

The father turned and gave his son another nod. By this signal, the boy removed his cap, revealing his shaven head.

From ten feet away, the mandarin did not appear impressed.

"His head is full, truly, but so are the heads of imbeciles," he said. "We are in greater need of worthy eunuchs to serve in the Emperor's court than of scholars. These at least perform the function of transmitting information of which we might make use. Our numbers dwindle, so we must place every agent in the position where they will do the most good for our cause."

Lieu Po'tu, risking the mandarin's displeasure, quickly pointed out the boy's eyes. "Excellency, your most humble servant requests that you examine my son's eyes. Like his mother, Fang has inherited the Eye of Imposing Will. First he learned to master small animals and then his playmates."

"Yes? I suppose a child of your wife should inherit this skill and hopefully he has mastered them like my Second Minister, Ki. Let me see him closer."

Lieu led his son to the mandarin's dais. Fang looked up, studying the old man's lean face, his scarcely open eyes, his two-pronged beard.

The mandarin flicked his long-nailed hand and the boy felt himself lifted by his father onto the dais. With a slight nudge, Fang stepped closer to the nobleman.

Suddenly, the mandarin's hands were all over the boy's freshly-shaven head, feeling, seemingly measuring, his skull by touch. The boy's eyes widened only slightly in response to this unusual manipulation of his cranium. Then the mandarin looked closely, deeply, into the boy's eyes. The boy stared back, not breaking his gaze.

"Just as his mother, as I recall," said the mandarin. Then he commanded, "Blink."

The boy did so.

"Blink twice. Rapidly."

Before Fang could respond, his father said, "Blink as your mother taught you."

The boy closed his eyes. He then opened the outer lids, yet left his inner, transparent eyelids shut.

The Mandarin Shu allowed his own eyes to widen slightly. The hint of a smile graced his lips for the first time in decades. "I am impressed with the boy's head. Truly, he has within him the blood of Liu Lei, as a child of On-yan'jing should. I foresee the boy achieving great things and some day becoming one of my most valued retainers. For now, send him to study with the Green Hats in Tibet."

Lieu Po'tu bowed low. The boy did also, after a nudge.

So it was proclaimed, that third day of May, in the four thousand, four hundred and seventy-first year of the Celestial calendar.

* * *

At five years of age, Fang desired only to impress his father. Lieu, already greatly impressed by his son—as he had been impressed by the boy's mother—wished a great position for young Fang. He hoped the boy would learn the many skills necessary to advance the goals of the Order, and he could do that best if he first learned from the "Green Hats" of Tibet.

Lieu knew that if those strange and reclusive aesthetics could impart their knowledge and skills to Fang, the boy could better protect himself from enemies. Even enemies who dwelt closer than he cared to think.

Yet with his wife, On-yan'jing, Lieu revealed his concerns. These, she shared. Before he was to be sent to Tibet, On-yan'jing had told Fang the most curious of legends.

"There lived in the time of the Five Dynasties and Ten Kingdoms," she said, holding him in her grasp, "two sisters who were serpents. These sisters were not the lesser snakes that scurry under rocks, but rather they were Great Serpents, descended from the Four Great Dragon Kings of Old. The eldest was known as Madame White Snake and the younger was called Madame Green Snake.

"One day, White Snake found a handsome young man, Xu Xian, and determined that she would have him for her own. Taking the form of a beautiful maiden, she seduced him and they were to be married. However, before the wedding, a Taoist priest named Fahai discovered that White Snake's beauty was an illusion. Her true form, revealed in the reflection of a stream, was that of a great serpent, covered in white scales.

"Fahai told the young man what she was, but Xu Xian was too smitten to care. Therefore, the priest took it upon himself to destroy the creature if possible. The wise man kidnapped Xu Xian and used him as bait. When the snake in the guise of a woman appeared to rescue her lover, she and the priest battled with weapons, with poisons, and with magic.

"However, White Snake proved stronger than Fahai expected and he had no choice but to flee. While in hiding, Fahai heard the legend of the dragon-handler, Liu Lei, who had captured two dragons and made them obey the will of the emperor. To do this, Liu Lei devised a potion of garlic and vinegar, which all serpents abhor. This potion Fahai brewed and he returned to the Celestial Empire. There, he once more battled White Snake. This time he used the potion and immobilized her. Fahai then petitioned the king to build Leifeng Pagoda, and there to imprison her immortal body forever.

"However, her sister, Madame Green Snake, had escaped the exorcisms and binding of the Taoist priest and she remained free. Later, she found a human lover of her own and from their union came a race of dragon-men. In the earliest generations, these traits included scales or tails, forked tongues and a poisonous bite. In time, her descendants were to all appearances human but imbued with other traits of the draconic race. The immortality of the true Great Snakes was not passed on to their human descendants, though they aged but slowly.

"From the ninth generation of Green Snake came I, On-yan'jing."

No one who saw On-yan'jing would confuse her for a serpent. Rather, she might be mistaken for a fifth sister of the Four Beauties of Cathay. Her form was lithe and tall, her bearing and demeanor noble. Her coiffure and attire were never anything but elegant. Only her emerald green eyes and double eyelids hinted of her otherworldly nature.

And her blood flowed in the veins of Fang.

2. Education

As ordained by the mandarin, Lieu Fang's mother and father made clear to him that he would be taken to a faraway land and continue his education there. He expressed no objection, as he had been raised to follow instructions. After Fang said his farewells to his playmates, his father lifted him into the back of a cart.

"Do not be afraid, my son," said his father, fighting to keep his own lip from trembling.

"I am not afraid," said Fang. "I shall do all that is asked of me."

The boy bowed to his father. The mother remained silent, as was her wont. The parents stood solemnly as their only child rolled away, watching them.

For weeks, for months, Fang rode in that cart, fed by an aged couple who never spoke. Over wild rivers, across frozen deserts, and through towering mountains, he rode, until they at last came to a massive building or city of black stone. The entire structure seemed to hang precariously on the side of a great rock in the middle of snow-capped pinnacles. There he was lifted down and set before the gates. The cart rolled away without him, back to where it had come.

Fang stared at the great bronze doors, noting the geometric designs, of which he was unfamiliar. He looked up to the towering ramparts. He looked all around. Fang seemed to be the only living person in this strange land.

Yet at last, the giant bronze gates opened. The men and women within wore swaths of green or black cloth and curious green hats. These hats covered the back of the head and had no bill but rose above in a cone that pointed forward. One of these men, upon whose hat was attached a gold emblem, like a spider or insect, came up to Fang and looked down at him.

"Greetings, Fang," said the bearded ancient. "We have been expecting you. I am Haong, Archimandrite of Yian-Ho, citadel of the Kuen-Yuin."

Once inside, Fang found himself in a city like none other, laid out chaotically—or rather laid out to a scheme and plan unfathomable to mortal minds—filled with temples, modest homes, and towers, hugging both shores of a broad and beautiful river across which spanned several small bridges, each separated by a thousand feet.

From each temple sang the sound of golden bells, laughing in the slightest of breezes. Here and there were circular fountains, bordered with stonework upon which were carved strange sigils and inscriptions or the bas-relief of a terrible monster. Or god.

Standing in what appeared to be a broad civic center, with dozens of levels of temples, Fang looked up at a massive structure, half-built of massive masonry and half-carved from a great mountain, all stacked one upon the previous. This central temple stood out as the largest and greatest.

Fang's attention was drawn back to the Archimandrite, who then introduced him to a threesome in black robes, emblazoned with a gilded sigil.

"These are to be your new teachers, Fang," he said. "Sister Wuo-tu, Brother Zeng, and Sister Yingli. Do as they say and they will teach you well."

The Archimandrite turned and departed, and Fang would seldom see him during his stay. Sister Yingli then showed him to his room, which was to be his alone. There Fang was stripped of his pajamas and bathed.

* * *

Outside the citadel, the winds howled and raged. The cold turned one's blood to ice and the snow obliterated one's vision and pelted like flung stones.

Yet within the great citadel, the sky seemed to have but a faint overcast. The air may have been cool, but not cold. Many inhabitants went about nude or in loincloths or in fetching shifts, usually dyed black. Likewise, Fang was given no clothes.

To and fro went the people of Yian-Ho, each a priest or priestess of the Kuen-Yuin or their devotees. According to the histories that Fang would learn in the following months, their secret society had originated not in Cathay, nor even in Asia, but in a great continent long since lost beneath the waves. Mostly these priests walked in columns, their hooded heads down, chanting nearly inaudible verses. As Fang passed by them, even when they collected fruit or vegetables from the gardens that grew between houses, the people of Yian-Ho were mostly silent and introspective.

In those first days, Fang learned where he was to sleep and to hurry to class when he heard a certain gong. It would be difficult to ignore, as all other students hurried to their class *en masse* when the gong sounded.

Walking to class barefoot over the smooth flagstones, Fang observed other occupants, not only novices like himself, but some tall and mysterious like Yingli, invariably clad in black, if they were attired at all. Their sashes could be green or black or occasionally undyed, likely denoting either rank or duties. These last were clad in outer robes of green over another of black, though some had sashes of either color and many wore sashes of plain cloth.

Many of the robed throng of a certain rank carried a golden ball, hanging from a black or green sash about their waist. Their robes were green or black or some combination of those two colors, depending upon their station and duties.

Fang made these observations covertly, yet, he realized, they ever watched him—they watched everything. Therefore, he decided to be forthright and query Lady Yingli of the various ranks and duties.

"The inhabitants of Yian-Ho are many and varied," said Yingli. "Many acolytes such as yourself have come here to learn our ways

"Many are the fantastic tales of Yian-Ho," Yingli told him, "even those told within these walls. Songs and poems proclaim that a thousand bridges cross the river, which is said to stretch longer than the distance from the Earth to the Moon. The floors of the great fane," she added, "number seven hundred and seventy-seven."

Fang, being both curious and observant, counted only twelve bridges across the river. Of the river's length, he discounted the mention of its length without bothering to take measurements.

Although never allowed to enter the temple complex, from outside he counted an impressive but rather more modest twenty-one. Perhaps, he considered, more levels had been dug into the mountain beneath, but never found any evidence of their existence.

"Certain places are forbidden to enter, upon pain of death," Lady Yingli explained. "Those forbidden are the Fane of the Sleeper and the Palace of the Archimandrites."

An immense structure, the fane had been built in an utterly alien design from a strange green-black stone. It bore six towering spires and a central edifice from which sometimes issued a pale greenish glow. The doorway was huge and seemingly without any gate or barrier or guard. Nothing would stop anyone from entering the fane, save rumors of punishments.

Atop the uppermost temple, a great sigil of greenish brass or bronze overlooked the city below. This sigil bore the image of a stylized kraken or devilfish, reaching out with half a dozen tentacles. Fang found himself curiously uncomfortable at the sight of this symbol.

Fang did not resist when his tutors pulled him away from the great fane. Instead, they showed him the gardens and parks and fountains that graced the wide, spiraling streets. He noted that the sanitation in most modern cities could be improved by emulating that of Yian-Ho.

"Amongst the Kuen-Yuin," instructed Sister Yingli, speaking to an assembled group of students, "the highest leaders are the archimandrites, who are given the task of administration of this citadel."

As Fang's father was an administrator among the Order of the White Peacock, he came to think of the seldom seen archimandrites as akin to his own father.

"One of these archimandrites," Yingli continued, "is ever assigned the role of absolute ruler of the Kuen-Yuin—the Dzil-N'bu, who dwells in the highest tower of Yian-Ho. Of the archimandrites, the Dzil-Nbu is renowned as the oldest and greatest amongst us, and our leader. The first Dzil-Nbu was Zanthu, may his name be venerated. He founded our city in the days following the destruction of Mu, the world's first continent."

Rather than challenge this last statement, Fang presumed that Mu had more correctly been the first continent to host the human species. During his entire time in Yian-Ho, Fang would never once lay eyes upon the Supreme Master of the citadel.

In time, Sister Wuo-tu gave Fang a simple black loincloth. For the next three years, Fang learned the language of Tibet, and of the barbarians that surrounded the land, Turkic and Russian. From her, he learned more of the Principles of the Sublime Order of which his father was a bureaucrat. They told him of a First Seven, which preceded the current Council of the Seven, but no more was said of this irrelevancy.

In the open courtyards, Brother Zeng practiced hand-to-hand fighting techniques with young Fang. He also instructed the boy in climbing and hiding himself in the jagged rocks that surrounded the citadel, lest he be found by any band of cannibalistic pygmies that oft times led hunting forays against the Green Lamas.

Sister Yingli taught him to meditate in ways at variance with any of the Buddhist practices in the land, focusing his mind on whatever goal eluded him. In her laboratory, the ascetic instructed him in the brewing of the most noxious of poisons from the most common of plants and minerals, and she instructed him in the medical treatments of the Indian doctor, Sushruta. Yingli and Wuo-tu jointly taught him the means to transmutate one element into another. "This may prove expedient," Yingli explained, "should you require gold."

In his third year at the lamastery, the Archimandrite Haong himself instructed the boy of the history of pre-Cataclysmic times and ancient prophecies, of which the Hindus of India and the Buddhists of Cathay have retained but a dim memory. In the ancient library, Fang read of the forbidden technologies that the Kuen-Yuin had amassed throughout the ages. Among these were innumerable poisons and potions, and the means to empower and focus energies within various rock crystals and gems. Such energies, it was alluded, were once employed to levitate stones, or empower flying machines, or send out beams of fiery death to destroy entire armies. Alas, various pivotal details were often absent from these narratives, and this absence was not lost on young Fang.

Looking over such scrolls, young Fang said to his teachers, "I will make these better."

The sisters exchanged a glance. His Celestial teachers might have scoffed, laughed, or even beaten the boy for such hubris, but the Green Lamas of the Kuen-Yuin did not ignore omens.

3. Homecoming

Fang did not recognize the old man at first. It was only his mother he recognized, for she had not aged in three and a half years.

"Welcome home, Fang," said his mother, On-yan'jing. "Your father and I are most pleased to have you once more in our house. I see you have grown. You are nearly as tall as I."

Fang bowed to her. He then and looked at the man he knew must be his half-forgotten father. He bowed.

Lieu Po'tu grinned and grasped Fang's shoulder, a rare display of affection for the staid diplomat.

"Your mother speaks true, Fang," he said. "We have missed you."

Then it was Fang's turn to speak. "Why have I been summoned back? I have not completed my studies. There are still secrets which the lamas have not revealed."

Fang's parents exchanged a glance. His father could not hide his disappointment. His mother could. As such, it was silently agreed that she should answer.

"Fang, there is also much you must learn here. There have been signs, long ignored, of an impending clash with ambitious barbarians who are fueled by greed and delusions of superiority. While the Manchurian emperor and his court can only admire the gilded goblet from the West, they fail to see the poison in that cup. It is the will of the Mandarin Shu that you take your place in the ranks of the Sublime Order of the White Peacock."

Lieu nodded in agreement.

Fang remained unconvinced. "What has that to do with me? I have learned of empires that existed long before Cathay and others that will exist long after Cathay is a forgotten memory. I have read books written before the first man came into being. The lamas are the wisest people in the world and only from them might I obtain complete mastery of their teachings."

Now it was his father who replied. "Do you think you were sent to study with the lamas of the Green Hats so that you might become a monk? No, you have learned their secret histories and their banned prophecies so that one day you might act to bring those prophecies to fruition. It has been decided that your intellect and keen observation might serve more practical purposes. For this to happen, we need you among us."

Fang's green eyes flitted once to his mother, then back to his father.

"You would have me save the land from the foolishness of its own emperor and his advisors and all his armies?"

His father nodded. His mother only stared.

Reluctantly, Fang conceded and bowed. Long had he known that his destiny would be unlike any other.

4. The Balance of Nations

By the time Fang achieved his ninth year, he appreciated not only his people's ancient culture but the forward-thinking of the Western powers. Upon his return to Hunan Province, he began to study English, French, German, Latin, and Greek. He impressed his tutors with his mastery of the barbaric tongues.

Fang's father had been a member of the Order of the White Peacock since he was only a little older than Fang. Although Lieu had never trained with the Green Hat lamas, he had impressed his teachers and was made an official in the mandarin's court at an early age. From that day to this, Master Lieu had not advanced in his position.

However, Fang's mother had not failed to notice the intellect and wisdom of the young diplomat. In a manner foreign to the ways of the Han people, she picked him to be her husband. Truly, she was not as other women.

"The mandarin of the White Peacock is without a spine," On-yan'jing said to her husband one day in their garden as they took tea. The plum blossoms had withered unusually early, telling of an icy winter to follow. "He lolls about on his throne, dreaming of past glories and hoping that our destiny manifests itself. This is the time to act yet he does nothing."

"Have you forgotten that I once advised the mandarin to place our allies, either the Dacoits bandits or the worshipers of Kali, in the court of the Tipu Sultan?" spoke Fang's father, in hushed tones. "Have you forgotten how he scoffed at my suggestion? The mandarin would not hear of it, being incapable of seeing beyond the borders of Cathay. At times I think he has forgotten that the Seven are seven, not two. For this advice, have I been denied the position of honor that I have earned in his service. I can advise him of no new course of action."

"I have not forgotten," she said, without emotion. "I know full well how the mandarin has failed the Order, lo these many years. If one would study the ways of the barbarians, one could not fail to see their greed and duplicity. They covet the riches of Cathay and they will stop at nothing to have them."

"Yes, yes," her husband agreed. "The British and French ambassadors speak of nothing but Turkish opium and how they might sell it in our cities.

"Our spies in the emperor's court tell us that, of late, the British wish to strengthen their alliance with the western Turks so as to bolster their position against the Russians. They want to fatten their purses as well. To do both, they hope to expand the trade in opium, which they buy cheaply in Turkey and India. But not even the British wish to have opium in their land. Instead, they demand that they be allowed to sell it in Cathay. The emperor refuses, but the foreigners insist. Have they no idea what that poison does to a man?!"

"They know," she said. "They do not care. They care only for the riches it might bring them."

He nodded in resignation.

"If only the mandarin would listen," she continued. "But if you will not speak, who can convince him?"

Fang, sharp of ear, had hidden himself nearby where he might listen intently. He gave his mother's words consideration.

* * *

"I agree with your assessment of the barbarians," said Fang, the next day. "Yet still I admire the British in many ways."

"Do you, now?" queried his father, sitting at his writing desk. "How so?"

"I admire their ambition, their ingenuity, and their willingness to change. Most of all, I admire their queen, who is young and intelligent and augustly named Victoria."

Unlike others in Cathay, even others in Europe, Fang knew that a woman would prove the better leader of a nation. Of an empire. Of the world. He knew this for he saw every day how a woman could be superior to a man.

"Remember, Father," he said. "It has been prophesied that one day all the World will be united under the single hand of a Universal Ruler—and that hand will belong to a woman."

The Order of the White Peacock and its allies in the Council of the Seven had long striven to make this prophecy come true. At times they advanced women to rule their far-flung nations, such as the first Salome, Cleopatra, Zenobia, the Empress Wu, and others. Other times, they aided ambitious men like Huang Di, the Pharaoh Sesostris, the Emperor Lieu, Alexander, Al-Muqanna, or the Great Khan Temujin—all empire builders whose vision knew no bounds. These men, it was hoped, would unite the nations of the world, but at the pivotal moment, the Order would replace that king with a queen.

Thus far, all such schemes had failed.

The nine-year-old Fang's opinion of Queen Victoria did not diminish on the fourth day of September, of the year 4475, when word was received that Great Britain had declared war on the Ching Empire of Cathay.

5. Fang and Foot

In the court of the Hunan mandarin, young Fang and six others assembled to be inducted into the Order of the White Peacock and to receive their orders. On his throne, the Mandarin Shu sat, grimly waiting. News of this war troubled him greatly. Flanking him were his advisors, the ancient and diminutive Senior Minister Weng and the broad-chested Junior Minister Ki.

One boy, two or three years older than Fang, bore a fearsome countenance, enhanced by his black pajamas and shaven pate. This was Hei Hu, who had already killed three men, all enemies of the Mandarin Shu. It was he who had been introduced first among the novices. Fang, the youngest and who had thus far achieved nothing to benefit the Order, was left for the last.

After each had been introduced and made to swear to uphold the precincts of the Order, the Mandarin raised his hand on which rested a silver ring with a great emerald. No one spoke. A few stopped breathing.

"All of you know that Cathay has been at war for several months with barbarians from across the ocean," he said. "They will not cease meddling in our affairs. Opium is illegal and the penalty for smuggling this poison into the empire is death. Yet these British barbarians unload tons of their poison in our ports and attempt to unload even more. On the word of our illustrious emperor, Commissioner Lin ordered their ships seized, but this act has only led to a declaration of war.

"We have informed our allies within the Ottoman Empire, and to divert the British, they have lately caused trouble in Syria. Alas, with the defeat of Muhammad Ali, the barbarians have returned. Therefore, we must tend to this crisis ourselves.

"It has taken the British fleet months to assemble their armada in Singapore. It took their foreign gunboats only days to subjugate Zhoushan Island and capture it with ease. Listen to me, you young recruits. We must not allow the barbarians to advance further, and that is why you have been inducted at so young an age. We will instruct each of you how best to aid the emperor and defend our land from this foreign incursion."

Unbidden, Fang stepped forward and bowed low. The mandarin raised an eyebrow. All others looked at him and this act of disorder.

"Lieu Fang, do you wish to speak?"

"Yes, honorable mandarin," he replied. Only then did he straighten and look his master in the eye.

"Exalted Mandarin," Fang said, "a wise man would ask, when is the advancement of the Celestial Empire the goal of the Order? Cathay must be made to serve the Order, not the other way around.

Also, a wise man would remind the mandarin that the emperor is not Chinese; he is Manchurian. Their ways are not our ways."

In the silence that followed, a spider's step might have been mistaken for a thunderclap. But this silence lasted only an instant, before Weng, the mandarin's principal advisor, spoke.

"This child is allowed to instruct the Hunan mandarin?! Is he to speak treason?! Does he not know who is the enemy of our people? Would this babe in 'open pants' tell us to throw wide our gates to the barbarians?!"

A murmuring—a growl rather—passed from the collective throats of nearly all those gathered in the throne room. Fang's father was silent, frozen with disbelief—not of his son's opinions, but that he would ever be so foolish to express them.

The Mandarin Shu raised his emerald-graced hand once more. Once more, all was silent.

"Does the boy Lieu Fang wish to say more?"

Master Lieu prayed his son would remain silent. His prayers went unanswered.

"Yes, honorable Mandarin," said Fang. "There is no treason in informing our most gracious mandarin that this war between the Ching and British Empires is an opportunity to advance the agendas of the Order. It should surprise no one that the British devastate our cities, for their mortars are far superior to any Chinese cannons. Their gunboats are faster and well armored. Sitting in the center of the Pearl River, none of our cannons can reach their gunboats, but their shells rain death upon the people.

"The British ships act as floating warehouses at the mouth of the Pearl River, waiting to offload. The Chinese navy can not catch them for our war-junks are awkward on the ocean waves.

"Not only do the British have a tactical advantage, but many aspects of their society are far superior to those of the Chinese. Contrary to common belief, the more foreigners that are allowed within the land, the more we might learn from them. The Westerners reward innovation and ingenuity whilst Cathay under the Manchurians remains stagnant and the common people do not trust the foreign Manchurians. Surely the emperor, if his eyes are open, will see the need to implement the changes necessary to advance Cathay—I speak of changes which are in accord with the goals of the White Peacock. Does the most serene mandarin wish to hear my outline of these goals?"

A pause followed. All eyes fell upon the mandarin.

"No," said the Mandarin Shu. "I have heard enough of this nonsense. Minister Ki speaks true when he says this cross-eyed whelp speaks treason. Master Lieu, it is not for your son to correct his betters. True, our defeat at Zhoushan bodes that the Empire needs more guns, but our traditions must be maintained at all costs. And who cares what commoners think?!

"The Order of the White Peacock is a Chinese institution. The goals of the Order are Chinese goals. We shall abide in our places to await the appearance of the Coming Teacher and reach out our hands only when the empire is threatened. Master Lieu, perhaps your son has spent too much time among foreigners, learning their ways. We regret having wasted a perfectly good eunuch by sending him to Tibet! Were he not already inducted into the Order, we would correct that mistake!"

The mandarin stared coldly at Lieu. Ki Ming smirked. Lieu Po'tu fought to keep from trembling.

Fang bowed low and said no more, though he wanted to tell the mandarin that the Order of the White Peacock existed long before Cathay rose along the banks of the Yangtze.

"I beg your forgiveness, Sire," said Fang's father. "I assured you that the boy will be punished for his unworthy remarks."

And with that, they departed, Lieu pulling Fang along by the arm. Afterwards, in the courtyard, Fang received the ridicule and scorn—emphasized by more than a few blows—of the other boys who'd been inducted this day.

"Coward!" said one boy as he shoved Fang. "You will not defend your own land!"

"The emperor's armies outnumber the barbarians ten-to-one!" said another, shoving him to the ground. "We can not fail!"

"His green eyes will not let him see the truth!"

"Maybe we should cut them from his head!"

And maybe they would have, had Hei Hu—the Black Tiger—not interjected a foot into each of their five faces. With that, they quickly dispersed.

Hei Hu took Fang by the arm and led him behind a decorative wall, away from prying ears. There, in a small garden, he spoke to the younger boy.

"You are right, Lieu Fang," said Hei Hu. "We must fight to preserve our ways—even if our ways must change. When has the Order ever sought to keep the Celestial Empire in the stagnant state imposed by the Manchurians?"

Fang blinked. He saw that Hei Hu had not understood what Fang had meant, not fully at least. Was everyone in the Order so dense? But Fang knew this was not the time to turn down a helping hand. Or a helping foot.

“Ever since Shu became mandarin,” said Fang, “if my honorable father is to be believed.”

* * *

Fang and Hei Hu, like all inductees into the ranks of the Order of the White Peacock, listened for any news of the Celestial Empire's struggle against the invading barbarians. To this end, they acted as spies in the vicinity of the British ships, docked and awaiting more troops, more supplies. In the following months, that news only continued to worsen.

After taking the pivotal island of Zhoushan, the British naval commander, Superintendent Elliot, used it as a base from which to launch further attacks. Fang learned that upon securing the Portuguese colony of Macau from Chinese invasion, the British had now set their sights on the great port city of Canton.

With the new year came new fighting along the Pearl River. Fang observed Chinese junks capable of carrying one or two matchlock cannons sunk with a single, well-aimed cannonball. Fortresses that had withstood Mongol hordes were reduced to rubble. Armies of thousands were scattered before the volleys of a few hundred riflemen. The steam-powered gunboats of the British floated over the shallowest of water and no Chinese gun could penetrate their ironclad hulls.

News came from Hei Hu that Wham'poa Island, close to Canton, had been lately captured with ease. The Chinese generals amassed tens of thousands of men to defend Canton and build defenses, but no one knew if that would be enough to protect the city.

Yet good news came in April, when the rival commanders, Elliot and General Yishan, agreed upon a reasonably fair peace treaty: trade was to resume and Zhoushan Island would be exchanged for one called Hong Kong. If their treaty were enacted, Canton would be saved.

Within hours, the Mandarin Shu entered the emperor's private chambers in the Forbidden City as easily as any palace servant. The Manchurian emperor of Cathay did not respond to him as a servant, however. Although Shu bowed first, they both bowed equally low.

“Illustrious emperor,” said Shu, getting directly to the point without the litany of compliments and well wishes a lesser courtier would employ, “we have heard that the traitor Yishan has made peace with the British.”

“He has,” said the Dao'guang Emperor, clutching the treaty he'd been sent. “What am I to do?”

“To such a display of rebellion, the only response is to command your men to exterminate the enemy, retain Hong Kong island at all costs, and regain every lost inch of land. The Empire must never concede land or honor to barbarians. If Yishan does not obey, have him beheaded."

"Yes! I will do so!" And with that, the emperor tore up the treaty unsigned.

On the other side of the world, the Foreign Secretary Lord Palmerston would soon do much the same thing upon viewing the preliminary treaty. In the chaos that followed such backtracking, the British set their sights on Canton once more.

Hearing this, the Mandarin Shu ordered Hei Hu and others to dive under British ships by night, drill holes in their wooden hulls, and thus sink them. Such methods had proved fruitful in the past, but always they had been performed by the Dacoits of Burma. Hei Hu would first need to learn how to swim.

Before any action commenced, Shu reported his plan to the emperor. "As you see, Your Majesty, I have the situation well in hand. Worry no more. The foreigner devils shall be driven from our land within a fortnight!"

The emperor smiled upon his favored mandarin and gifted him with a snuff box of red jade. However, among the servants, the courtesans, the guardsmen, and the eunuchs in the chamber with them, there was at least one who thought the mandarin's bragging would make for interesting gossip. In short time, that gossip reached the ears of Superintendent Eliot.

Thus, the endeavor ended in failure. British marksmen, warned of the attack in advance, shot anything that moved in the water that night. Hei Hu was one of the few survivors.

"This is an outrage!" screamed the Mandarin Shu, stomping around his own throne room, the next morning. The servants dropped to the floor and seemed to bury their heads in the marble floor. They would, if they could. "My own agents have revealed my plans to the enemy! I shall have a dozen of these worthless operatives executed!"

And he did so, over the next weeks, putting more effort into this endeavor than the prosecution of the war. Only Hei Hu escaped, finding refuge with the family of his young friend, Fang.

"Every battle is a defeat," said Hei Hu, "but every defeat reaches the emperor's ears as a great victory."

"Of course," Fang's father replied, "for the emperor rewards news of any defeat with death."

"I would expect that of any emperor; but does the mandarin of our Order also wear blinders?"

"Alas, so it would seem."

6. The Enemy Advances

"Like Canton, Amoy has fallen to the foreigners," said the Mandarin Shu, in the second year of the war. "The island city was well-prepared for a naval assault, but it fell when the British sent in their infantry. After destroying the city's defenses, they abandoned it."

The news did not get better in the ensuing months, Fang noted. A British transport, the *Nerbudda*, and a brig, *Ann*, each ran aground off the coast of Taiwan. Their mostly Indian crews were captured, but rather than hold them for ransom or offer them back as a gesture of good will, the vindictive emperor ordered the men beheaded. This act fueled British hatred of the Chinese like nothing before.

"The city of Ningbo is not a great city," said Lieu to his wife and son, "but it contains the largest cannon factory in the Empire. More important, Ningbo stands on the path to Nanking, a major city and trading center."

In October of that year, the people of Ningbo surrendered to the invaders without a fight.

At last, when even the Mandarin Shu realized the emperor must be made aware of the true situation, he spoke to him, giving the Son of Heaven a clear view of the real threat to the empire. This did not encourage the emperor to sue for peace, however. He ordered Ningbo to be retaken and he sent in the army to do so.

"What a disaster!" Shu bellowed in his throne room. All others remained silent. "The emperor's troops were slaughtered to a man! Now British ships sail up the Yangtze unimpeded and loot the imperial tax barges. They besiege Wusong and Baoshan, leaving a clear path to the great city of Zhen'jiang! What more can go wrong, thanks to the incompetence of my agents?"

The answer to that question came in June, when he heard of the fall of Shanghai, the largest and most important trading port in the empire.

* * *

In Shanghai, where the Yangtze River met the vast Pacific, young Fang noted that the seeming human chaos that proliferated along the busy docks belied the quite orderly commerce that forever took place here. As always, lounging sailors, haggling merchants, and sunburned fishermen filled the docks, all watched over by sing-song girls on the nearby balconies. But now there were great numbers of soldiers as well—soldiers in the red or blue uniforms of the British Army and Navy. Here, Fang, now eleven, kept his head down but his eyes open.

Shanghai had fallen, but that meant that now agents of the White Peacock had easier access to British soldiers and officers. As he spoke English and had sharp ears, this could allow him to learn their plans.

As always, clusters of boys hung about the docks, here and there. Like Fang, these boys kept their eyes open for any opportunity. Sometimes they would become employed as stevedores or messengers. Just as often, they would pick a pocket or run off with the spoils of an unguarded fishing boat.

Fang, in tattered pajamas and a coolie hat, had no interest in seafood or employment. He spotted a nearby group of four boys, sitting on barrels and crates, waiting until they would be chased off. He quickly joined them.

"Are you working on the foreign ships?" he asked, feigning a wide-eyed countenance. "They say the barbarians are very rich and they will pay gold if you polish their buttons."

The other boys, all about Fang's age, laughed at him. Fang, playing his role as a naive youth from the hinterlands, only stared back at them.

"Listen to this peasant, fresh from his farm!" one of them, the largest, said while laughing and shoving Fang's shoulder. "He thinks the British will share the gold they steal! We are lucky if we get even a few copper pieces for lugging their traps and cases!"

"He is a fool and a smelly farm boy," said another. "just take a look at his—" The boy stopped, his face registering shock and superstitious fear as he realized the newcomer had eyes the color of emeralds.

Fang wasted no more time on them. He allowed his inner eyelid to close, capturing their youthful minds. Scarcely educated and with no training against the mesmeric gaze, the boys were immediately enthralled.

"Where do the British plan to go next?" he demanded.

The other boys had not been consulted or informed about the plans of the British military, but over the last two days they had heard a word here and another there. For Fang, that was all he needed.

Fang left them to ponder what had just happened, hurrying along the crooked streets of Shanghai. Young Fang was indeed not trained to be a monk; rather, his training made him a perfect spy. Acting upon his father's instructions, Fang had entered Shanghai to learn what he could. Now he knew the primary goal of the foreign army.

“The word on every tongue is Zhen'jiang,” Fang reported back to his father, not a half hour later.

The elder Lieu mulled over this news, occasionally looking at his wife. She stood unmoving, beautiful, wise, and silent. Zhen'jiang, Lieu knew, had rested mostly serenely on the banks of the great Yangtze River, in Jiang'su Province for nearly three thousand years. Soon, that serenity would end, he knew with certainly.

“Zhen'jiang is the largest and best fortified city beyond Shanghai,” Lieu said, nervously. “It guards the heart of the Yangtze River, and beyond Zhen'jiang lies the great city of Nanking. This is where the next battle will be fought.”

Lieu took a cloth and wiped the perspiration from his lip. “If Zhen'jiang falls,” he added, “Nanking will fall. If Nanking falls, Peking and all of Cathay will fall! The British already know this!”

Lieu immediately sent word to the Mandarin Shu that the British intended to lay siege to the pivotal city of Zhen'jiang on the Yangtze, from where they might easily march on to Nanking—and then the Imperial City of Peking. Lieu hoped this intelligence would alleviate the mandarin's anger at Fang's outburst.

The Mandarin Shu sent a different reward for this advance information. Shu's message was succinct: “Lieu and his family will be sent to Zhen'jiang. Retain control of Zhen'jiang at all costs. Undermine the foreign army by whatever means necessary.”

Upon reading this edict, Lieu looked up at his wife and child, stunned. “The Mandarin Shu wishes a terrible fate upon this family,” he said.

“At least he had not made Fang a eunuch,” his wife commented dryly. “Yet.”

Fang’s eyes shot her direction, briefly.

“With what army will we defend Zhen'jiang?” Lieu asked, upon reading the message again. “What navy? All the guns of Zhen'jiang were sent to defend Wusong, but there they were captured. What am I to do? I am no assassin. I am a scribe. A librarian!”

“The mandarin has sentenced us to our doom,” said his wife, with a calm finality. Whether she truly felt such serenity within is a matter of some debate.

* * *

Five thousand soldiers—Han, Manchurian, Mongol, and Hui—had been sent to defend Zhen'jiang. Lieu attempted to speak with the commander of the armies, but he could not find which of the generals was truly in charge. Nominally, Hai Ling was the Supreme Commander, but rival generals ignored his orders. Traditionally, the

Han Chinese troops under the Green Standard refused to fight beside the Mongols and Manchurians of the Eight Banners, whom they considered semi-civilized. In turn, the conquering Manchurians considered the Han to be soft and overfed. Even within the Eight Banners, the Muslim Hui troops were reviled. As such, no general had true control of more than a thousand troops. Even among the better trained Green Standard Army, their weapons were more likely to be swords and polearms than smooth-bore muskets.

"No cannons, no rifles, and no leadership," said the despairing Lieu. "With this we are to combat the finest army of Europe? We must flee."

"If we flee," On-yan'jing said, "every assassin of the Seven Societies will make it their highest priority to find us. They would not spare Fang."

"And if we stay? Can we save Fang then?"

She did not answer.

7. The Siege of Zhen'jiang

Early on the twenty-first morning of July, the defenders on the walls of Zhen'jiang spotted a flotilla of seventy British ships approaching from downriver. Even before, thanks to Fang's espionage and his own observations, Lieu had known this armada would be on its way here. Once more he sent word to the mandarin, telling him that the situation was hopeless and that their best hope would be to evacuate to Nanking and make a stand there. The mandarin's answer arrived a day later: he ordered Lieu and his family to stay in Zhen'jiang and save the city.

"It is a death sentence," Lieu declared.

British mortars began shelling both fortresses which flanked the city. From two miles away, Fang watched those shells strike the walls and roofs of the forts. He adjusted his binoculars to see fires erupt and men leaping from the broken battlements. Within an hour, both forts lay in ruin.

After a few short skirmishes, Fang saw the British take all the high ground surrounding the city. There, they set up their artillery. Fang returned to the house where his father had stayed, to report the British advance. Mortars sailed overhead, leaving streams of smoke in the skies and death where they landed. The bombardment shattered layers of tiled roofing and exploded within, obliterating entire families in an instant. Fires and screams filled the streets.

"The Green Standard Army fights fiercely with such weapons as they possessed," Fang informed his father upon his return, "but the

British have no difficulty scattering them from the suburbs outside the ancient walls."

Lieu shook his head grimly. "To make things worse, for once the British outnumber our armies, two-to-one. Hundreds of Chinese soldiers have fled, leaving the defense of the city to the brave but ill-trained Manchurian Bannermen."

One of Hei Hu's runners arrived with news, but before he could speak, a distant rumble reverberated across the city. After a heavy sigh, he explained. "Once they'd cleared the western walls of defenders, the British engineers planted powder kegs at the centuries-old gates. Now they have set them off."

"No doubt," said Lieu, "the explosion blew the from their hinges. Already, foreign troops pour into the city!"

Yet Lieu expected this and gambled on a desperate ploy. Within minutes he was in the nearby garrison of the Bannermen, where he identified himself as an emissary of the Mandarin Shu to the Manchu commander. The general immediately bowed to the scribe.

Lieu did not wait. "General, you must call all your men to this garrison. Stay hidden, remain silent, and return no gunfire. Take no action against the enemy until you receive my order."

The general, without comprehension, bowed in acceptance of these orders. Outside, the bombardment continued, but the Bannermen laid low and waited.

The waiting was not long. The British ran riot through the streets, shooting anyone in sight, man or woman, ever advancing on the district of the Manchu garrison.

At Lieu's order, the Manchurians poured out of their garrison and ambushed the surprised British troops.

A dozen British soldiers and sailors fell the first assault. The rest fell back. In seconds, the Redcoats realized that the wild Manchurians had them pinned down.

The British quickly regrouped, however, and a pitched battle ensued for some hours. When the Manchurians ran out of powder—which was soon—they launched themselves on the remaining thousands, waving and thrusting their bladed weapons. Not one sword or spear reached its target; the British riflemen easily shot down their holders.

Lieu had hoped the British losses would be greater, but it was a foolish hope. Already, even more British reinforcements arrived and the tide of battle had shifted. A few hours past noon, he left the Manchurian camp and returned to the walled villa that had been his home these last few weeks. There, On-yan'jing and Fang awaited him.

They saw at once the anguish in his face.

"The city is lost," said his wife.

Lieu could not even bring himself to nod.

"I know not what to do," he said, his voice barely audible.

"I will fight them, Father," said Fang, now twelve. He snatched up a stout pole, a worthy quarterstaff, and hefted it with determination.

"You will not," said On-yan'jing, firmly. She turned to her husband. "We will escape through the tunnels. When the fighting stops, I shall make my way to the camp of their General Hough and poison him."

Lieu stared for a moment, letting the meaning of her words sink in.

"You will give yourself to this foreign devil?"

"Agents of the White Peacock have done so before," was her simple answer.

"You will not succeed. Even if you do, they will capture you. They will kill you!"

"Only after I have poisoned their leader."

Lieu felt a tightening in his chest, his throat. His beloved wife had the best plan for defeating the enemy, but even this was foolhardy and likely to succeed only in her death. Yet he could think of no other way to stop—or even slow—the British advance.

He was about to give her his answer when an explosion in the street outside thundered in their ears. Lieu and On-yan'jing ran to the windows.

Outside they saw soldiers with pink faces and red coats advancing down the street. All fled in their wake, unless they were shot first. Yet it was not simply the sight of the foreign army here, so deep within the city, that stunned the Lieu family. The British were coming from the wrong direction.

"They come from the north!" Lieu exclaimed. "They have breached all the gates of the city! There is no avenue of escape!"

On-yan'jing had no time to reply before a bullet shattered the frame of the window. Lieu pulled his wife and son away. More bullets struck the house.

"The gates of the house will not stop them," said On-yan'jing. "We must go to the tunnels."

Lieu nodded in agreement, but then said: "I will slow them."

A British cannonball shattered the lion-guarded gates of their house, followed by the gleeful whooping and hollering of the English and Scotsmen. To Fang, they sounded like all the demons of Hell.

"Take Fang!" Lieu ordered.

“No!” Fang insisted, the only time he ever defied his father. “I want to fight with you, Father.”

“Go!” Lieu commanded, pointing to the inner chamber.

Fang did not budge.

On-yan’jing did not wait. She knocked the quarterstaff from Fang's hands, grabbed him by the collar, and dragged him along with her.

Lieu ran towards the front gate of the citadel. There he had earlier planted small barrels of black powder in the roof over the gate, for just such a contingency as this. He hoped to bring down the gate on the heads of the barbarians—but his heart sank as he saw it was too late. The British were already kicking aside the shattered beams that had been the gates. The British would be inside before he could so much as light the fuse.

In the outer courtyard, a half dozen of Lieu's guards, armored in leather and bronze, with ornately-forged polearms in hand, rushed forward, prepared for pitched battle. The British, in their red coats and tall black hats, rushed through the shattered gates, firing their rifles. There was no battle; there was only slaughter.

British rifles could fire with more accuracy than the Chinese muskets, thus killing at a greater range. They had one other advantage; they had bayonets, and the British troops had no hesitancy in using them, on dying guards, on gardeners, on Chinese children. Lieu drew a sword, of which he had limited training....

Inside, On-yan’jing pulled Fang through the inner courtyard and into a room on the far side of the house. There she slid a hidden clasp which allowed a portion of the wall to slide back, hoping to reveal the stairs leading to a tunnel.

They were met with clouds of smoke. The house on the other end of the tunnel—maybe the tunnel itself—was on fire.

On-yan’jing shoved the door shut. Holding Fang's hand, she rushed to the other escape route. The entire city could not be on fire, not yet. Odds were, this route would be safe.

Before she got to the second tunnel, she found her path blocked by Redcoats.

“Well lookie here, mates,” said an English soldier, a grin sliding across his face. “Looks like we got us a bloomin’ Chinee doll.”

The other men mimicked his evil grin and moved closer.

Fang, every bit as tall as his mother, broke out of her grasp and stood before them, defiant. This is what he wanted—all eyes on him. He closed his eyelids... then opened only one set of them.

"Stop, you men," he said in clear English. "Turn around and leave."

There were too many. Fortified with a lust for blood and rape, fueled by adrenaline, their minds were not ripe for subjugation. Angered, Fang could not concentrate.

Ere Fang could attempt another course of action, he was quickly backhanded and fell. The Redcoats laughed.

Another man reached for On-yan'jing's gown. "Let's see if 'er tits is yellow," he said.

She turned her green eyes on him and he stopped in his tracks. With a lightning fast flick of her hand, she slashed the man with her nails.

"Ow!" the man cried, suddenly revived, clutching his own hand. "She cut me. It burns!"

"Damned foreigners!" snarled a flame-haired Scotsman in a kilt as he stomped towards her. A pair of his mates flanked him.

Fang was on his feet once more, seeking to protect his mother. A flying kick knocked the first Scotsman to the marble floor. Whirling like a Dervish, Fang kicked another man, toppling him into the one behind him.

That was all. A tall English sergeant brought him down with the butt of his rifle.

"Stupid monkeys," he declared.

On-yan'jing reached behind a great bronze urn and pulled a hidden switch. A panel in the ceiling swung open and a net, studded with barbs, fell on the British soldiers. Mostly unharmed but frightened, they squirmed and knocked each other to the floor, squealing as the barbs jabbed their skin when they attempted escape.

Taking advantage of the moment of chaos, On-yan'jing grabbed the dazed Fang and hoped to flee into the second escape route. At that same instant, one of the soldiers attempted to help the fallen man she had slashed. He bellowed his discovery to the attention of the others.

"Billy! 'E's dead! 'E's been poisoned!"

The man's purple and green wound proved this true. On-yan'jing did not possess poison glands, but rather she brewed myriad poisons and applied them to her nails, which she ever kept sharp.

"She done killed 'im!"

"The 'eathen bitch!"

On-yan'jing pulled Fang by his collar as she hurried to a dragon-carved door. This door led to the second escape route with many other doors that would slow any pursuers. But before she could open the door, another soldier freed his rifle, aimed at her back, and pulled the trigger.

On-yan'jing stopped suddenly as a fifty caliber slug ripped through her heart, silencing it forever. The report assaulted Fang's ears. Blood splattered across his face as the bullet exited her chest. He blinked the blood out of his eyes and looked up at his mother standing there, frozen.

Slowly, On-yan'jing looked down at her only child. How she had regretted not seeing him all those years in Tibet. She wished to touch his face once more. She extended her hand... Then she fell, landing on top of Fang.

The remaining soldiers were now free of the net. Not one of them would admit aloud that they'd been unnerved to see the woman stand so long after taking a bullet in the heart. The tall sergeant growled at the one who had shot On-yan'jing.

"Ya bleedin' piker! Now where's our fun?"

"Shush yer gob. There's plenty o' dollymops 'ere abouts," he said, giving a nod in the direction of the inner courtyard where the serving girls cowered. The other man shrugged, clearly disappointed that he would not have the opportunity to violate a beautiful noblewoman.

The other men went off to find comfort for their nerves in purloined wine or acts of mass rape upon the servants. Only the tall sergeant lingered, snickering at the sight of Fang, struggling to get out from under his mother's body.

Then Fang saw his father as he ran into the hallway. Lieu stopped, seeing his wife dead, his son splattered with her blood. "On-yan'jing!" he cried.

The tall Englishman turned and fired without hesitation. Lieu stumbled forward a few steps and fell next to his wife, the mother of his child.

Fang, rolling out from under his mother, took no time to look at his father. As the sergeant sought to reload his rifle, he launched himself at the man who shot his parents.

The sergeant, having fought lascars and Sikhs before ever setting foot on Chinese soil, was quick to react. He blocked the boy with his unloaded rifle as if it were a quarterstaff.

Fang only grasped the rifle with both hands, swinging his feet together into the man's belly. The Englishman fell with a groan.

Fang was on him, clawing, scratching, ripping one of his eyelids with a sharp nail.

"Augh! Get yer yellow claws off me, boy!"

With a strength he had not known he possessed, Fang tore the rifle from the desperate sergeant's hands. Fang launched himself once more, sinking his teeth into the man's throat. The Englishman fought with everything he had to stop the animalistic attack. It was not enough.

A moment later, Fang rose up, English blood dripping from his lips. He had killed the man with an instinctual, yet non-venomous and flat-toothed bite. This man would be the first Fang ever killed. He would not be the last.

Fang saw his father raise his hand weakly. He was still alive. Fang rushed to his side, even as the smoke began to thicken in the room.

"Fang..." his father gasped. "My son..."

"Father, I will avenge you."

Lieu shook his head with the strength he had left. "No. I forbid it. Forget revenge. Purge it from your heart."

The dying man grasped his son's hand and said, "Flee... Survive... Remember the Protocols always and promulgate them."

With that, the light left his eyes.

Fang released his father's hand and rushed to the open tunnel entrance.

8. Aftermath

Weeks later, the war ended. For the first time since the Manchurians themselves invaded, Cathay had been defeated by a foreign power, casting a great shame upon the empire. The Ching Empire ceded Hong Kong and twenty million pounds to Great Britain under humiliating terms. Chinese ports were now forced to allow the sale of opium, essentially turning tens of thousands of their own people into addicts.

As he watched the victors raise the Union Jack over the palace of Zhen'jiang, twelve-year-old Fang recalled his father's final words. Likewise, he recalled the Archimandrite telling him to wait, to let fate take its course.

This, Fang would not do. From now on, if a thing needed to be done, he would dedicate all his energies into making it happen. He vowed to aid the Order to more active intervention with and against the Western Powers, primarily the British.

"*The Protocols of the Order of the White Peacock must ever be promulgated, not the stagnant empire of the Chings. Cathay is but one nation in a world overflowing with nations. The goal of the Order has ever been to eliminate all nations, that we might unite the many races of mankind as one. The prophecies herald a new and better world, but*

I will not stand by and wait for these events to unfold. The prophecies will come true because I will make them come true."

Fang looked at his hand—the hand that killed the British soldier who had so brazenly killed his father and others. He heard the foreigner's last words in his mind.

It was then that he gave up his childhood name. On that day he took the name of Huang Zhou.

The Yellow Claw.

HIGHER EDUCATION

1. Recovery

The city of Zhen'jiang lay in smoking rubble. In the days after the fall of the city, the British looted the armories, the garrisons, and the treasuries. The storehouses of rice and other foodstuffs were thrown open and the Redcoats fed like swine while the Celestials starved. Anything the English and Scottish troops did not steal was stolen by the surviving Manchurian and Mongol Bannermen.

Within those ruins, Hei Hu, the Black Tiger, found a half-naked youth, ragged and dirty, whose eyes reflected no warmth.

"Fang! Lieu Fang!" Hei Hu called as he ran to the boy.

He stopped short, seeing the *dao*—machete—in the younger boy's hand, pointed at his heart. Narrow green eyes regarded the assassin.

"Fang! Do you not recognize me? It's me, Hei Hu. Put that down."

The youth did not lower the weapon. Instead he only said, "I do not know the name of Lieu Fang, a boy who could not save his family from the foreigners. I am now Huang Zhou."

Hei Hu snorted. "Yes, a good name. But put down that sword before I take it from you."

After a moment's pause, Huang Zhou did so.

"Your honorable father is dead, then," said Hei Hu. "Well, he was not a warrior and this is a time of war."

"The war is over," corrected Huang Zhou. "This is a time of humiliation."

Hei Hu grunted. In a few words, Huang Zhou told him what had happened since last they saw one another, a month earlier. He told how the mandarin had ordered his parents to single-handedly stop an invasion and they had failed. The city was overrun and an ignominious treaty followed. Huang Zhou did not feel compelled to add that he had lately murdered a few British soldiers whenever he found one alone.

"Now you are an orphan," said Hei Hu. "You have no family but the Sublime Order."

Huang Zhou did not reply. Neither did he argue.

* * *

The Celestial Empire had been broken by her enemies. It seemed only natural to Huang Zhou to abandon the land and return to the bleak expanses of Tibet that he had come to love in his youth. Alone and upset, the forbidden citadel was the only place left where he felt at home.

He packed in a satchel what little he still possessed: a water sack, a bag of rice and his writing implements, and began the slow and arduous journey to the roof of the world. Along the way, he found himself anticipating once more the study of alchemy, transmutation, and other subjects referenced most obliquely in passing.

As he neared the citadel of Yian-Ho, Huang Zhou spotted small piles of stones—seemingly nondescript unless one had been trained in their meaning as he had. These, he knew, were intended as markers for the Tcho-Tcho people, a kind of Central Asian pygmy. Whether these markers denoted tribal boundaries or the comings and goings of men or animals, or if they held a religious significance, only the Tcho-Tcho knew—and they did not share their ways.

These mysterious people were small and wiry, and could enter a house via any opening. Putting such skill to use, the Tcho-Tcho people had long been accredited as the finest assassins in the world; even better than the assassins of the Sublime Order of the White Peacock, who, after all, might allow a tree limb to fall on their heads from time-to-time.

One might think the Sublime Order would seek out these Tcho-Tcho and bring them into the Council of the Seven, as they would make excellent allies. Indeed, they and the Council were known to have many common enemies. However, Huang Zhou knew there existed between the Tcho-Tcho and his allies in the Kuen-Yuin branch an ancient and bitter animosity.

Still, he wondered how the Tcho-Tcho might become even better assassins. Maybe if they were smaller yet.

* * *

Without allies, wearing clothes of stolen yak skin, and living off the land, Huang Zhou walked and climbed for much of a year, being hopeful of climbing the mountains in the summer months. Several times over the last weeks of his journey, he had begun to wonder if he was lost. Each mountain seemed much the same as the next and could easily hide an entire citadel in even the best weather—and the weather was seldom the best.

Yet at last Huang Zhou found himself once more standing at the kraken-carved gates of Yian-Ho. This place was a building, a walled city, a monastery, and the capital of the Kuen-Yuin, the heart of the Si-Fan—the oldest organization on Earth. He called out to those inside, speaking in the Tibetan tongue.

A moment later, he called out one of the phrases he had learned of the original, precataclysmic language that these people still sometimes spoke.

He waited all day.

He slept before the gates all night.

In the morning, he ate the last of his food and continued to wait. Only at noon did the massive bronze gate open. Huang Zhou jumped to his feet.

Framed in the gate, stood an archimandrite—one of six who governed the citadel. The ancient wore the same sort of green robes and tall green hat that he had worn the day he first met him, seven years prior. No doubt, archimandrites of the Cult of the Kuen-Yuin had dressed much the same for a thousand generations.

"You were not expected, Huang Zhou," said the wise man. His voice held no more warmth than the ice-capped mountains that surrounded them.

Huang Zhou bowed deeply. He knew better than to ask how the archimandrite knew he was no longer Lieu Fang, for they had means of knowing what they needed to know of the outside world. "I ask ten thousand apologies for disturbing the meditations of the most serene Archimandrite," he said. "I have become an orphan and I would continue my studies. I have no other home."

"War makes orphans of many," said the ancient. "That which the fates have dealt us, we must bear. Take with you this knowledge when you go forth in the world."

Huang Zhou stared at the old man for a moment. "Serene Master, am I no longer welcomed?"

"Is this where you are needed? Is this the path upon which you have set your foot? Would you study our ways to achieve the betterment of the world or to have revenge?"

"I do not want revenge. My father forbade it with his last breath."

"Good," said the archimandrite, "for not even an ocean of blood can drown the fires of revenge."

"So you will let me enter?"

"No, Huang Zhou."

"Master! I have no other home. I have no country, for Cathay has buckled under the boot of the barbarians."

In a few words, Huang Zhou told him what had happened in the Celestial Empire. The archimandrite expressed his interest by watching a pair of sparrows fight over a grain of rice that the boy had dropped.

In despair, Huang Zhou cried out, "The emperor has failed Cathay! The mandarin has failed the Sublime Order! Both have failed to bring us any closer to the prophecies. Why should we serve them?"

The archimandrite casually regarded him. “It is not the way of the Sublime Order to hold petty rivalries and envy. Siddhartha said, he who envies others does not obtain peace of mind.”

“Master, the way of the Buddha is not the way of the Council.”

“True, young one, but neither are the teachings of Siddhartha in opposition to our own goals. He knew of us and shared many of our goals, if not our methods, for he taught only of the enlightenment of the man, never of Mankind.”

“Master, I promise to work for the betterment of mankind. Having a home and access to the secrets of the Kuen-Yuin will greatly aid me in this endeavor. I am only one person and the British have great armies and a greater navy. Would you not have me learn the secrets of the First Seven?”

The archimandrite shook his head. “No matter how many books we give you, still you do not learn that which is most important. Listen to me, Huang Zhou, the affairs of nations are trifling matters. Wipe these thoughts from your mind. Rather, remember the history you have already learned. Let Cathay and England and all other nations pass from the world, as Rome and Egypt and Atlantis have all ceased to exist. In the end, there shall be but one nation on the Earth and it shall be guided by a single hand, and that hand shall be guided by the Sublime Order.”

“If so,” Huang Zhou countered, “then the history of the Sublime Order is ten thousand years of failure.”

The archimandrite gave a single, solemn nod of his head. “Considerably more than ten thousand years. But remember that this is only because our goals are the most lofty. Remember, 'Nothing great was ever gained with ease.'”

“The Buddha said that?”

The archimandrite considered the question before saying: “I think it was Benjamin Franklin.”

Huang Zhou's only response was to stare.

For a change, the archimandrite broke the silence. “My son, you have shown that your heart is not with us; rather it is within the corporeal world, for there your thoughts ever return. Yet there, and only there, will you advance the ultimate goals of the Seven. You will then be prepared for when the prophecies happen in their course.”

Huang Zhou stared without blinking. “I have learned that nothing will be achieved by waiting for the prophecies to occur. The prophecies must be made to occur.”

The archimandrite relented. Possibly, he even smiled a bit. “You have learned indeed. Follow your own path, my son.”

The archimandrite stepped back inside and the gate closed. After a moment, Huang Zhou turned his back on the citadel and began to walk his path alone.

2. Cathay Again

Huang Zhou returned to Cathay rather faster than he ascended, as he now traveled downhill, and he was evermore focused on his ultimate goal than before. To sustain himself, he drank melted snow and hunted birds and at night he stole what villagers failed to secure.

Upon eventually returning to Hunan Province in the central portion of the Celestial Empire, Huang Zhou once more took up his studies with his masters in the Order of the White Peacock. These studies included history, botany, zoology, engineering, chemistry, and optics, and in all these subjects he surpassed all other students. During these next few years Huang Zhou did his best to avoid the attention of the spiteful Mandarin Shu, who never forgot or forgave any slight, even those of a nine-year-old boy.

From his friend Hei Hu, he learned more of the Wuxia arts, though the older boy easily knocked Huang Zhou's feet out from under him every time. The Minister Ki Ming, who was ever demeaning towards him, was charged with teaching him something of alchemy and the brewing of poisons. Despite Minister Ki's haughtiness towards Huang Zhou, the youth admitted the man's knowledge of poisons often surpassed even that of the Green Lamas.

Huang Zhou read of the properties of the poisonous Black Lotus and the *aglaophotis* from which he might brew cures for maladies of the body, mind, and spirit. He learned of the notorious *upas* tree, so poisonous that even its shadow could kill all who stepped upon it. In those same Burmese jungles grew a plant rumored to bestow the secret of the *elixir vitae.* From Africa came both *taduki*, and the curious sickle-shaped leaves of a plant valued by the pharaohs, should they wish to arise as a living mummy. Of all of these plants and more, Huang Zhou knew he would need to find them and test their seemingly miraculous attributes before he could determine the veracity of such claims, but he also knew better than to scoff.

In the entourage of Minister Ki was a girl, Po Phie. Her family had been prosperous, but they had lost everything in the late war with the British aggressors. Now she had been given to the mandarin's household as a seamstress.

Phie came to the attention of Huang Zhou after his tunic was torn during a particularly painful lesson with Hei Hu. He went to the servants' quarters and found the girl at her sewing.

"Po Phie," he said, "I have torn my shirt. Can you fix it now?"

The girl looked at the torn shirt. "Yes, master," she replied.

As she sewed his sleeve back in place, Huang Zhou took note of her simple but not unattractive features. Finished with her work, she rose and handed the repaired article of clothing to the young scholar with a bow. Taking the tunic once more, he also took hold of her hand.

Startled, the girl looked up at Huang Zhou, perhaps confused, perhaps frightened.

"Look into my eyes, Po Phie," he said, in a firm voice. His inner eyelid closed over his green eyes, forming opaque orbs that held her gaze. "Minister Ki has commanded that you obey my wishes. Within your heart and within your loins there burns a flame. Only I can quench this fire—with fire. Do you understand?"

Had the girl not felt some attraction to him, Huang Zhou could not force her to give in to his wishes. Charmed as she was by Huang Zhou's compelling green eyes, she answered.

"Yes, sir."

"Remove your gown."

Without question, she did so.

Po Phie was the first girl with whom Huang Zhou had intimate relations and he was her first as well. After he finished with her, he studied her nude form, slumbering upon the bed, his eyes drifting slowly over her unbound hair, her pale, smooth skin, her slender limbs, and her feet.

Moments before, his attention had been on other parts of her body. Now, without her tiny shoes and socks, her feet were exposed clearly to him for the first time. Stubby and twisted, with the toes folded under the ball of each foot, after years of having her feet bound in such a position, they were deformed beyond repair. She could never run from a man. She could walk only by hobbling. This ancient custom may have made the feet of women beautiful—to some eyes—but it certainly kept women subservient to men. Any man wishing to take advantage of her need only step on her sensitive and hideous feet.

Such was the custom of the Celestials, but Huang Zhou despised it. His own mother had never been made to mutilate herself in such a manner, and pity to any man who might have sought to make her do so. As said before, his mother was not like other women.

Seeing the girl's deformed feet angered Huang Zhou. He looked away from her sleeping face, lest she open his eyes and see the shame in his own. In using his power over her, he felt he had taken advantage of her, the same as those who had crippled her. Had he oppressed her as the British oppressed his people?

Although he had not the ability to subjugate anyone, still Huang Zhou resolved to never again use his ability to influence minds to make a woman give in to him. He would save those abilities for when he needed to advance the cause of the White Peacock.

* * *

At last, the masters of the Sublime Order had taught Huang Zhou all they could. Upon achieving his seventeenth birthday, he knew he must leave Cathay should he wish to learn more.

He'd considered traveling the Silk Route to Persia, where he'd heard of a heretic they called the Báb, who defied the imans by decreeing that all religions had merit and that the truest religion would, by necessity, be an amalgamation of them all. More to Huang Zhou's interest was a beautiful young lady called *Táhirih*—the Pure One—who'd publicly become an acolyte of the Báb and had been proclaimed something of a female messiah.

Yet no matter where he traveled, he would need the permission of the Mandarin Shu—whose wrath he'd incurred as a child. As the mandarin had a long memory, Huang Zhou knew he must chose his words carefully and be prepared for any trap.

The forbidden palace of Sang-Wah stood on a hillside, well outside the walls of Changsha, capital of Hunan Province. There, several agents had gathered to report to Mandarin Shu their findings concerning the comings and goings of the British and French trading vessels. Upon finishing, the mandarin would decide how much of this information was to be passed to the emperor's ears. Not much, Huang Zhou knew, based on his father's admission.

Hei Hu gave a report of the failure to assassinate a particular warlord who had proved overly cooperative to the British and their lucrative opium deal. As the mandarin understood that the task was unusually difficult, he ordered that only one of Hei Hu's operatives be executed.

After that, Huang Zhou came forward and kowtowed low to the Mandarin Shu. Shu, stroking his forked, white beard, allowed Huang Zhou to remain in that position a full minute before responding to the gesture of obeisance with a faint nod of his aged head.

"The boy we knew as Lieu Fang wishes to speak once more to his betters, I see," said the powerful nobleman. "Has he learned his lessons or does he still follow the path of his father who failed us in Zhen'jiang?"

Huang Zhou felt his muscles tighten upon hearing these words, yet he slowly straightened. He looked at the sneering face of the wizened old man. Upon the mandarin's head rested a fur-lined cap topped with a ball of pink coral, thus denoting his rank. Emblazoned upon the mandarin's green robes, a peacock of white silk shimmered.

"Honorable mandarin," said Huang Zhou, "once, you explained the symbolism of the bird that graces your robe. You said that as the peacock fans out its feathers in a proud display, so too do the branches of the Sublime Order spread out and cover all of Asia. The peacock is white for only from the color white can all other colors have their origin.

"Today, I hope our exalted mandarin will remember this wisdom. I also hope you and your honored officers will look beyond Asia and see the entire world.

"Honorable mandarin," Huang Zhou continued, "as you know, the Council of the Seven has not confined itself to the Celestial Empire. At times we have reached out and expanded. We have brought into the Council such secret organizations as the Dacoits, the Thugees, the Hashashim, and the White Lotus."

"Of course the serene mandarin knows this," commented Minister Ki, harshly. "Do you think he is a fool?"

"This humble scholar would never underestimate our gracious mandarin," replied Huang Zhou to Ki.

Turning again to Shu, he said, "To continue my words without the chirping of spring birds, I will add that the mandarin is also no doubt aware that the Council maintains relations with certain other organizations, outside of the Council of the Seven. Among these were the Knights Templars and most recently, the Illuminati of Bavaria. The Templars have passed from the world, alas, and with the Illuminati we have lost all contact."

"Yes, yes," said the mandarin, not failing to display his annoyance. "And so?"

"Illustrious Mandarin," Huang Zhou continued, not bothering to mention that it was the mandarin's neglect that caused the Illuminati to part ways with the Sublime Order, "many times wise men from the West have become known to us. Among these were doctors and learned men who followed the precepts not of Hippocrates but of a Brother Nicholas of Poland, in the time of the Yuan Dynasty."

Huang Zhou paused to judge the mandarin's response. The mandarin kept a straight face, never showing if he had a clue about what Huang Zhou spoke or not.

"Mandarin, I have heard late rumors from the Western barbarians of curious experiments and marvelous inventions, mostly originating from the regions near the University of Heidelberg where Brother Nicholas founded his brotherhood. I suspect his order may still exist and can be found today. I believe their inventions and amassed knowledge can be of aid to the goals of the Sublime Order of the White Peacock. I propose to travel to the West and become a student at this university so that I might rediscover this brotherhood and bring them once more into our fold."

Immediately, Minister Weng interjected his thoughts. "It would seem this young pup prefers the barbaric West to his own culture in the East."

The mandarin shared Weng's contempt. "Yes, again the infant would chase after our enemies, for whom he shows such admiration! Well, these days our emperor's armies clash with the Sikhs on the westernmost border. Perhaps if he is so fond of dealing with barbarians, I should send him there to undermine the efforts of those fearsome warriors."

Or die trying, Huang Zhou finished the mandarin's thought in his mind. He had no desire to go to India and fight in a meaningless skirmish. He knew his talents would be better served by learning more about the Westerners. But Huang Zhou had learned his lesson years ago, and he knew better than to say such things aloud to the mandarin.

Rather, Huang Zhou said: "Noble mandarin, I have already studied these fearsome Sikhs. The Sikhs rarely start wars, but they are often known to finish them, as the Mughal overlords of India discovered. The ferocity of the Sikhs is not only a trait of their men, but also of their women. Surely my most august and informed mandarin will know the famous story of how General Mai Bhago sought out forty deserters and shamed them into returning to her army, then leading them against the Mughals at the Battle of Anandpur. Such a warrior-woman is of a rank with Lady Fu Hao, Queen Penthesilea, Hua Mulan, the Truong sisters, Joan of Arc, or Qin Liang-yu."

The mandarin rested his head on his hand, clearly bored by the history lesson. Still, Huang Zhou continued.

"But I must ask my serene mandarin, what if such a warrior-woman exists among these Sikhs today? And what if she is the one prophesied to be the Universal Ruler of which we are to support and promote? Surely then our efforts would work against the Protocols. Please clarify for this most humble servant, if this is what the wise mandarin wishes."

The Mandarin Shu raised his head. Although silent for a moment, his eyes widened and flitted back and forth.

"No," said the mandarin with a hiss. "Of course that is not what we wish, you dullard. How could you think such a thing? Have you learned nothing from all your studies in the East, Huang Zhou? Maybe a Western school will knock some sense into your head! Go find one and let me see you and your backwards logic no more for a while!"

Huang Zhou bowed low, then turned and departed. The mandarin only stared coldly at the retreating form of Huang Zhou, glad to be rid of him and his logic.

Outside of the mandarin's chambers, Huang Zhou spoke with Hei Hu. "This is what I have learned from the Westerners. It is called *sophistry*."

3. His Journey to the West

And so, Huang Zhou left Hunan Province with a satchel containing a few implements, necessary travel papers, money, sundry supplies, and only one spare shirt. He took a barge down the Xiang River to the Yangtze and then overland to the Pearl River and from there to the coast. In the Portuguese-held colony of Macao, off the southern coast of Cathay, Huang Zhou boarded a ship.

By the time he sailed through the Straits of Malacca and around the Horn to Lisbon, he had a firm grasp of the Portuguese language. From Lisbon he took another ship to the port city of Rotterdam. Employing the German that he already knew, and eagerly learning more every day, he rapidly made his way up the Rhine. Two months after leaving the mandarin's court, Huang Zhou found himself in the Grand Duchy of Baden. This was no coincidence. Nothing in the life of Huang Zhou was ever a coincidence.

The Sublime Order of the White Peacock and the other representatives of the Council of the Seven might have had their origins in Asia, but at times in the past they had reached out and expanded. Certain organizations which had been allied with them in the past had their roots in the West. One of them had been founded here, within the confines of the University of Heidelberg in the year 1265, as rendered by the Western calendar.

Here in the West, the year was not 4484, as proclaimed by the Celestial calendar. Here the year was only 1847. Huang Zhou accepted that many people of the West were two thousand years behind Cathay, but not all of them.

Initially, Huang Zhou found the enrollment process confusing, but he knew a generous application of gold would smooth things out. Universität Heidelberg was nothing if not cosmopolitan, but a few well-placed gratuities helped smooth the enrollment process.

"You are not the first Easterner to matriculate at Heidelberg University, Herr Chow," said a dean, handing him papers to sign. "We even had a Hindoo a few years back."

Huang Zhou made no comment about the mispronunciation of his name, but he was interested to hear that there had been other Asian students.

"Indeed? While I would like very much to share a room with another of my race, I believe it would better advance my knowledge of your ways and customs to berth with a German student."

The dean nodded, without looking up from his perusal of the paperwork. "That will prove no problem, Mein Herr. At this time, you will be the only Celestial at the university."

"I see."

Huang Zhou bought a suit cut in the German style and presented himself in class the next day. His schooling included many of the same subjects he had studied in Cathay, but here his focus was on medicine and anatomy. In a Buddhist society, the dissection of corpses is considered a great offense. In the West, corpses could be hacked and sliced and cut into the smallest pieces and then boiled into corpse fat or preserved in jars of alcohol. The only statute governing the matter was that the bodies must come from executed criminals.

While Huang Zhou's presence caused some curiosity amongst his classmates and instructors, his polite demeanor precluded significant consternation. Upon reaching the age of seventeen, he bore a striking appearance: aside from his Far Eastern features, he had a broad head, a long face, and hawkish nose. His eyes, even without revealing the inner eyelids, were unique and imposing. He rarely smiled or revealed any emotion and this made many people uncomfortable.

Indeed, he knew it would bode well to ingratiate himself with his fellow students and faculty. He regaled the philosophy and literature students with tales of his homeland and extrapolations of Confucian and Buddhist teachings. Students of chemistry he tutored, for he knew more of the subject than their instructors. In his medical classes, which were his primary purpose for picking this institution, Huang Zhou studied vigilantly and impressed his instructors to no end. Yet when it came time to be examined, Huang Zhou made certain that he missed two or three questions on an otherwise perfect test. Thus he never incurred the jealousy of other students.

This was good, for Huang Zhou roomed with three other students. Herzog and Hoffman were bright but Ingersoll had interest only in girls. As for his schoolwork, Ingersoll paid Huang Zhou to write his papers. The first semester passed without incident.

* * *

Inside a snow-dusted tomb in Paris, the hand of a breathing, living man took a sheath of centuries-old papers from a hand long dead. The man glanced at the pages, then at the corpse whose casket stood in the tomb within the Cemetery of the Holy Innocents. He bowed to the corpse and departed.

The man discovered that the words written on those pages to be a play in two acts. The *Dramatis Personae* called for four male speaking roles, four female, several extras, and, curiously, one character to whom no gender had been assigned, despite being called a king. The first act was decently well written, even insightful, certainly engaging enough to want to read the second act. Oh, but that second act was unlike anything ever set to paper. Hours later, after reading the entire play, the man went insane.

The following morning, he furiously set about making copies of the play, hiring actors and actresses, and engaging a theater for the performance of the play. He would be the director.

Weeks later, in February, "La Roi en Jaune" was performed one time. Of the two hundred in the audience, a hundred and seventy-seven went insane. Ten had died of shock. Twelve others had been stabbed or strangled before the play ended—the director being one of them. None had managed to keep both their wits and their lives, except a stable boy who had snuck in and fallen asleep before the first act had ended.

The survivors spilled out into the streets of Paris, accosting passersby, grabbing them by the lapels and revealing what they had seen. Without the full context of the play, most of these bewildered pedestrians were only left bewildered. But many did go insane.

The mania that ensued in the weeks and months to follow spread forth like a wave, ever diminishing, yet ever spreading, crossing the borders of nations and the barriers of language. Soon thousands were caught up in the fervor, setting off revolutions in Paris and spreading across Europe by spring.

Revolution spread across the land like wildfire and all Europe seemed mad. Common workers cried out for the blood of the wealthy and powerful. Riots and reprisals became common. For months the revolutionaries mounted initial successes, taking over governments, and hanging their former officials from lampposts or tossing them out windows.

* * *

The newspapers reported riots daily. Because of the troubles across the land, classes ended earlier that year. Taking advantage of this, Huang Zhou made plans to return to Cathay, despite knowing that travel was unsafe while revolution swept the land. As he traveled through the states of Baden, Hesse, and Prussia, he saw masses of layabouts with banners but no actual violence. From the port city of Bremen, he booked passage to Shanghai on a fast steamer, via the Horn.

During his travels, Huang Zhou studied translation books. Through them, he gained a grasp of Latin, and its daughter languages: Italian, Spanish, and French. He also perfected his English, which was essential, if for no more reason than most of the translation books available had English as the base language. *Hardly a surprise*, he thought, *as the British people are on the march across the world.*

Once more in the Celestial Empire, Huang Zhou ignored the castle of Sang-Wah and the company of the mandarin. Rather, he went straight to Peking and visited his former sparring partner, Hei Hu, from whom he caught up on the latest news of Cathay. Universally, it was bad. However, Huang Zhou's primary goal for this return trip was to engage a warlord's daughter for a great task, but that is a tale for another time.

His stay was brief. Despite the advances in travel, Huang Zhou had scarcely time enough to speak with the girl once before boarding a steamship bound for Panama. There, he crossed from Pacific to Atlantic by mule, where he hired another ship to take him to Bremen. During the return trip, Huang Zhou spent much of his time in his cabin, studying Arabic, Hebrew, Farsi, Hindi, and Urdu.

Once more in Heidelberg, he ignored the rioting and revolution outside the university's walls. It meant little to him if Europeans murdered each other by the droves or not. His focus was on higher goals than mere revolution. Nonetheless, he wrote a detailed report of what was happening and passed this on to couriers who would carry word across Europe and Asia in just a few weeks.

In the fall, classes resumed. However, none of his searches, none of his careful hints and suggestions, yielded any trace of that brotherhood of scientists and doctors which had brought him here in the first place. He began to wonder if that organization had gone extinct. And if so, he contemplated what might be required to revive the Brotherhood.

* * *

In Vienna, a bloodthirsty general proclaimed that if the rebels "will not hear the voice of the Lord, they will hear the voice of the cannon!" With that, he began the bombardment of his own capital.

By year's end, all the myriad revolutions had collapsed from within. There were no reforms. Nothing changed that year, save that now the graveyards overflowed.

* * *

"All the girls want to meet you, Hang Chow," announced Ingersoll as he walked into the surgical theater the following September.

Huang Zhou barely glanced up from his dissections. "Who are these girls of whom you speak?" he asked. "Why should they want to meet me?"

"Dumb-head! They have never seen a Chinaman before. Ilsa wants to draw you; she's very talented. And Gretchen wants to know how you walk upside down."

"I do not walk upside down."

"Oh, she thinks all Chinamen must walk around on their hands because you live on the other side of the world."

"That is foolish."

"Yes. She's an idiot. But so much the better, is it not so?"

"How so?"

"You'll find out."

That night, in the rooms he shared with Ingersoll, Huang Zhou met the four frauleins as arranged. The girls were all students at Frau Klefman's School for Young Ladies and all came from good families, he was assured, and they were all very pretty. Gretchen, Gerda, and Astrid all had cascades of blonde hair and admirable depths of decolletage which they displayed very close to his face. Ilsa was brunette and she wore spectacles while she sat on the bed and made sketches of him.

The blondes all listened with oohs and awws and giggles as Huang Zhou told his stories of far-off and exotic Cathay. He also explained the concept of gravity to a doubtful Gretchen. Ingersoll kept their wine glasses full and Ilsa continued to sketch.

Huang Zhou felt it unfortunate that none of these girls would be allowed to attend classes at Heidelberg. Although Chinamen might be allowed to study there, women were not, no matter their race.

"Ilsa, do not forget to make his eyes slanted," Greta chided between slurps of Pinot Noir.

"I will not forget," Ilsa quietly responded. She, like Huang Zhou, drank only tea that night.

"I thank you, my dear," he replied. "I can assure you that all Han Chinese have what you might consider to be slanted eyes. Green irises, however, are considerably more rare in the East than the West."

Greta licked the liquor from her lips and said: "Is it true the pudenda of the Celestial women are sideways?" Astrid and Gerta giggled. Ilsa's eyes widened.

"No more often than the pudenda of Occidental women," Huang Zhou assured them. "My studies and dissections have confirmed this fact."

"My brother says Chinamen all have slanted genitals, to match their slanted eyes," said Astrid, after her third cognac. Ingersoll blustered and coughed. The sisters laughed loud and outrageously, but Ilsa only blushed and ducked her head below her sketch board.

Huang Zhou had heard similar uneducated remarks before and becoming angry would be beneath him. Figuratively gritting his teeth, but with no change in expression, he said: "Dear lady, your brother, though he might be most astute in all other matters, has likely never beheld the organ of any Chinaman, thus I fear he has been misinformed. However, I confess that my own organ does have a noticeable bend to the left whilst in a state of arousal. Perhaps I was spied upon and it is to this that he refers."

The girls and even Ingersoll went silent, all blushing. Ilsa, however, peered over her sketch board and looked at Huang Zhou. Or rather, she studied his crotch.

Ere the night was over, Ilsa had completed half a dozen fine sketches of Huang Zhou, though only half of them showed his face. Unfortunately, one of those had been marred by a smudge of blood from her maidenhead.

* * *

Another year and with it another semester gained Huang Zhou more knowledge of the West and more friends. Word out of Persia revealed that half of all Bábists had been massacred and the Báb himself was in hiding. Táhirih had been placed under house arrest. Huang Zhou wondered if, had he went to Persia rather than Germany, he could have saved her from that fate and used the Bábists to reunite with the Khurramites and thus promote the plans of his own order.

Another summer not only meant more time for him to pursue more languages and read more books, but the opportunity to take a steamship across the Channel. Rather than embarking from Calais, he chose Kiel, purposely hoping to have a longer voyage. He spent most of the two day trip in the engine room, learning how the device operated in actuality and not just theoretically, as he had already read of this in books.

In England, Huang Zhou rode on a great conveyance that moved along rails pulled not by mules, but by a large engine. The "Rocket" was every bit as unsubtle as the people of Europe, but also as innovative and forward-thinking.

On his way back, he stopped in France, and flew in a balloon. From the gondola's vantage point, he made several sketches of his observations from overhead, intending to share them with Ilsa when he returned to Heidelberg.

Before that, however, he allowed himself brief visits to Vienna and Venice, including stops at the new Chinese consulates, where he made himself known to the officials. Through these consulates, he sent to the Mandarin Shu sealed missives containing the latest scientific journals and samples of the most recent chemical discoveries, including titanium, chromium, and uranium.

There came no reply.

4. The Mentor

The following September, in the dissection theater, the apron-clad professor carefully performed an autopsy. He explained each step of the process, displaying each organ and explaining its purpose.

"The intestines, as you can see," he said, "consist of both smaller and greater portions. Here, Herr Berg. Take hold of this end and walk over to the door. Herr Rauch, take the other end and go to the other door and we will measure how long—I said take the ends, both of you! Hurry!"

The two young men did as ordered, albeit with little enthusiasm. Ingersoll was made to bring the end back to the first student, for the large operating theater was still not large enough across to contain the entire intestine. When the small intestine had been stretched to its limit, Huang Zhou volunteered to take the ell-stick and mark off the length seven times and a portion more. Thus it was found that the organ, stretched in such a manner, measured twenty-two feet.

Of course, the professor might have simply read off the measurement of the small intestine but, with this display, the students were not likely to forget. Having only himself graduated a year before, Professor Hans Teufel was the youngest of all the professors. He taught nothing by rote, but rather he excited the imaginations of his students with autopsies and surgeries. He did not simply demand that they memorize the organs of the bodies and the humors they contained, he asked that they apply what they had learned to new and unknown situations.

Some students hated Teufel for the challenges he threw before them. Huang Zhou, however, excelled in such an educational environment and Teufel quickly recognized him to be his best student. The respect was mutual.

"Revered professor," said Huang Zhou, one day after class, "I came to the West so that I might advance my education of those subjects which we of the East lack. At one time, the medicine of the Celestial Empire was far greater than that of the West. We made herbology and acupuncture into sciences, whilst European surgeons only sought to bleed every patient for every malady—including anemia.

"However, like all great empires, ours suffers from resting upon its laurels. Chinese medicine has not advanced in centuries, held back by Buddhist reverence for cadavers. Here in the West, doctors may dissect all the bodies they wish."

Teufel scoffed in ill-humor. "I wish it was as simple as all that. If we had a sufficient number of bodies to dissect, we would certainly train more physicians, perhaps even common surgeons, in the practice of medicine. We might also have a better understanding of why so many blood transfusions fail to save the patient."

Huang Zhou knew of what Teufel spoke. "As the only bodies available are those of executed criminals," he said, in irony, "perhaps one should hope for more crime."

"That's about what it would take. But think of the experimentation we could perform, without so many restrictions. We might see if Long's claims about ether hold true under all circumstances—or chloroform, or nitrous oxide. Or is it better to perform surgeries without anesthesia, to enhance healing, as some insist?"

"Such experiments would, perforce, need to be performed upon living subjects."

"Yes, but the human brain and the brains of animals are far too different. We'd learn very little."

"And to conduct such experiments upon human subjects would be a violation of one's Hippocratic Oath—*Do thou no harm*," Huang Zhou said, throwing out the name of the Greek doctor as a challenge.

Teufel took the bait. "Oh yes. Dear old Hippocrates. Just think of all the suffering and death that could be avoided were it *not* for those strictures."

"I often have."

Prof. Teufel looked at him, perhaps seeing him truly for the first time.

"Come to my house tonight, Herr Chow. I'd like to speak more."

Huang Zhou agreed.

* * *

A concierge allowed Huang Zhou into a small two-story house in a respectable but not ostentatious tenement house, as would be expected for a first-year professor. Teufel welcomed his prize student and, after offering him a glass of wine—which Huang Zhou politely declined—they sat down in the study and talked, only after Teufel sealed every window and door.

After discussing many aspects of medicine, anesthesia, and research in general, Prof. Teufel and Huang Zhou confirmed one another to be like minded. Indeed, with only a little more prodding, Teufel admitted that the Brotherhood of Nicholas still existed and that he was indeed a member.

"I'm told that our membership now consists of only a dozen or so men of science and medicine," Teufel admitted. "And these are scattered all over the map of Europe. But I tell you, Chow, of late their discoveries have been amazing."

"I would agree," said Huang Zhou. "And are you aware that a similar organization exists in the East?"

Teufel stared blankly, for once. "No, I am ignorant of anything like that. Is there?"

"Indeed. I speak of the Council of the Seven of the Si-Fan, which is held to be the oldest organization on Earth. At least, some of the seven branches can lay hold of that claim."

"Amazing. And yet, well, of late… China has fallen behind. Wouldn't you say?"

"To the great shame of my people, this is true. The reasons are myriad. For one, the Council has fallen out of contact with your Brotherhood."

Huang Zhou went on to ask of certain men of whom he suspected might have been members in the past. These included Adam Weishaup, founder of the Bavarian Illuminati.

"I am aware that Weishaupt had some sort of connection with the Brotherhood," Teufel said, nodding. "Although his not-so-secret society was more concerned for social changes than scientific research, we do have the Illuminati to thank for the French Revolution and exposing the secret work of the Jesuits. Many of the changes that the Illuminati put in place now encourage the various sciences and technology. The Illuminati came to have many benefactors, dukes and counts. Too bad they were slandered out of existence.

"The freedoms espoused by Weishaupt's society encouraged many of our greatest minds. Being allowed and encouraged to look further than his textbooks, Wohler derived organic compounds from inorganic material. Morton has invented a gas to make surgeries painless. Faraday has single handedly revolutionized the science of electricity and magnetism. There are more discoveries every day."

Over a claret, Teufel told Huang Zhou about some of the Brotherhood's other members and their researches. These included the Englishmen, Dr. Robert Knox and Andrew Crosse. Knox had conducted some of the most advanced research into dissection and grafting before his school was shut down by the authorities, over accusations of grave-robbing. But the most amazing experiments of all were those of Andrew Crosse.

"Crosse placed a volcanic rock in a solution of potassium silicate and hydrochloric acid in a hermetically-sealed aquarium," Teufel explained. "He electrified the solution with a Voltaic pile, so as to stimulate electrocrystalization, hoping to generate the same chemical reactions that occurred in the primal earth. It worked. He created life."

Huang Zhou, who took only tea, stared at his instructor, his features as impassive as ever. Teufel smirked.

"Hard to believe, is it not so? But it is true. Crosse recreated the experiments many times."

"Professor..." Huang Zhou began.

"Fah, Crosse was not the first; only the most recent. Others have attempted to create life—or to revive the dead. Rabbi Loew is said to have created a living man of clay. Maybe it's just a legend—who knows? But Chillingworth also tried to revive the dead. He came close to succeeding, too. And Franken—"

Teufel cut himself off, suddenly realizing he had said too much.

Huang Zhou, however, did not miss the slip. "Who is Franken?" he asked. "Another student here?"

Teufel glanced at the second story windows. Then he leaned close to Huang Zhou and spoke in a hushed voice: "No. Frankenstein. He matriculated at Ingolstadt in Bavaria, a few years before it was shut down. Indeed, he was the reason it was shut down.

"You see," and here Teufel lowered his voice even more, "Victor Frankenstein conducted that experiment which is the Holy Grail of the Brotherhood. Frankenstein… created life. No, not simple *acari electricus*. He created... a living *man!*"

Huang Zhou was not one to show surprise or fear or even doubt. His expression shifted nary at all from hearing these words. But Teufel could not have missed the slight widening of those unique eyes.

"That was fifty years ago," Teufel added. "I'm surprised you have not heard the story; an Englishwoman even wrote a book about it, although they've passed off as a romance."

"I must find this book and read it."

* * *

Soon after, Huang Zhou expressed a desire to sail to England to meet Crosse and Knox. Teufel, however, dissuaded him.

"Both men lay under the shadow of scandal," he said. "And if the English newspapers enjoy anything, it's a good scandal. They both keep low profiles these days. I doubt if either man will conduct further experiments in their chosen fields. At the moment, I am unaware of any other Brothers alive and active in the British Isles."

It did not matter, Huang Zhou soon realized. Teufel would go on to explain their theories, and how they might be applied through the Galvanic battery which Teufel had lately constructed. Huang Zhou hung on every word. The experiments of his professor had captivated his imagination. Expanding upon the theories of Galvani and Volta, he pushed Teufel for more information about the art of reanimation.

"Professor Galvani has determined that life is only a substance," Teufel explained, "It can be removed by death, but it can also be replaced, presumably by electrical current."

To this, Huang Zhou expressed doubts.

"Well then," Teufel said with a smug smile, "it seems I must show you the proof."

* * *

"The natural sciences are not my only areas of research," said Huang Zhou, one night after another carnal assignation with Fraulein Ilsa Gerber. "I have recently begun to study the supernatural realm as well."

Ilsa, now rather more worldly than when she first met the mysterious Celestial, smirked and said, "Oh? You would be a sorcerer then? Do not forget, they used to burn such people."

He nodded. "Of this I am aware; I have read the transcripts of the trials. However, I am not a practitioner of the supernatural, nor do I strive to become one. Rather, I have begun to study these newly burgeoning occultists, their table rappings, and visitations from the afterlife."

Huang Zhou did not tell the girl that the occultists had also begun to gain a following and showed influence over the wealthy and powerful of Western society. He pondered if these occultists might one day be united into some sort of cohesive organization that might benefit his Sublime Order.

"So this is why you read these kinds of books?" Ilsa asked, giving a dubious glance to a stack containing the works of von Reichenbach and Eliphas Levi.

"Precisely," he answered. "I considered seeking out Von Juntz and Ladeau, until I learned they both perished under unusual circumstances seven years ago. Curiously, in April of that same year, a Professor Enoch Bowen uncovered the tomb of the pharaoh Nephren-Ka, only to soon after cover it up again. Afterwards, he returned to America and founded a new and unorthodox religion, inspired by his discoveries."

"What sort of religion?"

"So far as I can ascertain, the church promulgates the advent of the imminent return of the Messiah."

"So they are the same as the Millerite church?"

"I would need to learn more before I can answer that. It would seem there are as many secret societies in the West as there are in the East."

"Wang, if you know of them, they are not secret, yes?"

Huang Zhou contemplated this logic. "You are most astute, my camellia bloom. However, certain criminal organizations such as the Black Hand and the Sicilian Mafia, purposely make their works known, so as to spread fear among the population."

"They are murderers, yes?"

"Murder is among their many petty, criminal pursuits. As such, I have no desire to pursue them further. Other secret societies of the West interest me more. Among these are the Illuminati, the Society of Leopold, and its offshoot, the Tribunal of Urbino. According to the few scattered references I have found, Papal authorities sanctioned this tribunal and their knights to search the world for various sprites and boogeymen that supposedly trouble the plans of the Papacy. As of the last century, the noble Vordenburg family of Styria were inducted into the ranks of this tribunal. They wage a crusade against witches and certain fabulous creatures of the Night: subterranean creatures that feed on the dead, men who take the shape of wolves, and most dubious of all, ghosts that rose from their graves to feed upon the blood of the living."

Ilsa gave a little laugh. "Surely no one believes in such things as vampires and werewolves in 1851!"

"Indeed, some do," Huang Zhou stated. "There was a werewolf trial in Spain only a few months ago. And during my researches, I have heard rumor of a pair of curious monster-hunters—as they proclaim themselves—one Hugo Krantz and his assistant, Edgar Frump."

Huang Zhou had also heard that these monster-hunters had but lately attempted to capture the escaped creation of Victor Frankenstein, only to have the creature turn the tables and nearly kill them. He chose to not mention their misadventure to the fraulein, lest she scoff at its veracity—or worse, demand proof. Nor was he compelled to tell her that recently, Mr. Frump ran afoul of a particularly sinister Hungarian nobleman named Dracole or Drakulya, and had not been heard of since.

"Interestingly," Huang Zhou did admit, "I have heard that Herr Doktor Krantz had been a student here at Heidelberg University. Yet the only record of a Hugo Krantz that I could find, referenced a man who had graduated in 1733."

"Oh. A grandfather? Great-grandfather?"

"Perhaps."

Eventually, Huang Zhou would conclude that occultists and monster-hunters offered little of value to his goals, given that they chased after spooks and fairies. Instead, he returned his attentions to the acquisition of the practical sciences.

* * *

In Cathay, where it was December of 4487, new troubles arose. Influenced by the influx of Protestant ministers, a ne'er-do-well named Hong had a feverish vision and due to this vision, he proclaimed himself to be the younger brother of Jesus Christ. As he was not the only madman in Cathay, he soon gathered thousands of followers to his cause.

These fanatics decreed that their foreign Manchurian overlords were demons in the service of Satan and they founded the Taiping Heavenly Kingdom, seeking to restore the native Ming Dynasty. The rebels easily took control of Guang'xi Province in the south where there had never been love for the barbaric Manchurians of the north. When the Ching emperor sent troops into the region, they were repulsed, thus challenging the emperor's already shaky authority

Hearing reports of these events from out of the Celestial Empire, Huang Zhou was momentarily tempted to return to his homeland and render his services. However, upon contemplating the value of his education, he remained. Cathay's destiny was not necessarily the destiny of the White Peacock.

In the following summer, Huang Zhou graduated near the top of his class—after purposely giving a few incorrect answers, so as to not incur the jealousy of his classmates—and graduated. He had now earned a doctorate of medicine. After graduation, Huang Zhou went back to his teacher and friend, Prof. Teufel.

"Noble Professor," he said, "I would ask that you return with me to Hunan Province and the Sublime Order of the White Peacock. It is my profound wish that you enlighten the Mandarin as to the existence and value of your Brotherhood. There is no doubt that when you display your experiments to the mandarin, he will accept this as proof of what Western science might accomplish."

"Ah. I am honored, my friend," Teufel replied. "However, I fear that long journeys rather interfere with my digestion. May I propose a different idea?"

5. Homecoming Gifts

Huang Zhou said his goodbyes to Professor Teufel, to his classmates, and to Fraulein Gerber. The professor was profound in both his sorrow and his well-wishes. Most of Huang Zhou's classmates were glad to see him gone, as they did not appreciate him scoring so high above themselves.

Ilsa, though, upon hearing the news, presented Huang Zhou with disbelief and tears. In his rooms, as he packed his traps, she vacillated between recriminations and hysterics.

"Do I mean nothing to you?" she said in reproach. "I thought you loved me. Even if you do not love me, please stay. Please!"

"I can not," he said as he reviewed his books, picking only those he considered necessary. "I have my duty."

"Yes, very well. I will go with you."

He did not look up, only considering which of the maps of the Vatican's basements and tunnels he would take. "You can not go to Cathay; it is not allowed for unmarried women. Also, you would not enjoy having your feet bound."

"We could be married," she said in despair. "Then I could travel with you anywhere."

Huang Zhou scoffed. "Your year 1851 is not a leap year."

"You are so cold! I think you have no soul!"

"I have a soul if any man does," he said, at last setting aside his packing. "I am not without feeling for you, my spring flower. I assure you I am pained to leave you behind. Yet pain is what I must accept if I am to fulfill my duty."

"Duty! Always duty! Do you care for nothing else?!"

"I care for many things, whether you chose to believe that I do or not. I care for you also, my dear. Yet we can be together no more."

Ilsa fumed and stomped her foot, but none of her arguments or theatrics stayed his plans. He sailed on schedule, without her. However, he took with him a sketch of Ilsa, a self-portrait he had commissioned during their time together.

* * *

In Cathay once more, twenty-one-year-old Huang Zhou found much of his homeland shaken by the Taiping Rebellion. By landing in the Portuguese colony of Macao and traveling through a circuitous route, he ignored these events as much as possible. Despite the war, he traveled rapidly, arriving once more in Hunan Province in only ten days. There he knew he must present himself at the palace above Changsha and stand before the Mandarin Shu to report on his findings and to receive his duties. Or sentence, depending on the mandarin's humor.

Huang Zhou realized something was wrong when he attempted to enter the gates of Changsha. A pair of blue-clad Mongolian Bannermen stepped out, with dao-staffs pointed at his chest.

"Huang Zhou!" their sergeant bellowed. "You are not welcomed in Changsha! So orders the Mandarin Shu. Enter under pain of death!"

Huang Zhou did not ask why, for he knew these guardsmen would not have been informed of the reason, and neither would they ask. He simply turned around and went back the way he had come.

He did not go far, however. He waited in a bamboo grove outside the city, along the road to Canton. He watched the comings and goings of farmer's carts or the sedan chairs of various aristocracy. He knew that as the carts would be searched for contraband, Bibles and muskets, the watchmen would not likely miss a tall scholar.

Taking the place of a court official or his fine lady would get Huang Zhou into the city, but he would need to hypnotize all four of the litter bearers. Difficult, but not impossible. However, disposing of the occupant in the sedan chair might prove more difficult.

At sunset, just before the iron-bound doors of the city were to be shut and barred, a small group of men were seen exiting the gate. At the head of this group, Huang Zhou spotted a tall figure, as tall as himself, striding confidently forward. The young man was imposing, clad all in black, his long hair pulled back, with scale armor, leather bracers, and a naked *dao* in hand. Huang Zhou knew this man: Hei Hu, his old friend. Surrounding him were four fighting men in black pajamas, with green sashes girded about their waists—members of the Tong of the Green Dragon, whom Huang Zhou knew by repute.

He had no doubt they were searching for him. It seemed that the Mandarin Shu had a change of heart; not only had he banned Huang Zhou, he had likely ordered his death.

Engaging Hei Hu in combat would be suicide, and no doubt, any one of his Dragons could best Huang Zhou in a contest of arms. In matters of stealth, however, he stood a better chance of survival. With that, Huang Zhou withdrew slowly, silently, deeper into the marshes and the tall shafts of bamboo.

Clearly, before he met the mandarin, he would need a dead man.

* * *

Days later, the Mandarin Shu took a seat upon his gilded throne. Flanking him, as always, were Junior Minister Ki and Senior Minister Weng, along with a bevy of finely attired ladies. Standing before him were Hei Hu, a dozen of Shu's personal bodyguards, and a handful of servants and courtiers. The green-shirted master of the Dragon Tong exchanged glares with the general of the Tenth Mongolian Bannermen in his ceremonial armor and bedecked with medals. Waiting patiently were businessmen who dared to ask some favor or another.

Today, another matter was in the forefront of the mandarin's mind.

"What have you learned of the whereabouts of Lieu Fang, who now calls himself Huang Zhou?" the mandarin demanded. "Why have you not brought him to me? We know he was at the gates of the city. How could you let him slip through your grasp?"

Hei Hu was quick to answer: "Merciful Mandarin, it was the Mongols who had Huang Zhou in their grasp. They needed only let him enter and take him unawares. Instead, they turned him away and now he is onto us."

"We obeyed orders!" the Mongol general, Sengge Rin'chen, growled. "Would you have us be like these bandits and defy the word of the mandarin? Nothing was said at the time about capturing anyone. We did as we were told—we kept the scholar out."

Mandarin Shu clearly did not care to have his orders repeated back to him. He slammed both hands down on the armrests of his throne.

"Silence!" he bellowed. "You would place the blame on me?! Such arrogance! Such impudence!"

The Mongol general held his place and his tongue. He would not, however, drop to his hands and knees and pound his head against the floor in subjugation like a proper Celestial. As such, the mandarin's next order would likely be a death sentence.

However, a crouched old man, swathed in robes of grays and browns, then hobbled forward. This being unexpected, everyone looked at him.

"Most gracious Mandarin," spoke the old man in a scratchy voice. "If you will allow a poor wretch to express a word, you will realize that this brave general is no more negligent of his duties than yourself. All I ask is your pardon to speak my piece and leave with my head intact, if it please my honorable lord."

“Yes, yes,” the mandarin said, irritably. “Go ahead and speak and keep your damned head.”

The stooped old man bowed. Then he rose up. And up.

Hei Hu blinked, seeing that the crouched old man was now as tall as he. Then, with a flourish, the stranger threw off his tattered robe, revealing one of green, cut in a simple yet austere fashion, befitting a scholar. An instant later, the long gray beard was shorn, revealing a youthful face and an impressive shaven head.

“Huang Zhou!” exclaimed the mandarin. “You are a fool beyond all imagining to come here!”

“Hei Hu!” cried Minister Weng. “Seize this traitor! Have him executed by the Death of a Thousand Cuts!”

Hei Hu drew his *dao*, the blade singing against the metal throat of his scabbard. He strode forward.

“Halt,” said Minister Ki.

Hei Hu did so.

The Mandarin Shu, stunned and confused, glared daggers at his third-in-command. But Ki Ming only reminded him: “Mandarin, have you not just granted Huang Zhou your pardon?”

The mandarin's eyes bulged in anger, but he kept his silence. Ki Ming's interjection reminded him that revoking his pardon not a minute after granting it would prove to everyone that his word could not be trusted.

Minister Weng seemed to concede the point as well. “Honored Mandarin, if you allow the young fool to speak, his ramblings will no doubt give you a new and better reason to execute him.”

The Mandarin Shu relented. Huang Zhou bowed in response.

He then rose and clapped his hands twice, quickly. Two coolies, earlier brought into the palace by Huang Zhou, entered the throne room. One carried a small table, the other a heavy box. The table was set in place and the box placed upon one end. The coolies quickly withdrew and Huang Zhou opened the box to reveal a mechanism within.

“This device is but one of the many things I have learned of in the West,” Huang Zhou assured the mandarin. “It will take but a moment to prepare.”

As Huang Zhou began connecting wires to the small machine, all eyes studied his actions. A few of the mandarin's people whispered questions to one another, but none could offer an answer. The coolies returned, walking slowly and carefully, carrying between them what initially appeared to be another box, this one covered with a silken cloth. This they sat on the other end of the table, then departed.

Huang Zhou methodically set up the equipment. Those watching noted that under the silk, a kind of aquarium lay mostly hidden.

"Honorable mandarin," said Huang Zhou, "I have these last four years sojourned among the people of Europe, learning their science and medicine. I have there found allies of whom the mandarin will no doubt see the value, for this most humble servant of the Sublime Order of the White Peacock has determined the continued existence of the Brotherhood of Nicholas."

This grand revelation was met with utter silence and apathy.

"The Brotherhood, as you will no doubt recall," Huang Zhou quickly continued, "is a kind of lodge or cabal that supports the advancement of scientific knowledge, disallowing certain strictures of the Greek philosopher of medicine, Hippocrates. Founded some six centuries ago by Nikolaus von Polen, a Dominican who conducted experiments with reptile and amphibian flesh, showing how the attributes of one creature might be passed on to another. From such inauspicious origins came an organization which promulgated many of Europe's greatest minds.

"Members of the Brotherhood included many wise men who defied the strictures of their age to advance the cause of science. Paracelsus sought to create a living homonculus in a bottle. Vesalius taught his students how to fabricate a man. The alchemist Dippel invented both pigments and poisons. Mesmer developed hypnotism. And Adam Weishaupt founded the Illuminati—a secret society dedicated to the overthrow of the Roman Papacy and the crowned heads that stifle Europe under threat of the flames of the Inquisition.

"More recently, Dr. Chillingworth has attempted to revive the dead with an electric current. Ah! You smirk. To be true, he failed, but Andrew Crosse succeeded, and he even created life in the laboratory. The men of Europe have done these things in the past and they will do more in the future.

"Profound and august Mandarin, I advise that you send emissaries to my friend Professor Hans Teufel and the others, asking that they be reunited with the Council of the Seven. Doing so, we would have access to their discoveries and we might also have agents within the European powers. Money will help to advance their research, all of which will be given for our benefit. My wisdom in doing this will be apparent."

The Mandarin Shu immediately scoffed at the idea.

"Can you not count," said the sneering mandarin, "you who would squawk like a rooster of your accomplishments? You speak of the Council of the *Seven*. We already have seven branches." Here he extended one finger after another. "We, the Sublime Order of the White Peacock. The wise Green Lamas of Tibet. The scheming White Lotus of Cathay. The thieving Blue Dacoits of Indochina. The murderous Black Thugees of India. The Yellow Phansigars of Afghanistan. The Purple, dreaming, Hashashim of Arabia and Persia. See? We have room for no more."

Huang Zhou only stared, wondering if the man was seriously halting the Council's progress because of a tradition involving a set number. And would he prevent a new organization from joining them only because they did not meet the dubious color-coding?

Minister Weng leaned forward from his position beside the throne. "Sire, this upstart once more wishes to empower our Western enemies by giving them access to our secrets. Clearly, these Westerner barbarians have nothing to offer us."

Huang Zhou did not wait for permission to respond. "I fear the mandarin is poorly informed by his advisors. Anyone who has studied our allies would know that the Thugees and the Phansigars are the same group, separated only by geography and language. The Dacoits are only bandits. These are included in our number only since the extinction of the fanatical Red Khurramites of Persia. As for the Brotherhood of Nicholas, they were part of the Seven for five hundred years and they have ever been loyal allies. It was only because we have not remained in contact with them that they have forgotten us."

Huang Zhou dropped and kowtowed once more, holding the position.

"Mandarin, you are older and far wiser than I, a humble scholar," he said from his nearly prone pose. "Yet I think the mandarin will be enlightened to see a sample of what I have learned in the West. At the very least, he will be amused."

Minister Ki here interjected. "Glorious Mandarin," he said, "it can do no harm to see what this nonentity has brought to show. As he says, it may prove amusing.

With a flippant gesture, Mandarin Shu indicated his permission. With that, Huang Zhou again bowed, then set about revealing his machinery. The courtiers craned their necks to see a flywheel connected by copper wires to various glass globes. Removing the cloth from the aquarium, Huang Zhou displayed a human arm, severed below the elbow. None of the retainers expressed shock, a testament to their training and lack of squeamishness.

Huang Zhou quickly placed the arm on a towel and clamped the stump in place, near where it had been severed. This completed, he put on rubber gloves and goggles and began to rapidly crank the flywheel.

Sparks flew. The Leyden jars glowed and crackled with electrical energy. When a sufficient charge had been achieved, Huang Zhou picked up a wire with each hand. He looked at the mandarin and his retainers with a hint of a smirk. Then he placed the wires on certain muscles of the severed arm.

The arm jumped, the fingers extending, quivering.

The wide-eyed mandarin also jumped. His retainers followed suit, all gasping in horror and backing away at the sight of a dead thing seemingly brought to life.

"Devilry!" cried the mandarin in a panicked voice. "Necromancy!"

"No, my wise mandarin," corrected Huang Zhou. "Science."

Of course, the dead hand was not given life but only electrified and animated by a galvanic battery which Professor Teufel had given him. After Huang Zhou explained this to the court, the Mandarin Shu reluctantly reinstated Huang Zhou as a member of the Sublime Order of the White Peacock.

With the wealth and sponsorship of the White Peacock behind them, membership of the anti-Hippocratic brotherhood in Europe grew over the next several years. With such support, their inventions continued to astonish the Mandarin and his court. In truth, a few times, the inventions astonished even Huang Zhou.

DHAKAR AND THE SHADOW MAN

1. Return to Bundelkhand (1849)

Upon learning of the death of his father, the rajah returned home. His journey had taken him from the bright and shining capitals of Europe to the most godforsaken splotch of land he could imagine: Bundelkhand, the land of his birth.

The sea voyage had been exhilarating, watching whales and dolphins at times, enjoying fishing from the railing, and enjoying consuming his day's catch in the mess. That was one of his favorite things about living in Protestant England for a time—the people did not relegate fish to Fridays alone.

After debarking in Calcutta, the rajah had ridden in a coach, followed by two wagons. One held his drafting table, a roll desk for writing, a favorite chair, oxyacetylene welding equipment, Davy lamps, voltaic batteries, dozens of pressure gauges, calipers, scales, and weights. The other held a few suits of clothes and his books on engineering, metallurgy, chemistry, and several other subjects.

His carriage had crossed several hundreds of miles, each dustier than the previous. Closer to his destination, the road twisted and turned as the hills grew ever steeper. The air was dry and burned the lungs. The people were uneducated and dirty. And yet, for reasons unfathomable, the British East India Company had its eyes on this place, thus far independent.

Bundelkhand was landlocked, and the thought chided him. The sea connected all the world and yet still held such mysteries. Yet such was his lot in life, it seemed. One should accept what one is dealt, according to the Buddha.

The rajah muttered a comment to himself about what the Buddha could do with his acceptance.

The journey ended with the rajah's coach pulling through the gates of Banda, the capital and his home. Eight weeks after he'd received the letter from his father's chamberlain, the rajah was home. A young *chokra* opened the carriage door and salaamed. The blare of a half dozen horns announced the rajah's return. The rajah, still in his finely-cut tail coat and top hat, stepped into the blasting sunlight, with cane and gloves in hand.

On command, a motley group of servants and hangers-on cheered and threw rose petals before the rajah's feet. A *mahout*—driver—led a decorated elephant forward and bade it to kneel, so that the rajah might enter his abode in the traditional manner. Another brought forward a silken pillow on which sat a brightly colored turban, festooned with strings of pearls and an ostrich plume.

The rajah eschewed the turban, but he did ride the elephant through the streets of Banda, for how often does one get to ride an elephant? The magnificent animal lumbered towards the nearby palace courtyard. Palace? Compared to Versailles or Buckingham or the Kremlin or any of the other fine edifices which he had seen, this place was a shack. His father's home had been painted a garish white and trimmed in red before he'd been born. As it came into view, he saw the place yellowed, faded, and chipped.

He scoffed at his own thoughts. In truth, it was a fine villa and it certainly towered over the squalor which surrounded it. Most people in this land lived in huts or lean-tos and here he was complaining about the size of his mansion.

Truly, the new rajah did not envy the wealth and opulence of Europe. Rather, he envied them their universities and libraries. He envied their knowledge even as he detested their greed and smug superiority.

Not all Europeans were like that, of course. Europeans were quite varied in their mindsets, as he discovered twenty years ago. One fellow might detest him for being a foreigner while another might seek him out for the same reason. Until receiving the news of his father's death, the rajah had been a student in various European schools for the last twenty years. He'd proven quite popular, despite his serious nature. The prince was thirty, young in the eyes of Europeans, but middle-aged in India, where so few people see their fortieth birthday.

Inside the courtyard of the palace, the mahout stopped the elephant with a tap of his long stick. To the blare of more horns, the rajah again dismounted and looked at the courtyard, now packed with servants in multi-colored garb. They delivered a lackluster but well-rehearsed cheer.

The chamberlain stepped out and announced him: “Hail, Dhakar Rao, rajah of Banda in Bundelkhand!”

The cheers redoubled. Musicians clacked their cymbals and strummed their zithers. Pretty, half-naked girls danced about him and decorated him with garlands of flowers.

Dhakar allowed this fawning, for he knew to do otherwise would be ungrateful. He even forced himself to smile once or twice. But he was glad when he was at last inside, away from all the adulation and merry-making.

Dhakar recognized the chamberlain, Vasanta, who had been his father's chamberlain. The fawning sycophant, now with a snowy white beard, eagerly seated the new rajah on a mound of embroidered cushions and offered him scented wine. Dhakar demurred with a slight wave of his hand.

"Thank you, Vasanta," said Dhakar, "but I rarely imbibe spirits. I would take a cup of tea, however, if there's any in the larder."

Vasanta, unused to such polite speech even directed to a high-ranking servant such as himself, nearly faltered. Regaining his senses, he bowed low and said, "It will be done, Sahib."

Vasanta all but ran to find a can of tea.

* * *

In the following days, the Rajah Dhakar Rao took once more to wearing Indian clothing—a gleaming white sherwani with matching loose pantaloons, and sandals. On some formal occasions, such as the laying of a wreath on his father's centograph, he wore a black turban. Other times he wore a simple tarboush, but most often he went bareheaded.

Dhakar's interest in fashion was far outweighed by his desire for modernization. He visited the compound's smithy, running his hand over the forge, looking at the dusty tools sitting in piles. He happily recalled old Akbar teaching him how to render ingots into implements. Dhakar then ordered the place demolished. A new foundry and workroom would take its place, with only the latest tool-making machinery imported from France, England, and Prussia.

Two weeks later, as the house was being painted sky blue, Dhakar assembled the several administrators who had formerly served his father. Tea and crumpets were served, but no one would misconstrue the assembly as a party.

"Gopal," he said, directing his attention to the commander of the city's garrison, "I am told that three tradesmen have had their carts rifled through and their wares stolen by bandits—and not a mile from the city's gates. Why do your men not patrol the roads and capture these *dacoits*—bandits?"

A hefty, middle-aged man with bushy mustaches, Gopal was dressed in a pink sherwani, a billowing white turban, and a broad crimson sash from which hung a gilded *tulwar*. Hearing the reproach, he sought to maintain his dignity.

"It is unheard of, Rajah," he said, huffing. "Never once under your father's time, nor in the time of any rajah I have heard of, has such a command been given. The garrison is to protect the city, not the countryside. Those that travel outside its walls do so on their own. Such a command as you give is without tradition!"

"I don't care about tradition," said Dhakar, calmly. "The command is given now."

Dhakar looked at all of them: Gopal, Ghanim the minister of the treasury, Sundaram the tally-man of the grain silos, and Rangam the chief eunuch. "In the short time since I have returned to Banda, I have seen the extreme poverty of my people and utter lawlessness of my homeland and I am appalled. It is worse now then when I was a child. Gentlemen, I vow to do something about it. For those of you who wish to aid me, I have many things I wish to have changed....

"For those of you who would not aid me as I see fit, I will accept your resignation."

Gopal and the others, unfamiliar with the concept of resignation, wondered whether the rajah meant imprisonment or execution. Not wishing to receive either fate, they all hastily agreed to Dhakar's terms.

* * *

One warm but not terribly hot day soon after, while sitting on a shaded veranda, Dhakar sat reading some passages of Chaucer's "Canturbury Tales" once more. Upon hearing the clatter of wheels and hooves, Dhakar looked up to see a coach approaching, decorated with orange streamers. This was led by a sharp-looking troop of soldiers with orange sashes, and with tulwars in hand. The site of these finely-trained men brought a pang of envy to his breast. Presuming some high-ranking official must be within the coach, he rose and went out to greet the visitor.

Standing at the top of the front steps, Dhakar had a better view of those streamers—they each bore an image of the elephant-headed god, Ganesh, holding a mountain in his human hand. Dhakar Rao smiled, recognizing the charge of the Maharajah of Jhansi in the north of Bundelkhand.

It seemed that the maharajah and his train had come to Banda to pay their respects. Rao was nearly a decade older, tall and stately, with the whiskers of a Rajput, which would put an Englishman's mutton chops to shame. His sherwani and billowing pantaloons were white, with a dusky orange turban and sash. His proud and calm demeanor bespoke wisdom. The Maharajah, once dismounted, held out his hand and aided his beautiful and younger second wife to step from the coach.

Along with Dhakar, Vasanta and the entire staff and all of Dhakar's retainers had come out to see the visitors. Dhakar pressed his palms together in supplication and bowed to his superior, and his staff followed suit, kneeling or bowing low, depending on their status.

"Please forgive this intrusion, Rajah," said the maharajah. "A bout of a trivial ailment prevented me from welcoming you to your ancestral home until now. I am Gangadhar Rao, maharajah of Jhansi and this is my wife, the Maharani Consort, Lakshmi Bai."

Dhakar bowed again. He was impressed with the man's genteel manor—nearly so much as he was impressed with the man's taste in women. Taller than most women, the maharani was proud and intelligent—he could tell that much at once from her manner, her stance, and her sharp eyes. Dhakar not only noted her striking features, but the scarf that hung over her hair, perfectly matching the shade of orange worn by her husband. He took her for barely twenty and he only a few years older, and they had been married for five years.

"I thank you for honoring my humble home, Maharajah," said Dhakar. "Please come in and I will have tea brought for us."

Inside, Dhakar quickly commanded Vasanta to prepare tea and bring platters of kebabs, a variety of vegetables, flat bread, curried rice, and flavorful pastes. He also had *chokra* boys brought in to fan the maharani, lest she find the 125 degree heat uncomfortable. The maharajah, he noted, bade the maharani sit beside him on a pile of cushions, as might a Sikh man. Certainly no Moslem, least of all a Moslem potentate, would dream of being seen with his wife sitting in a position equal to himself.

Seated, taking tea and nibbling on snacks, the maharajah first paid homage to Dhakar's late father and then complimented the dishes set before him. The rajah could only apologize for the fare, which, he assured them, was hardly up to the standards he had become used to in Paris or London.

Upon mentioning the European capitals, the usual response from Indians would be to say that he must be happy to be home and away from such places. Others would want to know all about his adventures there, which, they had no doubt, were of greater interest than anything that might occur here.

The maharajah, rather than making assumptions, asked him, "Which do you prefer, Rajah? Europe or India?"

Dhakar took a second to think before answering. "I must say that both Europe and our own land have many admirable qualities. In Europe there are many wonderful innovations, such as the railroad, the telegraph, the steamship, and other inventions. Mostly, I stand in awe of their fine universities and the education which, on some measure, is available to every child, no matter how common their station.

"At the same time, I never failed to be surprised by the ignorance and small-mindedness that I witnessed so often. That I was a rajah certainly impressed some few of the people I met, yet the next one would declare me to be a nigger—a pejorative term, as I understand it.

"Bundelkhand, indeed, all of India, is now my home and it is my intention as well as my duty to remain. It is beautiful here—we have not the smuts in the air that have come to plague the great cities of London and Paris. Yes, I am having a time of getting used to the heat once more, but that will come.

"But there is ignorance here as well," Dhakar continued. "I—Well, I do not understand why a man must ever be prevented from gaining a position in life when he has proved his worth, simply because his family is of another caste. Oh, it is true there are castes in Europe... but those are not hardly so rigid. Indeed, being born of a 'lower' class might be seen rather as a challenge. If a fellow has intelligence and ambition, he might, with effort, advance himself."

The maharajah, who was an educated man, nodded.

"And the women of Europe, Rajah?" the maharani asked, her voice refined and soft and yet strong. "Did any of them ever excite your interest? You dwelt there for twenty years and that is a long time for a man to do without."

The maharajah chuckled at his youthful wife's comment and they both looked to Dhakar for his answer.

Images of Solange and Gwendolyn and even the Donna Giovanna all passed through Dhakar's mind. Rather than comment upon them in detail, the rajah said, "There are in Europe many beautiful women, very different from here of course, Maharani. Yes, a few of them did turn my head... but I always knew one day I must return to India and I ever kept in mind that I must take an Indian wife."

"Has a marriage been arranged?" the maharajah asked.

The rajah set down his empty cup. "Father did arrange for a marriage," he said. "I was to marry the daughter of the Rajah of Bhopal. Alas, the poor child died of cholera a few years ago. Father did not settle on another bride for me and I confess I am relieved. I wish my wife to be of my own choice."

"And hers," the maharani added.

Dhakar bowed his head to her. "And hers, good lady. My years in Europe have shown me the value of having a man and wife in agreement."

The maharani graced him with a lovely smile.

The maharajah nodded as well, but then he spoke of another matter. "Rajah, we have heard you have begun reforms here in Banda."

"I have indeed, Maharajah," Dhakar said. "With all due respect to my late father and his sires before him, these reforms are long overdue. Already I have reduced the taxes on the commoners. It is they, after all, who toil the most—why should they see the least profit?

"After the grain is collected," he continued, "it will be sold outside the borders of the province only when there is a surplus. I intend most of it to go back to the commoners who have grown it. All business dealings are scrupulously monitored for fraud and smuggling.

"I also expect that every constable in Banda will go about his job vigorously, knowing that the death penalty is in effect should he be tempted to accept graft from the *dacoits*—bandits."

Dhakar then stopped, wondering how Gangadhar Rao might reply to all he had said. After all, tradition died very hard in the sub-continent.

The maharajah and the maharani exchanged a glance... and smiled to one another. This smile they shared with Dhakar.

"We are both impressed with these reforms, Rajah," said the maharajah. "Indeed, we are of like minds in all these matters. In some of these things, we have also made changes and it is our profound hope to make even more changes for the betterment of our people."

Dhakar found himself relieved. Having the maharajah as an ally rather than an enemy pleased him.

The maharajah seemed to be in accord, for he next said, "Let us then agree to act in concert, thus strengthening one another's position in Bundelkhand. Together, we may stand firm should any outside forces wish to interfere with our goals."

"Indeed, Maharajah," Dhakar answered.

To this the maharani added, "We wish only the best for Bundelkhand."

With that, they went on to discuss lesser matters: the coming of the monsoon season, the likelihood of a good mango crop this year, the cost of muslin, and a little gossip about the maharajah of Gwalior and his notorious graft. Then the Rajah Dhakar asked his guests if they would honor him by staying the night. They agreed.

Dhakar at once excused himself that he might have Vasanta prepare a fine dinner and make up the guest bedroom. Vasanta, like any good chamberlain, had anticipated the order and already had the servants and cooks working at their respective tasks. Dhakar grinned and slapped the man on the back.

At dinner, Dhakar was proud to display servants who happily served their master, addressing him with respect, but informally. The maharani assured the new rajah that he would witness the same treatment when he returned the visit to their home.

After a dinner of curried lamb, Gangadhar Rao proclaimed he had rarely had so fine a meal and that it was worthy of their empress, far off in England. Dhakar offered to share a brandy with the maharajah in his study, but the older gentleman pleaded tiredness and retired for the evening. The maharani attended him to his room.

Dhakar happily stood on his veranda, wafted by the evening's breeze. He sipped his liquor and considered that his meeting with Gangadhar Rao had gone well—better than he might have hoped. With a powerful patron like him, Dhakar felt he might make even more reforms. He would even begin some of the engineering plans he had drawn up while he was in Europe. There he had studied not only the construction of bridges but the nearly miraculous qualities of the galvanic battery and the voltaic pile. He had wild ideas of how they might be combined.

Dhakar then detected the sound of a soft slipper in the study behind him. He turned to behold the maharani once more.

"Maharajah tires very easily these days," she said, resting her hands upon the railing and looking out at the hills and ashoka trees, now lit only by the last vestiges of twilight. "The trip is not so very long, but it was harder on him than he admits. I thank you once again, Rajah, for allowing us to stay the night."

"It was but the least I could do, dear lady," Dhakar replied. "And I am glad that I could find a chance to spend more time with you."

She looked up at the taller rajah. Oh?" she said.

Dhakar smirked. "Indeed. I did not miss your intent when you asked about my interest in women."

Dhakar rested his hand on that of the maharani. Her eyes zeroed in on their hands before flashing back up to his.

"Rajah—" she began.

"We are both mature and worldly, yes? The maharajah is a fine man, of course, but he is older and hardly in the most fit condition, while you are young and vital. Surely he cannot keep your bed warm."

"Rajah!" she said firmly, pulling her hand away, her eyes flashing with stern rebuke. "That is no concern of yours. I truly love my husband and I need no other. As for my interest in your marital state, I confess I might be pleased to play matchmaker, now and then. And what woman is not? I have a young cousin who might catch your fancy."

Dhakar was immediately ashamed. "Forgive me, Maharani. I know not what came over me. Maybe the spirits.... No. No, I blame my actions on living in Europe for so many years and picking up their ways. They may preach a virtuous life from their pulpits and in their publications, but they seldom live up to such virtues."

"That is true of many people, whether they dwell in the West or the East," the maharani said, her anger already subsiding. "I acknowledge that you have picked up many ideas and customs in the West... but never forget that your actions are your own. No one makes you do anything against your will. Do not blame the British for that which you do with... a free hand."

Dhakar hung his head for a moment, feeling even more embarrassed.

"Yes, Maharani. You speak wisely. Still, I think India would benefit from the sort of reformations that the East India Company proposes."

"Yes," said the maharani. "Some of them."

2. Asha (1850)

Dhakar Rao maintained his region as an independent state, free of any military alliance with any other region, be they Hindu, Moslem, or Sikh, lest such an alliance draw him into an unwanted war. Most important of all, he kept the British out.

At the celebration of Holi that year, Prince Dhakar hosted a fete and invited every maharajah and rajah in the land to attend. Re-enacting the destruction of Holika, the streets were filled with spring revelers and bonfires. Clouds of pink and green and blue and red filled the air. Dhakar may have inwardly scoffed at the idea of celebrating the death of a demoness, but he was glad to see his people once more smiling and happy.

Among the attendees that year was Gurdev Dheri, a Punjabi potentate of marginal importance, who was passing through Bundelkhand on business. Once, this man had been a powerful maharajah, but those days ended with the fall of the Sikh Empire at the hands of the East India Company and their hirelings. Dheri presented an all white Arabian stallion as a gift for Dhakar, which he happily accepted and promptly named Zabu. In Dheri's train, however, was an even finer gem. This was his daughter, Asha.

Young, beautiful, with a confident stance and intelligent eyes, the girl instantly caught Dhakar's attention. He wanted to know more about her. Custom or not, he was determined to speak with her.

"Rani Asha, do you enjoy the festivities?"

The girl, whose head came up to his chin, bowed her head in respect and in acknowledgment of his title—but not in submission, he observed. He found he liked that.

"I do, Rajah," she said, with a comfortable smile. "The people are happy and carefree for at least one day, and your principality is troubled to spend only a few thousand rupees for colored dust."

Dhakar's own smile widened. "Maharajah," Dhakar said, referring to the man by his earlier title, "your daughter is most wise for a girl her age. I see she values not only the well-being of the commoners, but she also keeps her eyes on the purse strings."

The former Maharajah gave a good-natured laugh. "Indeed, Rajah. Like her mother before her, she never lets me spend a single rupee where it is not needed."

"This is good, Maharajah, for a woman's duty is to not let a man spend himself into debt."

They all shared a smile, then Gurdev Dheri led his daughter to view the festivities and bright, colorful clouds of dust that filled the streets. Even when the olive-brown girl was soon covered in yellow, pink, and purple powders, the Rajah Dhakar could not take his eyes off her.

* * *

Dhakar found some excuse to ride Zabu to the Punjab soon after, and he was invited to take tea with Gurdev Dheri at his estate, once finely designed and ornamented, now cracked and haphazardly plastered over here and there to hold it together. The tea, shipped from the base of the Himalayas, was an excellent darjeeling, and Dhakar pronounced it so. Still, he hadn't come here for the tea.

"Maharajah," said Dhakar, "your daughter is intelligent and beautiful. I would like to spend more time with her. Getting to know her better, if I may."

"So, you wish to court my daughter, as a European would?"

"I... Well, I suppose I do."

Gurdev Dheri smiled through his bushy beard. "This would be most agreeable, Rajah. We Sikhs do not often intermarry with those of other faiths, but I see you are a man of good heart, even if you are an infidel."

Dhakar managed a smile and did not bother telling the Maharajah that he had long since dismissed all faiths as a great load of foolishness.

Under the watchful eye of an escort, Dhakar visited Asha every day for the following week. They spoke of the weather, the blooming of the mangoes, and Asha brought up the expected revenue from the hundred acres of sorghum that her father had retained. Asha asked many questions about the Rajah's adventures in Europe and she was surprised he had stayed there so many years after his graduation.

"Honestly," he said, "I had begun to think I would make a home there. Paris, most likely, but maybe Vyones. Maybe Munich."

"Not London? Not Rome?"

Dhakar laughed. "Never London. The weather would be the death of me. Rome? Maybe, but I found Venice to be far more romantic."

With the subject of romance having been introduced, the two moved closer and spoke more quietly. The escort merely smiled to herself and looked off at Asha's nieces collecting mangoes in the garden.

In the course of the conversation, Dhakar admitted he'd had women before, a French actress and the daughter of an Italian conde. Adultery was considered a sin in her beliefs, and Asha told him so, but without judgment. "Rajah, if you stray no more, we will forget your past."

"If you so wish, Asha," he said. "But I want you to always feel free to speak or ask of any subject that you so desire. I would have no secrets from you."

"Very well, Rajah, if you wish," said Asha. "You are older than I. Would I be untoward to ask if you embrace the ancient custom of *sati?* If we would marry, and you pass into your next life, would you want me immolated on your funeral pyre to join you?"

Dhakar could not restrain his contempt for the idea that a woman should burn alive beside her deceased husband. "I would never want such a thing, Asha. It is a detestable practice, unknown outside of India. This is exactly the sort of barbaric custom that I intend to abolish. Thankfully, the East India Company has outlawed the custom."

Asha tilted her head, looking up at him with serious eyes. "They have outlawed the practice; they have not stopped it."

This intelligence surprised Dhakar. Moreover, it angered him. "Then I intend to follow their lead and make this the next of my reformations."

Asha smiled. "You are not only a wise man, Rajah, but a good one."

"And you, dear Asha, are so much more than a pretty face. But I admire your pretty face as well."

She continued to smile at him, unwaveringly.

* * *

That evening, after a dinner of curried vegetables, Dhakar Rao asked Gurdev Dheri for his daughter's hand. Dheri mulled over the decision.

“My daughter is very beautiful, yes? You must not be surprised to know that you are not the first man to ask for her.”

“Oh. I see.”

“No, Rajah; she is betrothed to no other. I would not give away Asha without knowing her thoughts on the matter.”

“Then, Maharajah, I will say that I would not wish to marry any woman who did not want me. Please speak with her, for though I believe she does wish to marry me, my heart may well deceive me.”

Gurdev Dheri smiled, closing his eyes. “Rajah is not only intelligent, he is wise. I shall speak with Asha and I shall base my decision on her feelings.”

Dhakar bowed to the wise old man, noting how the father's statement of his merits compared to that of his daughter.

At that moment, a tall, lean nobleman rode into the courtyard at the head of a troop of cold-eyed cavalry, whose livery was of green with gold embroidery. This nobleman dismounted with ease from a fine black stallion, allowing a lieutenant to grasp the reins. As the man strode up to the veranda, Dhakar observed he was at least five years younger than himself. His turban and gold-trimmed sherwani were silk and as white as snow. His pantaloons and broad sash were pea green. A scimitar in a gilded scabbard hung from that sash. With his bejeweled hand he stroked his short, pointed beard. The man had the face of a hawk and his eyes fell on Dhakar just as a hawk's might.

Gurdev Dheri introduced the two men.

“Rajah Dhakar, this is the Rajah Chambu Singh of Shaitanabad in Jalandhar,” Dheri explained. “He is my closest neighbor and our families have been the best of friends for generations.”

The two rajahs smiled cordially and bowed to one another. Still, Dhakar found the man's intense stare to be less than comforting. Then it occurred to him that Chambu Singh may have been one of Asha's former suitors.

* * *

A year after he returned to his homeland, the Rajah Dhakar wedded the Rani Asha in her father's mansion, every bit as humble as Dhakar's. Asha admitted she had hoped to be wed in the Golden Temple of the Sikhs, but this would not be allowed as Dhakar Rao was not of their faith.

The mansion and the surrounding courtyard, decorated for the wedding, were a riot of colors. Sikh nobility from all over the Punjab were in attendance. Many Hindu lords and ladies from Bundelkhand and surrounding regions also attended, including the Maharani Consort Lakshmi Bai, standing in for her ailing husband. One or two Moslem dignitaries were present, and all mingled together for the happy occasion. Only the Rajah Chambu Singh was conspicuous in his absence.

That night, Dhakar discovered that Asha had indeed saved herself for him. In contrast, he used his experiences in Europe to his advantage, and happily removed the obstacle to their wedded bliss. Asha found the experience more painful, but before their first night ended, her screams were not of pain but of pleasure.

Upon their return to Banda some weeks later, Dhakar gathered his officers and made an announcement. Standing at the head of a table, like a French dignitary at an embassy, he addressed Ghanim, Sundaram, Commander Gopal, and all of Gopal's captains.

"I wish to initiate many reforms for the betterment of the people of Banda," he continued. "Thus far, these reforms have included a reduction of the taxes and we have begun to build a new hospital for the poor. I thank you, Ghanim, and I thank you, Sundaram, for your work in these matters."

The two ministers pressed their palms together and bowed their heads to the rajah. He nodded to them, then turned to the commander of the garrison.

"But Gopal, the first thing I heard upon my return from the Punjab was how another baggage train was robbed and a girl taken—most likely raped and sold into slavery. Gopal, I will not allow Banda to be overrun by these bandits, these *Dacoits*. No! No excuses. I want them hunted down, arrested, and tried.

"I know Captain Gupta captured a pair of them just last week, and that is good. Now I want you to question those men, find out who their leaders are and where they are camped. I will not be happy until I have wiped out the *Dacoits*."

Gopal nodded his head vigorously. "It will be done, Rajah," he quickly assured. "I shall personally see to the questioning of the captive *Dacoits*." Indeed, with great alacrity, the garrison commander hurried off to the city gaol. There he berated his gaol-master and delivered a smack to his head.

"How can you be so negligent in your duties?!" Gopal demanded to the gaol-master. "If you wish to loosen the tongue at one end of the body, simply apply burning coals to the feet on the other."

Gopal was correct; the process worked quite well. In less than a week, the *Dacoits* and their leaders had fled the region around Banda.

Gopal admitted to Dhakar that they might return, but would not venture a guess as to when.

* * *

In his house in Shaitanabad, the Rajah Chambu Singh turned to the son of a *Dacoit* chieftain who served as his major domo. "Bring the monster to me," he commanded.

The young man prostrated himself low and said, "It will be done, *sahib*." He then rose and scurried off to the dungeons beneath them.

Whilst Chambu Singh waited, he turned his attention to his half-naked concubine, Baljinder, who was pretty, but not nearly as beautiful as Asha Dheri. Every day, Chambu Singh reminded Baljinder of this fact.

"I am not a man to mix business with pleasure," Chambu said. "It is far too easy to focus on merriment and lose track of business, which is far more important, yes?"

"Yes, *sahib*," she replied in a timid voice.

"Yes indeed, but this time I find that I can. I despise the Rajah Dhakar for winning the hand of the Rani Asha, and I wish him dead. Still, this is only a matter of the heart and I would never risk all I have for such trivialities.

"Rather," he continued, "the death of Dhakar Rao is now a matter of business. I may be a rajah but I am also a man with lofty goals and a firm commitment to duty. First among my duties, is patronage of the *Dacoits* of Shaitanabad."

At this time, India was infested with bands of *Dacoits*—bandits who robbed travelers and smuggled contraband from east to west and from north to south. There were many bandits in India and Indochina as there are in all parts of the world. But many bands of *Dacoits* had another cause besides mere thievery. These bands, along with their allies among the equally-outlawed Thugee Cult, believed in a certain ancient prophecies concerning the return of the goddess Kali—she who would herald a new era. She required only a single sacrifice—the death of the current world.

"Those who aid the goddess will be rewarded," Chambu reminded Baljinder. "Those who hinder her—or her devoted servants—are decreed to perish. To this prophecy, I have secretly dedicated my life, in defiance of the laws of the Sikh gurus.

"Now this Rajah Dhakar threatens our *Dacoits* in Bundelkhand. Should he prove successful, would not other rajahs take up arms against us as have the British already?"

Baljinder, finding the question too rhetorical to answer, simply lowered her head.

Chambu Singh took no offense at the girl's silence. He simply laid back on a pile of cushions and allowed his thoughts to manifest. The cushions lay on a Persian carpet and this laid on a stone dais in the throne room of his villa. He glanced about at the adobe walls that surrounded him.

"My villa is hardly as large or as fine as the mansion of that pretty-boy rajah of Banda," Chambu said, perhaps to Baljinder, perhaps to the walls themselves. "Maybe the palace of Banda will be mine when Dhakar is dead. Perhaps Dhakar's even more pretty wife will be mine as well, whether she likes it or not." Thinking of this, Chambu Singh licked his lips. Then he looked at the concubine kneeling by his feet.

"I hope I can break her will as easily as I broke yours, Baljinder. You never question my orders, do you?"

"No, *sahib*," she replied without looking up.

At last the major domo returned, now holding a length of chain attached to a bipedal creature. Chambu Singh could not think of this creature as a man, only an abomination, a walking skeleton of a man. The monster was now dressed in black pajamas and a hooded cloak of the same material, for the Rajah wished to see no more him than he needed. They had found him: nude, lean, and gaunt, with sallow skin and a face—a face of horror! Baljinder cringed and hid behind Chambu, covering her face with her shawl.

The monster's gaunt hands had been manacled together. Alongside the monster stood two *Dacoits* who should be holding the prisoner by his arms, but would rather face the Rajah's ire for disobedience than to touch the seemingly leprous creature. Thus far, the monstrosity had not offered any resistance. Indeed, he kept his head down, looking only at the floor.

The *Dacoits* stopped before the Rajah's dais. With a kick to the back of his knees, they bade the monster kneel before their lord.

Chambu Singh regarded the abomination. In his black robes and hood, he looked like a shapeless shadow on the floor. Singh regarded this shadow of a man with as much fear and disgust as his men, but also with a combination of amusement... and opportunity.

"*Cha'i'a Manukha*—Shadow-Man," he said, "with no gun and no knife, you killed four of my *Dacoits* before we could capture you. You impress me. Although you are an outlander, you say you were adopted by our allies, the Thugee. Certainly you have shown yourself to be a better assassin than my *Dacoits*, who are among the finest—so

I let you live. I promised you your freedom if you one day earned it. This is that day."

The Shadow-Man remained motionless, his head down, waiting.

"*Cha'i'a Manukha*, I want you to kill a man for me. His name is Dhakar Rao."

Slowly, the Shadow-Man raised his head. From under the hood he looked at Chambu Singh with red eyes. He nodded.

* * *

A week later, the full moon shone into the bedroom of the rajah and rani of Banda in Bundelkhand. The moon witnessed, as it had so many times, the fervent copulation of a man and woman in love.

Again and again he thrust, as the woman in his embrace writhed and lurched. Her sighs quickly became moans.

She grasped the rails of the English headboard, seeming to hold on for dear life. He thrust deeper, with more vigor than before, yet still he held back, refusing to release until she reached the same state as he.

At last, his thrusts brought her to the brink of ecstasy. Like an earthquake, she cried out, shaking the bed and waking sleeping birds in the trees outside. As she cried out once more, louder than the first time, he erupted, spewing like the whales he'd seen while crossing the ocean.

Outside, at the front doors of the villa, a proud Rajput stood watch over the courtyard, tasked with watching the shadows in the corners but mostly looking upward at the veranda overhead. He licked his lips under his heavy mustaches at the sounds coming from the open windows above. He envied his rajah and admired his taste in women. *By Vishnu, she is a beauty. Fah, if only I had a wife who looked like that. I would not have to bend her over the table and go in from behind every time. No, the rani has a face I could actually look at while I drive my big—*

The distracted guard had not seen the moving shadow nor had he heard the silent footsteps. He scarcely felt the silken scarf flit about his throat, but he felt it when it constricted, crushing his windpipe. He dropped his staff as he struggled, but it was caught in the spare hand of his assailant, lest the clatter alert any ear. The Rajput's eyes bulged, he grasped at the thin but powerful hand that held the scarf. He could not scream for help.

Not that the guards at the outer gate could have helped him. Already they were dead.

The Shadow-Man eased the Rajput to the ground. He looked up at the veranda overhead from whence came the carnal moans. He quickly scanned the exterior for a trellis or other means to climb up from the outside, but there was nothing. No matter, the front door opened easily. The intruder slipped inside, vanishing among other shadows.

The Shadow-Man wore no shoes, trusting like a Thugee that his bare feet would prove more silent than any shoe or sandal. They had taught him all their secrets and at all of them he excelled.

Inside the palace, the Shadow-Man padded silently past one slumbering guard after another, alerting no one. A moment later, he allowed the body of Rangam the eunuch to slump down among the women he guarded. Not one of them so much as stirred. The Shadow-Man let them be and silently mounted the stairs.

In the master's boudoir, Dhakar lay where he had collapsed, upon Asha. All either of them knew was the love and joy they felt at this moment.

The moment was short, as Dhakar just then became dimly aware of a presence in the room. He raised his head, half expecting to see Vasanta at the door, once more asking if all was well, as he had their first night together in their new home. Unbeknownst to Dhakar, the aged chamberlain lay in the hallway outside with a crushed larynx.

Instead, Dhakar's assurances died in his throat as he made out an ominous black shadow moving among the other shadows, coming from the door, looming closer. Silently and slowly the shadow moved, making Dhakar doubt his senses.

Maybe he would have remained senseless had Asha not screamed—clearly not a scream of passion this time, for she realized that a thing of horror loomed before them. Thus alerted, Dhakar also realized exactly what had entered their bedroom—an assassin. He did not bother to question how this hooded villain got here or why it had come. He needed to act.

So did the Shadow-Man. He knew the rani's scream would have alerted any survivors below. The garrote would be too slow—he unsheathed a flame-bladed *kris* and lunged.

In the same instant, Dhakar also acted, kicking the strange shadow as it lunged from the foot of the bed. The blow landed true, catching the assassin in the jaw, stopping his advance for an instant.

The Shadow-Man grunted, more from surprise than pain. The rajah had wits, he realized, and he would need to finish him fast. Conveniently, all the assassin needed was to break the skin—the poison on the blade would do the job from there.

He swiped with the blade, but the rajah darted away. The Shadow-Man leapt onto the bed, ready for a killing thrust with the diabolical blade.

But the naked rani attacked like a true Sikh, for whom a weapon is never far from her reach. She drove her own slim dagger into the Shadow-Man's arm, nearly making him drop his own weapon.

The Shadow-Man grunted once more and in the instant that followed he knew he now faced not one but two combatants. With more luck than skill, he might slay them both with a single slash, but already he heard footfalls and panicked voices from beyond the door. Already the rajah had reached for the *tulwa*r that hung over the bed.

He may have learned from the Thugees, but the Shadow-Man did not share their dedication to their goddess. His own hide meant more to him. Rather than continue the attack, only to perish at the vengeful hands of the remaining guards, the Shadow-Man broke off and leapt for the veranda.

Sword in hand, Dhakar gained his feet and took out after the assassin. Asha, letting her man handle the fight, now grasped a sheet to cover her front.

The Shadow-Man grasped the railing, ready to launch himself to the courtyard below. Yet he stopped for an instant, turned back, and hurled the poisoned *kris* straight at the heart of Prince Dhakar.

Dhakar's own blade deflected the poisoned dagger, which clanged upon the floor. He rushed forward, hoping to hack the assassin to bits.

Like a true shadow, the Shadow-Man had already vanished over the rail. Asha joined Dhakar and reached the railing at the same instant. They looked down.

Disheveled but unharmed, the Shadow-Man looked up at them from the courtyard. For an instant, just before he disappeared into his fellow shadows, Dhakar saw him without his hood in place.

A ghastly skull with burning red eyes glared back at them.

Epilogue

Having failed in his mission, the Shadow-Man knew better than to face the wrath of Chambu Singh—he had but one shot at success and he failed. He ran, he stole a horse from Dhakar's neighbor, then hid in the hills, the jungles, the deserts. Wearing a new disguise every day, he made his way through lines of Rajputs, Sikhs, Gurkhas, and vigilant English soldiery. He crossed the border into Persia three days later.

Back in Bundelkhand, Dhakar did not hesitate to continue with most of his reforms. He did delay his campaign against the *dacoits*, but he waited only until all of his men's muskets had been hand-rifled to hold the new Minié balls he had ordered. He promised them that they would not find themselves outgunned, even if they were outnumbered.

Within a month, every *dacoit* in the territory of Banda had been killed, imprisoned, or had fled the region. Yet never would any of the captives confess a word as to the identity of their true leader. Despite not knowing who was the real power behind the bandit organization, Dhakar declared his campaign to be a success.

Soon after that, the Rani Asha announced that Dhakar would have an heir.

XING'ZHEN

1. Youth and Beauty

Hunan Province, 1847.

The tip of the brush dipped into a small ink pot then rose and set onto a strip of rice paper. With graceful strokes, a series of singular marks appeared, and soon they became connected together with another. Beside this, a second pictograph was made. The calligrapher set aside the brush, which was quickly picked up by a servant to be washed and returned to the jar with the others.

Weeks earlier, this young man had been in the West, a student at Heidelburg University. On leave for summer vacation, young Huang Zhou meditated on the latest name he'd written as he watched the ink dry. He sat on a pillow before a small, short table in a sunlit room. The room stood almost empty, perfect for such meditations.

Arranged on the table were seven slips of paper, each bearing a single feminine name. He required no further notations; he had every known detail memorized.

Three of the names were Manchurian or Mongolian, and thus readily rendered into Chinese symbols. One name was Hindi and two others Farsi. The last name had proved the most awkward to write, but not terribly so. That name was Latin, but taken as English.

Huang Zhou reviewed the various slips of paper in turn, meditating some moments upon each name. Each had merits, he knew. Each had some detriment.

The last name, the English name, this one stood out in both merit and detriment. It might seem he would need to visit her first. The Manchurian and Mongolian names, however, were closer and easier to engage.

* * *

Peking, June of 1848.

The scents of jasmine and lotus wafted to the delicate nostrils of a young beauty by the faintest breath of air. The maiden closed her dark eyes and leaned over the row of immaculate flowers along the paved walkway. She inhaled the intoxicating mixture of scents and a smile graced her perfect lips.

Clad in a ducal robe of a Manchurian noblewoman, the maiden rose and looked about her father's enclosed garden. The tree-dabbled sunlight felt warm and relieving after a cool night. Xing'zhen disliked the cold nights of the previous winter, but these passed with the coming of summer.

So softly had the feet approached that the maiden was unaware of them until they were almost beside her. Flitting her eyes around, Xing'zhen of Clan Borjigit was not surprised to see the new girl, Dai'yu, who surely had the feet of a cat. The surprise was that she was not alone.

Dai'yu, scarcely two years older and newly brought into the household as a handmaiden, bowed low with her eyes directed at the cobblestoned walkway.

"Yes?" said the young Lady Xing'zhen, more annoyed at the interruption than alarmed, and clearly not afraid.

"Honorable miss," Dai'yu said, "I am instructed to introduce this gentleman scholar to you, so that he might present the greetings of the Mandarin Shu of Hunan Province. His name is Huang Zhou."

Dai'yu, without rising just yet, stepped backwards a few steps and allowed the man and girl to speak. In truth, Dai'yu's primary task was to act as his eyes and ears, already far more widespread than those of the Mandarin Shu's own spies—this arrangement had been made necessary as he could only return to the Celestial Empire during the summers.

Now, as Huang Zhou found himself regarding the duke's daughter, he confirmed the importance of his spy network. Indeed, Dai'yu's earlier reports had surpassed his expectations.

In turn, the girl Xing'zhen regarded the tall, slender form of this young Huang Zhou. His black robe was of a simple cut, denoting a scholar; his pea-green vest was lightly padded, befitting the early summer day. He wore a simple round skullcap. Only a few years older than her, his face was long and lean; his cranium broad and shaven. His nose was long and his ears appeared slightly pointed. Some trick of the light, no doubt, made his eyes appear almost green and filmy.

"I am unaccustomed to meeting strange men in my father's gardens," said Xing'zhen, unafraid and perhaps perturbed. "I know not this Hunan mandarin of whom you speak nor why he would send messages to me—I, who am but the daughter of Duke third class Hui'zheng of the Borjigit Clan."

Huang Zhou bowed to her in the fashion of a gentleman bowing to the daughter of a friend of equal standing. Once again on summer's hiatus from the European university he attended—and away from the revolution which then gripped that continent—he once again focused his attentions on his homeland. He then rose and looked the girl straight in the eyes.

"Honorable lady," said Huang Zhou in a deceptively soft, almost musical voice, "the attendant Dai'yu spoke incorrectly, but do not order her punished for I was not altogether clear in my instructions.

In fact, I do serve the Mandarin Shu, but I have traveled considerable distance to speak with you on my own initiative."

Suspicion grew subtly in the beautiful eyes of Xing'zhen. She glanced about, only to determine that the gardeners and maids that normally would be found attending to duties in the garden, were curiously absent.

Noticing this reaction, Huang Zhou dropped to his knees and prostrated himself before her, though not touching his head to the cobblestones. Not yet. Someday, perhaps, he would happily kowtow to her.

"Think not that I have come to abscond with you or in any manner corrupt you, Lady Borjigit," said Huang Zhou. "My ambitions are greater by far. Only allow me to speak and then declare if my ambitions do not coincide with your own." He then rose.

Xing'zhen nodded as the man straightened completely, nearly towering over her, which was not fully to her liking. Despite noticing her apprehension, Huang Zhou did not slouch in her presence.

Huang Zhou spoke to the young Manchurian beauty for the next hour, outlining his plans for her and his goals for the Celestial Empire. He explained precisely how he would go about doing these things—here a certain official would need to be bribed, there another would require threats, possibly blackmail. A great lady in Peking would require flattery or seduction to grant a wish—all leading to a point where Xing'zhen would be brought before a certain high-ranking Consort and her eunuchs. At that point, Xing'zhen would be required to display her beauty, poise, charm, and above all, discretion, in hopes of impressing the court favorably.

Xing'zhen of Clan Borjigit took it all in. Were she to become the emperor's concubine, she would hold a higher rank than any woman in the empire, short of being born into the imperial family. She had never dreamt of such a position. She could scarcely believe her fortune, but in no way would she be intimidated.

Huang Zhou then explained, in broad terms, the goals of the Order of the White Peacock, of which he was a member. He told her, in such terms as she might understand, their history, their connection to other far-flung societies, and relating to this, he told her how he had but lately studied in Europe and intended to return there soon, where he had learned of fascinating inventions. Most importantly, he related the Order's most important goal—that the ancient prophecies of a world united under a single hand be fulfilled for the good of all mankind.

In spite of herself, Xing'zhen covered her mouth and halfheartedly attempted to stifle a laugh. Huang Zhou raised an eyebrow.

“The idea amuses you, young lady?”

“I believe many prophecies, good sir, but this one I have never heard. Really, can you truly believe such a thing?”

“I do.”

She shrugged her eyebrow.

In the end, they agreed on most particulars and formed a loose alliance: Huang Zhou promised to have Xing'zhen brought before the Emperor's chief consort, whereby she might impress her and enter the Chamber of Imperial Concubines as one of their honored ranks. In turn, she would keep Huang Zhou informed about the inner workings of the Forbidden City—that massive, walled complex of palaces and courts that made up the Imperial government in Peking—all via a system of loyal messengers.

“I thank you, Huang Zhou, for this opportunity,” said the girl. “I shall not disappoint you.”

Huang Zhou bowed low to the girl once more, then departed without further word. Now it was time to visit the next candidate he had in mind for the role.

2. Other Candidates

Ere he set sail for Europe and his classes, Huang Zhou arranged to meet another lovely and slightly younger Manchurian beauty, this one of the Niohuru Clan. For the last two years, Huang Zhou had secretly funded young Lady Niohuru's education and grooming. He had made certain that much emphasis had been placed on teaching her to speak in public and to memorize litanies of historical events.

Huang Zhou traveled with Yao Ling, a worthy agent of the White Peacock and a capable valet who had lately come to his attention.

“Sir,” asked Yao Ling, “does our mandarin know of either of these young ladies and what you intend of them?”

“He does not,” said Huang Zhou, as they rode in a litter from one province to the next. “This is my doing alone. Of the Order of the White Peacock, only you and Dai'yu know of this or any other candidate whom I have picked.”

“I do not understand.”

“Then I must explain. Our wise mandarin and his counselors expect the foretold future Female Messiah to fall from the sky some day and only then will their great work commence. I, however, know that although this messiah's coming has long been proclaimed, she will be born and live as any other woman. Indeed, it is only logical that the purpose of the Council of the Seven is to raise and guide this future world teacher, making her the ruler of the world."

"I see."

Huang Zhou had spent years putting minor agents like Yao Ling and Dai'yu in place in various noble families. Most of these agents knew little of the Order of the White Peacock and certainly nothing of the Council of the Seven. They were not deemed of sufficient importance to know of such things, thus they would reveal nothing of great importance, should they be forced to speak.

"Lady Borjigit and Lady Nioruru," Huang Zhou continued, "are the two most likely candidates for this role. Both are young and presumably their minds will be easy to mold. Both are beautiful and capable of capturing a man's heart and mind. Both are intelligent. However, there are very few opportunities by which women might gain a position of power in the Celestial Empire. Are they both willing and capable of doing what needed to be done to take that opportunity? That still remained to be seen."

While not allowing himself to be swayed by omens, Huang Zhou did think it auspicious that this girl's family name, Niohuru, was derived from the Manchurian word for wolf. One would need the cunning, strength, and speed of the wolf to wrest control of the Celestial Empire.

The girl's family had not ridden the hill country of Manchuria for generations. After conquering the Celestial Empire in 1644, the Manchurian elite made themselves quite happy with the Chinese lifestyle—all while subjugating the Chinese people. The young Lady Niohuru had been groomed for fine things and her beauty, grace, and intelligence were all remarked upon.

As with Xing'zhen, Huang Zhou had seen to this grooming from afar. Upon learning of her qualities, his agents had contacted the girl's father and uncles and informed them that their master wished her to be trained in courtly manners and arts. When a member of the family asked too many questions, the path to her advanced education was smoothed by a healthy application of gold. Huang Zhou could produce all the gold he needed for his desires.

As the reports agreed that she was most talented in such skills as the lute and the zither, Huang Zhou determined it was time to pay her a personal visit. And now, they had arrived.

This visit was rather more formal than his meeting with Xing'zhen. They met in the house of her father, the duke, with most of the household present. Young Lady Niohuru wore a simple black gown embroidered with a Feng Shui emblem for longevity, *sans nombri*. Her hair parted in the center and hung aloft on either side of her head in a simple yet elegant coiffure.

Upon being introduced as a representative of the Mandarin Shu, Huang Zhou was allowed to address the fourteen-year-old girl.

"It is our understanding that you have shown aptitude in literature and calligraphy, honorable maiden," said Huang Zhou. "Is this true?"

"I am still learning, good sir," replied Lady Niohuru, with her eyes down. "And there is far more for me to learn."

He nodded. "Indeed, for the wealth of the world's knowledge is ever-growing such that one might read every work ever written and still there would be more to read."

The maiden's eyes widened. Then she lowered her head once more. "Sir, I have never thought of that. Clearly, I will never attain so much wisdom."

Huang Zhou stood impassive, not liking how the Niohuru girl had given up so easily. The Borjigit girl, Xing'zhen, had not once backed down to him. Still, as this one was even more beautiful—and thus more likely to capture the young prince's eye. He continued.

"I mean not to dissuade my good lady with the prospect of a daunting task. Indeed, I would rather that the young lady saw the vast wealth of history, governance, and science as an opportunity to better herself that she might go on to better all others with whom she would meet."

"Sir, that sounds only more daunting," she said. "I think I will read only poetry and a few classics from now on."

Huang Zhou left the house unimpressed. Lady Niohuru may have been quite intelligent, but he found her utterly unimaginative. Perhaps he could use her as a source of information, but he had doubts of entrusting her with a mission.

Yet by means of agents long-since planted within the Forbidden City, Huang Zhou soon arranged for young Lady Niohuru to be privately introduced to the emperor's son, Prince Yi'zhi, rather ahead of the official determination. The prince eagerly accepted his new gift. This decision proved fruitful, for at once she captured his heart, among other organs.

Afterwards, Huang Zhou confided to his agent, Yao Ling, "I've no doubt that the emperor-to-be will grant her every wish."

* * *

The Celestial Empire had never been a democracy. Even if Huang Zhou had wished it to be, it was never his intention to alter his homeland's form of governance. The form of government, he found, is irrelevant; only the people running the government is of importance.

Therefore, to advance the grandiose goals of the Order of the White Peacock, he simply decided he must place the Ascended Master of the World on the throne of China.

"Why make things difficult," he asked his acolyte, Yao Ling, who packed his traps, "when a simple solution presents itself?"

As it was a rhetorical question, the agent made no reply.

Huang Zhou sailed once more for Europe, having had but two weeks in his native land, so as to continue his European studies. Despite being far away in the fall, winter, and spring, he thoroughly groomed both Manchurian teenagers from afar. Following his instructions, Dai'yu and Yao Ling showed both of them how to contact and summon various agents of his, within and without the Forbidden City. Xing'zhen required little other education, for unlike most noblewomen, she already knew how to read the classics of Chinese culture, to write the thousands of Chinese characters with a brush, to play the lute and to sing like a lark.

The following summer, Huang Zhou returned to supervise both girls for a few weeks. He left the Niohuru girl to fend for herself in matters of intimacy, due to her youth. However, he placed considerable effort into personally instructing Xing'zhen how to perform the duties of a concubine.

Huang Zhou instructed Xing'zhen to watch and learn as Dai'yu performed the Delight of the Lips and Tongue upon Huang Zhou. After the first exhibition of this skill, Xing'zhen asked to perform the act herself, that she might become its master. This, Huang Zhou allowed. Under his tutelage, master the skill she did.

Afterwards, he allowed Xing'zhen to watch Huang Zhou penetrate Dai'yu in both the front and rear positions. This, however, he would not perform upon Xing'zhen, for it was essential that she appear before the emperor-to-be with her virginity intact.

Instead, he instructed the girls to continue their training with one another whilst he returned to duties of his own in the hinterlands. "Certain skills are universal," Huang Zhou explained, "whether performed with a man or a woman."

Huang Zhou assisted Xing'zhen and young Lady Niohuru by seeing to it that more than a few doors to the Imperial Court were opened so that the girls would always be in the right place at the right time. Posing as a civil bureaucrat of the third rank, he had made the acquaintance of Lady Kang'ci, the emperor's consort dowager. The shrewd Kang'ci was not one to be easily swayed, but she appreciated good advice. Huang Zhou saw to it that she spoke to no other advisor. From then on, he had her ear and could at least suggest a name here or an edict there.

The old emperor was dying. Soon, the emperor's heir, Prince Yi'zhi, would take take his father's place on the throne of the Celestial Empire. However, the prince had already married a Mongolian princess of the House of Sadka. Huang Zhou considered that this bride might be a threat to his well-made plans, yet perhaps, by luck, she might be as suitable a candidate as those he now trained. Indeed, due to her position, hers had been one of the names he had scribed on a strip of vellum, years earlier. As such, it would be only proper to meet her.

* * *

"Princess Sadka," said Huang Zhou, now dressed in the black-trimmed white robes and black hat of a Confucian scholar, "it is the hope of we scholars that every empress reflects the emperor's glory and wisdom. Thus we would now speak with you of your education and ambitions."

This meeting was held in one of several palaces that made up the Forbidden City. Huang Zhou had been allowed access to the princess by a simple deceit—he claimed to entreat the princess for funds to repair a deteriorating school in a far-off province. However, he had soon diverted the conversation to a subject closer to his heart. Although some members of her entourage raised their eyebrows, the princess seemed oblivious to his meandering.

"I have no ambition, but to be a good wife to my husband," she replied simply.

Huang Zhou nodded. "And no finer ambition could a wife have," he said. "And your education, my good lady?"

Princess Sadka paused to give the matter thought. Then she said, "It is proper for a lady of the court to sing well and play one instrument. I think no more than that is necessary. Correspondence is a matter for scribes. Father always told me that it is not good for girls to read and write anything more than love songs as there is no need."

"And this you truly believe?"

"I just said I did. Do you think that I speak false?"

"I beg Your Highness's pardon. I meant no insult. Quite obviously, you speak only the truth. Indeed, so obvious is it that you will make a suitable empress that my school need trouble you no further. May good fortune follow you all the days of your life."

Huang Zhou bowed low and backed away.

"Princess Sadka is not the Universal Leader," he said afterward to his acolytes, Lady Niohuru and Lady Xing'zhen in his private chamber. "Rather, she is an obstacle to those that might be."

This meeting was the first time the two teenagers had met.

Huang Zhou had hoped they would agree to work to each other's benefit, for the betterment of the goals of the Council of the Seven. In fact, he realized the girls were like predators, pacing, circling, never taking their eyes off the other for long. He admitted to himself that he was unsure of how to rectify this situation.

Yet soon they returned to the subject of the princess, whose position threatened all their plans.

"It would appear obvious" said Xing'zhen, "that this obstacle must be removed."

Niohuru stifled a gasp. Huang Zhou merely raised an eyebrow... then nodded.

Shortly thereafter, the princess and her entourage attended the La'ba Festival where she enjoyed a traditional bowl of diversified rice. Her bowl, being more special than others, had been specially made with the emblem of a gleaming phoenix at the bottom. She smiled upon seeing the fabulous beast revealed at the bottom of her empty bowl, for the phoenix had long been the emblem of the empresses of Cathay. She was unaware of the special material that went into the pigment, giving the phoenix its particular iridescent hue. This material had another attribute as well.

The healthy girl died at the age of eighteen.

"An unfortunate necessity," Huang Zhou afterward admitted to Yao Ling, "but soon, after a suitable period of mourning, a new flock of concubines will be necessary to ease the emperor's suffering. I intend that my agents, Xing'zhen and Niohuru, will be available to take their places beside the emperor-to-be."

ENEMY TERRITORY

The wretched stench of open sewage wafted through the air. Celestials in coolie hats trotted along with wheeled carts containing baskets of goods. Sing-sing girls leaned on the rails of verandas, scanning the streets for potential customers. Crows and rats fought over the corpse of a dead animal, indeterminable if it had once been a dog or a cat. Drunken sailors fought over some question about the number of aces to be found in a deck of playing cards. As he walked along the muddy, fog-shrouded streets, Huang Zhou ignored them all.

He had disguised himself as a coolie and traveled here, to the slums of London's Limehouse district, immediately after his graduation from Heidelberg University in 1851. Here, in a dark, dank back alley behind the Wing Loo Joss House, he stopped when he spotted a pair of men hidden in the shadows.

They looked at him with their thin, slitted eyes, then both struck one fist into the opposite palm and bowed their heads.

"Welcome, Master," said one of them.

Huang Zhou, now having attained his twenty-first year, contemplated that man for a moment. "Address me as 'Doctor', not 'Master', for I have yet to be given any other title. You shall aid me because it is your will, not your duty."

The young men both nodded in acknowledgment. These were Jun Lu and Tang Ho, men of the Order of the White Peacock whom he had summoned from Cathay to assist him. Their meeting this night had been predetermined a year earlier.

"I have picked both of you for your talents and for your proven loyalty to me," he said. "You are both aware that the Mandarin's policies have done nothing to advance the goals of the Society. Although I must soon return to Hunan, it is my hope that within the next two months I shall determine if the British queen is the one who is prophesized."

Both men, although trained to withhold their feelings, appeared surprised by this revelation. They long knew of the Prophecy, but had never imagined that it might apply to a Westerner, especially an enemy sovereign. Still, they bowed to him, never taking their eyes from his.

"Doctor," said Jun, "we shall not fail you."

Both men bowed again and he had them rise. For the rest of the night, Huang Zhou outlined what he would need from them: a secure place from which to operate, a chemical laboratory, tools for gardening, tools for picking locks, money, and other sundries. They had already secured lodgings behind the Joss House and had acquired most of the supplies they would need. From there, they might easily access the docks at Canary Wharf, with ships bound for every corner of the empire. Also nearby were the sewers with their myriad underground passageways beneath the Limehouse neighborhood.

However, Limehouse was not Huang Zhou's ultimate goal.

Huang Zhou contemplated many ways to enter Buckingham Palace. He made his way to both the British Museum and the Ashmolean, where he would study every crackled blueprint and every word written about Buckingham Palace, often going back a century or more. Within weeks, he knew the layout of every floor and the basements, from the day the first cornerstone was laid to the current arrangement.

He studied not only the current blueprints of the building, but the original floor plans and every change and addition that had ever been made to the building. He discovered a half dozen little known corridors, granting access to and from the sewers beneath and the roof above. He was scarcely surprised to see that the architects had considered many options for escape, should rebelling peasants or agents of the Pope attempt to lay hold of the monarch.

Yet in the end, Huang Zhou chose the simplest and safest means to enter the palace. He entered as a common gardener, the only employment available, he was assured by his associates, for a Celestial.

* * *

No doubt the hiring of Huang Zhou was similar to those Celestials hired by the British Navy and merchantmen for their knowledge of the straits through the islands of Indonesia and other seaways—that is to say, the Head Gardener thought only a Chinaman would know properly how to care for the Chinese sacred lilies, lotuses, and other exotic plants that grew in the royal hothouses. In a short time, Huang Zhou proved his skill in horticulture. The white lotus bloomed more lovely than ever in the British climate.

The gardens were vast and perfectly ordained. Trees and shrubs grew where they were planted and nowhere else. Perfectly-trimmed hedges following the inlaid stones that made up the miles of walkways. Flowers stolen from all over the empire bloomed nine months of the year. Not a leaf or a petal was allowed out of place.

After three weeks of watering and weeding, Huang Zhou had learned the queen's routine. Every Sunday after church, he observed the queen from a distance as she walked through the gardens of Buckingham Palace, never alone. Invariably she would be accompanied by a small retinue of ladies-in-waiting, maids, secretaries, the occasional minister, and the chief gardener. Huang Zhou noted that no guards were present. Despite a number of half-hearted attempts on the queen's life over the years, clearly the authorities felt that the palace walls were sufficient protection for their sovereign.

Late in June, an opportunity presented itself. The queen was attended by only an assistant gardener, a pair of ladies-in-waiting, and a maid pushing a perambulator. Huang Zhou knew he would not have many such opportunities. He gathered his things and approached.

The queen was not an imposing figure. She was short and had begun to put on the sort of weight to be expected for a woman who'd birthed seven children. Even in a billowing gown of deep blue crinoline and Italian lace, any who did not know her would scarcely suspect she was the most powerful woman on Earth.

Huang Zhou was almost immediately stopped by the head gardener.

"And just what do you got in mind, hm Johnny?" he asked, sternly, but in a low voice, so that Her Majesty's walk would not be disturbed.

Huang Zhou raised a multi-colored bouquet of flowers. "Flower for empress, yes?" he said, as simply as he could.

"No, there shall be no flowers. Not from the likes of you." The gardener snatched them away. "You get back to shoveling that manure and don't you dare think of walking up to Her Majesty's personage ever again."

Huang Zhou had little choice but to quickly bow low and comply.

* * *

Despite his quarry being so close, Huang Zhou saw that in such a massive palace, he might wait years before finding the perfect opportunity to address the queen—if ever. It was obvious that the head gardener was now watching him closer than before. The man had also found progressively more menial and odious tasks for him to attend.

Therefore, Huang Zhou returned to his original scheme. By night he gathered rope and some few tools and entered the basements. From there he opened a long-since forgotten egress, allowing him to slip into an architectural curiosity. He was then behind the very walls of the palace, a space created during some earlier remodeling, some ten inches wide.

It was not as easy to traverse as that might seem; joists and braces needed to be avoided, stepped over if he was fortunate, crawled under or climbed over if he were not. An hour's climb led to a dead end—but here he employed his tools to saw and then pry out some overhead boards. To work as silently as possible, he needed to make a single saw stroke then wait a half hour before making a second.

Seeing that this task alone might take months, Huang Zhou managed to sneak Jing and Tang into the palace by night. He had them work inside the walls during the day whilst he tended the gardens. Besides accomplishing the tasks much faster, any noises made during the day were more likely to be ignored.

Their efforts allowed them to at last climb up through the floorboards of a first story water closet. In and of itself, this was nothing, but it allowed Huang Zhou access to an otherwise secured hall. Making sure no one was present, he silently padded down the hall and into a linen closet. Here he removed a few nails in the paneling and found himself in a long boarded-up stairwell. Even the steps had been removed. Huang Zhou spent two days constructing a few steps that allow him access to the next level.

Here Huang Zhou could climb through a narrow passage which he knew would open onto a hallway adjoining the royal family's chambers. The passage was more narrow than the plans indicated, yet all he needed to do was round a corner....

Peering around that corner, Huang Zhou found himself staring at a brick wall. This was not in the plans! Had he made a miscalculation?

He reviewed each of those blueprints in his memory. No, he had not made a mistake—but would an architect have neglected his records? Was the addition of a fireplace the whim of a sovereign? Even so, such an edifice would be recorded. Perhaps instead, Huang Zhou wondered, he had found the back of a safe, filled with state secrets and unrecorded for that reason.

It mattered not. He would be unable to proceed this way. He admitted defeat and decided to return to the basement through the many passages.

At this point, he realized that he was stuck.

* * *

Some hours passed before Jun and Tang, noticing that Huang Zhou was late to return. Following his twisting and turning path within the walls of Buckingham Palace, they found him.

“Doctor,” whispered Jun, “what has happened?”

“Clearly, I am wedged into a space too tight to extract myself. Pull me free, but carefully—and quietly.”

Only one man could reach Huang Zhou at a time, and even Jun could not get a proper grip on him.

"This is not working," Huang Zhou said. "An application of a lubricant may help facilitate my freedom. Get butter or lard."

"Where is it to be found?"

"In the kitchens of course. From the basement, access to the kitchen is simple. Use the dumbwaiter. There are still a few hours, but hurry."

Jun passed on the instruction to Tang behind him. With a grunt, Tang departed.

Upon Tang's return an hour later, and with a generous application of lard, itself requiring considerable stealth and time to procure, and the cutting away of much of his clothing, they at last freed Huang Zhou. And scarcely a moment too soon—as they slid along the narrow passage, they heard people on other side, voices, footsteps. The first of the household staff had begun to awaken in the predawn hours.

Their urgency was tempered by their need for absolute silence. Being caught would spell the doom of their plans and their own deaths—and worse, the revelation of the existence of the White Peacock.

At last, Huang Zhou's men exited the palace proper even as the first hint of dawn warmed the east.

* * *

Looking over the floor plans once more, but now bolstered with his first hand knowledge of the chambers, Huang Zhou determined it would be impossible to safely enter any room of the royal family's chambers. Not allowing a thing like impossibility stop his schemes, Huang Zhou instead sought out yet another means to achieve his goal.

Jun and Tang listened stoically as Huang Zhou explained his intentions in the safety of the Limehouse lair where the two men commonly resided.

"Although it would be best to speak directly with the queen, there are other options," he said, outlining his next plan to his acolytes. "I need merely put my ideas into her mind."

He told them his intention was to simply produce a slim book, in English, which he would then leave it in some place that the queen could not fail to find it. This book was simply Huang Zhou's own translation into English of an ancient Hindu religious text, telling of the coming of a future Maitreya, the world-teacher who would bring together all peoples of the world—plus certain additions which the Council of the Seven had seen fit to include.

Scholars knew that the prophecy of the Maitreya was a late addition to the teachings of the Buddha, and for this, many dismissed the prophecy. However, Huang Zhou knew that the prophecy existed long before the Buddha and had only been grafted onto that philosophy. Indeed the Council of the Seven, the oldest organization on Earth, was founded to promote and bring about this prophecy.

Yet some few details found in the original source material differed from those texts associated with the Buddha. One detail in particular, which the monograph made quite clear, was that the coming Maitreya—or at least the Chakravarti, the ruler under whom Maitreya would be born—would be not a man but a woman under whose hand all the world would be united.

This book was not solely limited to Buddhist texts, but included several fragments that had come down from the dim prehistoric past to Celestial philosophers. Furthermore, correlations were made with the fervent cult that worshiped the strong female goddess Kali. No doubt when the queen read of these similarities, she would once more allow the free worship of the dark goddess in India—which would allow the cult to grow again.

One night, Huang Zhou entered a printer's shop and began setting type. Operating the printing press until the wee hours, he printed a single copy of this book. In the morning, there was no clue left behind that anyone had been there.

This had been his hope all along; to simply put into her royal hands a book of the prophecy. *Once she sees it, her curiosity will be piqued*, he thought. *The queen is an intelligent woman; thus, she will not fail to see the resemblance between the coming Maitreya and herself. What other woman has so much of the world already under her hand? Can there be any doubt that Queen Victoria will be the coming Maitreya?*

Such a book once convinced the Empress Wu that she was the Maitreya. Would Queen Victoria be less cognizant?

* * *

Huang Zhou composed a brief letter, explaining that the book was a gift from a devoted servant from within the Celestial Empire, in hopes that Her Majesty would contemplate the portions within that spoke of her. Leaving some mystery as to precisely what those portions were, he felt, would encourage her to read the entire work. He folded the letter and tied it with a white ribbon.

Initially, Huang Zhou considered hypnotizing some servant, perhaps a maid, perhaps a higher-ranking butler, perhaps even a lady-in-waiting, and compelling him or her to leave the book and letter for the queen to read.

After two failed attempts, however, Huang Zhou gave up on that tack. It seemed that members of the royal household were unusually devoted to their sovereign and thus successfully resisted his hypnotic powers. Not only could even a simple upstairs maid resist, but now one of the butlers clearly had suspicions of Huang Zhou after the attempt.

Fortunately, the butler never made those suspicions known. He might have, had he not taken a misstep whilst catching a trolley car after being jostled by a coolie. The coolie disappeared into the crowd and was never found to be questioned.

Just as Huang Zhou was a man of unusual talent, so were all of the members of the White Peacock. Upon settling upon the idea of entering the queen's study or private library, he then determined to put to the test Jun's ingenious skills with his lockpicks.

Sneaking through the curious labyrinth of hidden tunnels and passages to the upper stories, Huang Zhou and Jun came to a hallway they'd entered before. Twice they paused and hid as armed sentries passed by.

At last they came to one of the rooms which they did not fear to enter at night—no one slept here, for this was the queen's private study. The door was locked, as expected, but Huang Zhou silently put Jun to work on the problem. A moment later, Jun pivoted the internal tumblers to their correct positions and opened the door.

They entered and looked about in the dark. Huang Zhou found the queen's beautifully carved rolling desk, carved with the emblem VR. He even attempted to open the lid but of course it was locked. Rather than testing Jun's lockpicking skills, Huang Zhou simply laid the book in the center of the desk and placed the letter atop it.

Seconds later, they were gone, leaving no hint that they had ever been there.

* * *

In the morning, the book and the letter were discovered by the queen's secretary. Being of a keen mind and seeing anything out of place, Mr. Derby immediately handed the articles over to the chamberlain.

The queen's chamberlain would never consider reading Her Majesty's correspondence. Instead, he turned it over to the captain of the guard. As this exchange took place in the gardens, Huang Zhou, pretending to trim some bushes, had the opportunity to observe them.

Thrice before, attempts had been made on the life of the queen. The captain had heard of poison pen letters; perhaps this was one of those. He flipped through the book quickly, scanning a few pages, his brow furrowing, more in ignorance of what he read than disapproval. Yet still he disapproved. “She needn't know about all this,” he declared.

Not wishing to take any chances, he took both book and letter to be burned.

Snipping away, Huang Zhou's expression turned to outrage as he watched him do so.

Despite this action, the captain's remark was quite telling, Huang Zhou divined. For the first time, he realized that the queen was being kept from information about her own empire. Those surrounding her filtered reports from China and India, leading her to believe all was blissful.

The British authorities kept their monarch in ignorance, the same as their counterparts in China!

Huang Zhou began think of new schemes to engage the queen. Perhaps a disguise would allow him to—

Then the Chief Gardener stepped in front of him, his eyes flaring, his lips pursed angrily. He would not raise his voice, though, for fear of alerting the queen.

"You piker," said the man in a seething whisper. "You can't do a thing right. You done nipped off 'Er Majesty's prize roses, didn't you, hm Johnny?"

Huang Zhou looked down to see that he had indeed, lopped off a half dozen of the prize blooms.

"Well that's it, right," said the gardener. "It's the sack for you."

That was all. The Chief Gardener led him off to the shack which served as both a tool shed and an office. There, the man rang a buzzer, and soon after the Captain of the Guard and a burly pair of beefeaters made their presence known. They escorted him off the premises, and none too delicately did they go about it.

* * *

It might take weeks to rewrite and republish the book. Huang Zhou, now sporting a few bruises, knew he had no time to make another copy—he needed to return to Cathay soon. He cursed himself for not making at least a second copy. Still, having additional copies only meant that those who were unworthy could lay their eyes upon the secrets of the White Peacock and the Council of the Seven. Farthest from his desires would be to alert the world of his intentions.

Huang Zhou admitted to his acolytes that his mission had ended in failure. To himself he admitted that he failed because he was too naive about British politics.

"I have much to do in Hunan Province," he said to his agents as he packed. "However, you two will remain behind here in Limehouse. You will continue to fortify your positions. You will recruit more and more adherents and helpers, but tell them no more of the Society then they need to know. Most important of all, you will report your findings to me in Hunan Province, that I might be kept aware of everything that occurs in this land. Lastly, in case the queen might indeed prove to be the fabled World-Teacher, I would have you protect her from future assassins if at all possible."

"Yes, Doctor," said Tang Ho.

"Doctor," asked Jun Lu, "if the English queen is truly not the World-Teacher, does this mean the cause is lost?"

"It means nothing of the sort," Huang Zhou said without emotion. "You will recall, I have five more candidates."

THE HAREM OF THE EMPEROR

When the Radiant Path Emperor died a month after his son's bride, his youthful son, Yi'zhi, was enthroned as the Xian'feng or Universal Prosperity Emperor. The bestowed name would prove anything but prophetic.

After this second period of mourning ended, it was time to find official consorts for the new emperor. Huang Zhou, now having graduated from Heidelburg University, and dwelling once more in Cathay, had prepared for this. In the assemblage of magnificent palaces that lay within the walls of the Forbidden City, he gathered the girls he'd groomed. Within the elegant and shimmering Chamber of Imperial Concubines, he brought them to Consort Dowager Kang'ci. There, they and each candidate would be regarded by Lady Kang'ci, resplendent in her scarlet gown, elaborately decorated with dragons and phoenixes. By her side stood Huang Zhou.

"You've an eye for beauty, Huang Zhou," said the Lady Kang'ci, admiring his candidates along with the others. "I trust your judgment concerning their grace is every bit as astute."

"I believe you will find no fault in either my judgment or in the young ladies I have selected."

"Of that, we shall see, sir. Remember, only three will be selected."

Huang Zhou bowed his head to her.

With a loud clap from the hands of Kang'ci's chief eunuch, the first of two dozen girls was brought before the Consort Dowager. Each of these girls bowed to the mistress of the harem and was then questioned. Many were dismissed upon the first stutter or stammer. A few, if they bore some flaw, or they exposed clumsiness, or if they hesitated to respond to a question, were dismissed ere they had a chance to speak.

Neither of Huang Zhou's candidates were dismissed, as they had both impressed Lady Kang'ci. Eventually, in June of 1852, the Consort Dowager reduced the number of potential candidates to ten and then the three who would remain and serve.

Lady Kang'ci commanded both Lady Niohuru and Xing'zhen to enter service to the new emperor. In the Chinese custom, she renamed Lady Niohuru as Lady Zhen and Xing'zhen was given the name of Noble Lady Lan. This elevation was an important public consideration, for Huang Zhou intended both girls to be seen in court—and heard. He knew it would be prudent to have both consorts in place, should anything go wrong for either of them.

Along with these two, another was picked, a fifteen-year-old lady of the Manchurian Tatara clan. Young Lady Tatara had not advanced via the machinations of Huang Zhou; indeed, he had never met her. Still, he saw no reason to be concerned of her yet.

In the Imperial Courtroom, the three new concubines stood together, wearing the traditional champagne-colored gowns which declared their positions to be official. The three of them bowed in unison to the emperor. He grinned at each of them and did nothing to hide the erection under his voluminous but loose robes.

By some accounts, the emperor deflowered all three concubines the same night, one after another.

* * *

On a warm day, Huang Zhou sat at his low desk and scribed a set of instructions for his agents in various parts of the world, including a new agent in Brazil. After a time, Dai'yu knelt beside his desk and waited. With a nearly imperceptible nod, he acknowledged her.

"Doctor, I would ask an impertinent question," said Dai'yu. "Are the girls' desires aligned with your own? Is it truly their wish to be sex slaves?"

Continuing to run his brush gracefully over a large sheet of paper, Huang Zhou said, "In all the world, are women ever anything but the chattel of men? Do they get what they wish? In the Imperial Harem, at the very least they will be pampered, dressed in the finest clothing and jewels, given the finest food. They will be adored."

"By the emperor, yes," she interjected, knowing her master would wish her to speak her mind. "No other is allowed to see her."

"Perhaps not, my graceful swan with the mind of a wise owl, but it has ever been thus and it is not our goal to change this custom—not yet—but rather to exploit it."

Here Huang Zhou stopped and set down his brush. He regarded Dai'yu, looking up at him.

"You have done well," he said. "You found the means to prove yourself the equal of any man—as a member of our order. But you know that no woman in the Celestial Empire—or the rest of the world—has significant opportunity by which she may alter their fate or improve her station.

"The two concubines I have chosen have great potential, for they will be in a position to exert considerable influence over the empire. While remaining behind the curtain like empresses before them, they can dictate laws and reforms. They can advance and promote officials favorable to our goals. Unlike the emperors of the past, they will not be lead astray by vanity and the desire for bloodshed.

"I believe women will prove better leaders of men than men themselves."

Dai'yu bowed to her master, then departed to her tasks.

* * *

Two years later, as Huang Zhou engaged in selecting and training new agents to serve under him, he received a message from Lady Lan—once Xing'zhen. She informed him that she had advanced within the harem to the rank of Concubine, Third Class, and was given yet another new name, Lady Yi. However, she admitted, Lady Zhen had achieved an even higher rank: Concubine, Second Class. Soon after, she reported that she had become Noble Consort Yi, only for Zhen to be ordained to the highest rank of all—she would be proclaimed as the new empress consort of China.

Even though his favored candidate had not risen as high as he had hoped, Huang Zhou welcomed this intelligence; at least one of his candidates would likely advance to the position to which he had planned for her. As always, he kept close watch over the goings-on of the Forbidden City. His agent, Yao Ling, was unqualified to serve in the Chamber of Imperial Concubines, but Dai'yu made an excellent lady-in-waiting. Dai'yu kept Huang Zhou informed of all gossip and passed along messages to his agents in the emperor's bed. With Dai'yu's help, Huang Zhou periodically secretly made his way to the chambers of Noble Consort Yi.

He greeted the emperor's consort with a bow and a blessing, then sat beside her. He gripped her arms and brought her close, pressing his face against hers.

Yi scoffed. "You think that because I am a concubine of the emperor that I might be yours as well?"

"I do not, Noble Consort," he said, pulling back to regard her. "My ambitions are greater than even this. Yet do not think that my ambitions are for myself."

"Yes? And what are these vaunted ambitions?"

He stood, looking at her very seriously. "You know full well. Nine hundred years ago, the Empress Wu Ze'tian knew of certain prophecies that foretold of such a time when all the world would be united under a single hand, a universal ruler. And that—"

"That hand shall be the hand of a woman," Yi said, by route. A thousand years before, the Empress Wu had spoken those very same words. In a different language, Cleopatra had spoken them as well.

Huang Zhou stood and bowed to her wisdom.

Noble Consort Yi moved close to him and looked up. "A girl can be deflowered only once, and His Majesty has already seen to this.

Still, a concubine might require further training so as to best serve the emperor."

"Indeed."

Yi smirked. "I require more practice with the position of the Bucking Horse."

Huang Zhou was happy to instruct Yi in the technique several times that night.

* * *

A year later, Huang Zhou was not pleased by the reports he'd received from within the Forbidden City. Neither of his candidates proved to be the emperor's favorite. Instead, most of the emperor's considerable attention fell on Lady Tatara. This was good in one way, however, for now his two candidates no longer considered one another to be their chief rival.

In time, Lady Tatara became with child and the emperor was obliged to find other places to plant his wick. Yi, she who had been Xing'zhen, saw an opportunity and she did not let it pass her by. Trying the various techniques taught to her, Yi soon gained the majority of the emperor's attention.

Yi's position only improved when Lady Tatara did not produce an heir to the throne, but instead had a daughter. Huang Zhou was not surprised; the herbs he had placed in her food guaranteed that she would produce only female children.

* * *

During this time, Huang Zhou strengthened his place in the Order of the White Peacock. He placed agents not only in every province of the Celestial Empire, but in far off lands. Every month, ofttimes more often, he received reports from Tokyo, Calcutta, Isfahan, Cairo, Istanbul, Paris, London, New York, the gold fields of California, São Paulo, certain secluded islands, and numerous other locales of interest. He knew the schedules of every ship to traverse the Atlantic and the Pacific. He received every scientific journal published in Europe and America, which he read and memorized and in the margins he added comments and corrections.

His eyes and ears were everywhere, yet nowhere was his attention more focused than on the boudoir of the Noble Consort Yi, once named Xing'zhen.

* * *

In April of 1856, the imperial midwife stepped out of the women's chambers, intending to make an announcement to the Emperor's ministers and chief eunuchs in the more public foyer where they waited. However, immediately outside the door, she was intercepted by a tall man. She recognized this figure in the hallway, mentally comparing it to an upraised serpent in her mind. She knew he had not been granted imperial permission to be there—his authority was higher. She quickly bowed.

"What news have you, midwife?" asked Huang Zhou. He had stood in the wings of the Pavilion of Beautiful Scenery for the last two hours, waiting for the news.

"Noble Consort Yi has given birth to the Emperor's son, Master," said the midwife.

This came as good news for both Huang Zhou and his favored candidate, Yi. As Empress Consort Zhen had failed to produce a male heir, there would be no choice but for the throne to pass to the child of Noble Consort Yi.

Without nodding, Huang Zhou asked, "The noble consort is well?"

The midwife almost scoffed as she led him within to see the mother. "The child is small but healthy enough; he will live. As for the noble consort, it was an easy birth—but they say an easy birth is an inauspicious sign."

"Only for the child," he said.

Stepping inside, Huang Zhou did not so much as glance at the squalling infant, who might well one day become the Celestial Emperor. The child meant little enough to him, save that his birth now elevated Yi—once Xing'zhen—to an even greater position in the Celestial Empire.... and potentially, to become the most powerful woman on Earth.

GUNBOATS, OPIUM, AND ARSENIC

1: Old Enemy, New War

Ye Ming-ch'en stood taller than most Celestials—an illusion achieved with his elevated shoes. His girth, however, was quite genuine. He wore traditional deep blue robes, ornamented with gilded trims and a large round *feng shui* emblem, declaring him to be viceroy of Canton in Liang'guang Province and imperial commissioner, one of the highest-ranking officials of the Manchurian Ching Empire. His black skullcap, trimmed in ermine and surmounted with a ball of pink coral, showed him to hold a rank equivalent to a mandarin. This was misleading, however; his rank was considerably greater. Indeed, only members of the royal family held higher official ranks.

Yet Ye Ming-ch'en knew his true master. This day in October of 1856, as a visitor entered, Ye dropped to his knees and bowed, bopping his head against the floor.

After a moment, Senior Minister Weng bade the old administrator to rise. Weng took the opportunity to sit in the office's only chair—the one belonging to Ye. The imperial commissioner would not dream of expressing an objection. Minister Weng, he knew, held the position of second-in-command in the Order of the White Peacock. Only Mandarin Shu of Hunan Province and the emperor held higher positions in the Celestial Empire.

"Gracious Minister," said Ye Ming-ch'en, "I am profoundly honored for you to once more grace my office. May your ancestors bestow upon you their blessings."

Weng acknowledged the compliment with only a lengthy blink. Then he spoke.

"Ye Ming-ch'en," he said, "a recent incident in the harbor of Canton has come to the attention of the venerable mandarin of Sang-Wah. He wishes me to report what has happened and how it will be dealt with."

Ye breathed a little more comfortably. He felt confident that the mandarin would be pleased with how he had handled the situation thus far. He was only puzzled how Minister Weng might know of this incident in Canton, then traveled from Hunan to the Forbidden City in scarcely forty-eight hours—but he knew better than to ask details.

"Noble Minister," he said, "a junk now called *The Arrow*, well-known by my officers to have formerly been employed by Chinese pirates, has been spotted once more docked in Canton. Correctly, we ordered the Chinese crew arrested and the junk commandeered.

"That very day, the British consul, Mr. Harry Parkes, lodged a complaint with my office. He claims that the junk was indeed purchased by the British and flew their hideous flag. This is untrue and ridiculous. Moreover, when the British bought the ship, they bought the services of the original crew of twelve as well.

"I gave consideration to the complaint and released nine crewmen, only recently hired. I assured Mr. Parkes that the last three were members of the original pirate crew as well as rebels of the Taiping Insurrection. They are to be summarily tried for piracy."

"And Mr. Parkes' response?" Weng asked after a brief pause.

Ye Ming-ch'en recalled the black-suited white man's heels clicking, his curious swivel, then his imperious back turning on him.

"He left," Ye replied. "That was all."

Minister Weng, slowly stroking his long, thin beard, regarded the Imperial Commissioner. Ye Ming-ch'en tried to think what he might have done wrong.

Then Weng nodded. "This is well," he said. "I shall inform the mandarin that the situation is well in hand."

Ye Ming-ch'en, relieved, bowed to the representative of his master, who then departed.

* * *

A week later, Ye Ming-ch'en heard the echoes of British cannons as they began the shelling of the forts which had long provided protection to the city of Canton. By the end of the day, all four forts lay in ruin.

Not twenty-four hours later, Minister Weng and his aides once more stood in the Imperial Commissioner's office. There, he informed Ye of what he had learned in the past hour.

"Upon leaving your office, Consul Parkes immediately sailed down river to the British Fleet at Hong Kong. From there he ordered the attack on our forts."

Ye gasped in disbelief. "They would not dare! This is an outrage!"

"An outrage indeed, Imperial Commissioner," said Weng, "but clearly there is little which the barbarians would not dare. Furthermore, it is not only the barbarian navy that attacks the city, but their army is also on the march to your city. Furthermore, I have learned that the captains of these British armies have demanded that their troops be allowed inside the city. This then begs the question of how you intend to deal with this matter."

Ye Ming-ch'en verily fumed. "Enter Canton?! Never! They will not be allowed!"

Weng nodded in approval, then watched as Ye penned an order

to the commander of the Canton garrison, telling him to bar every gate into the city and to ignore any request by the British to allow troops inside. He sent it off with one of Weng's aides.

"I will accept no further insults from these barbarians, Minister Weng," said Ye Ming-ch'en. "Let the mandarin know he can depend on me."

Weng was pleased. "Excellent, Ye Ming-ch'en. You must rid China of these English. Issue a bounty for British soldiers and soon they will either all be dead or they will be pushed back into the sea! Do not trust your own people, for coolies are eager to receive British silver, even if it means aiding the enemy."

Upon receiving word of Ye Ming-ch'en's response—or rather, the lack thereof—the British Navy began a full-scale bombardment of Canton itself. Imperial Commissioner Ye then issued further orders that all commoners were to commit sabotage and terrorist attacks against the barbarian invaders at all their places of business and military bases throughout the province. He even offered a bounty for every British head brought to him.

2. Rebellion and War

At dusk some months later, two men looked over the flaming panorama of Canton before them. Once more, the smoke of a hundred fires rose from the burning city. As had happened during the Opium War, the forts flanking the city lay in utter ruin.

Hei Hu—the Black Tiger—nearly as tall as his compatriot, but broader in the shoulders—had but this day hurried to Canton, eager to collect Ye Ming-ch'en's bounty while also serving the whims of the Sublime Order. Alas, despite his speedy horse, he arrived in time only to see the walls of Canton shattered and its houses in flames. His companion, Huang Zhou, had a mission of his own, once he heard of the capture of the *Arrow*. Both young men, disguised in the pajamas and coolie hats of common fishermen, watched the bombardment from a distance.

"The barbarians again wage war upon us!" Hei Hu exclaimed. "Have they not taken enough from us with their unequal treaty?!"

Huang Zhou calmly surveyed the advancing red-coated army, the thundering cannons, and the flotilla of great ships on the river.

"We have seen this before, Hei Hu," he said. "It should come as no surprise that the British wish even more of the riches of the Celestial Empire. It also should come as no surprise that they picked this time to invade."

"Yes," Hei Hu grumbled, laying low as they spotted a small

troop of red-coated soldiers marching nearby on their side of the river. The infantrymen would not see through their disguises, but they might enjoy a bit of target practice.

Upon Huang Zhou's return to his homeland in 1851, he found the Celestial Empire shaken by the Taiping Rebellion. A young man named Hong, having failed three times at his civil service exams, allowed himself to become Christianized by foreign missionaries. The experience drove him insane, and after a series of feverish visions, he declared himself to be the actual brother of Jesus Christ and the forthcoming Heavenly King. Although the same missionaries who had converted Hong declared him to be a heretic, he somehow managed to convince some thousands of peasants of the truth of his claims.

"As Hong's cause is as much political as it is religious," said Huang Zhou, "his rebellion is bent on establishing a Taiping Heavenly Kingdom. This rebellion has spread across southern China and threatens to form a pincer attack with the British forces to overthrow the Manchurian Ching Dynasty."

"That's crazy," Hei Hu said, perplexed. "The British and the Taipings do not fight together."

"They do not fight together, but they fight the same enemy—the Emperor. Along with this Taiping insurrection in the south come others to the north and west. Some rebels are recognized by the red turbans they wear, others by the long knives they carry. Taking advantage of the crisis in Peking, the Muslim civil servant Du Wen'xiu began the Panthay Rebellion in Yunnan Province. These rebels agree upon nothing except the overthrow of their Manchurian overlords. So now, in this time of internal strife, the British Empire has once more chosen to wage war on the Celestial Empire."

Hei Hu scoffed. "Yes, of course. I know all this. The British Empire continues to grow more vast and more powerful, while the Ching Empire of China only stagnates. Opium pours into the streets, leaving the populace addicted to the foreign poison."

"The Celestial Empire has grown weak," Huang Zhou added. "Like the great and powerful yak that grows old, tigers and wolves will smell this weakness and exploit it."

Hei Hu fumed. "We must not allow this! I shall do as the Imperial Commissioner has ordered," Hei Hu vowed. "I shall assassinate the barbarian soldiers, one at a time and collect the bounties!"

"You will do this by yourself?" Huang Zhou asked, showing no hint of sarcasm or disbelief.

Hei Hu snorted. "I have been given command of the On

Lung—the Tong of the Green Dragons. That is all the army I require. Will you join us?"

"As you say, my friend, you have all the army you require." He then bowed to the senior agent of the White Peacock.

* * *

As Hei Hu stated, Master Leung, the head of the On Lung, had vowed to supply him with twenty fighters, to serve him in any way they could. These he encouraged with the promise of riches from the office of the Imperial Commissioner.

Huang Zhou, however, had requested only two agents, Yao Ling, the most clever and most subtle of assassins in the ranks of the White Peacock, and Dai'yu—Black Jade. These he had himself trained over the last few months.

Years before, Hei Hu had introduced Huang Zhou to the On Lung, the most notorious tong in the slums of Shanghai. Huang Zhou had more recently observed these men practicing hand-to-hand combat, and agreed that they might prove worthy allies. His interest, however, focused far less on their pugilistic men than on one of the girls among their ranks, the concubine Dai'yu.

Unlike Hei Hu or the men of the On Lung tong, Huang Zhou soon recognized her quick wits and ambition. He asked Master Leung of her and was told that when a particularly promising student was spotted in the ranks of a rival fighting school, Dai'yu promptly seduced him and convinced him to join the ranks of the On Lung. Another time, upon being asked to get a message into a castle of Yunnan Province, she brazenly disguised herself as the mandarin's concubine and rode in on his sedan chair—only to deliver the message and disappear. In the guise of a young guardsman, she escaped before the mandarin knew of her arrival. Huang Zhou decided to make use of these skills, placing her in one of the minor noble houses as an attendant to a certain Manchurian duke, the father of a potential candidate for the emperor's concubine.

Similarly, Huang Zhou found himself impressed by Yao Ling, who came recommended as a fighter, a scholar, and a spy. Months before, a minion in the service of the White Peacock had learned of a secret plot, he departed in the night, hoping to sell the information to a certain warlord who operated a warehouse filled with British opium. Yao Ling, however, saw to it that the man never arrived at his destination. Beyond his abilities as an assassin, he had a sharp mind for the many new technologies which Huang Zhou enjoyed showing to him. Huang Zhou knew he'd selected the two finest and most humble of the agents in the ranks of the White Peacock.

"During the first invasion by the British," said Huang Zhou to these agents, "my father was given the same task as I, that is to raise a siege with but with insufficient resources. His wisdom told him the only way to succeed at such a task would be to strike not at an army of thousands, but at the head of that army. This then, is what we shall attempt."

Yao Ling grunted and nodded assent. Dai'yu made no motion, yet Huang Zhou saw that she had caught his use of the word "attempt" rather than "do". Anyone should know the task was nigh impossible.

Huang Zhou presented his plan. They would sail downriver to Hong Kong, then enter the compound of the British governor, Sir John Bowring. To be allowed to pass, they would disguise the junk as a cargo ship and themselves as merchants taking supplies to the British headquarters. They even flew the Union Jack.

Huang Zhou and Yao Ling wore the baggy outfits of common coolies and Dai'yu dressed as a sing-sing girl. Once within the compound, it was hoped, they would learn the whereabouts of the governor and the number of guards around him at night. Hopefully, he would be unfaithful to the vows he'd made his wife, and Dai'yu could seduce him. She would then drug his brandy and leave. It was best that he take his nightcap well after she left, thus allowing them time to escape before the alarm was sounded. Such was the plan.

And the plan might have succeeded had their junk not been intercepted on the river by Taiping revolutionaries.

3. Taiping Rebels

The pungent smell of dead fish wafted from the shores of the Pearl River, where men unloaded their daily hauls as they and their ancestors had for thousands of years. Today, however, they stopped and looked up, watching a fast-moving war junk overtake a smaller vessel.

Ropes with grapples flew across the rapidly shortening distance between the two junks. The curses of the boarding party echoed over the sluggish water. Aboard the civilian craft, Huang Zhou realized they had no way to escape. He had just enough time to quickly scribe a message and attach it to the leg of a pigeon. He had no doubt it would reach its destination—he had bred the bird himself.

As the rebels heaved their ropes and pulled the smaller vessel closer, Huang Zhou quickly huddled and spoke quietly to the other two. A moment later, after the two junks collided, the rebels boarded their quarry. They roughly handled Huang Zhou and Yao Ling and bound their hands with stout ropes. Huang Zhou expressed no concern as the men gleefully reached under Dai'yu's cheong-sam and searched her. Dai'yu had expected this, but she squealed as if she had not. Just then, the captain of the rebel war-junk waddled over to them, a pistol and dagger displayed in his sash.

Ng looked more like a fat butcher than a rebel captain, perhaps because that is what he had been before hearing the calling of Hong and his Taiping revolutionaries. He had become a war-junk captain only because no one else wanted the job, and he was momentarily unsure of what to do with prisoners.

One of the mates ran up to him, gripping his knife. "Captain! You must kill them! They are spies of the barbarians!"

"Shut your mouth!" Ng bellowed, waving his own curved knife. "You don't tell *me* what to do! I'm the captain here, not *you!*"

The other rebel dropped his head in shame, having lost face. Ng glared at him for a moment more, before barking, "Take these three prisoners and lock them in the hold."

Thus, for no other reason than Ng's vanity, the lives of Huang Zhou and company were spared—for the moment.

The other rebels reached for Huang Zhou and his compatriots. Huang Zhou glanced at Yao Ling. Suddenly, despite his bonds, Yao Ling lunged forward, falling at Ng's feet.

"Master!" Yao Ling cried out to the captain, "I beg of you to speak!"

Huang Zhou also lunged forward with his bound hands, nearly grabbing Yao Ling by the collar before they stopped him. "Silence, dog!"

"No!" Yao Ling said, gasping in terror. "Do not let him touch me! He has poison in his pockets!"

"Poison?!" Captain Ng exclaimed, his eyes wide with surprise. The men holding Huang Zhou released him and backed away.

"This is rubbish," Huang Zhou said calmly. "Do not listen to him; he is crazy."

"I **will** listen to him," Ng said, glaring. "Separate them. Bring the short one over here."

Two of the men lifted Yao Ling to his feet and pulled him to the front of the junk. Two more kept a seething Huang Zhou in place with the points of their dao-staffs.

"Tell me what you know," Ng demanded.

Yao Ling hurriedly nodded and quickly bowed his head. "Honorable master, this man is a devil! He is part of a secret society—the British attack on Canton is only a ruse! It is really a trick to draw out the Taipings! It is true, father! The Ching Emperor and the British barbarians are secret allies!"

Ng and all his men gasped aloud.

"Dog son of a dog-mother!" Huang Zhou snapped, his face contorted in anger. "I will have your tongue cut out for such lies!"

"No!" Dai'yu interjected, her voice spitting invective. She moved away from Huang Zhou, and sent him a look of unmitigated hatred. "Yao Ling speaks true, Captain. This man, his true name is Fang. He is a devil indeed."

Suddenly she whipped her head around to face Captain Ng. "But do not think Yao Ling is any less of a devil! The plot was his idea!"

"No!" Yao Ling said, his eyes suddenly wide with surprise. "You lie! You try only to save yourself, you she-serpent!"

"I can prove it!" Dai'yu countered. "I have documents signed by both of them and the barbarian governor—you need only take me back to Canton and I will show you!"

"They both lie," said Huang Zhou. "Master, they are both *Hui*—Muslims—who plot to assassinate the leader of the Christian Taiping Revolution—Hong himself!"

"Wh-wh-wh-what!!?" Ng's eyes bulged. The folds of fat in his face jiggled as he looked back and forth and back again at the threesome.

Huang Zhou and the other two fell silent. The guardsmen looked to their captain, then to each of the captives, then back to Ng.

Captain Ng's mouth fell open and his eyes flitted back and forth. Stunned by these multiple, conflicting revelations, he struggled to find words. It would be some moments before he made a decision.

"This is clearly a greater conspiracy than I thought," he said. "Maybe.... Maybe not.... I do not know! But I know we must determine the truth. We will take them all to Heavenly King Hong and let him get to the truth! He is a holy man—he will know the truth!" On Ng's command, the war-junk changed course and headed to the port of Fumen with the smaller junk in tow.

In the hold, Huang Zhou, Yao Ling, and Dai'yu were separated, then bound hand and foot with rope, and their hands tied to rings in the hull, away from one another. They were kept in different corners of the dark hold—but they were kept alive. That was the purpose of their well-trained charade, and that was all they needed.

Less than an hour later, they heard a faint sound from outside the hull, muffled by the lapping of water to all ears that had not strained to hear it. A moment later, those ears heard a few faint sounds from the deck above: a thud, a grunt, another thud, a few words of alarm—

suddenly cut short. Then came another thud and another, and then a scream. This was quickly followed by panicked voices, running feet, a clash of blades, then more screams... and silence.

The silence did not last for soon they heard several splashes in the water. This was interrupted by footsteps rushing rapidly down the steps—then the door burst open. It was Captain Ng, his face livid with fright—and blood. He held his pistol as he would a club. With his other hand, he attempted to keep his intestines inside his slashed-open belly.

He failed, and they spewed out onto the floor. Ng then fell upon the prisoners and gasped out his last few breaths.

In the doorway there now appeared the broad-shouldered Hei Hu, in his black fighting clothes, and four of the Green Dragons, a bit bloodied themselves, but nothing life-threatening. The delay caused by Huang Zhou and his acolytes had proved sufficient. Alerted by the pigeon's message, the Dragons had pulled themselves aboard in the dark of night. Ten minutes later, Huang Zhou and his companions had been saved.

As their bonds were cut, Huang Zhou was not surprised that so few Dragons, operating with stealth, could slay five times their number. It only surprised him that Hei Hu had arrived with so few; after all, there could easily have been a hundred rebels on the two junks.

Huang Zhou bowed to Hei Hu. "I thank you, my brother."

Hei Hu nodded in response, then asked, "Why did the captain not kill you?"

"Although I knew your men would find the pigeon I sent off," Huang Zhou answered briefly. "I also knew this oaf of a captain would decide to execute us, so I conspired with my acolytes to confuse him. Thus, he would wish to keep us alive until our arrival. Or yours."

"I see."

"I confess I am surprised to see you led so few men here," said Huang Zhou. He left the next question unasked.

"The mission to murder the British in Canton failed," Hei Hu admitted, when pressed. "Most of the Green Dragons were shot before they could get in position to assassinate the British. Even the Dragon leader, Master Leung, is dead. To my great shame, they ended up killing no one. They are fine fighters, greatly talented, but they are not trained in stealth and the British numbers were too great. Only these four escaped and I was nearly captured. However, one of the Dragons, Red Tiger, risked his life to save me. So you see, Huang Zhou, we have both failed the mandarin in our duty."

"Delayed, Hei Hu," said Huang Zhou. "I have only to continue my mission."

Hei Hu shook his head. "Your plan would have failed also, either now or later," he added. "We have learned that Governor Bowring has doubled and tripled his guards in Hong Kong, and no Celestial is allowed within his palace."

Huang Zhou mulled on this until Hei Hu, the Black Tiger, motioned another man forward.

"Huang Zhou," he said, "this is my brother of the Fist, Red Tiger. He is next in command of the Green Dragons."

The man of whom Hei Hu had spoke, was rangy and bare-chested, with a shaven pate, save for his long queue. Despite his membership in the Green Dragon Tong, the sash about his lean waist was the color of blood. The glare on his harsh face seemed permanently fixed in place. The Dragons who flanked him seemed equally cordial. Huang Zhou bowed to the Red Tiger. The Tiger returned a bow, though not nearly as low, as one might return the bow of an inferior.

"We have lost many good warriors," Hei Hu admitted, "but we must still deal with the barbarians. I have consulted with Minister Weng and we have settled on a new course of action to stop them. With those members of the On Lung we left in Shanghai, I will not only rout the British from Canton, but I will also collect the bounty for killing the most Englishmen."

"Let us hope Governor Ye Ming-ch'en is not captured first," Huang Zhou postulated. "If so, there will be no bounties from him."

"Someone will pay the bounty, once we are victorious. Minister Weng has decreed that victory is inevitable if we cleanse Hong Kong of the English scourge. You are not the only one to see the value of poison, Huang Zhou. Weng, who is by far your master in the art of poisoning, has supplied me with all the poison I will need to kill every Englishman on the entire island. I plan to kill them all in one day!"

Huang Zhou said nothing; he had already calculated the odds of Hei Hu's success.

4. Eye to Eye

British gunboats, armed with breech-loading guns and heavy mortars, threatened the defenses of the Ching Empire. To reach Canton, British infantry and cavalry crossed the vast oceans by ship. British power, both here and in the far world, depended upon shipping—and keeping those ships afloat. Therefore, Ki Ming, minister to the mandarin of the Society of the White Peacock, planned to destroy the British fleet.

To this end, he sent two of his agents to pose as dock workers.

Daily they reported back to Minister Ki the comings and goings of the foreign ships, the contents of their cargo, and their armaments.

Another pair of agents, posing admirably as sing-song girls, returned with even more important information—the comings and goings of the captains of those ships. They soon reported that all of the captains intended to meet on the deck of the *Furious*, the flagship of Lord Elgin, the British High Commissioner to China. This day, the *Furious* lurked in sight of the forts that flanked the entrance to Canton, some twenty miles from the sea, and that meeting was to be held tonight.

"There can be little doubt that the captains gather to receive instructions for an imminent attack on the city," Ki Ming proclaimed to his acolytes. "This may be the only chance to slay all the captains in a single blow!

"Use no dynamite," he continued. "The *Furious* must burst into flames to show everyone that they are doomed to failure! The barbarians must be made to know the fate they will receive for attacking the Celestial Empire! Catch all of them before they can escape! Put fifty barrels of flammable oil inside the ship. Drill a hole in the ship's hull and run a fuse to the outside, away from the docks. At my signal, you will light the fuse and swim away to my junk and escape." Then he added, "And make it look like an accident."

The six agents, not daring to point out the contradiction of sending a public message while making the thing seem an accident, nodded their compliance. Then they left to attend their mission. Like Minister Weng, Minister Ki had picked a company of spies, saboteurs, and assassins from among the White Peacocks. To help him repulse an invading force of a dozen warships, hundreds of guns, and ten thousand men, Ki Ming had been allowed the aid of six agents of the White Peacock.

Yet he knew that if he was cunning, and his agents dedicated, such a task was not impossible. One had but to devise a plan and act upon it at the critical moment. A bit of luck would not hurt either. Yet Ki Ming knew better than to rely on luck.

Ki Ming was then left alone with his thoughts. And doubts. *Would it work?* he asked himself. *Yes*, he realized with an inner sneer, *if fortune favored every single step of the plan.*

Alone, he walked from the dock to a waiting rickshaw, contemplating the nature of fortune. He rode to a large but nondescript house and entered. For many years, this place had been one of the secret headquarters of the White Peacock, and for the last several days Ki Ming lived here, plotting every step of his mission.

Inside the house, no servant greeted him, for he hired none. He knew it would be better to cook his own meals than risk having a commoner in the house who might divulge the comings and goings of his agents.

Today, as Ki Ming walked down the hallway, the sound of a fast-moving ratchet—then another—caught his ear. Ere he could react, a pair of bamboo walls dropped from hidden recesses in the ceiling, with a sudden, great crash. One landing in front of and another behind him, he found himself in a cage, his movement blocked. Had the house always possessed such a contrivance that he was heretofore unaware? Or had it been installed in only these last two hours that he was absent?

As the echo of the portcullis faded, Ki Ming's sharp ears detected the softest of steps approaching. He turned to see Huang Zhou appear from behind a screen, flanked by Dai'yu and Yao Ling.

"Huang Zhou!" fumed Ki Ming. "How dare you! Truly you must be mad to attempt to capture me. What ransom do you hope to achieve?"

Huang Zhou stopped before the caged minister. "Minister Ki," he said calmly but firmly, "I do not *attempt* to capture you; I have succeeded. Yet you are most correct, sir; I do hold you for ransom. This ransom only you can pay—I will grant your release if you pay to me an hour in which you will listen to my words."

Ki Ming lowered the inner eyelid of his own orbs, casting a baleful glare upon Huang Zhou and his agents. The two agents stiffened, but that was all. Huang Zhou only scoffed.

"You have no power over my loyal agents, Ki Ming," he said. "Waste not your time attempting to subvert my agents, for I have trained them to withstand such abilities. My mesmeric abilities are far greater and more pure than your own."

Ki Ming heaved a sigh, and his eyelids returned to normal. Then, noting the sturdiness of the bamboo bars, he gave his captor a single emphatic nod.

"Excellent, Minister Ki," said Huang Zhou. "First, I have the misfortune to inform you that your scheme to assassinate the captains of the British fleet is doomed to failure."

Ki Ming bristled and clinched his fists, yet he said nothing.

"The British have sharp-eyed marksmen posted on every ship," Huang Zhou continued, "anticipating attacks from the water after Hei Hu's failure of last month. For fear of thievery, coolies are never allowed into a ship's hold unsupervised—thus your men will be unable to plant any explosives or barrels of oil. They will certainly be unable to drill a hole in the ship's hull. You have only condemned six worthy agents to their deaths."

The minister was livid. "How did you know my plans?!"

Huang Zhou scoffed once more. "By a method almost embarrassingly simple. Whilst you thought your junk to be safe in the water, Yao Ling swam up to it, placed a cup against the hull and heard every word you said."

Ki Ming gasped, not expecting his plans to fall apart so easily. "But... what else could I do? I follow the orders of the mandarin!"

"And you would have followed those orders to the pits of Hell," Huang Zhou commented flatly. "Now it is best that you recall your agents so that their lives are not wasted in a futile effort."

Ki Ming lowered his head a bit, keeping his eyes riveted on the younger man. Then he grunted in agreement.

Huang Zhou ordered the portcullis raised. For the remainder of the allotted hour, Huang Zhou spoke to Ki Ming of the future of the Order of the White Peacock and the Celestial Empire.

5. The Extra Ingredient

January of 1857 found both Tigers, Black and Red, in Hong Kong. Minister Weng, they strongly suspected, stood on the nearby mainland, waiting and watching.

"This is not how I like to face my enemies," said the rangy Red Tiger, commenting on the attire of a common laborer which he wore.

"Nor mine," replied the tall and athletic Hei Hu, as they walked down a dark stairway to the cobblestoned street in the pre-dawn hours, "but Minister Weng's plan cannot fail. By this time tomorrow, the entire British squadron will be dead!"

Curfew was in effect and strictly enforced, but the red-coated British soldiers allowed the two men to pass. After all, they were obviously bakers, for they carried a large flour sack. They needed to get to work if there was to be any bread for the soldier's morning toast.

Through a back gate off Queen's Road, they entered the E-Sing Bakery, the only business open at that hour. Both had been employees here for less than a week, replacing a pair of bakers who'd met with unfortunate accidents. Neither of the Tigers were particularly adept at the art of baking, an art largely unfamiliar to many in the south of the Celestial Empire where rice was the staple. But this large and prosperous bakery had a special clientele.

Since the end of the first Opium War, Hong Kong had been a British possession. Here they docked their ships and established their government offices and their businesses—most of which related to the distribution and sale of opium to the Chinese people. These foreigners may have enjoyed Chinese tea, but they had little taste for rice. They demanded bread.

The proprietor of the bakery, Cheong Ah-Lum, was already on site, and immediately began ordering his two newest workers to this or that task. It was soon clear he was not greatly impressed with them. However, they were always prompt, so he would not dismiss them just yet.

"It must be today," Black Tiger whispered, when he had the chance. "We cannot depend on Cheong's good graces much longer."

Red Tiger nodded as he opened the flour sack they had brought with him. However, this sack contained no flour.

They added the sack's white powder into the sacks with actual flour. They mixed this together and stirred it with water. They rolled out the dough, forming hundreds of loaves of bread. Other employees were tasked with making the finer pastries and treats.

Dozens at a time, the loaves were baked. One batch would be pulled, only to be replaced with a new batch. Cartloads after cartloads were filled. Just before dawn, those carts rolled along the crooked streets of Hong Kong. The first cartload of bread was delivered to the great house of Governor Bowring and his family.

Inside the houses of the colonists, cooks sliced and toasted the bread and applied jam. They could not have guessed that today's batch contained one extra ingredient.

Back at the bakery, as Baker Cheong handed out coins to his employees, he noted that the two least competent of them had left without waiting to be paid. He shook his head and went about counting the day's profits.

Meanwhile, in the stomachs of Governor Bowring and his wife, among others, the arsenic churned. They fell ill, became dizzy, and—as Hei Hu had used ten times more arsenic than necessary—they vomited up the poisoned bread ere it had a chance to kill anyone. That miscalculation gave various households the opportunity to sound an alarm and prevent many others from eating the bread at all. Runners carried messages from house to house, telling those who had eaten bread to stick their fingers down their throats.

A hundred or more Englishmen and women were sickened, but not one died. Cheong Ah-lum was ruined and villainized, despite being utterly unaware of the plot.

6. The Trial

When the disastrous news of the Hong Kong debacle caught up with Hei Hu, he immediately notified Senior Minister Weng. Weng, in turn, was obligated to report the matter to the Mandarin Shu.

Despite the hundreds of miles of mountains and winding rivers, they received a reply within a day; even the sluggish mind of the Mandarin Shu had realized the advantage of installing a series of private telegraph lines across the empire. As a result, both Weng and Hei Hu were summoned to appear at the court of the mandarin in Hunan Province.

Despite misgivings, Weng and Hei Hu traveled as rapidly as possible, on steamships, junks, and carriages. They reached the towering stone pillars of Hunan in a week. The mountaintop citadel of Sang-Wah, surrounded by the towering mountains, stood both serene and aloof in its seclusion. Yet this serenity and peaceful facade masked the deadly heart of the Sublime Order of the White Peacock. Both Minister Weng and Hei Hu knew well that a dozen hidden archers had them in view at any moment. As they entered the palace, they walked over trapdoors or under dead-falls and they were greeted by bowing and respectful courtesans whose sharp nails were tipped with poisons far deadlier and fast acting than arsenic.

Within the throne chamber sat the elderly Mandarin Shu upon a gilded throne that bore an emblem of a white peacock, its tail feathers fully displayed. Emblazoned upon his green, silken robes was the same stylized peacock, in white. His beard was equally white and forked. Kneeling one one side were the mandarin's concubines, including his newest and favorite, the beautiful Sin Yee. But to Weng's consternation, standing on the other side of the throne was Junior Minister Ki Ming, stout and stern.

Weng and Hei Hu both bowed low to the mandarin. The mandarin bade them to rise, then turned his attention to Ki Ming.

"Minister Ki Ming," he said, "you may question Minister Weng."

As Ki Ming stepped forward on the dais, Weng and Hei Hu exchanged an uncomfortable glance. For one minister to question another in court was rare enough. For a junior minister to question a senior was unheard of. Ki, however, turned to the mandarin.

"Gracious Mandarin, with your kind permission, I would first put my questions to Weng's subject, the warrior, Hei Hu, the Black Tiger."

The Mandarin Shu nodded impatiently. Then Ki Ming questioned Hei Hu.

"Hei Hu," Ki said, peering at him with his hypnotic eyes, "you were ordered to eliminate the British presence in Hong Kong, that they might no longer threaten Canton. Yet you have failed the mandarin's wishes. All know you as a fine warrior and your loyalty has never been questioned. Yet once again, you have employed a heavy hand, as one who would squash a mosquito with a sledgehammer. Only you would use ten times the arsenic than necessary. Now the opportunity for us to wipe out the British of Hong Kong in one fell swoop is lost! They will be only more wary of any attempt to eradicate them! The penalty for this is death!"

Hei Hu watched each of the guardsmen around him as they tightened their grips on their dao-staffs and tensed, ready to lunge should the word be given. Some of these men he had trained.

Hei Hu bowed to the mandarin. "Honorable Mandarin," he said in an unwavering voice. "gladly will I accept any punishment you wish to inflict upon my unworthy self. Yet I would be remiss in not informing your venerable self of the true cause of the debacle."

Ki Ming turned to the Mandarin Shu, who raised an eyebrow. He then nodded to Ki Ming.

"Hei Hu," he said, "tell the mandarin what you know of this matter."

Hei Hu rose and faced the mandarin.

"Glorious Mandarin, I did as I was commanded—by Minister Weng!" he said, seething more at the accusation of fault than any thought of the punishment should he be found guilty. "It was he who told me that I must add one full cup of arsenic to each bag of flour. I have his instructions here!"

With that, Hei Hu displayed a small scroll, delineating Weng's instructions—and in Weng's brushstrokes.

"What is this?" Weng exclaimed, his eyes widening. "Let me have that!"

"No!" Ki Ming snarled. "The mandarin alone shall see this document!"

Ki Ming took the scroll and handed it to Mandarin Shu. Weng blanched as Mandarin Shu perused the document. He positively shuddered as Shu's eyes rose and regarded him.

Shu glowered at Weng. "What do you have to say for yourself?"

"It is not my fault, venerable Mandarin!" Weng cried as he beseeched Shu's throne. "I... I just wanted to be certain! I know nothing of these modern poisons. I am an herbalist, not a chemist!"

Ki Ming scoffed. "Honorable Mandarin," he said, "we now see that the fault is less that of Hei Hu, but instead that of Weng. Hei Hu is no master of poisons, but he never claimed to be." Then Ki peered at his trembling rival. "But you, Weng! You should know better!"

Minister Weng quite jumped in his sandals.

Ki continued. "You have unleashed Hei Hu's brutality when you should have employed the subtlety of Huang Zhou! In the last thousand years, few agents among the White Peacocks have mastered the art of poison better than Huang Zhou. Huang Zhou, once your student, would never make such a mistake. Why did you not task *him* with this scheme?"

"I... I..." Weng faltered. Under his heavy robes, his knees knocked.

Shu glowered at Minister Weng. "I have heard enough. What do you have to say for yourself?"

"Mercy!!" Weng cried.

Wishes are not always received.

* * *

Ki Ming retired to his chambers in the palace of Sang-Wah in the mountains above Changsha in Hunan. He ordered tea brought to him, and after it was placed on the table of carved ebony, he dismissed his servants.

As he sat, a panel slid open and a tall figure in a green robe entered. Ki Ming regarded the younger man, even as he poured two cups of tea.

Huang Zhou bowed, then rose.

"The trial went well, I understand."

Ki Ming smirked. "You understand correctly, my friend. Minister Weng has been executed and I am elevated to the position of Senior Minister. Hei Hu was admonished, but he retains his title and his life."

Huang Zhou sat beside Ki Ming and took a cup in his hands. "I am pleased that my plan went as well as we might hope."

7. In the Court of the Mandarin

Even before Huang Zhou heard of the disastrous failure of Hei Hu in Hong Kong, he had given up on assassination plans, for he knew that no number of assassinations in Asia would stop the plans of the colonists in Great Britain. Besides, the outcome of the current Opium War held little concern for him, but rather he focused on the future of mankind. Rather than murder Englishmen, he intended to focus on the goal of awakening the World Leader.

Huang Zhou had spent the last two months in deep contemplation, fasting and meditating as he studied the ancient—even prehistoric by some considerations—tomes in the vast libraries of the Order. He had learned much, but far from everything he would need to bring about the vague prophecies.

"But who is she?" he asked his disciples, Dai'yu and Yao Ling, rhetorically. "Has she been born yet?"

There, in his apartment within a mandarin's villa in Shandong, overlooking the Yellow Sea, Huang Zhou regarded the missives he'd lately received from his agents in London, Jun and Gau. Whilst they had made progress in securing the loyalties of various Limehouse entities and constructing—or discovering—secret tunnels that might one day be useful, they were no closer to gaining access to Queen Victoria. In truth, Huang Zhou would have been surprised if they had.

Closer to home, in the last few days the British had attacked Canton, leaving the city devastated and aflame, its people blown to bloody bits. Vast armies of British and their American allies poured into the burning city. One American captain defiantly raised their patchwork flag over the residence of the Imperial Commissioner, Ye Ming-ch'en. Ye was captured later that day, trying to climb over the back wall, much to the glee of Consul Harry Parkes.

"The turmoil of this second Opium War may prove an excellent opportunity to reform the White Peacock," Huang Zhou said. "Mandarin Shu remains obstinate, constrained in the old traditions, even working against the goals of the Order, which shall only lead us to defeat. His latest blunder is to sacrifice his highest ministers and most proven agents on an impossible task. I believe Minister Ki Ming and the Black Tiger share my concerns about the mandarin's ability to lead us.

"I have convinced Ki Ming that change is necessary by showing him the many things I have learned, and how they might be used to further the goals of the Sublime Order. Yet even he remains hesitant to challenge the Mandarin Shu."

"Senior," asked Dai'yu—for women were ever allowed to speak, equal to the men in Huang Zhou's retinue, "is the mandarin now our enemy?"

Yao Ling flashed his eyes from Dai'yu to his master.

"Our venerable mandarin is not the enemy," Huang Zhou stated clearly to his subordinate. "However, it has fallen to us to enlighten his mind. We must ever believe that the mandarin can be shown the path of logic and innovation. Now, while the British have called off their attack on Canton, I must attempt one last time to sway the mandarin's mind."

* * *

Upon returning to the mist-shrouded mountains of Hunan Province, Huang Zhou once more regarded the figures of dragons and tigers, unicorns and phoenixes as he walked along the tiled floors of the mandarin's palace. Twenty-two years had passed since he first entered this chamber, led by his father.

Huang Zhou presented himself before the dais of the Mandarin Shu and bowed. The usual guardsmen, administrators, clerks, scholars, and courtesans stood about, staring impassively at the curious agent. With a flick of his hand, Shu indicated he should rise.

"Huang Zhou," said the mandarin, "I understand you have been deeply immersed in your studies. I recall the miracles you brought back from the West. Now I would have you show me the many new technological marvels you have discovered and how they might be used to benefit the Celestial Empire in its war."

Huang Zhou bowed his head. "I have none, your serene Grace."

The mandarin's eyes flashed, confused. "None, you say?"

"Indeed, Your Grace. I have sequestered myself these last months in the great libraries of the Sublime Order, where I have studied how, in the past, agents of the Order did not confine their efforts solely in Asia. Agents of the Order could be found in the courts of the pharaoh and at Rome. Such discoveries as I have made might further the goals of the Order. However, I sought no weapon of war, for war is not the answer to the goals of the Council of the Seven."

The mandarin's eyes widened. Before he could speak, Huang Zhou continued.

"Noble Mandarin, war threatens the Celestial Empire once more and we must realize that defeat is very likely. Yet the goals of the White Peacock are greater than any one nation, even our own. If China is lost to the barbarians, we must focus our attention elsewhere. We must not ignore our allies, the Dacoits, the Hashashim, the Phansigars, the Thuggees, and those few Khurramites which have survived. We must support them. We must also look to organizations of the West, such as the Anti-hippocratic Cabal and the Illuminati.

"Serene Leader," he continued, "I envision the Council of the Seven as a single entity, and the organizations which I have named serve as the arms and legs of this entity. The Kwen-Yuin of Tibet serve as the heart and soul of the Seven and provide our spiritual guidance. The Sublime Order of the White Peacock is the head, and thus it falls upon us to lead the rest, to instruct them, and to encourage them."

When Huang Zhou paused, the Mandarin Shu laughed—loudly. No one else in the chamber moved.

"So who is the prick of this great creature of yours, Huang Zhou? Hm? Tell me that!"

Others laughed along with their mandarin, and most of the

ladies giggled behind their fans, but in Huang Zhou no motion could be seen. He waited until they once more became silent.

Then Huang Zhou spoke. "If a mandarin of the White Peacock wishes that his advisors make their reports in the form of schoolboy insults, then clearly he no longer has the goals of the Council of the Seven first in his heart."

Huang Zhou, for one of the few times in his life, had allowed anger to dictate his response. There came an audible gasp from everyone else in the throne room. The Mandarin Shu, his eyes dancing between confusion and fear, settled on anger.

"How dare you!" he bellowed, finding his feet. "You accursed whelp! You attempt to make me look like a fool!? I shall make you regret your upstart tongue!"

Already, Ki Ming had backed away, his face ashen. Hei Hu, unbidden, had laid hold of Huang Zhou's arm. Red Tiger took hold of the other.

"Take him to a cell!" the mandarin yelled, in a most decidedly un-serene manner. "Have him thrown in a cell until I can think of a worthy form of execution! The Death of the Slow Slicing may not be sufficiently slow for such calumny!"

* * *

Huang Zhou sat in the bottom of a dark hole, too small for a tall man to lay down properly. Absently, he wondered what hour of the night it was. The only glimmer of light came from an overhead grate, and that was none too bright. In past centuries, this cell likely sat under a latrine.

There was a small but heavy door at the bottom, through which he had been shoved. This had a simple lock and he might have attempted to reach through the tiny window and pick the lock from this side, had he not been deprived of his possessions, including all of his clothes.

The grate lay a full ten feet overhead. He tried climbing up the walls, hooking his fingers and toes in the stonework. The process was slow and ultimately futile. The grate was iron and firmly bolted in place.

Huang Zhou attempted to meditate, yet found himself distracted by his situation. Rarely had he ever become enraged, and now it seemed doing so had only caused him to forfeit his life. This he did not necessarily regret, as he hoped that his sacrifice might cause others to contemplate the things for which he was willing to die. Perhaps they would challenge the incompetent mandarin and set the Order on the right course once again. Then again, perhaps they would be even more afraid to act, once they'd seen him executed.

Would the mandarin have him executed first thing in the morning? The middle of the following night? Or would he be left here for days and weeks, as the mandarin hoped to stretch his suffering to the greatest length.

Huang Zhou briefly pondered the form of the actual execution. The Death of the Slow Slicing, he knew, was far from the worst way to die. Blood loss would usually bring about death in as little as ten or fifteen minutes. Most likely longer, for him.

There was no purpose served in thinking of it, of course; the thing would happen and he would likely have no choice in the matter—much the same as any man's death. Rather, Huang Zhou closed his eyes and attempted to sleep.

At some point of time, he awoke as a faint sound came to his sharp ears, from above. He opened his eyes, looking up at the grate. With the passage of time his pupils had adjusted and the dim, distant lamp light seemed brighter—yet hardly bright at all.

Whilst resigning himself to his fate, he nonetheless hoped that no one intended to use the cell for its original purpose. He stood up, preparing to dodge any substance that might fall his way.

He then detected the faint echo of a subtle foot. Then he saw a movement—and an unknown hand. It dropped something through the grate, then disappeared.

Huang Zhou caught the falling object ere it struck the floor. It was a key.

Epilogue

Dawn found Huang Zhou on a stolen horse, riding through the jagged mountains of Hunan Province, on the road that led to the Silk Road, the quickest overland route west.

Due to the death sentence over his head, Huang Zhou intended to flee China for a time. He would make his way to India, where he intended to find the Thuggees and Dacoits of India that he might incite rebellion. Such a rebellion would divert the attention of the British, allowing China to strike back against them.

More importantly, Huang Zhou hoped to continue his search for the future World Leader. He already had a candidate in mind.

One day I will find she who is to become the Universal Ruler and I will work to advance her to that place where she is prophesied to sit. Then, as an afterthought, he thought, *If I can not find her, I will create her.*

Huang Zhou had no doubt that a woman could do as well as a

man as the future leader of the entire world. Perhaps better. If he had any doubt, he need only to think of the hand that had dropped the key into his cell.

A hand both slender and graceful.

DHAKAR THE VISIONARY

1. Bundelkhand (1851)

The women shooed the rajah out of the Rani Asha's bedroom, knowing he would only be in the way with his fretting. Downstairs with the men, including the rani's gray-bearded father, the Maharajah Dheri, the rajah continued to pace and scowl at the others.

The other men only laughed good-naturedly at the Rajah Dhakar, soon to be a father for the first time at the age of thirty-three.

"You chide me," Dhakar said to them, "but have you never worried when your wives gave birth? So many things can go wrong!"

"I was nineteen when my wife gave birth to my first child," said the elder maharajah. "Asha followed not two years later. I have never worried, but only let the women handle their own mysteries. They are more experienced at having babies than us."

The other men all laughed with the maharajah. Dhakar forced a smile—which dropped as soon as he heard his beloved Asha scream from above.

He moved for the stairs, but the others held him back. With smiles on their faces, they shook their heads and said, "Relax" or "All is in the hands of the gods."

Dhakar Rao, who did not believe in the many gods of his Hindu ancestors nor the one god of his Sikh in-laws, felt no comfort. Nonetheless, he sat down and waited, making only furtive glances towards the stairs for the next hour.

At that time, one of the midwives descended the steps with a bundle in her arms. Breaking into a wide grin, she announced to the rajah that he now had an heir.

Soon, Dhakar sat beside his wife as she nursed their newborn son. Though she'd been through an ordeal, Asha giggled as she saw Dhakar's tears of joy.

"He is beautiful, yes Dhakar?" she said. "I can only hope that he will prove as worthy to the people of our city as his father."

Dhakar smiled at her. "I will leave him a better land than my father left for me."

* * *

In the months to follow, Dhakar Rao doted over his son as much as he doted over his wife and his research into engineering, metallurgy, and voltaic piles. The rajah, educated primarily at Heidelberg, the Sorbonne, and Cambridge, had continued his studies as best he could on his own in India. In truth, it mattered little where he studied, for most of his research now involved experimentation and practical application in the workshop he'd constructed on his plantation, near the outskirts of Banda. No book had been written that told of the things Dhakar planned. As he scrawled various notes and drew plans, it amused him to consider that one day he would have to write such a book.

Although by no means haunted by the attempt on his life a year earlier, Dhakar took sensible precautions. He had replaced the guards and others who had been murdered by the lone assassin with twice their number. They made their patrols both night and day, and he made sure they were well armed and trained. He had ordered locks to be added and lanterns lit in every corner of the compound.

In the meantime, Dhakar commissioned an English artist to paint Asha and the baby, Bani, together. For the sitting, Asha wore her most elegant sari and held the baby as she posed. Upon viewing the completed picture, Dhakar happily awarded the artist double the agreed-upon sum.

Asha resumed her role as mistress of the house and household. She supervised the kitchens and kept correspondence with other nobles in the region. She maintained order and settled disputes between townsfolk, allowing Dhakar to spend more and more time with his plans and his foundry. Asha tended to the bills as Dhakar purchased curious gadgets and devices from faraway ports, then welded them into new and unfathomable shapes.

* * *

Dhakar Rao had inherited his fiefdom upon his father's death. This consisted of the sprawling city of Banda, some thousands of acres of farmland surrounding it, and a few adjacent villages. Bundelkhand rested, mostly serene, in an arid portion of the Ganges Basin, in the north of the Indian Subcontinent. Sagar, in the south, and Jhansi to the west, were the principle cities. Allahabad sat farther to the East, and Kanpur—or Cawnpore, as the British called it—to the north.

Banda, centuries ago the capital of Bundelkhand, had little to appeal to the senses today; it had a marketplace, waddle huts, and tens of thousands impoverished people, the same as any other city. However, Dhakar had plans by which he might supply Banda and other cities with all the food as they needed.

One day, Dhakar met with the British Resident of Banda, a man named Cockrail, who also held the position of Joint Magistrate over the District, whether Dhakar wanted him there or not. Dressed in a lightweight suit, vest, and cravat, the magistrate made a dashing figure, despite the sweat running down his face. Cockrail had not been placed in the role of Resident by the East India Company, but directly by the

British government. Neither Banda nor Bundelkhand were under EIC control, but that did not stop the British from planting their administrators in their midst. Dhakar knew why. Not only did the man serve as an administrator, he could be, when necessary, a spy. Dhakar danced verbally around the question over a noonday meal.

"Yes, yes," Cockrail said, laughing good-naturedly. "I'm to observe and report on every little matter here in Banda. Glad to say there's little enough to report. I do like the way you're handling the place, Rajah. Quite the improvement over your father's way of doing things, if you don't mind me saying so. Shouldn't complain, though. The old boy was getting on in years; still stuck in the old ways, what. But I do like seeing you taking an active role in the running of the town."

"I thank you most heartily, Magistrate Cockrail," Dhakar replied with a bow of the head. "I wish nothing more than to improve the lot in life of my people."

Cockrail smiled. "I must say, your English is impeccable. Quite a bit easier than going through translators. I'm getting better with my Hindi, though, don't you think?"

"Indeed, Magistrate," said Dhakar, feigning a smile. Besides the matter of the resident's competence, Hindi and Bundeli were not quite the same language. "You shall speak it like a native in no time."

Cockrail laughed again. "Don't know about that. Just need to be able to get directions in the marketplace, don't you know?"

Dhakar forced another smile and nodded, then they finished their meal. Before they parted, Dhakar shook the hand of Mr. Cockrail, glad that he had made a friend of this important man. Over the next few years, they would dine together a number of times, with Dhakar always bringing Cockrail's attention to various needs in the city of Banda and in the province of Bundelkhand. As a result, the two men saw to it that money sent from Great Britain went for the improvement of roads and the propagation of an improved postal system.

* * *

"Dhakar, what is this?" asked Asha one day, walking into his workshop and displaying a receipt. "Why have you spent seventy thousand rupees on valves and gauges?"

Dhakar looked up from his drafting table. "Have they arrived? It's about time."

"Yes, they are in a crate. The men want to know where they may set it down. But why do you need so many of these things?"

Dhakar stood up and hurried for the door. "I may need more before I am finished, my beloved. I just hope those oafs are careful.

One can't find these things in India, you know. I must order them from European manufacturers."

Asha followed him into the courtyard, waving her bare arms. "I think you have gone mad from the sun, always walking about with nothing on your head!"

Dhakar turned, walking backwards for a few steps. He grinned at her and said, "Just keep a look out for the levers and hinges I have ordered. I will tell you everything, soon."

* * *

Indeed, not long after the baby's first birthday, Dhakar took him and Asha for a ride to a wide portion of the river Ken, away from Banda proper. Stopping, they looked out on the glistening waters, surrounded by rough hills and a scattering of trees.

Asha cradled the baby in her arms, looking out over the river. She rested her head on her husband's shoulder.

"It is very beautiful," she said.

Dhakar nodded. "Yes. I just doubt that it's deep enough. I think I would prefer Lake Lakha Banjara, by Sagar, for my first prototype."

Asha pulled away slightly so she could look up at him. "What do you mean? What prototype?"

He smiled, perhaps smugly. He then opened a leather tube and produced several large sheets of heavy paper with numerous illustrations and draftsman's notes and laid them on the seat of the coach for her to peruse.

His explanations flew forth rapidly, seemingly without rhyme or reason and without any order she could determine. She caught only snatches of what he said: "...voltaic piles... rows of galvanic batteries... electrical power... a turbine engine... a hull the size of an elephant... rivets that have passed the most extreme pressure tests... exploration of the last secret realm... iceboxes to preserve specimens... entirely new species... a crew of only two at first, but someday maybe twenty, maybe thirty... barracks... observation deck... and we need only catch what we eat!"

Asha grasped his arm, stopping him there, steadying herself. She took a moment for her mind to stop reeling.

"It is a ship??" she asked, incredulous. "It will sail upside-down?? Those trinkets that you brought from Europe, they will make this contraption work?"

"Upside-down?" Dhakar repeated, momentarily confused. "Oh no, I explained it badly. I mean it will not sail at all. There are no sails. It travels under the water by means of a screw. That is how I intend to explore Lake Lakha Banjara. According to the East India Company's geologists, their soundings indicate a depth of twenty-five feet in places."

Asha had yet to be taken in. "And the lake, however beautiful it is, has such treasure at the bottom that you must spend a million and a half rupees to find it?"

Dhakar smirked. "Lakha Banjara has no treasure that I have ever heard of. The treasures I hope to find are greater than all the rupees in India." He took her free hand in his. "The treasure I seek is a new world, the world beneath the sea. I plan to explore this world, which no man has ever seen. Asha, until we see this hidden world, no one truly knows what is down there. There may be unknown minerals, unknown creatures. If nothing else, there will be fish and seaweed—enough to feed millions of hungry people throughout the world.

"But we won't know until we take a look. This vessel is only a prototype for a greater vessel which I hope to build. Then we can begin the exploration of the sea, not just a lake. What do you think?"

Asha looked out over the river once more. She looked at the plans he held. She looked at the baby. Finally, she looked up at her husband again.

"I did not know I married a madman," she commented dryly. "Such is my *karma*, I suppose. If you are to give fish to every staving child in India, then you will need a madwoman beside you, Dhakar—or you will never get this thing finished."

* * *

With Asha's moral support, Dhakar next sought out a bright and eager young engineer straight from the university, Sandeep Lal. Dhakar apologized for the salary that he would pay the student, as even he began to see that his funds were not endless. Lal adjusted his spectacles and studied the plans, then listened to explanations as to how the project might actually come to fruition.

Amazed and inspired by what he saw, Lal said, "Rajah, I would aid you for free, just for the honor of being involved in such a project."

Dhakar slapped the young man on the back. "Don't be so rash. A man must eat if he is to build. But while I promise you will not starve, you will most likely lose some baby fat."

Soon others would aid Dhakar in his work: Hari Babu, the best student of physics and chemistry to ever graduate from the University of Bengal; Anup Khan, a master draughtsman, experienced in bridge-building, who quickly improved on portions of Dhakar's plans; Masud, a railroad mechanic and welder with years of practical experience on engines; and Chundawat, a sailor who had piloted steamships up and down the Deccan peninsula for the last decade.

With their help, Dhakar began construction of the frame for what Asha called his "Iron Water Buffalo".

2. The Boiling Kettle (1854-56)

Later that year, old Gopal retired and a far younger Captain Ram Gupta succeeded him as Dhakar's chief of the garrison. Preferring the clear-cut European military tradition, Dhakar gave him the title of general.

"I am not being pretentious by giving you such a title for the first time in the history of Banda," Dhakar told him, afterwards. "Military structure is no small matter these days. Every rajah in India has his own army to protect his interests. Armies abound throughout the subcontinent. Smaller ones might be overrun easily."

"Yes, *sahib*," said General Gupta. "The East India Company has three major companies of soldiers, the Bombay, Madrat, and Bengal. These companies are each about two hundred and fifty thousand strong. They consist of men from all over India, but with large numbers of Punjabis and Gurkhas, all led by British officers. These are backed up with a few battalions that are exclusively British."

Dhakar nodded, pondering the matter, though his mind kept flitting back to a problem with the propeller. Maybe it just needed a more constant supply of oil or grease to keep it from seizing up.

"Rajah...?" Gupta asked.

"Yes," Dhakar said trying to bring back his attention. "How many men do we have in Banda?"

"Two hundred and fifty, *sahib*."

"I see. Is that enough?"

"Enough for what, *sahib*? Two hundred and fifty is maybe enough to keep the *dacoits*—bandits—out of the town. It is not enough to keep out the Company."

"No, I suppose it is not." These days, the men of the East India Company often marched into parts of India where they had no business. And they had a habit of not leaving.

"Rajah, do you wish me to find more *sepoys*—soldiers? There are enough layabouts to double the garrison."

Dhakar quickly did some numbers in his head. "No. I need to purchase better valves and a new monitoring system for the pumps. We have enough men to keep peace. They are guardians of Banda, after all, not all of Bundelkhand. Actually... can you dismiss some of the men? A hundred? Fifty? Honorably, of course."

Gupta, like any general, gasped at the thought of losing any men for his army. Yet, as he had been but newly commissioned with the task, he made scant argument. Eventually, rajah and general agreed to dismiss fifty men. The money saved would be used for the *Iron Buffalo*.

* * *

Dhakar and his craftsmen poured themselves into their work, completing the frame and hull of the ship in a year—a hull that would stand against incredible pressure. Afterwards, they began the more difficult part of installing the engine, electric batteries, and rudder—and making them all work together. Dhakar's crew brainstormed, drew up new plans, assembled, disassembled, argued, and brainstormed some more. They agreed to dismantle a sizable portion of what had first been constructed and enlarge the tail end so they might move the engine further back. Everyone agreed that would facilitate a better arrangement, but now the controls would need to be reworked to compensate for the greater distance from the helm.

Some months short of the *Iron Buffalo*'s maiden voyage, word came that Dhakar's friend and superior nobleman, Gangadhar Rao, the maharajah of Jhansi, had died after a long illness. This occurred the day after he adopted a son and heir.

Dhakar and Asha, along with emissaries from all over India, and a few from Britain, France, and even one from China, attended the funeral and gave their condolences to Rao's widow, Lakshmi Bai. With the death of the maharajah, custom obliged her to forfeit the title of maharani consort. She would now be the maharani regent for her young son, Damodar.

The lovely young maharani stood stoically as she conducted the ceremony and lit the funeral pyre. Gone were the days when she might be obliged to lay beside his corpse as it burned. Lakshmi never cried, but nonetheless this strong woman appeared troubled.

Dhakar knew why. With Gangadhar Rao dead, the British East India Company might now claim that his province had been abandoned and in abeyance. According to the Doctrine of Lapse, which the Company had imposed over all of India, unbidden, any region whose sovereign died without blood issue became the property of the Company. They had done so in the past.

Would they make such a claim over Jhansi?

* * *

They did. In November, by writ of British law, the British Resident informed the widowed Lakshmi Bai that she no longer had a claim to the capital of Bundelkhand. She lost her wifely title of maharani and only retained her inherited title, rani. Under British law—the law applied to Indian subjects, not the British themselves—her son, being adopted, had no claim to the throne and she would not be considered his regent. A British officer, Captain Skene, politely asked her to vacate the palace.

Her reply was, "I will not give up my Jhansi."

Afterwards, a troop of East India Company redcoats moved into the palace and the fort. They brought down the red triangle of the Jhansi flag and replaced it with the Union Jack. The rani moved out of the palace, but she remained in the city. Lakshmi Bai may have been officially powerless but she remained vigilant and optimistic, writing letter after letter to the new governor and his ministers, arguing her case and citing various British laws. She also wrote letters to her fellow nobles, informing them of the indignities to which she had been subjected and reminding them that their turn might be next.

When not writing letters or sending envoys to London, Lakshmi Bai watched the goings-on, ever speaking to the men and women of Bundelkhand. Over the next several weeks, more and more of them would come to listen.

* * *

"I worry for our rani, Lakshmi Bai," Dhakar said one day, not long after, as he and Asha took tea on the veranda. Bani sat at the same table, slurping away at a bowl of paneer and rice. "According to her letter, with the maharajah's death, the East India Company has invoked their clause of revocation upon Jhansi."

"They cannot," Asha declared, scandalized. "It is against our ways. Even should a rajah or maharajah pass without issue, the crown is passed on by his decree not his bloodline. He and Lakshmi had a child."

"By adoption," he stressed. "And no, it is all very legal—according to the treaty imposed upon us by the East India Company. They claim Gangadhar Rao's lands are abandoned."

"They take ever more lands, Dhakar! Already half of India is occupied by Company troops. Soon there will be no part of India left for the Indian people!"

"Asha... there are no Indian people. There are Hindis, Marathi, Bengalis, Gujartis, Punjabis, Gurkhas, Tamils, and a hundred other peoples, and all enemies of each other. India has not even a common religion. There are Hindus, Jainists, Muslims, Sikhs, Christians, and a few Buddhists or Jews. And the castes—Kshatriyas, Brahmins, Rajputs, untouchables—some not allowed to speak together! There is no unity in India and I fear there never shall be, for there is not even a common tongue with which to communicate. Small wonder that first the Mughals and then the British found it so easy to take over this land."

Asha looked at him firmly. "That does not make it right."

Dhakar said nothing more.

* * *

The following February, three years after birthing a son, Asha gave birth to a girl, Savita. Young Bani took it upon himself to rock her cradle and to make sure the baby had sufficient blankets. His parents chuckled.

"Bani is barely out of the cradle himself," Dhakar noted, "and already he rocks it for his sister."

"He will be a good father some day," Asha commented proudly.

* * *

In October, Dhakar pointed out an item in the newspaper to his wife. Unlike many women in India, Asha could read and write, and in four and a half languages. English being the language she half understood, he translated.

"War has once more broken out in several provinces of China, not two weeks ago," he said. "They rise up against their British oppressors."

Asha at once grasped the ramification of this news. "The British forces are now split between two nations. They will be unable to bring the full force of their empire against us. This is the time for Lakshmi and the others to make demands. Dhakar, this is wonderful news!"

Dhakar chuckled. "Asha, your mind has become political from spending so much time with Lakshmi."

"You are surprised, Dhakar?"

"I am impressed. You and she are both very admirable women." Then he smirked a bit. "I am glad to have married one of you."

"Oh? And did you marry the right one?" Asha asked petulantly.

Dhakar took her hand. "I know I did. I've a hunch that Lakshmi would never allow me on top."

Asha laughed. "Maybe tonight you will *not* be on top."

He grinned. "I can live with that, now and then."

* * *

Whilst the Widow Lakshmi Bai composed yet another to-be-ignored letter to Governor Canning and consulted a book of English inheritance law, her chamberlain stepped into her study. He did not bow.

"Rani, there is a man to speak with you," he said, in a stilted tone.

Lakshmi lifted her eyes from her papers and looked at him, unbowed. "A man? Who is this man?"

"Rani, there is a man to speak with you," he repeated in the same manner. She noticed that he did not look at her but at a nondescript portion of the wall behind her.

The rani got up and walked around her desk, eyeing the unusual gaze of the chamberlain. She took down a *tulwar*—sword—from another wall, before marching out to the foyer.

She stopped suddenly as she spotted a figure who could only have been the one responsible for this curious incident. Attired as a Brahman scholar, yet of no race of India, he stood a full head taller than her, formal and attentive, one might even say regal. Upon his shaven head he wore no headdress, for already he bore a crown. He gazed coldly, stern and confident, yet with no hint of arrogance.

Lakshmi raised her sword as she regarded him. "Who are you?" she demanded. "How dare you hypnotize my servants! ...Do I know you?"

The man bowed to her, never allowing his eyes to leave hers. Then he rose.

"We met briefly, Lakshmi Bai, at your husband's funeral," he said in perfect Bundeli, but with a faintly musical accent. "Since that day I have watched you from afar and taken note of your trials and tribulations and my heart is heavy for the wrongs foisted upon you. It is with great honor and supreme expectation of our mutual fortune and benefit that this wayfaring intermediary makes his presence known to you once more."

With that, he bowed again, never displaying a hint of emotion.

Lakshmi lowered her sword then laid it on a small table. "My ally, Singh, told me of you and I will speak with you, *sahib*. He told me of your Order and I agree that we may help one another. Please enter and we will have tea and speak of our respective needs and benefits. You like tea, I am certain."

The man replied with the faintest nod of his head.

"Thank you, Rani," he said. "However, if it please Your Highness, my given title is Doctor."

3. India Under the British (1857)

"Bite the cartridge!" the British sergeants bellowed to their troops of the 19th Native Infantrymen. They had assembled one February morning on the training field of the Meerut Garrison, north even of Delhi, to explain how to operate the new Enfield rifles and their Minie bullets. Coating the cartridges with grease rendered the bullets safer to handle and easier to load. Biting and then tearing the cartridge allowed the gunpowder inside to ignite when struck by the firing pin.

However, this would lead to a problem that no one in the Company had foreseen. The *sepoys*—Indian infantrymen—noticed a taste in these new cartridges. Back in the barracks, they spoke of it.

"The new cartridges taste rancid," said Inderjit, wrinkling his nose and sticking out his tongue.

"Yes, they do," agreed Banerjee. "They are soaked in grease, yes?"

"What kind of grease?" asked Fawud, suddenly alarmed. "It must not be lard. The Holy Koran forbids us to consume the fat of an unclean animal. Consuming swine will prevent my soul from entering Heaven!"

"Or tallow," said Banerjee, a Hindu, becoming equally worried. "Cattle are sacred animals; to bite into their flesh—or even the fat of their bodies—is therefore sacrilegious."

"And we Sikhs do not eat any kind of meat," Inderjit added. "But let us find out. Let us go ask the lieutenant."

They did so. The British lieutenant, with his boots up on his desk, took a moment to look over one of the pamphlets that accompanied the boxes of cartridges and read through it.

"Well now," he said. "It seems some are greased with tallow, some with lard, and some with beeswax. I do hope that satisfies your idle curiosity. Now back to your posts."

The men did not return to their posts. Instead they each went among their respective fellows and told them, indignantly, that the British were forcing them to consume animal products, either lard or tallow. Hearing of this, all and sundry agreed that there could be only one reason for the British to do such a thing.

"Eating this grease will corrupt our souls from the inside out!"

"Yes! Whether we are Hindu, Mahomedan, or Sikh, we will become infidels, damned to perdition for all eternity!"

"With our souls damned, they give us but one choice for salvation—we must convert!"

"They want to convert all of India to Christianity! But Christianity is a false religion!"

* * *

The next day, the *sepoys* of the 19th Native Infantrymen staunchly refused to take rifle practice—a thing unheard of. Nine out of ten fighting men in many brigades of the British East India Company were native *sepoys*. These soldiers protected the interests of the EIC and the lives of their employees. The British hierarchy adjudged it no small matter to have the *sepoys* in revolt against their masters for the first time in decades.

Word of the incident passed from one end of the garrison to another, and rapidly spread from one end of the subcontinent to another via the newly constructed medium of telegraph wires and newspapers. Across India, officers were aghast—and worried.

Seeing that their oversight had led to such outrage, commanders of the EIC were quick to recall the new Enfield rifles. Over the next weeks, they ordered the guns rebored for larger rounds and the offending cartridges were discarded. Word would be sent to the manufacturers in Delhi, Bombay, and Mysore to henceforth employ only the more expensive beeswax.

Nonetheless, no explanations, apologies, or changes in manufacturing protocols would change the situation that had arisen. The offending cartridge grease was not the only reason for the *sepoys* and the general population to resent the East India Company.

Half of India had no contact with the EIC and their policies. Few in the south cared what happened in the north. Even within territories under EIC control, many Indians were quite happy with how things were run—the British had provided hundreds of thousands of soldiers with gainful employment and they had made many reforms—outlawing thieving bands of *dacoits* and the murderous cult of the Thuggee. They had maintained peace between the Mahomedans, Hindus, and Sikhs by encouraging tolerance.

Nonetheless, many natives had come to distrust the EIC for other policies. *Sepoys* were at times asked to take up arms against their own people. Pensions were small and native soldiers were not allowed to rise above the rank of sergeant and they received pitiful pensions no matter how many years they served the East India Company. They were forced to cross the sea to fight, thus corrupting their souls, according to the Hindu belief.

Other grievances included the seizing of land from native rulers like Lakshmi Bai, British land reforms that stripped nobles of their patrimony of generations, and the disgraceful treatment of its native soldiers and others. That condescending British attitude did not help either.

* * *

Dhakar Rao heard the clatter of rapid hooves from beyond the compound walls. He looked out a window of the workroom to see a small body of cavalry ride into his compound. At the head of this troop rode the youthful Rani Lakshmi Bai. She wore the clothing of a *sowar*—cavalryman—though her hair flowed loose and windblown. Most of the riders were women and similarly attired. Behind her sat her adopted son, age five, holding onto his mother's waist. Most dangerous of all, the rani held the orange flag of Jhansi, festooned with an image of the god Hanuman holding a mountain in his hand.

Standing beside Dhakar, Lal said, "By Vishnu, I have never seen women as *sowars*."

"Nor have I," he said, grinning and handing the blueprints to his assistant before stepping out. "But by Vishnu or not, I find I like it."

The rani handed the reins to her cavalry commander, a woman named Jhalkari Bai, who might have been the queen's twin. Lakshmi leapt from her horse and strode up to the steps. There, Dhakar hurried to greet her.

Lakshmi Bai smiled brightly. "Rajah, it is good to see you. Where is Asha? I must see the new baby."

That and training with her troops another would be the public reasons for her visit. Whilst they were all at tea, Lakshmi took Asha's hand in hers and revealed another reason for their long ride to Banda.

"Asha," Lakshmi asked, "I know you can ride a horse. You said your father wanted you to learn. Would you like you to join my cavalry? Once you are able to ride again, of course."

Asha's expression showed surprise. Dhakar had no expression.

"Dear Lakshmi," said Asha, "I am flattered that you think of me. Father let me ride, yes, but it has been years." She looked at Dhakar.

Silently called on to respond, Dhakar said, "I admit it would be good exercise. But maybe it is too soon after giving birth."

Turning back to Lakshmi, Asha said, "I must defer my answer until after Savita is weened."

"Of course," Lakshmi said as she rocked the baby. "I understand that it is too soon for you. Well, I came to Banda to see Asha and the baby, not to recruit another *sowar*."

But that evening, Lakshmi Bai revealed yet another reason for her ride to Banda. Privately, she spoke with Dhakar in his study.

"I am glad to be back in Bundelkhand once more," she said. This land will always be my home."

"We are glad to have you in our home once more, Rani. And it is nice to see our sons playing together."

"I only hope the children of the future will be so happy as these."

Dhakar smiled before saying, "May it be so."

“I have ridden to the Punjab, where I spoke with Chambu Singh and others, to judge their loyalty. I intend to secure the future for my son, and for all the children of Bundelkhand, by returning to the throne of Jhansi.”

Dhakar's smile dropped. “Lakshmi... that is impossible. Yes, they committed a great atrocity by stripping you of your title, and I was among those who wrote letters of protest. But the East India Company will not approve of you just walking back into the palace of Jhansi.”

“I will not walk in, Rajah. I will charge.”

Dhakar took a deep breath before responding. “Rani, I cannot help but wonder if you have taken all factors into consideration.”

“I have. After they deposed me, I petitioned Governor Canning and his ministers—most would not even speak with me, a mere woman. I tried to negotiate and they laughed at me. My envoy in London was not allowed to enter Parliament. Now I will take action. For the last year I have raised an army in secret. Taking Jhansi will not prove difficult, Rajah. The Company has seen fit to post no more than three score troops in the city, trusting that there will be no trouble there. But nine out of ten of those troops are native to India. I know my people are loyal. They have come to me, swearing their allegiance. They desire to wrest Bundelkhand from the hands of these invaders.”

“Rani, I admire your courage and intelligence. But the British will only send in more troops. Many more.”

“Of course. I expect this. But what if others arise?” she asked, standing by the large globe in the center of his study. “What if all India throws off the yoke of British oppression?”

Dhakar laughed until he saw the flash in her dark eyes.

“Forgive me, Rani,” he said, attempting to suppress a smirk. “As I recently said to Asha, India is not a nation, but an assemblage of nations. No one can ever get everyone in India to agree to anything.”

The rani's hand drifted over the globe. “Dhakar, we have learned from our mistakes of the past. I assure you that I also expect assistance from others. Others who wish to stem the tide of growing British power and repay them for their atrocities.” He noticed her hand encircle India on the globe.

“Rani, are you serious? Because if you are, I do not want Asha to join your little play cavalry. Yes, there have been mutinies here and there. It's not the first time. Consider the mutinies at Vellore and Barrackpur—nothing came of them. This is serious business. Talk like that could get people killed.”

“Play cavalry,” Lakshmi Bai repeated with no apparent emotion. “I assure you that my troops, be they women or men, are not playing. But I will not press you at this time. I see in your heart that you sympathize with my plight yet you will not join us."

"Us? You speak of your troops in Jhansi?"

"Not them alone. Our allies and resources are more than you realize. Forgive me, that is all I can say."

Dhakar did not ask any more. Only the next day, after the rani and her cavalry rode off, did he speak to his wife, telling her of the conversation.

"Asha," he said, "I do not want you to join Lakshmi's women's cavalry."

Asha bowed her head.

"I hope you are not angry with me," he added, "but the rani is playing a dangerous game. She could be arrested if the EIC finds out she wants to reclaim her throne. I hope you understand."

"Yes, Dhakar, I do," Asha said, looking at him. "I have qualms of my own about Lakshmi's schemes. I support her in my heart, but I also fear the wrath she will incur."

4. Revolt!

On the evening of March 29, 1857, a month after the meeting between Dhakar and Lakshmi, an incident occurred at the Bengal Native Infantry in Barrackpur near Calcutta in the east. There, a *sepoy* named Mangal Pandee, enraged upon learning the rumor of the lard-ridden cartridges, attempted to rally the other *sepoys* against the British officers. When they hesitated, he took it upon himself to attack a lieutenant with both sword and pistol. Other officers called their troops to restrain the mutineer, but they hesitated, possibly because they sympathized and possibly because their weapons had been stored in the armory for the night and Pandee still held a loaded pistol. Another officer intervened and a wrestling match ensued. Eventually, a few of the men restrained Pandee and threw him in the brig.

Of greater concern of the East India Company's officers was that so many of Pandee's fellow *sepoys* had refused to follow orders. As a result, they ordered that the entire unit be dismissed with dishonor for their antipathy. With that order, men who had served the EIC for five, ten, even twenty years, were now stripped of what little pension they might have hoped for.

After a few other little mutinies arose across the subcontinent, the commanders of the EIC decided to not only hang Pandee and dismiss his company, but to announce the punishment to every battalion across the land.

The British officers decided that logically this would get results.

* * *

"The *sepoy* known as Mangal Pandee," announced a colonel of the native soldiers stationed in Meerut north of Delhi, a week after Pandee had attacked the British officers, "for having mutinied against the East India Company, for attempting to arouse his fellow *sepoys* of Barrackpur to mutiny, and for attempting murder against a Christian subject of our Gracious Queen, has been tried for these crimes and has been most justifiably hung by the neck until dead."

The colonel stopped to take a sip of water before reading the rest of the orders. *By the Savior, even for India it's hot in May*, he reflected. During the pause, a few of his captains and lieutenants became aware of some grumbling among the native troops. At once, the officers rapped several turbans with their riding crops and harshly ordered the soldiers to remain silent, in an effort to draw the men's attention to their superior officer. After all, these men needed to know what fate might befall them should any of them get it in their heads to follow suit.

The colonel continued. "Upon review of the inaction of the *sepoys* of the Thirty-Fourth regiment of Bengal Native Infantry, for refusing to stop the mutinous Pandee, the unit has been disbanded..." Here he paused for dramatic effect. "*...with dishonour*. Let there be no doubt—the same will happen to you lot. God save the queen."

The pause did have a dramatic effect. After the proclamation had been read, the native soldiers gathered in groups, discussing the ramifications of this action by their British overlords.

"So they will disband us also?" asked the Hindu, Banerjee, incredulously. "They will send us home with nothing? We already protested and refused to eat their bullets. Will they hold that against us and force us to disband before we retire?"

"No pay and not even our pensions?" asked Fawud, the Mahomedan, equally aghast. "I have served the British for twelve years, and now I will lose my pension if even one man steps out of line?? I have seven children to feed."

"Don't we all?" countered Inderjit, the fatalistic Sikh. "Or more? But the British listened to our protest and they have already stopped making the cartridges. Maybe they will—"

Fawud interrupted Inderjit. "You Sikhs will always lick their boots! You're good for nothing but inventing false religions!"

"You will not stand with us?!" Banerjee asked, scandalized. "May all the demons of Naraka feed upon your bones!"

Inderjit stared incredulously at the men he'd considered his friends. They continued to revile him until he simply walked away, shaking his head.

But Fawud and Banerjee and thousands more continued to discuss their grievances long into the night. Anger had simmered for years in the many provinces under the flag of the EIC. Now that anger threatened to boil over.

*   *   *

On the following Sunday evening, the tenth day of May 1857, the English officers and regulars of Meerut relaxed, as they always did on the Sabbath. Unusually, the numbers of British to native *sepoys* were nearly equal, but this did not dissuade the natives from their plan. As the sun set and the air cooled, the officers prepared to attend evening services in the local church and the common British soldiers drifted to the pubs. None had their weapons on them.

Knowing this, the native soldiers, to a man, rose up in mutiny and attacked them. Not only *sepoys*, but common people soon joined the fighting, killing unarmed British officers and infantrymen when they were found alone. If native servants of the officers attempted to hide or otherwise protect the British, they too were killed. If the rebels, both *sepoys* and townsfolk, could not engage the British in battle, they employed arson to burn down their houses and barracks.

Even the native chief of police supported the rebellion, refusing to arrest rioters and looters and even unlocking the cell doors so long as his prisoners promised to fight against the EIC. They heartily agreed and with that act five hundred beggars, thieves, and *dacoits* were unleashed upon the hated English.

The juggernaut of rebellion rolled on from that point. Only hours after the revolt in Meerut, rebellious *sepoys* made their way down river to Delhi, the traditional capital of the old Mughal Empire. Hearing word of the events in Meerut, the *sepoys* of the city revolted by dawn—and in Delhi, the native soldiers far outnumbered the British.

By afternoon, the rebels had set nearly every British structure in Delhi to the torch. The garrison had been burned to the ground, and only a few dozen surviving British troops and their families managed to escape to the outskirts of the city. Within the walls, only one military installation still stood, the most prized of all—the East India Company arsenal.

A handful of ordinance officers inside knew they could not hold off a siege for long—but they would not allow the weapons and powder to fall into the hands of the mutineers. Instead, they set a fuse and ran for their lives.

Not even the nine fleeing officers would have predicted how great the explosion would be, as three of them were killed instantly. A few hundred civilians in their surrounding houses were likewise blown to bits in that instant. Many more were left dying. Once the echo of the explosion faded, those not deafened for life heard the screams of half a woman. Nearby, her crying child reached for her but without hands.

Yet the blowing of the powder house availed the EIC troops little. Many weapons and even powder managed to survive and the rebels salvaged it from the ruins and from dead bodies. Any *sepoy* who thought of remaining loyal to the Crown now joined the rebellion. The ever-growing number of mutineers and rioters continued to search for any remaining British through the night, lit by a score of fires. Within days, the rebels indisputably controlled Delhi.

To legitimize the rebellion and to unite the divergent forces, the Muslims among the leaders of the revolt decided to restore the Mughal emperor. Bahadur Shah Zafar had been forced to abdicate the throne thirty years earlier. The Muslim contingent among the rebels unfurled their dusty green flags which bore the charge of a golden lion. They marched to his palace in Delhi and stood outside in their thousands, calling his name.

"Zafar! Zafar! Come with us and reclaim your titles! The Mughal Empire will rise again!"

"Go away!" extorted an old man in green robes and turban from his window. "This is not the house you want."

The rebels saw they would have a hard time convincing him. So, when they discovered forty Englishmen hiding in a basement, they took them to Zafar's mansion by night and murdered them all, practically under his window. With the sunrise, everyone in Delhi assumed that Zafar's men must have killed the English. Zafar then knew his only hope of forestalling a British rope around his neck would be a successful revolt. He had no choice but to restore himself to the throne.

When news came to them of this bizarre stunt to get Zafar on the throne once more, Dhakar found himself somewhat amused. Asha did not share his sentiment.

"Dhakar, we Sikhs resent the Mughals for a century of oppression, war, and forced conversions to Islam," she explained. "My people will never support a return of the Mughal Empire. Any Sikh who may have thought of joining this revolution will now join the British."

* * *

Every British man, woman, and child of Delhi had been killed. Word of the victory spread across India like wildfire and every tongue spoke of revolution. When news came to Jhansi in Bundelkhand, the Rani Lakshmi Bai wasted no time.

The rani presented herself once more at the office of Captain Alexander Skene, the political officer of the EIC forces in Jhansi and commander of the 12th Bengal Native Infantry.

"Sir," she said, "I am very afraid for what this rebellion means. It may spread here and then we are all in danger."

"Madame," said Captain Skene, "I will do everything in my power to protect you and your household, the same as everyone else in Jhansi. Now, if you'll ex—"

"But what if this is not enough?" the rani implored. "I must be allowed to raise an army to protect my house, my lands, and my people. They say the rebels have gone wild and they kill every man, woman, and child."

"Y-Your own army? Preposterous. We can't have you, a private citizen—and a woman, to boot—giving guns to a great lot of men over whom the Company has no control."

"Yes? And if I raise an army of women? Do you worry that I am unable to control *them?*"

When the captain finished laughing, he said, "Well, if you want to raise a little army of women, dear lady, I think we can let you have them. Might be fun to see what you come up with."

The Rani Lakshmi Bai pressed her hands together and bowed to him. Then she departed.

Within the hour, Lakshmi Bai, along with her loyal commander, Khuda Ali, and the rani's women officers, Jhalkari Bai and Uda Devi, went through the streets, speaking to every young woman and many middle-aged ones too.

"Women of Jhansi," said the rani, once they had gathered in her compound, "I speak to you not as your queen, but as your sister. I speak as a mother. I will raise the only army which the British allow—an army of women!"

The rani's words left many eyes, many mouths, wide open. She did not wait for their minds to fill any void with doubts and fears.

"Young unmarried women of Jhansi," she continued, "our land is in the hands of invaders—they take every rupee they can get and they impose their wills over us—like a rapist! Yes, and many times their soldiers have had their way with the women of India—many of you know all too well of what I speak! The time has come that we can stop them. You are full of life and energy. Your wills are not yet broken.

Our brothers and fathers in the armies of Delhi and Meerut have risen up and slain their overlords—are we women to do less?

"Join me, sisters," she continued. "Join me and when the moment is right, we will stand beside our brothers in Jhansi when they too rise up against the British!"

They cheered upon hearing this speech from the deposed queen. Eager to join the cause, many a young woman of Jhansi joined her army. Even some older women joined, never before having the opportunity to prove themselves the equal of any man.

A few men stepped in, refusing to allow their daughters and wives to go, but many of these relented after fiery arguments or heapings of insults from those women and others. A few of the larger matrons not only enlisted, but dragged their husbands along as their porters.

Before the end of the week, two thousand women had assembled in the courtyards of a dozen of the rani's most loyal supporters. Under the watchful eyes of Khuda and other warriors who had once served under the late Maharajah, a thousand and a half women trained with sword and lance. Another four hundred trained under Jhalkari Bai as *sowars*—cavalrymen. Or cavalrywomen, in this case. The last one hundred trained with Uda Devi—as snipers.

Under cover of darkness, Lakshmi Bai went to the men of the garrison, common soldiers who'd once served under her husband. Some had retired, many had been dismissed by British officers, and others became *sepoys* in the armies of the EIC. In a corner of the star fort of Jhansi she spoke to them.

"You men have given everything for the British company and what have you received? The wages of a common farmer and the hatred of your neighbors! If you stay in the army until your beard is long and gray, you will receive only a paltry pension and never will they allow you to become an officer.

"These British take ever more of our land, reaping the profits and heaping nothing but contempt upon us. They rewrite our laws and abolish customs that have stood for thousands of years and they call this reform. They topple those who have ruled the land wisely for many centuries and they call this reformation of our land rights... but you get nothing for these reformations. Nothing! No one profits from these reforms except the British!"

"Oh sure," said a burly Bengali, clearly unimpressed. "You want your throne back, Rani. But you ask **us** to die for it!"

A few voices began to murmur. These Bengals were not native to Bundelkhand, but had been brought in from the east, as the British ever did—thus their loyalties lay elsewhere. The rani knew she must appeal to their shared interests.

"Native troops all over India are in revolt, open or hidden," she said. "Will they rise up against their oppressors and you will do nothing? If you, the native Company men of Jhansi, switch sides and join us, I promise that you will be joined by many thousands more, no more happy with the British than I. The garrison here has only fifty officers and maybe two hundred British enlisted men; the rest are natives like yourself."

All these things she said threw kindling on the fires already lit in their hearts. Many of the men nodded, yet a few still grumbled. Those grumbles must be stifled at once. The rani continued, falling back to the religious argument, so close to the hearts of so many.

"Fah! They make you cross the sea any time they wish—a forbidden thing in the Hindu religion. They force you men to consume beef and pork on their bullets that you might become infidels like them! Did you relish the taste so much that you are willing to burn in the flames of Naraka?! If you object like Mangal Pandee, they hang you. And even if you do nothing like his regiment, then you are cashiered without pay and without even the pittance of a pension you have earned!"

She paused, looking at first one man, then another. She saw their anger rising, their eyes inflamed. She had no intention of letting that flame die out.

"Men," she said, waving a pistol, "the next time the British tell you to march and kill the people of India, remember who truly deserves to die!"

Roused by these fiery words from the beautiful queen, the *sepoys* rose up to a man. Immediately, they began to rupture drums or steal bugles that might be used to signal other troops in a hurry, they slipped wooden wedges under the garrison doors so that the Englishmen could not escape, and they overpowered a guard and stole many of the muskets from the armory.

Throughout the night, revolt silently grew in the streets of Jhansi.

5. Revenge of the Rani

In the predawn hours of May 24, 1857, Captain Alexander Skene of the 12th Bengal Native Infantry awoke to the sound of a tumult outside his window. In only his nightshirt, he quickly slid out of bed and looked out his window. In the scant light, he saw scattered plumes coming from a few large fires in the streets of Jhansi. Thirty feet below, natives ran all about—*and at this hour!* Blinking the sleep out of his eyes, he saw that many of these were *sepoys*, still wearing their uniforms, now disheveled. Others wore civilian clothing, often only a loincloth. All were armed with muskets, swords, spears, or axes. Not a few carried torches.

Even as he donned his trousers and boots, the captain ran out to the top of the wall, where he found his men. From below he heard the murmur of a thousand angry voices.

"Secure the gates!" he ordered. "I've some inkling of what's going on, and I won't have outsiders stirring up trouble in my city."

As only English and Scottish troops were given charge of the gates, the majority of them hurried to confirm them shut and the bolts thrown. A sergeant saluted the captain and made a report.

"Sir, it's not outsiders going about," he said. "It's our own *sepoys!* They've went and mutinied, sir!"

"Damnation," said Skene. "Where's that boy with my jacket?"

"I can't say, sir," he said, then turned to the nearest recruit. "Private, get the captain's jacket and step lively! Captain, them wogs has set fire to the garrison. We think they're burning alive at least a score of our men."

"The Deuce!" Skene then looked over a nearby parapet to get a better view of the goings-on in Jhansi as dawn broke.

Below, some hundreds of *sepoys* with swords, muskets, and torches in hand, sought out their former commanders. When they found British officers or any other Englishmen—and many English businessmen had set up shop in the profitable subcontinent—the rebels killed them.

Captain Skene, throwing on his red jacket, bellowed for his missing boy to get his hat. He then left the sergeant and made his way to his Bengali troops along the walls.

"Man the cannons, you dolts," he said, firmly. "Be prepared to fire upon this riffraff."

The captain's orders were not obeyed. Rather than fire upon their fellow Indians, the fiery-eyed native troops rushed upon Captain Skene in a body and took hold of him by the arms.

"Now see here," he said, scandalized. "You'll unhand me at once!"

Unhand him they did not. Skene struggled, he kicked, yet still they pressed him against the parapet. They lifted him, squirming like a fish, by arm and by leg.

"Confound it all!" he bellowed. "This is most irregular!"

The Indian natives hurled him from the walls. He continued to rebuke them, remarking something about "damned impudence", until his stiff upper lip smashed on the cobblestones below.

* * *

To their credit, the British forces held out for another eleven hours, but their efforts proved futile. Lakshmi's saboteurs had made sure their kegs of gunpowder had been replaced with sand. Far outnumbered by the rebellious native infantrymen, and forced to fight with saber and lances after their powder ran out, the last remaining EIC officers eventually waved a white flag and asked to parley. The rebels granted this request.

A dozen surviving British officers filed out. From within the officers' quarters, wary rank and file English soldiers watched carefully.

"To whomever amongst you is accredited as leader," said one of the surviving lieutenants, barely able to withhold a sneer, being forced to bargain with people he considered savages, "we offer to cease fire. We ask for the opportunity to abandon this... city... with our families and our belongings."

The Rani Lakshmi Bai languidly rode forward on her black horse, Baadal, to face the sneering officer. Before she answered him, she translated the officer's words verbatim, for the benefit of her own officers and her people.

When her people grumbled and snarled, the rani raised her hand for them to remain silent. About to speak, she stopped as she spotted Commandant Khuda, running up to her.

"Rani!" Khuda cried out, in rage. "Before they surrendered, these infidels spiked every cannon they could get their hands on!"

The rani knew spiking to be a simple process; one merely takes a common iron nail and hammers it into the touchhole of a cannon. Upon breaking off the head of the nail, the cannon is then rendered unusable by one's enemies. Having learned of this action by the British, Lakshmi Bai's made the logical decision.

"No," she said to the EIC officers. "As you have left us without weapons to defend ourselves, we do not consent for any British to leave with either your weapons or your belongings. Yes, and I think you soldiers should not be allowed to leave with your lives either."

The lieutenant froze for a second but it took no more than a second. No translation need be given of her next command.

"Fire!" cried Lakshmi Bai, pointing with her sword. No one questioned the orders—they fired. Every British officer in Jhansi dropped as a hail of lead balls ripped through his body.

Lakshmi Bai only sat on her horse as the maddened, screaming *sepoys* and others charged into the officers' quarters. The English enlisted men inside returned gunfire only sporadically—The main fighting lasted but a few minutes.

Still, a few holdouts remained. A handful of enlisted men had retreated to a nearby granary and continued to fight with swords, after native *sepoys* set fire to the barracks. Lakshmi then spotted a wounded EIC lieutenant, attempting to crawl away. She walked her horse over to him, tightening her grip on her sword. She recalled meeting him and his wife, once or twice, for tea.

* * *

Triumphantly, Lakshmi Bai returned to the palace not an hour later, intending to once more raise the flag of Hanuman over the roof. However, upon riding into the courtyard, she found it filled with British subjects. These were not EIC soldiers. Every single Englishman in Jhansi, be he soldier or civilian, had been hunted down and killed.

Even if her people had not informed her, the rani would have recognized them as the English women of Jhansi, women she knew. She'd taken tea with many of these women, as she implored them to persuade their husbands to listen to her case.

Now, fearing for their lives and the lives of their children, the women had gathered in the courtyard of the palace. But now the palace had been restored to the Rani Lakshmi Bai and no longer in the hands of a British commander. Now the jubilant rebels paraded Skene's mutilated corpse through the streets beyond the compound's gates.

At once, all of the women begged for refuge, for mercy. Looking down at them from the strong back of Baadal, the rani raised her hand for them to fall silent and they did so.

"Who amongst you would speak for the rest?" asked Lakshmi, in decent English. One Englishwoman stepped forward, only to fall to her knees before the rani—an act of supplication she'd never before performed.

"Most gracious Rani," said Mrs. Barrington, clutching her young children to her bosom, "we ask for mercy. Please grant us refuge. Please don't throw us to those mad rebels. They're running wild and murdering everyone! You are a mother, the same as I—the same as most of the women here. For God's sake, have mercy!"

The Rani Lakshmi Bai, still clutching a sword from which dripped the blood of Lieutenant Barrington, said, "Much like the Emperor Zafar, I wanted nothing to do with this revolt when it began. I asked only to be given Jhansi and be left in peace, but this you British have refused to allow. I will consider your plea, and I want to protect you all—I do. But I will remind you of the answers that I received when I pleaded my own case. Know that you may have to do as your Bible tells you and reap what you have sewn. Now I must cut down that hated flag of yours and restore the flag that rightfully belongs over Jhansi."

Ten minutes later, an orange triangle of cloth, bearing the image of the ape-god Hanuman holding aloft a sacred mountain, unfurled once more over Jhansi. From the roof, Lakshmi Bai looked down at her city. She saw the thousands amassed below, looking up at her, proud and free once more. She saw their determination and zeal. She saw they would make a great army, men and women both. Lakshmi Bai raised her sword overhead.

"Jhansi is mine again!" she cried. "I now implore the Hindus, in the names of the goddesses Ganga, Tulasi, and Salikram—and I implore the Mahomedans by the name of Allah and the *Koran*—and I entreat all of you to join together in destroying the English for their warfare against us!"

The people of Jhansi roared in support of their queen. Huddled among them, the Englishwomen trembled.

* * *

For most of a week Dhakar Rao and his family, along with his group of engineers and several workers had traveled west along the *ashoka*-lined road to Sagar, and a most curious sight their caravan made. The people of Bundelkhand stopped to watch the ten oxen and the massive cart pass by, marveling at the curious shape beneath the tarpaulins. Dhakar had ordered his men to haul the *Iron Buffalo* from Banda to Sagar and the shore of Lakha Banjara Lake. Yes, they'd heard rumor of trouble in Meerut and Delhi, but that was far away in the north. Still, for safety, he'd brought ten mounted riflemen, along with Lal and the engineers.

At the lake's shore, they backed the huge cart into the water. Quite a feat, considering the strength and stubbornness of the oxen being asked to walk backwards.

Asha watched while holding Savita and chiding Bani to not get too close. At six, Bani had inherited his father's adventurousness. An hour later than planned, the bulky steel contraption had been rolled into the water. Asha had expected it to sink out of sight at once, despite Dhakar's explanations about buoyancy and air bladders. It did sink somewhat, but slowly and the top section remained above water.

She watched as Dhakar opened the hatch on the top. Chundawat, the pilot, entered. Dhakar seemed about to follow him, then stopped. He jumped back on the dock and hurried over to Asha and the children. Grinning, he took her face in his hands and pressed his lips hard against hers. Then he snatched up Bani.

"Dhakar!" Asha cried out. "No! Not my child!"

"He's mine too," he said with a laugh as he ran with the boy. "I promise I won't drown him!"

For his own part, Bani laughed and waved at his mother, most likely enjoying her distress. Then he found himself placed within the strange metal contraption. His father followed him, then closed the lid, silencing Asha's cries and threats. A moment later, those watching heard a strange hum and they watched anxiously.

The *Iron Buffalo* moved off, farther into the placid waters of the lake. Then, the craft slowly slipped under the water, leaving only bubbles on the surface—and a livid woman on the wharf. Lal, the young engineer, found himself awkwardly steadying the Rani Asha as her knees gave way.

6. Nana to the Rescue

A handful of survivors from Delhi had made their way to Meerut and informed the commanders of the rebellion that had arisen. Due to the telegraph system running across the subcontinent, within a day every British Resident and magistrate across India learned that Delhi, the largest and wealthiest city in northern India, had fallen to mutineers. The British of nearby Meerut and other cities were aghast to hear of the mutiny, but they had their own troubles to deal with before they could mount expeditions to relieve Delhi.

No one in the EIC need be informed that the native infantry and cavalry in India far outnumbered the British, sometimes by as much as ten to one. Should they all mutiny, the British in India would be instantly, vastly outnumbered.

They therefore took measures to prevent the same thing happening in their own areas of influence. In Kanpur, some three hundred miles down the Ganges River from Delhi, on the blisteringly hot sixth day of June, the Magistrate and Collector Charles Hillersdon held a meeting of his officers to apprise them of the situation. The day before, several *sepoys* of the Kanpur Garrison had imitated their brothers in Delhi and began rioting.

"Cawnpore is home to not only a large garrison and well-stocked magazine, but a plethora of British businesses," Hillersdon noted, stating the obvious. "We'll be next on these mutineers' agenda. How bad is the situation, Wheeler?"

"The wogs have more anger than weapons," reported General Hugh Wheeler, the garrison's elderly commander. A short Irishman, he'd served over half a century, fighting Afghans and Sikhs, while speaking Hindi with the *sepoys* under him and earning their respect—or so he had hoped. On the other hand, his own men had plenty of reservations about the man. Wheeler had cuckolded a lieutenant serving under him and then, like King David, sent the man into an unwinnable battle to be killed. Wheeler had seven children with the man's half-caste wife, five whilst she was still married to the lieutenant.

"Thus far, two regiments, one of infantry and one of cavalry, have mutinied and abandoned the city," Wheeler added. "Rioting by locals has been confined to a few small neighborhoods. I've wired Calcutta about the situation; told them not to fret. Still, can't hurt to entrench the barracks for siege."

"Have the guard doubled and curfew set for sundown," stated Mr. Hillersdon, speaking to his staff and the officers of the garrison in his stifling hot office. "Then I want to bring in every Hindoo leader, chieftain, and soothsayer into this office and inform them of precisely the repercussions they might expect should they fail to keep their people in line."

"Here, here," said one of the collector's sycophants. The others murmured their agreement.

With a bit of trepidation, General Wheeler brought another matter to the collector's attention. "Sir," he said, looking sharp in his red coat and white trousers, "without the two hundred men we've sent to Delhi to retake the city, I fear we're more than a tad shorthanded. Even if we put every man on the walls, we can't hope to come near doubling the number of those already posted there."

"Damnation," said Hillersdon, frowning and looking down at the papers on his usually immaculate desk, as if he might will more soldiers into existence.

At that moment, an aide stepped into the office, bowed briefly and said, "Sir, the Nana of Bithur has sent a message. It's in English, sir."

The man handed a folded letter to the collector. Hillersdon opened it and read the contents.

"Ah," he said, relief showing upon his face, even as he patted it with a handkerchief. "At least we needn't concern ourselves about the good Nana. He's offering fifteen hundred Marathi infantrymen to defend the city's battery. Jolly good fellow. That should free up quite a few men for you, eh, General?"

The relieved general heartily agreed. One of the young clerks, however, silently recalled a different letter received only the day before, from the Chief Commissioner of Lukhnow, expressing his dark opinion of the Nana. The clerk, not confident of the reaction he might receive upon bringing up such a matter, decided to wait for a better time.

An hour later, the Nana of the Marathi people marched his army through the gates of Kanpur's battery under their orange banners. His men's uniforms were of common homespun and only the matching colors of their turbans distinguished them as an army. Nana Saheb appeared as a stout, serious-looking man, festooned in blue robes trimmed in gold with an ornate orange turban bearing gems and a tall ostrich feather. Befitting a commander in a time of fighting, he had a silver-handled scimitar and a brace of pistols tucked into his orange sash.

Inside the parade grounds, the Nana saluted the British colonel. The colonel returned the salute.

"My men are here to secure the battery," said the Nana.

"Thank you, Nana," the colonel replied. "We appreciate your help. Thanks to you, we'll be able to send my men to other duties now."

Nana Saheb bowed his head slightly.

Shortly, Nana Saheb and his men arrived at the fortified battery, surrounded by dozens of crates of muskets and several hundred barrels of black powder and lead balls. The colonel in charge noted that only one in ten Marathi soldier had a musket to defend the magazine and the powder house; the rest had only spears, *katars*, or *chakrams*. Still, getting any help he could gave the colonel relief.

The colonel nodded to a captain who then turned to his men and began bellowing orders. The Redcoats immediately fell into formation and marched out through the gates.

Intending to follow, the colonel turned to thank Nana Saheb again. However, he found himself distracted by the sight of the Marathi warriors opening the coffin-like crates and taking out the muskets.

"Nana," he said, "your men are not to touch our weapons. Control these fellows, will you."

Nana Saheb, descended from the last Marathi emperor, a dynasty that had overthrown the Mughals, only to be overthrown themselves by the British, raised his pistol and pointed it at the colonel's face. The colonel found himself more shocked than frightened—and he felt plenty frightened.

"I have secured the battery of Kanpur in the name of the Marathi people," said the Nana Saheb. "And in the name of the Emperor Zafar of whom I am a vassal."

The ramifications of the leaders of the Marathi and Mughal empires—rival Hindus and Mahomedans—working in union was not lost on the colonel. It meant that potentially millions of former enemies were now united against the paltry thousands of Englishmen. Realizing this, the colonel immediately emptied his bladder.

Thanks to Nana Saheb's ploy, his men secured a great store of guns, ammunition, and powder. Each of them would now be armed as well as the British soldiers—and there were far more of them. Weapons were not all that Nana Saheb took from the EIC—before the day ended, he also captured the Company's treasury. With that gold, he would afterwards be able to secure the services of many bands of fighting men who might be tempted to fight only for their own little town and then go back home. Under Nana Saheb's vision, these divergent mutinies could be forged into a rebellion that would push the British into the sea.

The streets of Kanpur ran red with British blood that day. By sunset, the Nana Saheb had control of most of the city. As for the overly-trusting Collector Hillersdon, the rebels made him watch as they gang-raped his wife and murdered his children, before they slit open his belly, ripped out his guts, and strangled him with them.

7. The Rani Rides

Having lit a fire in the hearts of the rebellious *sepoys* of Jhansi, the Rani Lakshmi Bai found she could not so easily quench that flame. She had given orders that the British women and children were to be unharmed, but the *sepoys* had not yet appointed leaders or even agreed that the deposed rani might be their new leader.

That night, the rani awoke to hear a tumult of angry voices and terrified screams in the palace courtyard. She ran to the window and threw open the netting.

Below, lit by some dozens of torches, she saw a hundred or more *sepoys* in the courtyard, taking hold of the Englishwomen, pulling some by their hair. Among the women who had been stripped naked, she saw Mrs. Barrington. Before the rani's eyes, two men held the Englishwoman. Another drove his wick into her. She screamed.

"Stop!" the rani commanded from above. "Let those women go! As queen of Jhansi, I command you!"

The maddened *sepoys* ignored her orders. Most of them could not even hear her for the bellowing and laughter of their enraged compatriots and the screaming of their victims. One man did stop what he was doing, but another pushed him aside and took his place.

The rani snatched up a silk *duppata* and threw it around her. "Jhalkari!" she said. "Get word to Commandant Khuda and have him bring round all the men he can spare! We must save these British women if we are to have them as hostages!"

Jhalkari Bai bowed and ran to carry out the orders. In the meantime, the rani grabbed up a sword and hurried down the stairs.

She did not make it to the courtyard before Uda Devi, in pantaloons and her own disheveled *dupatta*, intercepted her.

"Rani, these men are mad with revenge!" Uda said. "If you try to stop them they will kill you! Stay back, for Ganga's sake!"

"No!" the rani ordered. "I'll not have this blood on my hands!"

Lakshmi Bai pushed Uda out of the way and charged into the courtyard. She cried out for the men to stop, even as she smote several of the nearest ones with the flat of her sword. Already many of the women and children had been dragged outside the courtyard and into the street.

With so many men in the courtyard, the rani found her way through the crowd hindered. By the time she got through, the British survivors had all been dragged out.

Lakshmi attempted to follow them through the gates when suddenly a troop of her own men rushed into the courtyard.

"Stop those *sepoys*!" she commanded. "I will not have Jhansi become another Kanpur!"

The one hundred men poured into the courtyard, pushing her back before closing the gates behind them.

"What are you doing?" she demanded incredulously. "I am queen of Jhansi. Do as you are ordered! Where is Khuda? Who is in charge here?"

At last a captain appeared. He bowed solemnly before speaking.

"Gracious Rani," he said, "we have been ordered by Commandant Khuda to secure the compound and protect you from the rebels. If you would please return inside, you will be safe."

Livid, the rani shrieked. "Damn your orders! I am queen! Do as I command!"

It would take ten minutes of argument and threat before the captain finally relented and ordered the gates reopened. By then, the rani's hand maidens had dressed her more appropriately and her armorers had supplied her with a scale vest and helmet. Before they had the gate half open, she charged out.

She stopped cold. Behind her, the soldiers and the retainers all seemed to gasp in a single voice as they beheld the sight that lay in the street before the palace.

For the only time in her life, the rani's knees felt weak. She held onto her companions to steady herself.

"My people did *this*??"

* * *

The next morning, the Rani Lakshmi Bai reclaimed her sovereignty over Jhansi and her people rousingly accepted this news. Soon after, she received a message from the Nana Saheb telling her to remain in Jhansi and hold it against any efforts to retake the city. She almost laughed sardonically—*Did he think I would do anything else?*

"Of course I will hold Jhansi," she vowed to her attendants and to the gods. "But I intend to do more than just that."

* * *

Two days after Dhakar had the first trial run of his submersible craft, he and his family spotted the walls of Banda. After a long and dusty ride, the town came as a welcome sight.

Dhakar Rao and his family had ridden in the same carriage that had taken them to the river, but the *Iron Buffalo* had been left behind on the shore of Lake Lakha Banjara. The submersible now rested in a locked and enclosed shed attached to the dock, as Dhakar worried about thieves. Still, he happily held Asha and listened as Bani regaled his little sister with ever more details about his adventure under the water.

"Savita, there were trees on the bottom and there were weeds moving and they grew around an old boat with many, many fish swimming through it and lobsters and—"

"Crawfish, Bani," his father corrected, grinning.

"Yes daddy, they were crawling-fish. They crawled all over the boat."

"Crawl-fish!" Savita announced, giggling. "Crawl-fish! Ha-ha!" She squirmed and giggled more. Bani scowled at his little sister.

Savita's parents shared their daughter's laugh. It felt good to laugh again, despite the news they'd heard while stopped at a tiny village. Only this morning, before they left their inn, refugees from Kanpur had told them of the rebellion—to hear them, one might think half of India to be in flames. Some said that the garrison of Jhansi had mutinied. Away from the children, Dhakar and Asha had quietly whispered their worries for their friend, Lakshmi Bai.

Now, as the coach approached the city, Dhakar looked up to see hundreds of horses and their riders lolling about the gates. From a distance he worried that they were either British cavalry or revolutionaries, but coming closer he recognized the reddish-orange banner and its blazon of the god Hanuman—the flag of Jhansi.

The riders, both men and women, armed with swords, lances, and guns, stood and watched as he stepped out of the carriage and passed through them. The look of anticipation in their faces could not be denied. He noted his own men on the walls and behind the gate, unusually quiet. He could imagine their concern—after all, they were outnumbered. He shared those concerns, but he would let no one intimidate him out of his own city.

Dhakar walked up to the gate and almost at once encountered Lakshmi Bai, today wearing not only trousers, but a shirt of brazen scale mail and a small, tight turban on her head. Jhalkari stood with her and they both smiled brightly.

"Rani!" he said, clearly relieved to see her. "You have escaped Jhansi, thank the gods. You may have whatever sanctuary we can give you."

The rani and her companions were silent—for two seconds. Then the rani laughed loudly and her cavalry joined her. The response surprised both Dhakar and Asha.

"Rajah," said Lakshmi, smiling, "we have ridden for two days to bring you the news. It seems you have not heard already, but my city is free. The *sepoys* have mutinied in Jhansi. We are free. Free!"

All around them, the riders cheered, a deafening roar of joy. Dhakar found himself stunned to hear that Lakshi had joined the mutineers—but he did not intend saying so.

"Yes and greetings to you as well, Rani," Dhakar said, pretending to smirk at the enthusiasm that caused her to forget her manners.

"I ask your forgiveness, my friend, for I am overjoyed. Jhansi is free!"

"Dhakar, you should not tease the rani," Asha said, handing her daughter to a matron and then hugging her friend. "This is wonderful news that she brings."

"It is," Dhakar agreed with a smile. "Did the British flee the city? Or did you take them prisoner?"

The rani's smile dipped a bit. "They did not surrender."

Dhakar's own smile did not dip but completely vanished as her meaning sank in.

"May my riders and their horses take water?" the rani asked. "We have traveled far and fast and we hope to be in Sagar in three days."

"Of course. And I will have hay brought for your horses and rice for your men—I mean women—I mean... people."

Lakshmi laughed again. "Thank you, my flustered friend. My 'people' will be happy for anything they are given. May we go inside and talk while they fill their bellies?"

* * *

Inside, after a light meal, Lakshmi Bai and her cousin, Jhalkari Bai, retired to the library with Dhakar and Asha. On the other side of the room, Bani and Damodar helped little Savita build a fort of wooden blocks. But while the children happily played, Dhakar expressed his concerns.

"Lakshmi," he said, "I celebrate your victory, but I am also troubled. You are in an extremely dangerous situation."

"Dhakar, I know well the sort of dangers we face. But I would ask you if you know of the fire that burns in the hearts of the native troops of the East India Company? They are in revolt from one end of the subcontinent to the other. India will be victorious... but only if brave men like you join us."

"I..." he looked to Asha, saw her anticipation. He looked back to Lakshmi and Jhalkari. "I sympathize, of course, but.... You see, I've just had the first test of my invention and it went well, although there's still a problem with a sluggish valve on the port side and I really want to explore deeper waters before I start work on the... the... well, I have in mind a larger, actually much larger—"

"Dhakar!" Asha chided him. "You criticize Lakshmi and her brave riders for forming what you call a 'play army', yet you would play with toy boats!? The fate of all the peoples of India is at stake here!"

For the first time since the night he laid his hand on that of Lakshmi's, Dhakar felt shame. An emotion he did not commonly host.

"You are correct, my beloved," he said. "The revolution is, if anything, overdue. Yet I... I cannot help but be concerned. Rani, you may have won your city, but the British will only send in more troops to take back what you gained."

"You are right, Rajah," said Lakshmi. "Of course, the British will hope to reclaim Delhi and Jhansi both. I expect them to send more troops from their garrisons in the Punjab and we are prepared."

"Rani, I meant the British will bring more troops from England. They may even have the assistance of other nations, such as France."

The rani smiled indulgently once again, stepping around the globe. "Dhakar, I assure you that I also expect assistance from outside. All over Asia there are those who wish to stem the tide of growing British power and repay them for their atrocities." He noticed her hand drift over the globe and he saw that it briefly rested over a place east of India.

"Ours are not the only hearts that live to regain our freedom and dignity," she said. "Dhakar, you know that much good can come from the West, and I agree. But not at the cost of our freedom and our lives." She looked at the children in the adjacent chamber, happily playing. "And not at the cost of their freedom, either. You see this, do you not?"

Dhakar dropped to one knee and took her hand. He kissed it and looked up at her.

"I do, my Rani. I will aid you however I can."

Asha looked on with pride, even if she did not understand his adopted custom of kissing a woman's hand.

Although a decade younger than he, Lakshmi petted Dhakar's face like a mother. "Prepare for war, Dhakar. It is upon us."

8. Dhakar the Rebel

"Jhansi, Banda, and Sagar are the three largest cities in Bundelkhand," said Lakshmi Bai, the next morning, pulling on her gloves as she walked to where her *sowars* saddled the horses. "If all three are secure in our hands, the British might hesitate to take this portion of India."

"I am ready to proclaim independence from the East India Company," said Dhakar, walking alongside her. "But Sagar has a larger foreign garrison in her midst and their rajah has found it profitable to ally himself with the British."

"I know this, Dhakar, so we will bring together your people and mine and we will be joined by the army of Chambu Singh. That should convince the British to flee Sagar."

"Singh?" said Dhakar, surprised. "But the man's a Sikh. They're loyal to the British."

Lakshmi laughed. "Not all Sikhs side with the British, Dhakar. Your Asha is proof of this. Chambu knows that we will be victorious. Our goals align with his own."

Dhakar hesitated. It seemed that the goals of many had aligned these days. Still, those goals were different. Lakshmi wanted to rule Jhansi once more. Nana Saheb had wanted his EIC pension and titles returned to him and when he did not receive them he decided to revive the old Marathi Empire. Saheb's general, Tatya Tope, wanted nothing more than to kill Englishmen, the more the better. The Sultan Zafar himself only wanted to be left alone in his old age, but many around him wanted the Mughal Empire returned to power. But would the Mughals and the Marathis share India in peace? Maybe when tigers and wolves share a meal, Dhakar thought. And Chambu Singh...what goals had he?

Dhakar had no chance to ask the rani. Already she had mounted her sleek white horse, Sarangi.

"Farewell, Rajah!" she said. "I must scout Sagar and determine its strengths and weaknesses. We shall meet again, soon!"

And with that, she took off, her cavalry falling in behind her.

Dhakar waved. He even smiled. But he did not smile inside, for he knew what he must do next.

* * *

With the rani's encouragement, Dhakar Rao knew he must act. The EIC had only a small garrison in Banda and like every garrison of the EIC across India, its compliment comprised of mostly native soldiers, sometimes as many as nine out of ten.

However, the two hundred men in his own army would scarcely be sufficient to overthrow even the smallest detachment of EIC soldiers. He would need to raise an army of a thousand or more, if possible. Thus he called all the able-bodied men of Banda to gather before his villa that very day. With General Ram Gupta beside him, the rajah stood on the veranda and spoke.

"Men of Banda, all of you know what is happening in Delhi, in Calcutta, in Jhansi. Like never before, the people of India, no matter their caste or religion, have risen up against our oppressors. They will not fight alone. We will join them."

With a roar, they all agreed. Never before had Dhakar felt such a moment of pride and purpose. He looked to Asha and saw the same hope in her eyes.

On the fifteenth day of June, the native soldiers of Banda rose up and turned on their former commanders. Within hours, the people of Banda ran riot in the streets. Be they *sepoys*, merchants, farmers, beggars, or dancing girls, all cheered and swore allegiance to the rebel cause. Whatever that might be.

Except one. Magistrate Cockrail, the British Resident, presented himself before the Rajah Dhakar in his palace, while the light of distant fires glowed beyond the library's windows.

"Rajah," said Cockrail, very firmly. "I must insist that you speak with these unruly troops of yours. Tell them to lay down their arms and return to their barracks at once. They'll listen to you, Rajah."

"I cannot do that, Magistrate," Dhakar replied. "The barracks are on fire. The men would roast alive."

Cockrail did not hide his exasperation. "Rajah, this is mutiny! It cannot be allowed to continue unchecked. You *must* do something."

"You are correct, Magistrate." Then Dhakar turned to General Gupta. "Gupta, arrest the Magistrate and take him to the brig—if it's not on fire."

Stunned, Cockrail laughed derisively at him. "You're mad, Dhakar! These mutineers will never defy me—they haven't the courage."

Gupta made a gesture and two of his men took the magistrate by the arms.

"Wh-what's this?" Cockrail blustered, finding nothing funny this time. "Unhand me! This is an outrage. You'll not get away with this, Dhakar!"

"Take him away, Gupta," said the Rajah Dhakar. "If he resists arrest, shoot him."

Gupta nodded and pushed the British Resident out the door.

"Dhakar!" Cockrail cried out. "I thought we were friends!"

Dhakar stood resolutely until Cockrail disappeared from his sight. Then he slumped and looked away. Asha laid her hand on his arm, an offer of comfort, but the magistrate's words still stung him. He had thought they were friends, too.

"Dhakar," said Asha, "what good is it to live if we do not live free of tyranny?"

He looked into her beautiful eyes. Before he could reply there came the nearby report of a single gunshot. Dhakar hurried to the veranda and threw open the mosquito netting.

In the compound lay the body of the Magistrate Cockrail; General Gupta stood over him with a smoking revolver in his hand.

"He resisted, *sahib*," Gupta said, formally.

The echo of that shot continued to reverberate in Dhakar's head.

He closed the curtain and looked at Asha. "If the revolution fails," he said, "we have all signed our death warrants."

* * *

The juggernaut of the Great Revolt rolled out from the center of India, engulfing city after city. The fervor that Dhakar had put into the *Iron Buffalo* he now transferred to the Insurrection. The forge and the drafting table sat unused, despite the prototype being finished. Rather, Dhakar rallied his engineers and craftsmen to take up arms along with his troops, exhorting them to rise up against the East India Company that sought to bring all of Bundelkhand under their mantle.

Dhakar and the people of Banda quickly raised a proper Marathi army. Half of these were left to hold the city from attack. A week after he secured Banda for the rebels, Dhakar kissed Asha and his children goodbye, mounted his trusty Zabu, then led the other half of the army out through the gates of Banda. Asha took the hem of her *dupatta* and wiped her eyes.

"God grant you victory, Dhakar," she said.

A few days later, as Dhakar and his troops rode up to Kanpur, they quickly determined that the city had yet to be completely secured, despite three weeks of bombardment. Even with the beginning of the monsoon season, the rains failed to quell the smoke of a dozen raging fires that rose from the northern neighborhoods. From within the walls, he heard ceaseless gunfire.

Dhakar soon joined Nana Saheb and Tatya Tope at the siege of Wheeler's entrenchment. He had never met either of them before, but the word of Lakshmi Bai provided sufficient introduction.

The Nana Saheb stood tall, broad of shoulder and belly, and resolute in demeanor. He made an impressive figure in his ornately embroidered robes, his turban and sash the same color as the Marathi flag, his freely displayed jewels and medallions, and the matching sword and dagger secured under his sash. He had a complexion dark and smooth, with a mustache trimmed in the European fashion. And spectacles.

By contrast, Dhakar thought the older Tatya Tope wore the sloppiest turban he had ever seen. He wondered that it managed to stay on his head. His casual attire might proclaim the man scarcely a step above a common beggar. Yet this man had trained both the nana and the rani in the arts of warfare, in their youth.

"Welcome, Dhakar of Banda," said Nana Saheb, grinning broadly as he clasped Dhakar's shoulders. "We are happy to have you among us. With Marathi leaders such as yourself, this rebellion will not be just a matter of a handful of disgruntled soldiers turning on their masters. No! We will forge a true army and a true empire once more!"

Dhakar bowed to the man, thinking the fellow had ambitions.

Rising, he said, "I am happy to serve as I might, *Peshwa*—Viceroy. I have brought seven hundred men from Banda to aid your cause."

"Seven hundred," Saheb pondered, rubbing his shaven chin—the only part of his face shaven. "I hoped it would be more. Still, every bit helps. I thank you, Dhakar Rao. But I have not yet declared myself the *peshwa*—I only claim to be the vassal of the Emperor Zafar."

"My apologies, Nana. I am a better scientist than a rajah."

"Are you? How interesting."

Dhakar could not help but note the lack of interest in the Nana's voice.

Dhakar then followed them about, noting Kanpur to be a massive city. He quickly understood that taking it would not be a matter of shooting a single magistrate and a few English soldiers.

Soon after, Dhakar saw the Nana Saheb set out a plan for routing the enemy from their position by charging from the east. Just before they were to attack, the nana changed his mind, ordering the troops to move to the west and attack from that point. That plan of attack may have been better, but in moving, the troops were exposed to sniper fire and a dozen men were lost.

In the hours to follow, Dhakar witnessed Nana Saheb give orders, insist that his generals swear to uphold it—and an hour after, change his mind. Nor would he do this only once or twice.

Tatya, Dhakar saw, was a man of his word, but unquestioning in his loyalty to the Nana. Very soon, Dhakar had reason to wish these two men held each other's position.

Shortly, Tatya Tope and Dhakar left the nana to review their stocks of gunpowder.

"Over a thousand Englishmen remain barricaded in the north of the city," Tatya Tope explained to Dhakar as they walked. "Most are soldiers and officers, but many are civilians, plus women and children. Many British have settled in the city, operating EIC businesses. Many were born here and know no other home. Even so, the British position in Kanpur is untenable."

"How will you dislodge them?"

"Nana has a plan. He will present them with terms shortly."

However, in the hour to come, the Nana revised that plan, allowing the British to withdraw without a fight. "There will be less bloodshed that way," he said.

"We have them utterly surrounded," said Tatya. "Sure, they still have their guns, they can still punch balls out of lead sheets. But their powder is almost gone. They're already defeated," Here he grinned. "And they know it."

So did they, for that evening, the British commander, General Wheeler, sent word to the nana, offering a surrender of sorts. His offer of surrender included a provision for permission to pack up their belongings and weapons and depart the city. To the surprise of Dhakar and Tatya, the Nana agreed. Dhakar wondered if Nana Saheb had actually noticed the weapons clause in Wheeler's proposal.

"Find one of the white women we captured," said Nana Saheb. "Have her take a message to the general. Tell him that I will provide a flotilla of boats for the British to evacuate via the river."

Tatya bowed and went out to pass on the orders.

“Nana, you are most merciful and generous,” said Dhakar. “I hope the British will remember this generosity on your part.”

The Nana smirked.

By the next morning, under a gray sky that anticipated the beginning of monsoon season, everything had been set in place. Fifty good-sized rowboats had been pulled onto the broad shallows of the Ganges, at a jetty. This, the northernmost portion of Kanpur, sat outside of the city proper, thick with jungle growth all around.

Under a flag of truce, the British soldiers marched to the water's edge. Behind these, the civilian men, women, and children followed. At the head of the column, General Wheeler observed the rebels lined up on either side of them, cursing them and mocking them.

Watching from nearby, Dhakar could well imagine that General Wheeler no doubt felt relieved that Nana Saheb had allowed his men to retain their weapons. *What sort of surrender is this?*, he wondered. From a distance and with a lull in the rains, Dhakar saw Wheeler dismount, pat his horse a fond farewell, and get into the first boat. Whilst the rest of the regiment were getting into their own boats, he had the men in his own boat push off.

Then, just as Wheeler's boat approached the deeper, faster-moving water, while the rest of the British soldiers were getting in the boats but the women and children had not yet, Dhakar received a message from a runner.

Dhakar felt his blood turn to ice as he read the new orders. Thenana had once more changed his mind about the evacuation. These men, peacefully evacuating, were now to be killed, everyone of them... and by Dhakar's hand.

Barely had the gravity of the situation sunk in, than he heard a gun's report. From Dhakar's standpoint, he could not say who fired first, but at that moment, when the evacuees were out in the open and most vulnerable, the shooting began.

Seconds later, a pair of cannons, hidden in the thick trees, erupted. With deadly accuracy, they shattered two boats and any hope of evacuation for the British. Dozens died in the first volley of gunfire.

As the rain began to fall, Dhakar regained his wits and, as ordered, commanded his men forward into the water, drawing their weapons. Hundreds of British soldiers floundered in the shallows. These men attempted to regroup, and they got off a few shots, but clearly they were doomed. Dhakar's men and thousands more were upon the wounded survivors, with sword in hand. Nana Saheb had been clever—he had ordered the remaining Englishmen to be shot only if necessary, but hacked to bits if possible, to save precious ammo and powder.

Sloshing through the water, Dhakar went up to nearest British soldier. He raised his sword, even as the man looked to and fro, clearly confused by the events. Yet Dhakar hesitated.

The man then realized Dhakar was upon him. Man? More a boy, Dhakar thought.

The boy fumbled for his rifle, turning it one way then the other, to find his grip. Dhakar knew he must not let him do so.

In that an instant, Dhakar brought his sword down on the boy's head, hard. The boy half-screamed and half-gurgled. He fell backwards into the water. He did not get up.

All around Dhakar, men committed murder. With *tulwar* and *katar*, they hacked and stabbed, slaughtering the British. Dhakar, like Tatya Tope and the others, found himself caught up in the savagery. Some men he stabbed, many he hacked to ribbons as they attempted to defend themselves. Limbs he severed and faces he chopped as a cook chops a cabbage.

When it was over, nine hundred Englishmen had perished in the massacre, floating languidly downstream, the water now as red as their coats. The rebels took hostage the remaining two hundred English women and children, still on the shore. Among them were General Wheeler's two daughters, one of them a child, younger than Dhakar's son.

Afterwards, a blood-splattered Dhakar went behind a copse of trees, expecting to vomit. The queasiness passed, even as he noticed he'd somehow taken a shallow saber cut.

Dhakar went back to his men and had his wound bandaged. There, he reflected that war is neither noble nor glorious. Armies were not raised for the purpose of playing with kittens. In times like these, war is necessary. As Dhakar looked up to see a group of rebels running by, yelling and caterwauling incoherently, parading General Wheeler's severed head on a pike, he realized that hacking men to death, one after another, is what war is about.

Dhakar had seen such madness before, his last year in Europe, as men in one nation after another revolted against their various governments. He saw them kill and burn and he saw their governments strike back, killing and burning ten times worse. In the end, the streets were filled with corpses and nothing changed.

Nonetheless, Dhakar wasted little time informing the Nana that he needed to join the forces of Lakshmi Bai and Chambu Singh back in Bundelkhand. Seeing the rajah's pallid face, Nana Saheb granted permission.

9. Secret Alliances

A week after Dhakar's departure, British Army regulars, recently brought in from China, besieged the rebels in Kanpur. Seeing this, Nana Saheb ordered his loyal followers to shut the gates, throw the bolts, and man the walls. He then sent out an emissary to remind the British that the rebels had over a hundred hostages.

The British commander responded with a demand of the immediate surrender of the city. When Nana refused, the battle commenced and both sides fought fiercely. Despite a pouring deluge, the British field guns proved accurate. Within hours, breaches began to appear in the outer walls of the city.

"We cannot hold the city much longer," Tatya Tope advised. "We must prepare to evacuate soon."

"I fear you are right," said Nana Saheb, regretfully. "But before we go, execute the last of the hostages."

Tatya blinked. "The women and children, *sahib*?"

"Yes," the nana said, glaring out the window at the British encampments beyond the walls. "If the British will not relent their siege when we hold hostages, there must be no hostages for them to rescue. They must know that we will keep our word—or they will never concede their death-grip on us!"

The rebels spent the rest of July 15, 1857 raping and murdering the last of the two hundred English women and children of Kanpur. When the rebels were finished, the corpses were dismembered and thrown into a well. General Wheeler's eldest daughter were among these.

As per usual, Nana Saheb changed his mind and rescinded his order, realizing the world stage would condemn his actions. These new orders arrived too late for all except Wheeler's youngest, aged five, she being taken by a *sowar* as his new wife.

The next day, after Nana Saheb led his people out of the city, the EIC forces reclaimed Kanpur and hoped to rescue British survivors. Instead, they soon discovered their bodies, packed into the abandoned well. The officers, but especially the common foot soldiers, were outraged. In response to this atrocity, the British massacred not hundreds of Indian civilians, but several thousands.

* * *

Dhakar's infantry met with Singh's cavalry at a villa he'd commandeered roughly halfway between Jhansi and Sagar. Chambu

Singh wore a great turban bearing a clasp with a gaudy gem from which sprouted an ostrich feather. He wore a trimmed and pointed black beard, a crisp white *sherwani*, billowing trousers of pea green, and his shoes terminated in curled points. He'd thrust a brace of wickedly curved daggers in his green sash. Singh rode a black Arab charger with even more baubles than the Sikh rajah himself.

Upon dismounting, Singh and Dhakar salaamed politely to one another, each eyeing the other warily. Chambu Singh flashed a sly smile at Dhakar, yet he could not hide the cold cruelty and malice in his eyes.

Singh welcomed Dhakar inside his dry, warm home and ordered tea brought. Sitting alone, Dhakar allowed the mildly sweet and fruity beverage to sooth his parched throat. He looked up from his cup and smiled at Chambu Singh.

"This is excellent oolong, Singh. I see you have many varieties in your cupboard."

"Thank you, Rajah," said Chambu Singh. "A good host should keep a well-stocked larder to meet his guest's tastes."

Dhakar nodded. "I had heard most of the supply routes have been cut off due to both the revolt here and the uprising in China."

"This is true," he said calmly and carefully, "yet I have a supplier."

As ever, Dhakar mused, *this man keeps a tight lip.*

"I dare say, you have connections within the Celestial Empire, bringing you not only tea but information." Dhakar almost added, "and instructions," but he held his tongue when he saw the smile drop from Singh's face.

The two men locked eyes. Hatred that had simmered for years began to boil. Vague suspicions became firm in their minds. Hands slowly moved towards swords.

"Chambu!" said the Rani Lakshmi Bai, regal in billowing red trousers and orange *dupatta*, throwing apart the beaded curtain and stepping into the room. Dhakar started, not expecting the rani to be here. "You and your damned tea! You should be ashamed to have left such a clue."

Chambu Singh looked away, still angered, yet clearly chagrined. The rani then turned to Dhakar.

"Yes Dhakar, we have allies in China. Their goals are much the same as our own—to push the British into the sea! By rising up at the same time, we divide their forces and help one another. We cannot fail!"

"Who are these allies from China?" Dhakar asked. "Why do they wish to aid us?"

Lakshmi gave a nonchalant shrug of her head. "Their motive is obvious. It will aid their own struggle against the British if we draw away their troops, yes? And..." Here the rani sounded almost embarrassed. "Their envoy said something silly about... well, he thinks I am some sort of female messiah, long prophesized by their Buddha and others. The Maitreya. He said I am to herald in some sort of era of world peace. Of course I discount all this talk of prophecies—but it would be foolish to refuse his offer."

Dhakar said nothing more, but only glanced at Chambu Singh. He had expected this news of Lakshmi as a messiah to evoke a derisive laugh or a bawdy jest from the man's lips. Rather, the man looked stunned and truly reverent as he gazed upon the young queen.

"I have a plan to secure Sagar, so as to hold all of Bundelkhand," said the rani of Jhansi. "Here, I will show you."

Lakshmi went to the table where Chambu Singh had maps laid out. Over these, the rani unrolled a large cartographer's map bearing splotches of dried blood. It displayed the breadth of Bundelkhand.

"They will take the most direct route from Calcutta, along the Grand Trunk Road, which will bring them to Sagar," she said. "But we intend to meet them before they get there and divert them. By 'we' I mean the revolutionaries who fight with Nana Saheb and those of Emperor Zafar and my own, numbering a total of seventy thousand or so. Any that you can bring from Banda will be appreciated."

Lakshmi may not have seen Dhakar wince at the mention of his fiefdom, for she continued. "Immediately after, they must pass through certain narrow mountain passes, along the Sone River. There, on the hills above, we will be waiting."

"How do you know they will come through that pass?" Dhakar asked.

The rani smirked. "As a Sikh general, Chambu is privy to the plans of the British. He passes everything he learns to me."

She then pointed to a spot on the map. "I hope to attack them in this place—Kumbhanda Pass," she said. "See? They will become bogged down as they must snake left and right, and march no more than four abreast. If you and your men attack from the opposite side, victory will be ours!"

Dhakar looked from the rani to the map, then back. Clearly, this woman knew the land better than he. The gods themselves must have carved that portion of the canyon for no other purpose than an ambush.

"Lakshmi, you have the mind of a tactician. But do you have enough men and munitions?"

Lakshmi smiled at him. "Already I can count on four thousand men and women of Jhansi who have already sworn to aid me in this fight, and I hope to have many thousands more by then. Every day the British invoke more strictures and punishments on the peoples of India. They hang soldiers who dare ask for the same treatment as an Englishman. Everything they do brings about another insurrection. They have already lost, only they do not yet realize it."

Dhakar looked over the map. He estimated the number of troops the British might muster under the circumstances of the revolt and he considered the cover from fire her troops could expect. He even calculated the rate of fire from their respective weapons.

It would work, he concluded.

* * *

Not a week later, a British regiment advanced steadily along the Sone River amid the narrow and steep Kumbhanda Pass. The commander, Major Manderberry, had sent scouts ahead, looking for any ambush. As they'd not returned or fired a warning shot, he felt assured that his men were safe.

The first bullet buried itself in his brain. Under a hail of gunfire from the cliffs above, the regiment found itself pinned down and unable to advance. The sharpshooters, under the command of Uda Devi and Dhakar, fired round after round in quick succession. Dozens of Redcoats died under the hail of gunfire before the buglers could sound retreat. Dozens more died as they attempted to flee.

The Englishmen took cover in every available nook and cranny—yet which could only cover them from one side. They returned fire with equal skill, and after an hour, the Indian rebels found themselves running low of ammo, and they'd taken dozens of casualties. On Uda's order, they pulled back from the ledges and waited.

A British captain, seeing what the Indian rebels silently offered, sounded the retreat. Soon after the last Englishman had departed out of sight, Dhakar rejoined Uda Devi.

"We have repulsed the enemy," said Dhakar. "They have fled! Maybe it was not the massacre that the rani hoped for, but we need not worry about the Redcoats advancing through Kumbhanda Pass."

Uda Devi looked south, towards the dust cloud rising from the retreating columns of British soldiers.

"For now at least," she said, grimly.

* * *

However, when the rani of Jhansi sent an envoy to the court of the rajah of Sagar in August, she found his loyalty to the EIC and their profitable arrangement had not wavered. Soon after, Lakshmi Bai, Dhakar, and Chambu Singh brought their armies to Sagar as a show of power. On Singh's men, not a single item of green cloth was seen, for they marched under orange banners, disguised as Marathi troops. Though the rebel forces easily surrounded the city, the rajah ordered the gates sealed and his people fortified their defenses.

"We can only lay siege to the city and hope that the native soldiers inside will rise up and mutiny," said the rani, in the camp outside. "If not, then we wait and starve them out. We haven't enough cannons to breach the walls."

Dhakar disliked the idea of a protracted siege—they would be pinned down too long and too much could go wrong. Still, he saw no other option but to agree.

There would be skirmishes and Dhakar frequently found himself in battle, fighting alongside the queen of Jhansi whom he admired, and Chambu Singh, whom he detested. Others, like Uda Devi and her band of sharpshooters, picked off men at a distance with their rifles.

Again and again, Dhakar found himself caught up in the violence against the troops of Sagar. The Sagari regulars poured out in a sortie, hoping to draw Lakshmi and Dhakar within range of the British marksmen on the walls. The ploy nearly succeeded, and Dhakar took a grazing bullet wound in the leg.

In the weeks to follow, the rajah attempted other sorties and the rebel forces met them head on. Dhakar often found himself face-to-face with the enemy, hacking them to bits with his saber. Again he would be shot, and once he took a shallow cut from a sword.

* * *

One evening, in the rebel camp outside Sagar, Lakshmi Bai came to Dhakar as he sat by his fire. She asked about his bandaged arm and he assured her he'd received only a scratch and he would be fine. Then she sat by him.

"Dhakar, tell me more of this toy boat," Lakshmi Bai asked. "Asha has told me such fabulous things that I can scarcely believe."

Dhakar gave the rani a brief outline of the *Iron Buffalo*, confirming its capabilities and his half-forgotten ambitions. He mentioned his plans to build a bigger vessel, capable of traveling considerable distances under the sea.

"Rajah, such a boat could stop the British ships from bringing ever more soldiers and guns from across the sea!" she said, clearly impressed and inspired. "We could defeat them on the water before they ever set foot on our land!"

He drew a deep breath before speaking.

"Rani, I fear I must quash that idea. The submersible is not a weapon; I designed it for exploration. Even if I added weapons, it is too small, too slow."

"But this bigger boat—!"

"Rani, even under the best of circumstance, a craft capable of doing what you ask would take years to build. There is simply not enough time."

The rani relented and said no more on the subject. As she rose and walked off, Dhakar hung his head, sorry to have disappointed her. Upon thinking more, he felt even more sorry that the larger submersible had not already been built and made capable of doing precisely what she had in mind.

* * *

Early in July, Asha's prediction came true. The British had at last begun their counteroffensive against Delhi, launched from the Punjab in the northwest, largely manned with mud-soaked Sikhs loyal to the British crown. Along with these were hardened British veterans diverted from wars in the Crimea or China, brought to India.

As they marched to Delhi, after the monsoons had passed, the British soldiers fought in numerous skirmishes. Other times, they came across a dirty little village with no defenses and hung every man they found—thus guaranteeing that no one would attack them from behind. They attacked various forts held by the rebels and the defenders fled back to Delhi.

In Medieval times, the siege of a city could take weeks or months, sometimes years. In 1857, once a proper army came on scene, a siege might be a matter of days, sometimes hours. That Delhi held out until September shows how well Zafar and his Mughals had defended their city—indeed, at times it seemed the rebels might dislodge the sparse British forces from their positions. Yet, after even more British, Sikh, and Pakhtun reinforcements arrived, the outcome had been decreed.

The extra British guns hammered the walls and shattered the gates of Delhi. Mortars spread devastation well within the walls, killing indiscriminately. Seeing the north gate in ruins, Brigadier General Nicholson led the charge—only to fall to a sniper's bullet. Confusion and indecision being forbidden in the well-disciplined British army, another general immediately took command and the British entered the city.

Once inside, British troops crying, "Remember Cawnpore!" waged their war against not only the rebels but every shopkeeper, *mahout*, and beggar they came across. Every woman and girl insufficiently hidden would be violated over and over. Centuries-old palaces and entire neighborhoods were burned. By dusk, half of Delhi would be engulfed in flames.

The following day, British troops captured the elderly Mughal Emperor Zafar while he attempted to escape. The day following that, the British authorities executed his two eldest sons. As a gift, they presented the old man with their severed heads. After that, the Mughals sued for peace.

With the recapture of Delhi in September, the rulers of several rebellious states across India capitulated and begged the British for leniency. The cities of Oudh, Lucknow, and Agra, one after another, fell to the besiegers. Eventually, only Nana Saheb, Tatya Tope, Rani Lakshmi Bai, and Rajah Dhakar continued the fight.

With no Mughal emperor to lead the rebel cause, Nana Saheb declared himself *peshwa*—heir apparent to the Marathi throne. Tatya Tope, the Rani Lakshmi Bai, and the Rajah Dhakar Rao immediately swore allegiance to him.

In November, Tatya Tope attempted a second siege of Kanpur. A week later, facing fierce resistance from British regulars fresh from England, he had no choice but to retreat.

Tatya led his beaten and disheartened men south. He soon reunited them with those of Lakshmi Bai and Dhakar at Sagar, which still stubbornly withstood their siege. By then, Nana Saheb had ridden off somewhere, attempting to raise more troops.

The rebels had lost the great cities of Delhi and Kanpur. Sagar and Gwalior they had yet to take. Eighteen Fifty-Seven, a year that had begun with such promise, ended under the impending shadow of failure.

10. The Siege of Jhansi

In February, the rebels spotted a column of dust approaching Sagar from the south. Lakshmi's scouts rode out and returned within an hour. Confirming her worst fears, they reported that twenty thousand British army regulars under Major-General Sir Hugh Rose had arrived to relieve the siege of Sagar. Seeing this massive army after the last seven months of attrition to her own forces, the Rani Lakshmi Bai knew she would be caught between the two forces. She had no choice but to sound a retreat.

The cause is lost, Dhakar knew, and he wanted time to consider his options. *Surrender? Asylum in some foreign land? This constant warfare and the butchery I've witnessed from both sides only sickens me. I wish only to return to Banda and my family.*

However, the rani ordered him to attend her in her own city. “Jhansi will be the next target of the British, Dhakar,” she said. “It is larger and more valuable to them than Banda. We must prepare for a siege if we hope to retain anything from this rebellion.”

* * *

Not two full months later, in early April, Major-General Rose led his regiment to Jhansi. They stopped just outside of musket range and began to amass, facing the gates. From the walls of the city, the rebel leaders watched.

“Look!” Commander Khuda said, pointing to a nearby ridge. “The British will attempt to set up their cannons on the heights. Our mortars cannot reach them there!”

“I see that,” replied the rani. “And we cannot place our own cannons on our walls to reach theirs—these mud walls will crumble from the recoil after a few shots.”

“What can we do?” Khuda asked in despair.

Lakshmi Bai turned, rushing down the steps. “We must not let the British get those cannons in place! Dhakar! Have snipers give us cover!”

“Yes, Rani!”

Moments later, Dhakar watched as the rani raced out of the gates at the head of a troop of women's cavalry. They charged towards the heights overlooking Jhansi, hoping to rout the British ere they had a chance to encamp.

Captain Rodgers and Lieutenant Morton supervised the cannon placement, whilst taking a cup of tea. They watched the heavy iron cannons lurch and rock back and forth on their carriages. They nodded with approval as the British soldiers whipped their draft horses up to the heights. At one point, the ropes strained and the horses stalled.

“You men,” Morton ordered, “get behind the carriages and push.”

Four or five Redcoats began pushing each carriage, helping the horses to pull. The cannon in front began to move again.

Meanwhile, up the draw rode a fast-moving troop of Marathi cavalry, their steeds' hooves pounding a fierce and rapid beat. They'd covered half the distance before the British officers realized what was happening.

"Onward for Jhansi!" the rani cried, pointing her sword at the lumbering cannon train.

Rodgers blinked, scarcely believing what he saw. Morton retained his wits and rallied his men.

"To arms!" he yelled, finding his feet. "Fire on those riders!"

The men however, had their weapons slung across their backs or had laid them aside so they could push. They scrambled to free their rifles and take aim even as the Indian cavalry-women fell upon them. The outcome of such a skirmish is decided in a matter of seconds—and neither side had even one to spare.

"It's that damned Rani!" the lieutenant realized. "Shoot her!"

A swipe of Lakshmi Bai's *tulwar* cleaved Morton's skull to the teeth. A dozen British soldiers fell in that first charge of the wild lancer women.

Captain Rodgers ordered his bugler to call those troops amassed farther behind. The British cannon crews had found their weapons and fired. Half a dozen women cried out and fell from their mounts.

"Charge!" Lakshmi ordered. "Cut the ropes! Kill the gunners before reinforcements arrive!"

Uda Devi slashed the ropes of a cannon and it rolled backwards, crushing the legs of a pair of screaming redcoats. Jhalkari Bai hurled a spear at Rodgers, but struck his horse's neck instead. Both went down. The British gunners, realizing they must fight or be slaughtered, fell back and began to shoot with precision.

A dozen more warrior women of Jhansi fell from the British volley. Rodgers, regaining his feet, commanded the British troops to reload. Lakshmi stopped just long enough to appraise the situation.

The British forces had the rani's forces outnumbered and she spotted their cavalry approaching, threatened to surround her own. Seeing how things stood, Lakshmi had no choice but to call retreat or perish in vain. Her cavalry followed her down the draw, still being pelleted with British gunfire. Moments later, they withdrew behind the walls of their city.

Her people, seeing this retreat in the face of the oncoming battalions of Englishmen, all looked to her. Dhakar stood among them.

"Load and prime the cannons!" she commanded, though she and everyone in Jhansi knew that all thirty cannons had already been loaded and primed. "Take pitchforks and shove their scaling ladders away as fast at they are set in place!"

The rani's people ran off to follow her orders.

"Uda! Take your snipers to the towers. Pick off any Redcoat officers that you can."

"Yes, Rani," said the taciturn Uda Devi, who then hurried to carry out the orders.

Then Commander Khuda came running up to her—no easy task for a corpulent man.

"Rani!" he cried. "A British battalion has been spotted approaching from the north—they attempt to surround the city!"

Scarcely had the queen of Jhansi time to process this troubling news than she heard the fire of the British cannons and felt the impact of the shells on the walls and gates of the city.

"Pile anything you can find against the gates!" she commanded. "Wagons, crates, barrels!" Her officers and many commoners ran to comply with her orders.

"Jhalkari!" Lakshmi called out. "Come with me! I have a mission for you."

Dhakar noted that Jhalkari clearly had no idea what the rani had in mind, but she did not hesitate to obey.

Left to his own, Dhakar ordered General Gupta to set his five hundred remaining men on the walls, hoping to pick off as many Englishmen as they could.

"Yes *sahib*, but it will not be enough. If every bullet they fire hit its target, still there are too many of them."

"I know that, Gupta. I damned well know it. It's hopeless—but every Englishman we kill is one less to trouble Nana Saheb."

Ram Gupta bowed his head then scurried off to get the men on the walls. Dhakar followed them and took up a position towards the north end of the city where he saw the approaching British battalion. Only the extremely rough ground around Jhansi hindered the Redcoats from meeting up with their fellows and surrounding the city.

The British cannons fired relentlessly. The walls cracked and crumbled in places. The south gates had been shattered. The walls would soon be breached and the enemy would be inside, fighting hand-to-hand.

Indeed, Major-General Rose saw those many breaches in the walls of Jhansi and he smelled blood. Even before his army had fully encircled the city, he ordered his men into the breaches. The Indian rebels did everything they could to keep them out—throwing together makeshift barricades and pushing carts of burning hay into the breaches—yet nothing stopped the enemy. They were overwhelmed and no hope remained.

"Gupta!" Dhakar commanded, "Send most of your men down to the streets to stop the British!"

Gupta, knowing the plan had some merit, nodded and passed along the order to the captains. While men on the walls were largely protected against the enemy outside, fighting them from within the city would leave them uncovered and in the open.

Dhakar himself stayed on the roof, rifle in hand, hoping to spot Rose or other officers. Killing a single British officer would not stop the siege, but it could buy time for the rebels.

Then something outside the city caught Dhakar's attention. He spotted a small troop of riders exit from the north gate, which closed behind them. At their lead he saw a woman in the attire of a *sowar*, brandishing a sword. A smaller figure sat behind her, his arms wrapped tightly around her waist.

"Lakshmi," Dhakar said, the name passing his lips like the prayer of a dying man. Did she truly hope to stop an entire battalion with less than a dozen cavalrymen?

Then he saw the riders turn, dart through a ravine. A moment later, they appeared some distance away. Gupta ran up to Dhakar and also looked on.

"That is the rani?" he asked. "She has run away?"

"She must escape to fight another day." He turned and looked Gupta full in the eyes. "The rani's fate would be far worse than ours, should she be captured."

Gupta nodded grimly. He realized that the Redcoats now entering the city would be quick to associate the willful queen with the rebels who had committed the massacres at Delhi and Kanpur. They would want to take their revenge on her personally.

Instead, the British soldiers, unable to find the Rani Lakshmi Bai that day, would have to satisfy themselves with the indiscriminate murder of her people. From the sound of the screams below them, Dhakar knew they had begun.

Dhakar and Gupta aimed their rifles at the British below them and fired. Before either man could load their next bullets, they heard the roar of far-off cannonade.

In the next instant, a volley of hot iron cannonballs hit the rubble-filled wall. Beneath their feet, they felt the wooden walkway attached to the wall buckle and heave.

Both men toppled with the walkway, struggling to find something to hold onto that wasn't falling. The entire section of wall seemed ready to collapse.

Dhakar lost his rifle as he grabbed hold of a tottering beam. He held on for dear life as the beam creaked and fell, taking a goodly portion of the walkway with it.

A fifty-foot section of the walkway fell halfway, collapsing several barns and sheds below. The sudden stop caused Dhakar to lose his grip. He dropped onto a roof of branches and straw—which immediately collapsed under his weight.

He fell into a house, amidst a family of screaming women and children, who had thought they were safe within the city's walls. Dhakar, his fall softened by roof and people, quickly got to his feet.

"Get out!" he commanded. "The wall may collapse any minute!"

He rushed out without confirming if they followed or even heard his orders. He looked back at the shattered wall section. He spotted Ram Gupta climbing down the remains of a ladder. Between them lay a massive section of collapsed wall.

"Gupta!" he yelled over the din of screaming, gunfire, and distant cannons. "Be careful! I'm going to the palace—it's our last best defense! Get the men and catch up with me when you can!"

Gupta looked at him and nodded. "Yes, *sahib*!"

Dhakar turned and ran, armed with only a sword and a half-empty revolver. The city had become a scene of chaos as old men stood in the street and prayed to each of their thousand gods, as donkeys brayed and upset their carts, and as old women scurried about, wondering where they might hide their grandchildren from the seemingly unstoppable invaders.

The British had broken through the breaches here and there, but they found the fighting fierce. The rebels still had a slim chance if Dhakar could get to the palace and turn its guns on those breaches.

Through the maze of mud huts, he ran. Though separated from Gupta and most his troops, Dhakar knew that several dozen more had been stationed with Captain Chundawat in the vicinity of the palace. He had only to meet up with them, enter the palace, then turn the well-defended cannons on the breaches. He would be there in only a few minutes, if his luck held.

Suddenly from around a corner, a Redcoat roared and charged him with his bayonet. Dhakar deflected the blade with his own, then shot the man in the gut. He fell with a scream.

Dhakar saw that two more Redcoats in tartaned kilts had entered the alley and spotted him. Both fired and Dhakar sought cover behind the corner—yet one of the bullets struck him, tearing into his ribs, all too near his heart.

Dhakar stumbled into the wall. He panted, wondering if these were his last breaths.

One of the Scotsmen rounded the corner. Spotting Dhakar in distress, he stopped and grinned. Then he charged with his rifle upraised, its bayonet pointed at Dhakar's heart.

Dhakar shot him with his last bullet.

The other man appeared and raised his rifle. Dhakar hurled his empty revolver at the man's head—causing a burning wave of agony to shoot through the left side of his body. Obliged to duck, the man missed his chance at a clear shot.

Dhakar rushed him as best he could and had the man's barrel in his hand, holding it so that any shot would go astray. With his saber, he hewed off the man's arm. The Scotsman ran off, screaming and clutching at the bleeding stump.

Dhakar stumbled away, down an alley, clutching at his own wound. The bullet had missed his heart; he needed only to staunch the flow of blood. And escape.

In the distance, he saw the fluttering Union Jack at the base of the rani's palace—the British would take it before he could hope to get there. Jhansi was lost.

Like the rani, Dhakar vowed to escape or die trying. If the British had not yet completed the encirclement of the city, there was still a chance. He would only need to find his horse...

That was the last he remembered before passing out.

11. Crushed Before the Juggernaut

Baadal, the strongest of Lakshmi's horses, had been the perfect choice for a long ride. With her ten-year-old son, Damodar, strapped to her back, she rode hour after hour, that she might entreat with Jayaji Rao, the maharajah of Gwalior in the north. Thus far, the maharajah had given the rebels lip service and nothing more, but Nana Saheb had set his sights on this city. Within the city's ancient and exquisite fort, they might hold off the British for weeks or months, while gathering more and more troops to their side.

Normally a ride of a week, the rani charged on night and day, leaving Jhalkari and her cavalry behind. She hoped that the bulk of the infantry would have had the chance to escape alive and ready to fight.

Three days after they'd left Jhansi, within sight of the walls of Gwalior, Baadal stumbled and fell dead, causing Lakshmi and Damodar to tumble to the ground. Unharmed but for some bruises, Lakshmi pressed her hands together and said a brief prayer for the brave animal. Then she took hold of her son's hand and ran the rest of the way.

Entering the great city, Lakshmi made her way through masses of people waiting for handouts of grain, of which all had been distributed the day before. She saw piles of animal bones, sheep, goats, and horses, long since butchered. Today, the people were butchering their dogs and cats for food.

Within the palace, a dusty Lakshmi Bai found the maharajah of Gwalior lolling on a pile of silken pillows, surrounded by slaves who offered him dates and wine. A gramophone played in the background. Lakshmi presented herself to the maharajah, but he did not welcome her.

"I want nothing of your trouble!" Jayaji Rao said. "I should turn you over to the British, who have made for profitable allies. And I will if you do not leave my city at once!"

So Lakshmi and Damodar exited Gwalior. Some hours later, Jhalkari and the cavalry caught up with them. Before they could exchange more than a few words, they saw some hundreds of native soldiers and others spill out from the city.

Lakshmi and Jhalkari drew in their breath, hoping for the best yet uncertain of the outcome. They passed along the order to be prepared for an attack.

This day, the gods smiled on them. The leader of these few hundred *sowars* said, "We are sick of the British! We are sick of Jayaji Rao, the gutless coward! Rani, we have seen your courage and we wish to join your army."

Lakshmi, feeling grateful for any assistance she received, welcomed them. They camped without the city and wait for Nana Saheb to arrive.

* * *

Dhakar awoke in a small dank room, lit by a single oily lamp. His clothes and weapons were gone. An old woman, having heard him stir, entered through a beaded curtain.

"Do not get up, *sahib*," she said. "You are hurt very bad. Lucky my husband and I find you and drag you inside."

"I... thank you, *memsahib*," Dhakar said, wincing as pain shot throughout his body, simply from laying back down. "B-But I must get to my men. We have to form barricades. We can hold them off if—Ow! If we... can just..."

The old woman held him down with a single hand. Her husband, with a long white beard and only a loincloth, stepped in and knelt beside her. He asked if she needed help.

"No. He is too weak to walk. I will give him broth."

"M-my men..." Dhakar muttered.

"Your men are dead, *sahib*. They died three days ago, along with my sons."

* * *

Two days later, word came to Jhansi that British army regulars, under the command of General Whitluck, were on their way to Banda. Hearing this, Dhakar quickly thanked the couple who had nursed his wounds and left them. Although unfit to walk, let alone ride, walk he did, wrapped only in a homespun loincloth, bandages, and a turban of rough khaki. In such a disguise and with a week's growth of beard, he trusted that no one would recognize him.

In the streets, Dhakar witnessed the rape of Jhansi. British soldiers who could not take out their wrath on the willful rani, did so on any other woman and girl they could find. Any citizen who uttered an objection they shot. Clearly, many did object, for Dhakar saw pile after pile of Indian corpses in every street. He would later hear that five thousand men, women, and children died in the sack of Jhansi, and he did not doubt it.

Dhakar had no idea what happened to his horse, Zabu. Redcoats guarded the gates day and night, and allowed no one to exit. He waited some hours and when darkness fell, he picked his way through one of the breaches left in the walls. This too had a guard, but half sprawled in the rubble, drinking. Dhakar snuck up on him and killed him with an improvised cudgel. He then took the man's rifle and fled into the dark.

For days Dhakar traveled on foot, mostly by night, sleeping in a gully or under a clump of bushes. At last he came to a small camp, clearly refugees from the fighting. He wanted to join this family, to help them, to offer them his wealth for the suffering they had endured.

Instead, while they slept, he stole their horse.

* * *

On April 16, 1858, British army regulars, under the command of General Whitluck, began the bombardment of Dhakar's city, Banda. Fresh from England, these ten thousand troops set up their cannons and quickly shattered the gates of the proud city. After that, they marched into Banda and reclaimed it, vowing vengeance for the death of Magistrate Cockrail.

Throughout the day, they killed three thousand rebel soldiers and civilians. They violated twice as many women and girls. They stole everything they could find. If they could not steal it, they burned it. The British would not settle for victory, they demanded revenge.

That evening, Dhakar saw the glow of the fires as he approached the city on foot—on horseback, he would be too conspicuous. He had no doubt what he would find.

Dhakar had purposely neglected to shave since before the revolt collapsed and he'd attired himself in a sloppy turban and such robes as even the most aesthetic of *sadhus* and *yogas* would eschew. Despite the fifty thousand rupee bounty on his head, Dhakar's best friend might not recognize him.

He entered the city through a lesser gate, left unmanned by British soldiers who'd spotted some prize to pluck. Within the city, Dhakar saw fires without number roar through half the shops in the square. Dead bodies littered his streets. Chaos reigned as screaming women and children ran to and fro. A dozen times soldiers accosted him or shot at him from a distance. He had come by a butcher's knife and each time he met a British soldier alone, he killed the man. If he crossed the path of a troop of soldiers, he avoided them and left them to their looting.

At last, he came to his villa. An icy wave passed through him when he found the gates wide open and unguarded. Streams of smoke wafted from within.

He ran into the courtyard, spotted half a dozen small fires and several bodies. Amid the bloody corpses he spotted old Mrs. Patel, naked, sobbing, and covering her face in shame. On the steps lay the body of Hari Babu, his chief designer. Dhakar did not hesitate, but panting with dread, he ran inside his house.

The smell of smoke assailed his nostrils as he noted the furniture tossed about, the curtains shredded, vases shattered. One of the young maids he found stripped nude and sobbing over the corpse of her father, the chamberlain. With his heart in his throat, Dhakar charged up the stairs.

In their bedroom he found Asha, equally naked. Her arms and legs splayed and bruised, her nether regions splattered with gray-white globs, her throat a hideous ruin.

"*No!*"

Dhakar fell beside her, sobbing, screaming, his nostrils assailed by the stench of the emissions of a dozen men or more. Tightly he grasped her dead and ravaged body to his bosom.

The British, those champions of decency and freedom had done this? Or had it been their allies, the Gurkhas? Had it been her own people?

He knew the truth. It had been all of them, one after another.

Had it been a saber or a *kukri* or a *tulwar* that had slashed her beautiful throat? Did it matter?

The smoke grew denser. It would be so easy to let the fumes suffocate him, to go unconscious and drift away into the flames like a *suttee.*

Then a thought entered his mind. He laid her body down then ran down the hall to the children's room.

He found Bani first, his knuckles torn and bloodied. The boy had died fighting a foe he could never have hoped to defeat.

Lastly he found Savita. When he saw what they had done to the three-year-old girl before they killed her, something died inside the soul of the rajah.

Smoke filled the house. If he stayed much longer, he would die also. Did he care? Would he not welcome death, rather than to live with this memory?

No.... No, no, no! He did care! He would make himself care, for he remembered Asha's words, "*What good is it to live if we do not live free of tyranny?*"

The house would burn and that would be their funeral pyre. His gold, gems, and much of the art had been taken, but curiously they had left the portrait of Asha. Perhaps whatever sliver of humanity remained within them did not wish to see the eyes of she whom they had defiled. More likely, they feared to see her dead eyes staring at them with reproach.

The soldiers had started the fire in his study, using his books for kindling. Dhakar beat off the flames to make his way to his workroom outside. Fire threatened this structure as well, but he could still make his way inside. Some of his inventions had been stolen, likely for the brass fittings which could be melted down and sold. The rest had been smashed if possible.

Locked away in his hidden safe, his plans and diagrams had survived. Grimly, he thought that he could still make use of his plans—but something different than he intended before. These he snatched quickly, rolled them up, and put them into a round case. This he took with him—just before the roof collapsed.

Knowing that Banda held only bad memories, Dhakar gathered a few hidden handfuls of silver and the portrait of his late wife—all he had left of her now. Breaking apart the frame, he quickly rolled the canvas and put it in with his plans, then exited the burning building.

Before the night ended, Dhakar escaped the city.

12. Tumbling

The rebellion continued, but the rebels found the fighting ever more difficult against the better-organized British troops and artillery. Nana Saheb and Tatya Tope joined forces with Rani Lakshmi Bai and their combined Marathi troops made a stand at the city of Kalpi, southwest of Kanpur. Weeks later, their scouts found the troops of Major-General Sir Hugh Rose sluggishly approaching, though the rough terrain. They returned and reported the Redcoats to be ten thousand strong and ten miles away in the hills. Hearing this, Tatya Tope prepared the city's defenses.

On those walls, Lakshmi Bai and her second officer, Uda Devi, scanned the horizons with spyglasses. They spotted no Redcoats, but something did catch the rani's attention. She then hurried down the steps.

Unannounced, Lakshmi Bai entered the office commandeered by the nana. He and Tatya looked up from the map-cluttered desk. Lakshmi gave her superior officer a brief bow of the head.

"Yes, Rani?" said the weary nana.

"Nana," she said, "Uda and I see that you have no defenses to the north. The rear flank is wide open to the British."

Nana Saheb sighed. "Yes, yes. But the British are coming from the south. I will not waste my men when I need them elsewhere."

"Sire, the British will not fail to see an open flank," said the rani, astonished. "Rose is no fool; he will take any advantage we give him. Should he set up his cannons on those hills, his troops could easily pinch us."

"Yes, yes," said the nana, no longer hiding his exasperation. "If he does this, if he does that. We have real problems, Rani. Women giving me orders does not need to be one of them!"

Lakshmi Bai fumed for several seconds, then stormed towards the door, without bowing. Before she reached it, the nana barked out an order.

"You will leave your troops where I have ordered them to stand!"

She stopped for a second. Tatya Tope looked hard at the nana, but spoke no word. Without looking back at them, Lakshmi nodded. She then departed. Nana Saheb, having ignored her advice, then continued with his own plans.

Soon, the people of Kalpi saw dust clouds advancing from the south. Redcoats followed scarcely an hour later. As the rani predicted, the British did indeed spot the unprotected northern flank and set up their cannons on the ridge, largely surrounding the city. After the first few volleys, the Marathi troops found themselves in danger of being routed from two sides. Many fled in panic.

Defeated, Nana Saheb had little choice but to sound the retreat. He and some thousands of rebels hurriedly escaped the rapidly-closing cordon and Kalpi fell to the British. Upon entering the abandoned city, Major-General Rose found the wounded who had been left behind and hung them.

* * *

Miles outside the walls of Banda, Dhakar found four men waiting for him, all disheveled, bloodied, and filthy, like himself. These were Sandeep Lal, Masud, Niraj Khan, and Chundawat. Like Dhakar, they cried for the kind and caring Rani Asha and her children when they heard the news, for they had all grown to love the Rajah's family.

Not only had these engineers and sailors survived, but they were soon joined by some three dozen more. These were men he knew, who had all fought with Dhakar in various battles.

"Rajah," said Lal, "we all vow to fight for you until the bitter end." The other men, though exhausted, all nodded or voiced their agreement.

Dhakar could only fear that the end would be bitter indeed. Any one of these brave men, he knew, would gladly lay down his life for their rajah. That knowledge only made Dhakar sick, feeling unworthy of such devotion.

* * *

Under a blistering sun, Dhakar's general, Ram Gupta, had been led out to the artillery grounds. Redcoats tied his hands to the wheels of a cannon, with his back against the muzzle. He was not alone; twenty others, some men he knew, several he did not, had likewise been trussed up to cannons. These cannons, he'd observed earlier, were primed with a double load of gunpowder and chunks of rock salt. No cannonballs would be wasted. Ravens and feral dogs, having seen previous executions, waited anxiously.

Near him were strapped a Hindu and a Mahomedan. A tall Sikh sergeant came over to them. With only a glance, Gupta could tell these three men had a long-standing hatred.

"Maybe in your next life," said the Sikh, "you will listen to me."

The Mahomedan cursed a blue streak.

"In my next life and the life after," the Hindu said, "I will still rise up against tyrants and invaders—and you will still lick their boots!"

The Sikh only scoffed and walked off. Next, a list of crimes was read off by an officer in a language Gupta did not understand.

Then, at a command, several British gunners, in unison, set a flare against each of the cannons' touch holes.

The blast blew Gupta and the others to bits, flinging those bits across the artillery grounds, one arm flying to the left, one spinning to the right. The ravens took to the wing, catching pieces of flesh and entrails in the air. Seconds later, dogs ran to devour various chunks of flesh bouncing and rolling on the ground. Gupta's skull shattered on the ground and dogs fought for mouthfuls of his brain.

Justice had been served in the British Empire.

* * *

A month later, Dhakar and his loyal followers presented themselves to Nana Saheb, Tatya Tope, and the Rani of Jhansi. Lakshmi barely recognized Dhakar, now bearded, with wisps of gray, and his eyes aged and hollow. His men were no better. Still, the rebels welcomed even such a paltry force as this, given how desperate the situation had become.

Together, the rebel forces entered Gwalior State in June. At the gates of the city, they met resistance from troops loyal to the Maharajah Jayaji Rao. However, not all troops were loyal to this lackey of the EIC and within the hour, the maharajah found he had enemies inside his gates as well as outside.

The rebellious *sepoys* of Gwalior threw open those gates, allowing the army of Nana Saheb to pour in. Dhakar asked no one's permission, but immediately ordered his troops to charge in, with him at the head. Like never before, Dhakar charged into battle, slashing and hacking, left and right. Perhaps he sought death; if so, Death mocked him. He lived to stand beside Nana Saheb even as Jayaji Rao fled. Nana Saheb seized Gwalior, taking control of the city's impressive fortifications and there claiming for himself the title of *Peshwa* of the resurrected Marathi Empire. The rebels rejoiced, knowing this to be a great victory.

It would be their last.

* * *

Two weeks after the rebels took Gwalior, troops of the British Empire caught up with them. From the walls, the Peshwa Saheb, Tatya Tope, Rani Lakshmi Bai, and the Rajah Dhakar looked on as a massive British army began to spread out, rolling their cannons into place at Fort Serai, nearby.

The rani turned to an ashen-faced Peshwa Saheb, saying, “Listen to me this time, Peshwa! We cannot let them put their cannons in place. We must stop them now!”

“H-How?” Peshwa Saheb asked, faltering.

She looked first to him, then to her troops, who stood waiting for battle. To all of them she said, "Before their cannons are set in place, I intend to lead my cavalry out of the gates and break through their first line of attackers. We will charge the cannon emplacements at Serai before they get off a single shot. I will either be victorious or I will be among the first to fall. If so, let me be your martyr and continue the fight!"

Jhalkari Bai led a salute for her cousin, the rani. The cavalry of men and women waved their swords and lances and cheered. Peshwa Saheb nodded silently, not wishing to counter the rani again. If he did so and they failed again, he knew his own troops would desert him at once.

Dhakar stood a moment, wondering, doubting. Before Lakshmi could mount her horse, he stepped beside her. "Rani," he asked, "are you so comfortable, throwing away your life?"

Lakshmi gave him a tender smile. "Of course I am, Rajah. Should I fall, I will reincarnate to once more take up arms and fight against oppression. This is my destiny."

She mounted her horse and turned to face her troops. Never had Dhakar seen this fiery warrioress look so serene. Then she spoke to her people.

"We fight for independence," she said, raising her sword. "As Krishna says, if we are victorious, we will enjoy the fruits of victory; if defeated and killed on the field of battle, we shall surely earn eternal glory and salvation!"

Moments later, Lakshmi Bai and the cavalry flew from the gates of Jhansi. They charged the British flanks head on, hoping to prevent their use of the cannons. They met the surprised enemy in a hail of musket fire, under the roar of their Marathi battle cries.

* * *

On June 18, 1858, the Rani Lakshmi Bai fell at the Battle of Fort Serai just outside the walls of Gwalior. She had been shot in the back by a common British rifleman. She was twenty-nine.

Seeing the battle to be lost, the Peshwa Saheb ordered his troops to abandon the city and scatter. In the retreat, the British captured Tatya Tope—later, he would be hanged. Of Peshwa Saheb there were faint rumors from Nepal over the next several years, but he never again troubled the British Empire.

Dhakar had also fought on with his last score of men until he too ordered a retreat. He and his men rode from the flaming ruins of Gwalior in hopes of finding some safe haven.

For weeks Dhakar's last thirty men ran from the British and their bounty hunters, hiding in wild jungles and in abandoned temples. To their surprise, Dhakar led them to Sagar and Lake Lakha Banjara.

"I will not have the *Iron Buffalo* fall into the hands of the British," he explained. "If they find it and study it, they might build an even greater submersible, a weapon of warfare. Even if they do not use it against our people, they would use it against the other peoples they hope to oppress. This, we cannot allow."

So Dhakar and the others went to the lake and once more started the engines of the *Iron Buffalo*. The voltaic piles had drained somewhat in the last year, yet they needed very little energy for this operation. Wearing only loincloths, Dhakar and Chundawat powered the submersible out to the middle of the lake, with a rowboat in tow. Then Chundawat untied the small boat, got in, and rowed off a short distance.

Inside, Dhakar sealed the hatch and set the controls to begin descent. He sat there a moment, thinking the *Iron Buffalo* would make a fine tomb.

But no, he would not allow himself such luxuries. Before the craft reached the bottom, he opened its bottom hatch and swam out. The *Iron Buffalo* sank under the water, but Dhakar returned to the surface. He swam to the wooden boat and climbed in.

Dhakar had thought he would never again shed tears after losing his family. He was wrong.

After returning to the shore, he ordered his men to mount their horses again. They did so, riding ever westward, ever north, seeking the Punjabi border.

The Sikhs had allied themselves with the same British invaders that had crushed their empire, and many Sikh men found employment by fighting England's wars for her. For that reason, Dhakar hoped the British would not search for him in the Punjab, but there he knew the people and their language, taught to him by his late wife. Thus Dhakar led his men to the last place on Earth he ever thought he would seek asylum.

Dhakar rode for Shaitanabad.

13. Salvage

By November of 1858, the British forces had utterly crushed the Sepoy Revolt and even the last few holdouts realized that fact. Dhakar knew it. The British had won and they had placed a bounty on his head. For the first time, he employed a pseudonym.

Prior to the Sepoy Mutiny of 1857, forty thousand Englishmen and women lived in India. By the end of the mutiny, six thousand of them were dead. Tens of thousands of their loyal *sepoys* perished in the fighting against their rebellious brothers. Yet even those numbers pale before the half million slain by the British and their allies, be they *sepoy* or citizen. That number would double if one included all who died due to the accompanying plague, famine, and dysentery that has ever followed war.

The people of India had come closer to uniting than ever before. As a result, the East India Company ordered their unity shattered as few people would ever experience. Massacres and reprisals fell upon not only the *sepoys* who revolted, but common citizens as well. Women and children suffered even more than the men, as sexual abuse of the defeated is ever rampant at the hands of the victors. Of those who actually took part in the rebellion, brutal executions—hanging and blowing men from cannons—followed their defeat. Yet back in England, not all approved of the news from India.

"We are not pleased to hear of Englishmen committing wholesale massacres and depredations upon our Indian charges," said a cross Queen Victoria, to her ministers. "Upon learning of the results of the British East India Company's ghastly policies, we do hereby order Parliament to revoke their charter and dissolve all their holdings."

The British government decreed that the brutal East India Company to be no longer capable of controlling its holdings and should never again bring the Empire into a costly war. After several rounds of Parliament, the peoples of India became the direct subjects of the British crown. The country would henceforth by ruled by the newly formed British Raj. The armies would be reformed and reorganized. No longer would the occupying army consist of one Briton for up to nine natives. Rather, the ratio would be no less than one in four. Further, the *sepoys* would be allowed to advance to the ranks of officers, thus diminishing the inequality of the Indians who served them.

Her Majesty meant well, but for the people of India her reforms were too little and came far too late. It would take another ninety years and very different tactics to achieve a semblance of the goal of Indian independence.

Epilogue

For months, Dhakar and his last two dozen men ran from the British and their bounty hunters, hiding out in arid deserts and in the slums of a dozen cities. Dhakar led them ever westward, ever north, ever closer to the Punjabi border.

At last in Shaitanabad, Dhakar sought sanctuary at the court of Chambu Singh. Singh had more gray hairs and less patience these days. Indeed, on finding Dhakar and his men upon his doorstep, he promptly had them arrested.

"Your betrayal will be punished, Chambu!" Dhakar sneered, struggling futilely against the Dacoits who had laid hold of him. "In this life or the next! Would you sell me to the British for a pardon?"

"I require no pardon, Rajah," said Chambu Singh, calmly. "No one knows that I aided the rebel cause but for you and the late queen of Jhansi, may her soul find rest in her next life. My fellow Sikhs believe I only aided the British."

"Then why do you put me in chains?"

A wisp of a smile passed Singh's thin lips. "My cause is greater than this miserable rebellion of yours. I have my orders and I obey them. Fear not, for you and your men shall be allowed all the comforts you require and the means by which to continue your work."

Dhakar had ceased struggling and raised an eyebrow. "What do you know of my work?"

"I? Nothing. But others have caught wind of your little scrawls and scribbles. It is their wish, not mine, that allows you to live. Until their emissary arrives, you may have the run of my humble palace. Take one step outside its walls and it will be your last. Even if you should be so fortunate as to escape, I will have every one of your men crushed beneath the feet of my elephants."

Dhakar clenched his fists at hearing the threat. He would have throttled the life from Singh this very moment, had he any doubt that the Dacoits would fulfill his orders.

"Now," said Chambu Singh with a smirk, "let's see about making you presentable. You should receive a guest in due time."

"What guest?" he asked, suspiciously.

"A guest from the East."

MACHINATIONS

1. The Imperial Harem

Kuo, captain of the guards of the Chamber of Imperial Concubines, regarded the tall man who approached. He peered at his half-shaved head, his elaborate robes, his conical red hat. Mostly, Kuo sneered at the man's short steps and stiff gait. He faced the man—not that the word "man" described the fellow. He stood between the approaching fellow and the ornate doorway leading to the inner chamber.

"Who are you?" Captain Kuo demanded with suspicion. "I don't know you."

The robed man stopped and regarded him flatly. "I am Shun, honorable captain. I have been sent by Duke Hui'zheng to serve under the High Clerk. An Dehai, the Chief of the Eunuchs, was to have been here to vouch for me, but I have heard he has been called away to deal with some matter. Please, honorable sir, I must enter to attend my duties."

Kuo curled his lip. "I don't care who sent you or who you are sent to! Only eunuchs are allowed beyond this door!"

"Yes," said the man called Shun, with a quick nod of his head.

Kuo smirked. "Prove it."

The newcomer stared at the captain a moment. Then he reached down and lifted his robes, raising them up to his waist.

Kuo cocked his head and took a good look, despite how the sight disgusted him. This person, supposedly a man, had no more genitals than a woman. Only a slit appeared between his legs.

Kuo rose up and sneered. "So, you truly are qualified to go among the women. Then go."

The newcomer bowed his head low and walked past the captain. When he was around the corner and out of sight, he stopped.

The man identified as Shun relaxed his abdominal muscles and, with a silent wince, allowed his testicles and then his penis to descend once more.

He wiped perspiration from his face and took a deep breath or two. It had been easy to do this as a child. Of all his skills, the ability to retract his genitals was now the least favorite of Huang Zhou.

* * *

"If I cannot find her, I will create her," Huang Zhou once said, in hopes of finding and promoting the Universal Ruler who'd been prophesized in Antediluvian scriptures. For a time, he thought that the future ruler of the world might be the bold and courageous Rani

Lakshmi Bai of Bundelkhand, so he had aided her campaign with strategy, arms, money, and most importantly, information.

Alas, none of his efforts had been sufficient. The Indian Mutiny ended in disaster; the Rani was dead; the rebels scattered or broken or dead. Only Chambu Singh, who had kept his allegiance secret, managed to come out unscathed. The mutiny may have caused the British to postpone their war against the Celestial Empire, but now Cathay was again their target, and Huang Zhou determined that the cause of the Sepoy Revolt was lost.

He now turned his attention once more to his homeland in May of 1858. He returned to Hunan Province once more, there meeting with his sponsor among the Order of the White Peacock, Minister Ki Ming. Yet still, the Mandarin Shu offered a bounty for his head.

Shortly thereafter, British troops laid siege to the treaty port of Tien'tsin in the north. If Tien'tsin fell, the road would be open for the English to march straight to the nearby gates of Peking and the Forbidden City.

Therefore, by mutual agreement of the emperor and the Mandarin of the White Peacock Order, Hei Hu—the Black Tiger—was ordered to Tien'tsin. His task was to aid the Mongol general with the defense of the pivotal city. Attending him once more were assassins of the On Lung Tong—the Tong of the Green Dragons.

The Ta-Ku Forts of Tien'tsin had lately been constructed to protect the seaport against the invaders and Hei Hu saw to the training of their gunners. More important, Hei Hu employed the sort of deceit of which the Order of the White Peacock were masters.

They spread rumors that the forts had only skeleton crews in place and were unprepared for battle. The portholes of the Chinese guns were covered. Learning of this, a British armada of fifteen warships was sent to take the forts. On the morning of June 25th, the admiral of the flotilla nonetheless carefully approached the first boom of chains and heavy timbers that had been put in place across the river to stop them. This they cut through with ease and without a single shot fired from either defending fort. The first of four ships then steamed its way upriver to the second boom.

Secretly, silently, Hei Hu and his hidden men watched as the steel-clad British ships attempted to ram the next boom, as the first had been so flimsy. This one, however, had been constructed securely, with many thick chains double-wrapped around sturdy pilons sunk deep in the river. It held fast. While the other three ships drew close, and offered assistance and suggestions of what to do next, Hei Hu gave a prearranged signal. At once, the false porthole covers dropped, revealing a half dozen large Chinese guns on either fort. With a second signal, the Chinese guns fired.

A cannon shot rang out, the ball hitting the all-important bow gunner of the admiral's ship, taking off his head. Volley after volley followed from the forts, shattering one ship after another. Before it was over, six of the fifteen foreign ships had been sunk or run aground in the mud, including the British admiral's flagship. The admiral had been wounded, but he managed to narrowly escape in one of the surviving crafts.

The Mandarin Shu, General Rin'chen, and Hei Hu all considered this to be a great victory. Huang Zhou knew better.

"The British shall withdraw only until reinforcements arrive from India," he said. "Then they will return with vengeance in their hearts."

* * *

A week later, Huang Zhou's thoughts were not of war or rebellion. Rather, the grandeur and the immediacy of the Chamber of the Imperial Concubines filled his mind. One concubine in particular held his attention.

Removing the hat and wig that had aided his disguise as the eunuch Shun, he presented himself to Noble Consort Yi, she who had once been known as Xing'zhen. Today, as a woman and not a girl, she was more beautiful than ever. Motherhood had only enhanced her noble bearing and her shrewd intelligence.

On her knee, she gently rocked the emperor's heir as she regarded the tall man once more. She smirked.

"So, has my mentor paid the price to enter the Chamber of Imperial Concubines?" she asked, bemused. "I hope my humble self proves worthy of such a sacrifice."

Huang Zhou gave her a stare that had withered bloodthirsty warriors. Yet Yi did not flinch, at least not until her child began to scream.

"You frighten the baby, Huang Zhou," she said, comforting the child.

"The child is not a baby," Huang Zhou commented. "He is four years old, yet he fears his own shadow."

Yi shrugged. "And so? Do you come all the way to the Forbidden City, risking your neck and your dick, to criticize my abilities as a mother?"

"I care nothing for your ability to raise a child. I care only for your ability to govern a nation. And greater things."

She scoffed as she dried the child's tears with a silk

handkerchief. "Your ambitions are ever greater than mine, Huang Zhou. Do you truly believe the entire world will fall at my feet?"

"It is my belief that stranger things have happened."

Noble Consort Yi conceded the point. Huang Zhou then gave her a pair of long brass "nails", to be worn on her last two fingers. These nails were more that just decorations as any man who might attempt to interfere with her would learn.

"I wish you to remain safe," Huang Zhou said, "as I wish to guide your ambitions and achieve all our goals."

For the next two hours they drank tea while Huang Zhou delineated the Order's ancient past, as well as its current state and its likely future. He further related other matters which he felt she needed to be aware, such as the recent discovery of the planet Vulcan within the orbit of Mercury and his ongoing search for the Rajah Dhakar who he believed had survived the collapse of the Sepoy Revolt.

They reaffirmed their alliance: he swore to aid her ambitions and she promised to keep him informed about the inner workings of the Forbidden Palace. They then engaged in carnal acts for another hour or so.

Afterwards, Huang Zhou rose, bowed to the imperial concubine, then departed. By this time, Chief Eunuch An Dehai—Yi's favorite and a servant of the Order—had arrived and vouched for him to exit without incident—and without having to once more prove his qualifications.

Yet upon leaving the Forbidden City, Huang Zhou had doubts. It seemed to him that Noble Consort Yi had enjoyed and even relished his tales of the ancient past yet only tolerated his recounting of the events of the present. When he had mentioned the future, she ignored him altogether.

2. Panic in the Forbidden City

After his victory at Tien'tsin, Hei Hu went to Canton in the south, where he and his troop of agents again aided in the defense of that city, should the British attempt an invasion from their garrison in nearby Hong Kong.

Three American ships had also been ordered to the great, bustling port city of Canton to protect the American businesses there. Their orders also included the clear instruction of avoiding conflicts with the natives, and this they did. As they had encountered no problems for the few weeks they bivouacked within the walls, the American commander, James Armstrong, eventually gave the order to withdraw.

However, Hei Hu spotted Armstrong's second-in-command, Commander Foote, in a small rowboat, being transported to his own ship, the *Portsmouth*. For Hei Hu, the easy target was too tempting to pass by.

"Chow!" he cried to the best marksman in the garrison. "The American captain is escaping! Shoot him!"

Chow fired off round after round in quick succession. Some in the garrison thought he must be hunting birds and others thought he must be "saluting" the departing Americans. However, the distance was too great. None of the American sailors were hurt and only a few balls stuck in the skiff.

But American pride—always a delicate subject—had been wounded. Commodore Armstrong insisted that the Chinese be made to pay for their disrespect towards his second-in-command. Rather than retreat, the screw-driven sloops-of-war, *Portsmouth* and *Levant*, accompanied by the far smaller, but faster and well-armed warship, *San Jacinto*, steamed into position before the five forts on the Pearl River that protected Canton.

On November 16, the bombardment commenced. Over the next four days, four of the five forts were captured, hundreds of Green Standard soldiers were killed, and scores of cannons were captured. Many of these guns were turned on the Chinese, bringing about even more slaughter. Afterwards, they were spiked and abandoned.

Hei Hu noted that neither of the American sloops, but rather the small, screw-driven warship, *Jacinto*, inflicted most of the damage on the Chinese army, sending them running. While hiding amid the rubble, watching the small ship sitting in the river, untouchable, Hei Hu heard her crew howl in celebration. Rising up, fuming, unable to hold it in any longer, he cried out.

"May that ship be forever cursed!"

* * *

A year passed before the Anglo-French Alliance once more besieged Tien'tsin.

"Again??" the Mandarin Shu bellowed, upon hearing the news. "Hei Hu, can you not defeat them once and for all?"

Hei Hu dropped to his knees and bowed, stifling his frustration and anger as best he could. "Honorable Mandarin, I have done all I can with the resources I am given. I have twice repulsed the barbarian invaders with only the aid of a few Green Dragons. But now the British are joined by French troops and ships. The war goes badly and I cannot stop such an armada alone. I require assistance. Maybe more agents or a troop of worthy soldiers."

Shu rolled his eyes. "It is ever more excuses with you, Hei Hu. Can I not depend on you to raise a simple army?"

"Sire!" Hei Hu said, raising his head and trying to control his anger. "The emperor holds back the Mongol hordes at his command. He will not speak with me, but you have his ear. I ask only that you command him to send troops he already possesses!"

Shu leaned back on his throne, stroked his white beard, and gave thought to the proposition. Beside him, his chief concubine, Sin Yee, regarded the mandarin yet kept her council to herself until asked. She was not asked.

Eventually, at the behest of the Mandarin, the Xian'feng Emperor summoned the seventy thousand Mongol infantry and twelve thousand cavalry to reinforce the Ta-Ku Forts at Tien'tsin. With such forces, could anyone doubt the victory of the Ching Empire?

* * *

"Hei Hu's scheme is doomed to fail," said Huang Zhou.

Ki Ming nodded as he paced across the floor of his chamber. "But what can we do to save the city? I see no salvation."

"We shall do nothing to aid Shu's scheme, Master. We shall allow him to fail."

Master Ki stopped in his tracks, regarding his willful student with a gaping mouth. Rather than allowing him to find words, Huang Zhou explained.

"By failing to save Tien'tsin," he said, "all our members will see that the Mandarin is unfit to lead the White Peacock. Thus enlightened, they will demand change."

Ki Ming sat down, resting his chin on his fist for some minutes. Nothing held his gaze, and his eyes flitted first left then right. Ki Ming had long since known that the Mandarin was mistaken and dangerous, not only to the goals of the Order, but to all China. Now he realized that he and Huang Zhou might be able to do something about him. Something dangerous.

Finally, he looked up at Huang Zhou.

"So be it," he said.

* * *

"*They will only return.*" The words of Huang Zhou echoed in Hei Hu's mind.

By August of 1860, additional British ships, heavy laden with troops and guns, had arrived from India to once more aid in the third siege of the Ta-Ku Forts. Were that not enough, this time the British were joined by their French allies. Even the Russians agreed to take part.

The Celestial forces held for a time, but the English and French guns and mortars had greater range. They could sit downriver from the forts and fire with impunity—the Chinese cannonballs fell short of their targets and rested at the bottom of the river. The battle became a massacre and Celestials died by the hundreds.

Officially, the Americans were neutral, but once a renegade American captain allowed his crew to aid the gunners of a ship flying the Union Jack. It was the first time since before 1776 that the forces of the two former enemies had fought side-by-side. The American captain reasoned, "Blood's thicker than water." Before the onslaught from the steel-clad ships, the Ta-Ku Forts crumbled.

Later that month, the Anglo-French coalition shattered the walls of Tien'tsin and scattered the Mongol and Green Banner armies which had defended the city. Devastation and slaughter fell upon the city. Afterward, nothing stood between the invaders and the capital of the Ching Empire, Peking.

The Mandarin Shu was livid, screaming at all and sundry for their failure to save the tottering empire. Most of all, he railed against Hei Hu and ordered his agents to find the Black Tiger and bring him back to Hunan, dead or alive.

Not a single agent, upon hearing those orders, relished them. They knew Hei Hu had been given an impossible task. Worst yet, they knew Hei Hu to be the fiercest warrior and the finest assassin among them. Not a one of them would stand a chance against the claws of the Black Tiger.

* * *

By September, the British had pitched their tents outside the gates of Peking.

"The Celestial Empire will be overrun by barbarians!" said Empress Consort Zhen, formerly known as Concubine Niohuru. She stated the obvious as she surveyed the expanse of the Forbidden City. Servants and soldiers ran back and forth in the massive courtyard below her, attempting to bolster its ancient defenses. Beyond the gates of the capital, a huge foreign army amassed.

"Indeed, and what of it?" asked he who was forbidden to be there. "Cathay has been overrun by barbarians before, both Mongols and Manchurians."

"What?" the empress consort returned, instinctively covering the ears of her daughter, the young princess beside her. "I am a Manchurian."

"Your ancestors were every bit as barbaric as the British and French which now assail the cities of the Celestial Empire," replied

Huang Zhou. "These new barbarians will surely sack Peking as did your Manchurian ancestors before these and the Mongols before them. The proper question to ask is whether the forthcoming invasion is to the advantage of the White Peacock or not."

"I think it is not!" interjected Noble Consort Yi, who was also present. Her son, the emperor's heir, was off somewhere with one or another tutor, whose lessons he routinely ignored.

"I concur," he answered. "It is through the Celestial Empire that the goals of the Order of the White Peacock will best be advanced. Or to put it another way, my candidates for the forthcoming World Leader are both Manchurian. It is only fitting that there remains a Manchurian Empire through which one or the other of you may lead."

"Yes, but what does that mean for us? The foreigners have surrounded the city. There is no escape!"

"They have yet to completely surround the city," he replied calmly. "There remains an avenue of escape."

"Run away from these barbarians?" Empress Consort Zhen said, aghast at the thought.

"Run or die," said her fellow consort, Yi, before Huang Zhou had the opportunity to express the same thought.

Concerned for Yi and Zhen, his candidates to become the forthcoming World Leader, Huang Zhou had traveled to the Forbidden City in hopes of saving them from the doom that was fated to fall upon the capital. He could not save Peking, but he could save these two—if they allowed him.

"Noble consorts," he said, stepping to them so that the three of them stood in a triangle, "the Imperial Court must gather their belongings and be ready to leave within the hour. Order your servants to pack your belongings in the caravan I have assembled outside. Take only the most essential items for we can spare no time. The city's gates are not yet barred against attack nor are the walls manned with sharpshooters, but they will be soon, ere the British guns begin to fire.

"Next," he said, and here he looked to Yi, whom he deemed far more influential and capable than Zhen, "implore upon the emperor the need to evacuate. Peking is only a city, but he is the Empire. Should he perish at the hands of these barbarians, the empire will collapse. This we cannot allow. If he does not leave willingly, I shall have him given a draught of an elixir which shall render him unconscious and he shall ride to Changsha over the back of a mule."

Zhen was shocked. Yi stifled a laugh before stating, "It shall be done, Master. I believe the emperor realizes the danger and will be amenable to keeping his hide intact, without the need to describe the colorful fate you would promise him."

"Good. Yet keep it in mind."

Then Zhen spoke. "Master, you would have us go to Changsha? Earlier, when we spoke of this contingency with His Serene Majesty and his councilors, it was determined that should it be necessary to flee, we would flee to Cheng'de."

Yi agreed. "It is better that we go to Cheng'de, as the palace is much better and there is not so much climbing in the mountains. Also, Prince Zai'yuan and the Imperial Court, insist that we continue to wait."

"Yes, Cheng'de the gardens and fountains are much more beautiful," Huang Zhou said, for once allowing his sarcasm to show. "What would the prince have us wait for? A British bayonet in the emperor's gut?"

"Those are his orders, Master."

"And has the emperor forgotten how to give orders in his own court?" Huang Zhou asked rhetorically. "I shall speak to this Zai'yuan at once."

He clapped his hands together twice, ending the brief meeting. Zhen went off to her duty, rounding up the court's servants and setting them to packing the essentials and loading the caravan. Yi, however, led Huang Zhou through the unusually chaotic halls of the Forbidden City, to the chambers of the Prince Zai'yuan, he who had been personally raised to the First Rank of councilors by the emperor himself.

Noble Consort Yi bowed to the surprised prince and his numerous assistants and clerks. "Lord," she said, "This man is Doctor Huang Zhou, and it is imperative that you hear his message."

With that, she bowed again and backed out of the room.

The stunned silence lasted but an instant before the courtiers turned on Huang Zhou. Then they spoke at once, nearly obliterating one another's tirade.

"Who are you?"

"What is this message, why is it important?"

"Why did a whore introduce you, even if she is the emperor's whore?"

Huang Zhou ignored the impertinent questions, viewing each and all of them through his lowered inner eyelid.

"Silence," he said.

They all ceased to speak, including Prince Zai'yuan. Save for the High Councilor himself, these were men accustomed to kowtowing and obeying the will of a dominate figure—and Huang Zhou was the most dominating man they would ever meet.

“We require privacy,” Huang Zhou said. Before Zai'yuan could reply, his courtiers, advisors, and clerks all filed out of the room. The prince stood and watched them depart, stunned.

When the last of them had departed, Huang Zhou stood close to Zai'yuan, looming over him.

“The safety of the emperor and the emperor's court is of the utmost importance,” said Huang Zhou. “You will aid the consorts, Zhen and Yi, in this endeavor.”

Zai'yuan, a man used to giving orders, not taking them, was not hypnotized. “How dare you!” he said, attempting to seethe, but in fact shuddering. “Who are you to give me orders?”

Huang Zhou regarded him a moment. The pause did nothing to soothe the prince's nerves. Then, leaning closer, Huang Zhou answered him in a calm and steady voice. “I am the man who will kill you if you forestall these orders in any way.”

* * *

With expediency, the caravan was loaded, although there was some argument between Empress Consort Zhen and the actual Empress over certain items to be left behind. As the drivers awaited the order to proceed, Huang Zhou found the two ladies at the final, overloaded wagon, waving their arms and flaring their eyes at one another.

“These perfumes came from farthest Araby,” said an aghast Consort Zhen. “They are worth their weight in gold! Even more!”

“I do not care, you mindless whore!” cried the livid empress. “This mirror has stood in the Hall of the Auspicious Hegemony since the reign of the Kang'xi Emperor!”

Huang Zhou decided the matter by hefting the case of Arabian perfumes and hurling it into the full-length mirror. With a loud crash, the priceless items were rendered into a fragrant pool of glass shards.

Huang Zhou turned to the startled ladies. In a flat voice he asked, “Are there any other issues which I might rectify?”

Neither lady voiced a complaint.

However, there was a dispute of greater importance, which the emperor, via his councilors, imparted to Huang Zhou. The emperor had decreed that the caravan would travel to the Summer Resort of Cheng'de and only Cheng'de. Standing with the resolute Prince Gong and the wily General Rin'chen was Noble Consort Yi.

“Honorable sirs,” said Huang Zhou, “it is imperative that His Gracious Emperor be brought to Changsha, where I can guarantee his safety, even should Queen Victoria herself lead every soldier and marine at her disposal.”

“But it is the emperor's will!” said Prince Gong, not afraid but clearly aware of the need to hurry. Both of them knew Huang Zhou by repute and they both had heard vague rumors of the Order of the White Peacock.

Noble Consort Yi moved between Gong and the agent of the White Peacock. She looked up at Huang Zhou, resolute.

"Cheng'de is closer," she said to him. "The path you propose goes through dangerous mountains and the horses will move slowly. Therefore, I have convinced the emperor to hold up in Cheng'de which is surrounded by mountains and therefore defensible."

Huang Zhou regarded the young whore, the beautiful and intelligent lady, the potential future empress of the world. He had wanted to bring them all, even the worthless emperor, to Changsha for safety, yes—but also to show off his abilities to the Mandarin Shu. Surely the mandarin would rescind his death sentence when he saw Huang Zhou's prize. Perhaps the mandarin would even grant him a proper title.

Instead, Huang Zhou bowed to Noble Consort Yi. To his chagrin, he admitted to himself that she was right: The emperor and his consorts would all be safer on the journey to Cheng'de.

Huang Zhou remained in Peking, for he still had a task to attend. Yet silently, he found himself annoyed with the Noble Consort.

3. An Empire Totters

The Celestial Empire found itself rocked not only by war from without, but by rebellions within. Some rebels had ancient grievances, others had new religions they wished to promulgate, but all these rebels agreed the Emperor and his court were incapable of dealing with the foreign invaders.

In the south, the Taiping Revolt grew day by day and the emperor's armies found themselves in flight. In the north, the Red Turbaned Rebels still held on. Worst of all for the Ching Empire, British and French troops marched unhindered from Tien'tsin on the coast to the Imperial City of Peking.

By September of 1860, the confident British Empire sent a team of negotiators ahead to Peking, in hopes of brokering a surrender with the Ching Dynasty. Consul Harry Parkes, popular with the British public after hunting down the despised Imperial Commissioner Ye Ming'chen and throwing him in the already infamous Black Hole of Calcutta, was clearly the man to lead the team.

However, the Xian'feng Emperor looked less kindly on the choice of the blustering and devious Parkes to negotiate anything. He ordered the British delegation arrested outside of Peking by the Mongol general, Sennge Rin'chen. On the orders of the Mandarin Shu, any pretense of diplomatic immunity was thrown to the wind. In a similar manner to the accommodations of the Black Hole, the Englishmen were thrown in dark, dank cells where they were beaten and tortured. Within a week, only Parkes and one other man were alive.

Someone at last realized this treatment of British officials would only inflame the advancing British troops and their queen, not to mention the British public. In the second week of October, Parkes and the other survivor were released and allowed to return to the British lines, an hour before the emperor's order for their execution arrived.

"The Mandarin Shu's plans have once again backfired," noted Huang Zhou. "This will only be to the advantage of the Order, in the long run."

"Yes, yes," Ki Ming agreed, nervously. "But the short run might get all of us killed."

Huang Zhou ignored his master's pessimism. "Shu's latest scheme has resulted only in a desire among the Western forces for revenge. To no one's surprise, Lord Elgin, the British High Commissioner to China, horrified by the emperor's treatment of England's ambassadors, spoke of entering Peking and destroying the Forbidden City. Fortunately, cooler heads prevailed and he instead issued orders that the Old Summer Palace outside Peking to be razed."

"The old palace?" asked Ki Ming, aghast. "Even that is a terrible loss! The treasures!"

"Indeed, yet this is the best for which we can hope. I shall make certain that everyone within the Order of the White Peacock knows that this idiotic blunder was caused by Shu, and Shu alone.

"At that time, I shall inform Shu."

* * *

The Mandarin Shu looked once more at the paper crumpled in his hand. The scroll had been delivered by a messenger he did not know. Obviously, it had originated from Huang Zhou, informing him that the British had designs on the Summer Palace, intending to have it looted and burned within a day.

"And, of course," railed the Mandarin, "the jabbering monkey's price for giving me this information is a pardon!"

The Mandarin's curses reverberated off the walls of the empty chamber and echoed back to his ears. Once the echoes ceased, the ancient halls were left in utter silence. He looked around, still marveling that he had found his palace abandoned this morning. Everyone in the Order had turned on him the day before. One by one, they had all left in the night.

Now, the Mandarin regarded the lavish but empty marble halls of Sang-Wah, the palace of the White Peacock, hidden in the hills above Changsha. He was utterly alone.

Hundreds of miles away, he knew, the Summer Palace of the emperors of China stood in the hills overlooking Peking. The serene compound spread over acres of beautiful gardens, ornate pavilions, glimmering ponds, and stone bridges, all designed with the finest of aesthetic concordance in mind. Within the expanse, numerous temples and shrines surrounded a sumptuous marble palace filled with a thousand years' collection of art, literature, and records.

Among those records, he likewise knew, lay the accords between the Order of the White Peacock and the Imperial Ching Courts. Alone or not, he had to take action—at once. Shu raced at once to Peking.

* * *

Through secret tunnels, of which neither Ki Ming nor Huang Zhou had been given any knowledge, the Mandarin Shu personally appeared within the Summer Palace. His last hirelings within Peking—not members of his own Order, for those had fled from him—informed him that the English queen had expressly forbade Lord Elgin from destroying the Forbidden City. Shu cursed this report, as he would rather watch the great complex of relatively modern palaces and treasuries burned to the ground than lose that which lay within the chambers beneath the ancient Summer Palace.

These records alone guaranteed that the Celestial Emperor would remain loyal, thus it was essential that they be protected—at all costs. Never mind that some of the greatest treasures in the empire were threatened, the alliance between that empire and the Order of the White Peacocks stood precariously near imminent collapse. Worse yet, if the plunderers discovered the thousands of documents contained in the secret vaults of the Summer Palace, the machinations of the Order of the White Peacock might be revealed to the outside world!

Shu found the pleasure palace of the imperial family to be every bit as chaotic as Peking itself—maybe worse. Here and there ran servants, carrying bundles of silken garments or chests of jewels. No! These were not servants—all of them had already fled. These were the high lords and administrators of the empire, scurrying to salvage anything they could.

He spotted a man—Yin Nao, a paid agent of the White Peacock in the past. Clutching a bundle of tally sheets and records, the man rushed through the gilded hallway. Holding up his hand, Shu stopped him as surely as a stone wall.

"Yin Nao, where is the emperor?" the mandarin demanded.

"His Majesty is gone!" the accountant cried. "A man came and led the court and household out just in time. The foreign devils are just outside and we have no defenses! We must go—now!"

"No," said Shu. "You will not leave until you tell me what I wish to know. Who was this helpful man who led our emperor to safety?"

"I-I do not know. I have seen him before, but no one knows his name. He is a confident of the Imperial Concubines. He is very tall and has the eyes of a snake—or a demon!"

Huang Zhou!

The Mandarin Shu allowed the man to leave, not caring if Yin Hao would be able to escape the fast-closing cordon of British troops. Rather, Shu made his way to the emperor's throne room, even as the roar of advancing soldiers echoed from beyond the all-too-thin walls of the palace.

The throne room stood pristine and unusually empty. He passed through without pause, hurrying down a private corridor into which he had not stepped for half a century. There he fingered a half-hidden niche, lifting a bit of delicate moulding, and bringing a faint click to his ear. He then slid an ornate paneled section of wall to the side. An aperture appeared beyond.

As the door behind him pivoted on weighed hinges and closed, he hurried down the steps. Overhead, the echoes of screams and hoots of laughter issued from outermost gates. The British had entered the emperor's Summer Palace. Shu knew of ways in and out of this palace that the barbarians could not imagine, but he had very little time.

He pushed open a heavy bronze door, pivoting on hinges set in place even before the Mongols held sway in this land. He closed it behind him, lest by some trick of fortune these new barbarians managed to get this far within the next hour. He knew he would need less than half that time.

He entered the large Chamber of the Secret Archives. Shelves on either side, laden with scrolls thousands of years old, he ignored. Catalogs of global explorations, stunningly ancient histories, celestial commentaries, sexual techniques, and scientific inventions meant nothing to him. His only concern was the dragon-carved cabinet at the far end.

The Mandarin Shu hurried to the cabinet. This ark held four thousand years of compacts, accords, records, reports, and transactions between the Order of the White Peacock and the imperial court—all the courts, be they Han Chinese, Mongol, or Manchurian. These records alone guaranteed that the various emperors would remain loyal—more important, if they fell into the wrong hands, their secret alliances might be revealed to the world! He took hold of the ornate lock.

It slipped loosely in his hand. Indeed, one of the small doors fell off. He stepped back and, with bulging eyes, viewed the interior of the cabinet.

Its shelves sat empty—save for a single sheet of paper. Shu did not want to read the words written on that paper. Yet he did.

> Mandarin, when I sought only to benefit the Order of the White Peacock, you sought to end my existence. Even so, I gave you the opportunity to change. Instead, you held the White Peacock where it has been since you took up your honored position, never changing and never growing. As such it has been mandated that a new order must arise of which you shall play no part.
>
> --The Yellow Claw

From overhead came the sound of wild soldiers tearing tapestries from the walls, grabbing what gold statuary they could, and smashing what they could not. Yet Shu heard nothing—his thoughts and questions overwhelmed his senses.

"I should have boiled him alive the day I first laid eyes on that accursed, big-headed freak!"

His words reverberated through the deep chamber, mocking him. As the echoes faded, they were replaced with the sounds of carnage, the laughter of rioting soldiers, the screams of women and eunuchs.

Shaking his head in disbelief, the mandarin turned and went back to the bronze door through which he had entered. He would find these rebellious agents of his and subdue them. He would prove to them that his will was not to be defied. He would have revenge on them all.

He returned the great outer door, set his hand on it, and pushed. It did not move. He tried to pull the lever but it did not budge.

The mandarin's heart seemed to lodge in his throat as he realized the extent of the plot against him. As the heat from the burning palace overhead became palatable, he realized that the Chamber of the Secret Archives was to become his tomb.

"Huang Zhou!!"

The echoes of his own voice seemed to repeat forever.

* * *

The emperor's Summer Palace was looted and burned to the ground on October 18, 1860, destroying millennia of priceless artwork. Anything made of gold or encrusted with gems was stolen by soldiers, only to be hocked for a night's worth of liquor or whores. Documents and rice-paper records dating back thousands of years had been engulfed in flames. If it could not be burned or shattered, it was pissed on. General Gordon would thereafter be known as "Chinese" Gordon, a term of honor for bringing the ancient empire to its knees, for on the following day, the Ching Empire agreed to Britain and France's terms of surrender.

On the previous day, as the foreign armies still marched to Peking, Huang Zhou had got word to Noble Consort Yi, telling her to convince the slow-witted Xian'feng Emperor to withdraw from the capital before he found himself on the end of an English rope. Yi, knowing that failure to do so would place the entire Imperial Court in peril, did so.

In addition, Huang Zhou had sent his companion-in-arms, Hei Hu, to safeguard their journey, this time to Rehe Province in the north. Fleeing the barbarians in such an ignoble manner, Noble Consort Yi would thereafter thirst for revenge against the Western powers, hoping to punish them.

Huang Zhou had remained, alone, at the Summer Palace long enough to discover the location of the hidden chamber and make off with one certain bundle of scrolls—the records of the dealings of the Ching Dynasty with the Order of the White Peacock. They were in his hand not an hour before Shu entered the chamber.

4. The Peacock in Full Display

"The war went most badly for the Ching Empire," said Ki Ming, shortly before he was to be officially accorded the title of Mandarin of Changsha—the *de facto* title of the leader of the White Peacock. "The Chinese had ten times the fighting men of the British and French, yet they took rather more than ten times the casualties."

Huang Zhou bowed his head. "Once again, the terms of the treaty are anything but equal."

Ki Ming blinked as an expression of resignation. Both men stood within the throne room of Sang-Wah, citadel of the White Peacock, awaiting the coronation to begin. The event had been delayed by the need for two items.

Huang Zhou and Ki Ming had waited a year for the flames to cool and for both the ground and the political situation to settle before returning to the ruins of the palace. By night they dug until they found the door to the Chamber of the Secret Archives. Within, the heat from the fires above had burned all the scrolls, artwork, and maps. The heat had also baked and mummified the body of the Mandarin Shu.

They took that which had not burned—the emerald-clasping silver ring that Shu had worn for the past seven decades. This ring Ki Ming took and placed upon his own finger.

Along with the matter of retrieving the silver ring, there was the need to acquire an actual albino peacock for the ceremony. The eyes and ears of the Order had scoured all of the Celestial Empire before one hatched at an aviary in Yunnan Province. That ceremony had been conducted yesterday; today's ceremony was another matter.

Servants entered now and unrolled a verdant carpet all the way from the throne to the main door. Walking along this, Ki Ming took his seat.

The rest of the surviving members of the White Peacock then entered the throne chamber, with Dai'yu and Yao Ling taking their place beside Huang Zhou on one side. On the other side stood Sin Yee, the mandarin's former courtesan. Even the albino peacock was present, although the bird's presence was not required today. The last to enter was Hei Hu, now in black leather armor, with a heavy dao—machete—strapped to his waist via a white sash.

Huang Zhou stood before the new mandarin and bowed to him once more.

"Mandarin," he said upon rising, "Hei Hu aided the emperor and his court to escape the clutches of the British aggressors, thus redeeming himself for the debacle of the E-Sing Bakery. Such an act should be rewarded. It is my humble suggestion that the ring of the successor, which formerly rested upon the hand of Master Weng, be placed upon that of Hei Hu."

Ki Ming nodded his agreement. In truth, Hei Hu's goals, being the overthrow of the invading armies, were ever more clear and obvious than Huang Zhou's own and therefore more likely to impress the members of the White Peacock. The goals of Huang Zhou were considerably more subtle and oblique, more ambitious, and thus unlikely to appeal to any but the most astute of minds.

Hei Hu strode up to the dais, stopped beside Huang Zhou, and bowed to the new mandarin.

Ki Ming nodded and indicated that he should rise. "Hei Hu," he said, "for the many services you have performed for the Order of the White Peacock, it has been decided that you shall be ordained as my heir and second-in-command. Step forward and receive this token of your new position."

Hei Hu did so. The Mandarin Ki Ming then placed the silver ring on the hand of the warrior. For thousands of years, the mandarin's immediate successor was always shown this honor.

The Black Tiger bowed again to the new mandarin, then briefly admired the ring and its emerald. Then, with something of a smirk directed towards Huang Zhou, he turned and took his place beside the mandarin's throne.

"Huang Zhou," said Ki Ming, "I thank you for your valuable advice and far-flung goals, but I believe Hei Hu to be more valuable to the White Peacock in practical matters. It is my hope that you accept him as my second-in-command."

Huang Zhou bowed. Nor did he smirk, even though it was he who had suggested to the new mandarin that Hei Hu be promoted, not he. Before this ceremony begun, Huang Zhou knew it would be better that Hei Hu be given the accolades than himself. Receiving such an elevation over his elder would only encourage resentment.

"I will obey the will of the Black Tiger as I would your own."

At present, this was the best arrangement that Huang Zhou could hope for. Hei Hu would forever be a thorn in his side if he was not promoted over him. And clearly, Ki Ming cared only about the technologies that Huang Zhou could bring to the White Peacock, not the innovations of society and government. Well, at least he had been pardoned and would keep his head.

For his life, Huang Zhou had Sin Yee to thank, she who had secretly loved him from afar. She whose slender hand had once dropped a key. For her courage and intelligence, Huang Zhou intended that she would become his bride on the morrow and stand by his side.

Yet Huang Zhou also realized that he would not always be able to rely on the White Peacock—and maybe not the other members of the Council of the Seven, as they currently stood. Henceforth, he vowed to forge their divergent, half-forgotten groups into a cohesive unit. He would do this with or without the aid of Ki Ming and Hei Hu. The aid of Noble Consort Yi, however, would be essential. Most important of all, he would now no longer be hindered by the restrictive policies of Mandarin Shu, may his ancestors hold him ever in their clutches.

"However," said the Mandarin Ki Ming, "you also shall be elevated, Huang Zhou. You may now take the title of 'Master'."

"I thank you, most illustrious Mandarin," said Huang Zhou, bowing. "However, I prefer the title of 'Doctor'."

ASSIGNATION IN SHAITANABAD

The Punjab, November of 1860.

For this meeting, the Rajah Chambu Singh of Shaitanabad offered his guest, Dhakar Rao, several suits of clothing. Still in mourning, Dhakar had picked a sherwani and trousers of black khaki, with a simple white sash about his waist. Upon his head he eschewed any turban or tarboush, choosing to remain bareheaded. He retained his beard, but this he had now trimmed and shaped to a point.

Dhakar Rao and his few remaining men had dwelt in the confines of the villa for nearly a year before Chambu Singh's long awaited guest had at last been able to free himself of obligations in his native land. During that time, the refugees had all been well cared for and all had healed—in body if not in mind.

On this day, after all the introductions had been made, the two rajahs and their taciturn guest retired to the library, where Dhakar presented his blueprints.

The doctor now sat at the large desk, silently reviewing each portion of the drawings, the lists of materials and other specifications, and blueprints for the facility where all the work might be completed. Curiously, he scarcely glanced at the lengthy tally sheet of the proposed expenses.

This sunlit room lay within a scented compound of the palace of Chambu Singh, who ruled this region with a bloody hand and had not read a book since he was a boy. Yet though he was a cutthroat, Chambu Singh knew his master and so rooms had quickly been made ready and a library assembled in short time.

This bandit leader sat apart from the speakers, munching on dates fed to him by a half-naked slave girl. The Rajah Singh, having no comprehension of "clockworks" and "white man's toys", simply sat and scowled on a richly-embroidered divan on the other side of the chamber, flanked by a pair of Thugee assassins. No weapon appeared in their hands, for none did they employ save the simple scarves around their loins.

On the other end of the large room, the doctor, who seemed unaware of the heat of the day—even in November—now looked up and regarded Dhakar at last.

"Your plans and diagrams are most intriguing, Rajah. I only regret that they are so far beyond your means to implement."

Dhakar Rao, to whom this comment was addressed, may have stiffened or blanched on the inside, but no sign of his feelings appeared outwardly. Standing in the hastily-assembled library and workroom, he merely said, “I have considered even this, Doctor. I can only hope that such wealth as I was able to escape with during the Uprising will provide much of the funding for the raw materials.”

“It will not,” said the Celestial doctor, with no sign of emotion. “I would not question your wisdom and innovation of design, only your understanding of rather more practical matters. Nonetheless, I spoke not of wealth, my good rajah. We have the means to provide our cause with all the wealth one might require. In truth, it is this new power source and the means to deploy it that will prove the most vexing.”

Dhakar had worked in a fervor these last six months on those plans, revamping and improving them. He knew the plans were feasible, but many other factors stood in his way. And yes, they mostly came down to money.

Dhakar had long seen himself a man of the future and the future, he long felt, lie in the West. In the West science held sway over superstition. But the men of the West, Dhakar knew, were far from admirable in all ways. They had given themselves over to greed and lust. They came to India not to share their knowledge, but to reap its treasures. The men of the West had come as conquerors and oppressors, rapists and murderers.

But were the men of the East very much better? Any better? Supposedly, this Celestial doctor had money, despite recent events in Cathay. Yet Dhakar had doubts—could he trust the man? The doctor’s goals and aspirations seemed nebulous, even outlandish—would it not make more sense that he intended to secure these plans from Dhakar and then sell them to the British or the Americans? Dhakar shuddered at the thought.

As he watched the doctor peruse the plans, he knew that India had not suffered alone. Every people over whom colonial flags flew were little better off than slaves. Trust him or not, Dhakar’s only hope lay with this Celestial doctor, who knew well the folly of standing against British guns.

Attired in a silken robe the color of emeralds, embroidered with rampaging golden dragons, with a simple black skullcap upon his fine head, the doctor lifted one of Dhakar’s sketches and analyzed every detail through his unique green eyes. Those eyes disturbed Dhakar in a way that bespoke the ancient fears and superstitions from which he had sought to free his people before the Uprising. Even Dhakar, who had studied at the finest schools of Europe, still felt a tinge of supernatural dread in this man's presence. A full decade older than the doctor, could not stop himself from deferring to the man, such was his strength of personality.

Today, two years after the collapse of the Uprising, these two men had come together, after a spy had informed the doctor of Dhakar's plans. Dhakar was in no way lax in his security; the spy that informed the doctor was Dhakar's host, Rajah Chambu Singh.

"You place much store in the power of electricity, Rajah," spoke the tall doctor. "Of all the elements in your plans, this intrigues me the most. With this, you present us with an innovation beyond its time and for that, I commend you, Rajah."

"Thank you, Doctor," spoke Dhakar. He was about to correct the doctor concerning his title, as it no longer applied after his homeland was overrun. But the doctor spoke first.

"However, I have the unfortunate task of pointing out an error in your calculations. It appears you have not made consideration for the human component."

"Sahib...? I don't follow."

"Men must build your machine. Men must be made to operate it. Those men must first hear in their hearts the same calling as your most worthy self. The men with you now, no matter their dedication, will prove insufficient for a craft of the size you propose."

"I'm sure they will come to me, Doctor, once they hear of my plans."

The doctor leveled his basilisk stare at the handsome and almost equally tall Dhakar. Yet the cruelties of the last few years had lined the rajah's face.

"As men flocked to your calling during the Sepoy Uprising?"

Dhakar had no answer to that. Of course men had flocked to him when he and other rajahs called them, only not nearly enough. More joined the side of the British and their guns. The majority of those who joined him went to their deaths. Dhakar could only stare back, but in his mind, for a moment, he saw only those dying men, he heard only the enemy cannons, and he thought only of all he had lost in the war: chief among these, his beloved wife and children. With them died his title, even his honor, for he had become an outlaw in his own land, his name cursed.

And so, he vowed revenge.

From another world, from within his own mind, he heard the curiously musical hiss of the doctor's voice. "Our cause is the propagation of the Council of the Seven, whose goal is the unification of all people of the world under a single banner."

Dhakar blinked once or twice, returning his thoughts to the present day. He noted the doctor was no longer in front of him.

He looked about and spotted the doctor once again sitting behind the table, looking once more at the designs, studying every detail. Now released from the doctor's mesmeric stare, Dhakar felt a tinge of embarrassment, perhaps danger. Who was this doctor, really? The stories from out of Cathay would have one believe him to be a wizard, a demon reborn, a fallen mandarin in disguise, or a master of men's minds.

This last, Dhakar now had no difficulty believing.

Without looking up, the doctor spoke once more. "My divers have retrieved your *Iron Buffalo* from the depths of Lake Lakha Banjara, should you require either a prototype or spare parts."

Dhakar's eyes widened in surprise. After the Mutiny failed, he had scuttled the *Iron Buffalo* for fear of it falling into the hands of the British. Yet this doctor had, with no great difficulty, retrieved it.

"I find no fault in your engineering, my prince," the doctor continued. "Indeed, I see considerable danger in your new schematics should they fall into the hands of our enemies. We can afford no more losses, you will agree. The men whom you called to you before were true in their hearts but few in number. For this alone did your cause fail. Be not ashamed; my countrymen failed in the second war over opium in Cathay as they failed in the first Opium War. Warfare is rarely the best way to secure one's goals."

Dhakar, in deference to his new patron, bowed his head in the Celestial manner and nodded. He could not challenge the doctor's wisdom. The doctor stood and acknowledged his bow, then continued.

"Your lack of loyal men we may acknowledge as a weakness but not a fault. Yours is a Great Mind and you share with the Society a common disdain for imperialism. We find your goals and ours to be compatible and most honorable. When next you seek to strike against the imperialists, it will not be your men who fail you, for I shall provide all you require. They will come to my call and yet speak the same language, for each will be handpicked from every corner of the Earth, and each of them will be devoted to our cause, Prince Dhakar Rao."

Dhakar, a man of strong will and determination, nonetheless breathed easier and allowed himself a slight, wearied smile in the presence of the great man. He remembered the woman under whose flag he fought so many battles—Lakshmi Bai. She had met the doctor and she had believed in his goals. Dhakar knew he could do no less.

He pressed his hands together and bowed his head. The doctor stood and returned the bow.

"I thank you, Doctor. We share the same goal—to make a better world. Clearly, we need one another."

"Indeed."

"However, I have lost my family and with them, my name. I wish no recriminations to fall on any who still bear the name of Dhakar. I must take a new name, so that, to all I knew in India, I will exist no longer."

A gleam of humor appeared in the doctor's eye. "So, like Odysseus, you will be a voyager on the sea, proclaiming yourself as No Man."

Dhakar smiled a bit. "Yes, Doctor. Only my travels shall be under the sea."

The doctor gave Dhakar a polite nod of the head.

"Now," asked Dhakar, "what must I do to continue my work?"

Without emotion, the doctor said, "First, you must die."

* * *

And so, the Rajah Dhakar Rao died to the world. Word went out from Bundelkhand that the fugitive rajah had at last fallen victim to his many wounds. A hastily procured body, was incinerated only after his compatriots emphatically identified it as that of the late rajah. A simple cenotaph would be erected nearby.

The living Dhakar now sailed on the sea for the first time in years. Despite his birth in a landlocked country, he had loved the sea from the day he first laid eyes on it. His destination was a small island in the Andaman chain, where a laboratory and a shipyard had quickly been erected, and where everything he needed had been brought. Eventually, a handful of equally disgruntled British, French, and Polish sailors would be sent to join Dhakar's company. Upon meeting them and knowing them to have as many grievances against their governments as he did, Dhakar happily accepted them. Despite these men arriving with differing languages, they all learned a new one, that they might all communicate together. Even more men would follow these.

As the Celestial Doctor had foreseen, Dhakar's destiny lay with the sea—or under it. Dhakar hoped the work would take his mind from his wife and children, from the torment they suffered. Now he would focus all his waking hours on his new project, the project that was the natural culmination of his schooling and research. It would be a new, better, far larger version of his *Iron Buffalo*. This then, would become his life's goal.

Despite Dhakar's love of his late wife, this new underwater craft would have a more fitting name than Iron Buffalo. His own name would change as well. Perhaps "No Man", as the doctor had suggested. Or, in Homer's original Greek, Nemo.

* * *

Five years later, reports appeared in newspapers on both sides of the Atlantic of a strange sea monster. Scientists theorized this giant creature to be a massive narwhal, able to ram and sink a ship. A number of warships sank to their doom upon being ruptured by this monster.

Interestingly, the monster showed a distinct hostility towards battleships flying the Union Jack.

The End

AFTERWORD

In this book, I've taken historical personalities such as the Dowager Empress Ci'xi of China, the amazing Rani Lakshmi Bai of India, and Queen Victoria of England, and events like the Opium Wars and the Sepoy Revolt, and attempted to give them life once more in these pages. Most people in the Western world today are utterly ignorant of these amazing events which did so much—both good and bad—to shape the world in which we live.

I've also taken various fictional sources and written pastiches of the characters, connecting them to real world events and people. To the best of my knowledge, all of these works are in the public domain. They include the following:

"The Phantom of the Opera" by Gaston Leroux, "The Maker of Moons" by Robert W. Chambers, "The Raja and the Tiger" by Clark Ashton Smith, and, notably, "Twenty Thousand Leagues Under the Sea" and "The Mysterious Island" by Jules Verne.

Possibly other novels have also provided inspiration. I'm not telling.

The prophecy of the Maitreya, the coming World Leader or World Teacher is true and a part of Buddhist thought. While modern Buddhists do not necessarily believe the Maitreya will be a woman, they don't refute the possibility. Among others, Empress Wu—the only reigning empress in Chinese history—believed that she was either the Maitreya or that she could achieve the position.

Likewise, in India, thousands of Hindus worship Kali, the misunderstood goddess of destruction, and they believe that her return is immanent. At that time, the world will be destroyed—for the purpose of creating a new and better world.

I took these beliefs and a few others, and combined them, as if they were all based on an earlier, original prophecy. More on this will appear in future works.

But Wait, There's More!

We've not yet seen the last of Huang Zhou!

Huang Zhou next appears in the novel, "Monster of the East", the third book in the **Legend of Frankenstein** series! Can even the brilliant mastermind withstand a monster that should not be?

Then, in the next installment of **The Forbidden Chronicles**, Huang Zhou returns to England, hoping to once again influence the queen and thus gain power over the world's greatest empire. His acolyte, Dr. Ahn, rescues a scientist from the ruins of his jungle laboratory and they begin to research the mean to create a new breed of killers.

In Russia, Huang Zhou meets a genius who might open up new worlds… and the brilliant young Viscountess Halyna. But can even she melt his cold heart?

When the martial artists of China rise up in rebellion, the representatives of the foreign nations make their last stand—but the woman Huang Zhou loves is trapped with them. What chance do they have against twenty thousand of the finest-trained fighters in the world?

Once more in China, Huang Zhou matches wits with the woman he set in place to be the Mistress of the World—only to find she may have outwitted him! And what happens when Halyna finds herself trapped inside the besieged embassies during the Boxer Revolt?

Against the backdrop of the first Russian Revolution, Huang Zhou courts both the Czar and the revolutionaries and he battles Halyna's sadistic brother. Read his next series of incredible adventures in **THE RETURN OF HUANG ZHOU*!***

Excerpt from THE RETURN OF HUANG ZHOU….

As Huang Zhou worked on his plans and diagrams in the laboratory, he noticed in his peripheral vision that he was under observation from the doorway. His eyes shifted to the small, nearly hidden figure.

"Come to me, Princess," said Huang Zhou.

The four-year-old girl did so, then bowed to him. She looked up at him, waiting his next instruction.

"Did your mother send you to fetch me?"

Little Nu shook her head. Like her father, she bore a broad brow and intelligent green eyes.

"What do you wish, Princess?"

Looking up at him, she said, "Mother says you are older than grandfather."

A tiny muscle in Huang Zhou's right eyelid briefly moved, seemingly of its own accord.

"Your mother is correct," said Huang Zhou, after a moment. "What brought about this discussion?"

"Mother said he rides horses and has a big house in the leg-a-shun."

"Legation. Akin to an embassy. Say it correctly."

"Legation."

"Yes, he does. And he has an even finer house far away in the Crimea. I was a guest there for a time."

"Oh."

Huang Zhou regarded Nu for a moment. "Daughter, do you wish to meet your maternal grandfather?"

"Yes, Father." "Very well. Find your mother and tell her I wish to speak with her."

The little girl bowed low, then hurried off.

A few moments later, her mother, adorned in a silken cheong'sam dress, appeared in the laboratory and bowed.

"Master," she said, "you sent a small child to summon me, I believe."

"Halyna," Huang Zhou asked, looking up from a microscope which he'd come to realize was of insufficient power for his needs, "you know that your father, Count Pavel Zaroff, has arrived at the Russian legation to command his business dealings as he once commanded the cavalry. Do you wish to see him again?"

"I do know, Master," Halyna Zarova replied. "And no doubt, he is running various business matters, as has long been his wish. I have mixed feelings.... My brother, Yuri, is in Manchuria where he is fighting martial artists and Chinese bandits."

She sighed. "Master, I think I would rather not deal with anyone who sells opium to your people."

"I appreciate your loyalty, my sunflower," he replied. "However, the child must meet her grandfather. It is unfair to her to do otherwise."

"Yes, Master," Halyna replied dutifully, then bowed. "I shall have the servants prepare for the trip to Peking."

Huang Zhou nodded and looked once more into his microscope.

Read more in THE RETURN OF HUANG ZHOU!

About the Author:

Perry Lake has made up stories about monsters and the supernatural since he was a small child. You would think he'd grow out of it. His tales of ghosts, vampires, ghouls, strange laboratory creations, and more have thus far been collected into eleven books and three inter-connected series: **The Legend of Dracula**, **The Legend of Frankenstein**, and the **Krantz Family Chronicles**. Expect more to follow.

Mr. Lake's fiction and non-fiction work includes three articles in *FATE* magazine, *Orion's Children*, about ten stories in the weekly news magazine *Off The Record* (the haunted house story got a great deal of attention), and the prestigious *Journal of Dracula Studies*. He even won third prize for a *Doctor Who* screenplay submitted to the *Writer's Digest* screenwriting contest. The judge, by the way, was J. Michael Straczynski, of Babylon 5 fame, who knows a thing or two about a good story arch.

Lake is also the creator of *Cassiopeia The Witch*, a small press comic, relating the adventures of a modern-day Wiccan practitioner and lesbian. As Mr. Lake has a fondness for drawing the female figure, Cass spends much of her time without clothing. For over forty issues, Cass tangled with the evil Devil's Children, the intolerant Army of Light, the zombie-raising Professor Boudac, plus various vengeful ghosts, ravening werewolves, walking mummies, and inhuman cryptids. She's even clashed with Larry Johnson's *Madame Boogala.* Cass will soon reappear in a series of reprints!

Lake's other comic book work includes professional comics published by Rip-Off Press, Carnal Comics, and Eros. He wrote and/or illustrated parts of several *Demi the Demoness* titles, including *Demi's Strange Bedfellows* and *Sex Squad.* Cassiopeia appears in four of these.

Mr. Lake survived the 2018 Camp Fire that destroyed the city of Paradise, California. Not letting a little thing like that dissuade him, he got out through the flames with his laptop and all his stories.

MORE FROM PERRY LAKE!

Dracula I: HIS FIRST CENTURIES

Beginning with a quartet of tales featuring the psychopathic Vlad the Impaler, witness his despicable acts and brutal death. When the infamous Doctor Faust raises Vlad from the dead, Dracula finds himself enslaved by Faust's magicks. Can he ever be free?

Upon his coming, **Dracula** establishes a new vampiric bloodline, raised from those of noble bearing and ruling temperament. But will they be enough to defeat the powerful, millennia-old vampires who already rule the Night?

Dracula II: HIS WOMEN

A king needs a queen—maybe three of them. Vlad Dracula is no different and now he sets his sights on a bevy of beauties for his court. Count Dracula seduces Katya and Clarimonda. He meet his match in evil, the Countess Elizabeth Báthory. And, at last, Dracula meets his greatest love—Mircalla Karnstein.

Twenty short stories of seduction and terror, featuring women who will love you to death.

Dracula III: PLOTS & SCHEMES

Dracula and his vampire hordes plot and scheme to enslave the world and rule the Night! Varney the vampire finds himself trapped between Dracula and his own personal demon!

Dracula strives to expand his fledgling kingdom, only to once more clash with the Vordenburg clan. But this time, Baron Vordenburg finds an unexpected ally—the son of Dracula!

Dracula turns his attention to France, the most powerful nation in Europe, now in the decedent last days of the monarchy. There, he forms an alliance with the powerful magician Cagliostro! With these arch-fiends allied, do the crowned heads of France have any chance of survival?

Dracula IV: INTO THE MOUTH OF DEATH

Countess Mircalla Karnstein and Laird Ruthven join forces to seduce a beautiful heiress and turn her into one of the Undead. The crusading Vordenburg clan hunts vampires in Serbia, if only they can convince a dying old nobleman to help them. Lenore, goes out on her own, becoming the muse of a famous poet—only to fall into the hands of a pair of ghouls.

Once more, the Vordenburgs attempt to stop Dracula's plans—

but can they stop a wave of madness spreading across Europe? Countess Mircalla goes in search of the last of the Karnsteins. When the last Vordenburg stands in her way, will Dracula and Elizabeth Báthory be able to stop him?

Against the backdrop of the bloody Paris Commune, Dracula hatches his most ambitious plot, leading to an epic battle against the oldest and most powerful vampiress of all—the undead deity who created him—LILITH!

In the foggy alleyways of Victorian London, a killer stalks the night in search of blood—driven to perform an unearthly ritual. See Dracula's actions right up to the opening chapter of Bram Stoker's novel!

Ghouls 0: GHOULS AMONGST US

From the dawn of time they come: creatures hidden in the depths and the darkness. Even the famous Hunchback of Notre Dame and the infamous Phantom of the Opera appear. Eventually, ghouls enter the modern world where they become... our saviors?

Ghouls I: HUGO KRANTZ, GHOUL

Meet Hugo Krantz, devourer of human flesh. Hugo will encounter other ghouls, diabolical noblemen, sword-wielding actresses, and vampires. He will plunder ancient tombs and attempt to revive the dead using the latest tools of science.

Ghouls II: KRANTZ & EDGAR

Hugo Krantz—scholar, entrepreneur, and bon vivant; Edgar Frump—slovenly brute and glutton. Two completely opposite fellows, except for their fondness for human flesh. See them encounter the immortal Voodoo-Queen, Marie Laveau! The Jersey Devil! Spring-heel'd Jack! All together in one book!

THE NIGHTMARE OF FRANKENSTEIN

Beginning minutes after the conclusion of Mary Shelley's novel, the Monster of Frankenstein strives to learn the secrets of his creation. Along the way, he battles ghouls, witches, and the legions of the Undead! Trafficking with mad scientists and madder sorcerers, he will be captured by fiends and forced to battle other monsters in the arena of death!

MONSTER OF THE WORLD

In these seven stories, the Monster of Frankenstein battles a vile Gypsy witch with the power to command demons! In Egypt, he meets and beds Nitocris, Queen of the Mummies!

Then the Monster plunges into the swamps of the Deep South and strikes out for the Wild West, hoping to make a new home for himself...and profit from hunting gun-toting outlaws! But will a deranged preacher prove to have the fastest gun?

MONSTER OF THE EAST

On the streets of the Barbary Coast, Emperor Norton I discovers and befriends the creation of Victor Frankenstein. Will they be able to defeat the nefarious cult of Asian devil-worshipers that has taken root in the city? Then, in an epic tale, the Monster and a mysterious girl cross the vast Pacific Ocean to to China, where they engage tongs and missionaries. Traveling inland, they encounter "hopping ghosts" and the Yeti, and learn of a secret society bent on world conquest! In Tibet, the Monster discovers a hidden citadel of cannibal pygmies—who may hold the secret of his creation! Standing in his way is the oriental mastermind known as... *Huang Zhou!*

FRANKENSTEIN VERSUS THE MARTIANS

The boisterous and egocentric Professor Challenger, the hero of "The Lost World", has studied alien technology and tangled with mad scientists. Calm and aloof, the psychic investigator Dr. John Silence, has investigated ghosts, cat cults, and Canadian werewolves. Now, the nameless Monster of Frankenstein seeks them both to learn the truth behind a world-wide cover-up of the most devastating event to ever strike the Earth.

But what about the criminal genius Phantomas? Or the would-be conqueror of the skies, Captain Mors? And how do Dr. Frankenstein and Count Dracula fit into everything? Will they join forces to save the Earth? Or end up killing each other?

AND COMING SOON—
THE RETURN OF CASSIOPEIA THE WITCH!!

www.ingramcontent.com/pod-product-compliance
Ingram Content Group UK Ltd.
Pitfield, Milton Keynes, MK11 3LW, UK
UKHW041855190726
13854UKWH00002B/923

9 781737 504139